# GIDEON'S TREE

# TREE

## EMMY'S STORY, Part 15

By
Kenneth Lee McGee

For Pastor Herb and Carolyn Ireland
God sent you to our church.
His timing is always perfect.

A special thanks to the people who helped with some technical issues. Thank you Beverly Saylor, Jim Rouse, Gina Lamigo and Teresa Wisnieski.

Thank you Sue Midlock for creating the cover. If you want to see more of her covers, check out her Facebook page Your Book Cover.

I want to thank the people from my church who have graciously allowed me to include fragments of their lives as inspirations.

I want to thank my wife Sheila for being my toughest critic.

# Chapter One

Kenny Colwell finished the last of his coffee. "Want another cup?"

"Warm me up, please," Emmy said.

Kenny refilled his cup, added some to his wife's half-filled cup and stared out the window. "We could go for a walk after the rain stops. It's not that cold for November."

"Maybe later. I don't want you to feel you have to stay in the band because of financial reasons. You aren't, are you?"

"Not at all." Kenny sat down.

"We would be all right if you never made another dime from the band," Emmy said. "We have trusts for the kids, and our investments are solid. We could cut back on expenses."

"I could get a job teaching music."

"I could get my education degree and teach school."

Kenny laughed. "Who are we kidding, Em. My dream has always been to be a rock star."

Emmy's blue eyes sparkled. "I know, and if you keep working at it, one of these days it might come true, m'lord."

Kenny stared into Emmy's eyes as they sat in the breakfast nook drinking their morning coffee. "Some people might actually think of me as a rock star, m'lady. Fridays At Five is a name recognized the world over."

"There are lots of people in this world who are easily deluded," she teased.

"You are so funny," Kenny said. "What time do you have to leave?"

"Practice starts at ten, so we need to leave around nine thirty. Why? Do you have something in mind?" Emmy stood up and ran a hand through her husband's thick hair. "You need a haircut, and there are only three more Saturday rehearsals before the kids' Christmas program."

"The kids are still sleeping, and it's only seven thirty." He moved his eyebrows up and down in a suggestive manner.

"Are you doing your Groucho impression again, or are you trying to wiggle your funny-looking ears?" She picked up his empty coffee cup, and took it along with hers into the kitchen. "Should I make more, or was that enough?"

"I'm good," he answered. "We might get a couple inches of rain according to the weather report I heard."

Emmy rinsed out the cups, placed them in the dishwasher, came back to the breakfast nook and stood behind Kenny. "If it was colder, this would be snow and we could use the snowmobile."

"I should call to see if the shop is finished with it."

They both turned as they heard a siren. Seven-year-old Kevin Michael Colwell entered the kitchen on his hands and knees pushing a rather large red firetruck.

"Why are you up so early? This is Saturday. You can sleep longer," Emmy said and then put her hands over her ears. "Turn that thing off before you wake up your sisters."

"I didn't realize it would be so loud," Kenny shouted to be heard. "I never would have bought it otherwise."

Kevin Michael turned off the siren and scooted into the breakfast nook. "I'm hungry. Can I have some ice cream?"

Emmy rolled her eyes. "Just because your father sneaks some ice cream for breakfast once in a while does not mean you are allowed. I can make pancakes or bacon and eggs. There's cereal in the pantry and fresh fruit in a bowl on the island. You should eat a banana before they get too ripe."

"The bananas are still too green. Do we have blueberries? I can fix my own cereal, but I want blueberries," Kevin said.

"You know where the blueberries are," Nearly ten-year-old Isabella Marie said as she walked into the kitchen while rubbing her eyes. "What was that loud noise? It woke me up."

Emmy glared at Kenny.

"I can take it back," he said.

Kevin picked up his new firetruck and showed it to the younger of his twin sisters. "It was this, Isa. Didn't it sound awesome? It sounds like a real siren."

"It sounded like a loud toy," Isabella said as she rolled her eyes. "Is there any coffee left? I need some caffeine to help me wake up."

Emmy frowned at Kenny.

His eyes widened as he shrugged.

"Who let you drink coffee?" Emmy demanded.

"Father James let us have some of his," Isabella answered without realizing it might get him into trouble.

"When was this? I'm going to confess to murder and then kill him," Emmy said.

"Last week sometime. We didn't drink very much. Heather didn't like it, but I did."

"What didn't I like?" Heather Rose asked as she opened the fridge and pulled out a quart of Weber's Dairy chocolate milk. She poured the milk into a glass and then shook the empty container. "We need more."

"There should be more milk outside the service door. I heard the delivery truck earlier," Emmy said. "Would you rinse out that bottle and put it with the others, please?"

"It's raining," Heather said as she looked out the window above the kitchen sink. "I don't want to get my hair wet."

Kenny looked at his twin daughters and grinned. "Your hair looks just like your mother's did when she was your age. Long, dark and curly. She always put hers in a ponytail or a braid."

"I want to get mine cut short like Mommy's is now. It's too hard to brush it." Heather tried to run a hand through her tangled hair.

Kevin Michael set his firetruck on the granite-topped kitchen island and grabbed the empty milk bottle. "I'll get the fresh milk. I don't mind getting wet."

"Do not play in the rain," Emmy warned. "And wipe your feet in the mudroom."

Kevin raced out of the kitchen.

"Do you really want to get your hair cut?" Kenny ran a hand through Emmy's still curly but much shorter dark hair.

"It needs a trim at least," she answered.

"I don't want to get mine cut," Isabella said. "I like it long."

"Should I make blueberry pancakes?" Emmy asked as she walked into the pantry. "We have fresh blueberries and some of that special maple syrup."

9

Kenny winked at Isabella. "How about chocolate chip pancakes instead of blueberry. Aren't you tired of blueberry pancakes?"

Heather and Isabella giggled.

"Blueberries are good for you. Chocolate chips aren't," Emmy called out from the pantry.

"How old was Mommy when she first ate blueberry pancakes?" Isabella asked as she snuggled up to her father.

"I think she might have been ten or so," Kenny answered.

Emmy walked out of the pantry with all the ingredients needed to make pancakes from scratch. "I was older than ten. I was fifteen, and your mother made them on Christmas Day." She set everything on the countertop close to the stove.

"Do you still order blueberry pancakes when you are on tour with your band?" Heather asked.

"If they're on the menu," Emmy answered and then turned around suddenly.

"Look who's here!" Kevin Michael shouted as he dashed into the kitchen.

Mickel Boyanov walked into the kitchen with hands on his plump belly and his short, wiry, gray hair dripped from the rain.

"Father James!" Heather and Isabella rushed over and wrapped their arms around him.

"Did you take off your shoes, and why on earth did you let the girls drink coffee?" Emmy put her hands on her hips and frowned at her half-brother. "Are you growing your beard back? You better not give Kenny any ideas. I don't like kissing him when he's got a heavy beard."

"You always kiss Daddy," Kevin Michael said.

"I removed my shoes," Father James said as he hugged the girls. "And I thought I would grow my beard since it's going to be winter soon."

"How did you get here?" Heather asked. "And where is the chocolate milk?"

"I forgot it," Kevin Michael said. "I'll get it."

"My old Civic still runs," Father James said. "I thought I would go to rehearsal if that's all right with you."

10

"You should get rid of that old thing. What year is it?"

"It's a 1998 sedan, and it still runs like brand new. I can't see spending money for a new one."

"Are you coming to our program?" Heather asked.

"I won't be able to make it, so I want to watch you rehearse," he answered.

"Father James has to preach at his church on Sunday just like Pastor Tyler," Kenny said.

Isabella checked out Father James' bluejeans and flannel shirt. "Are you in disguise? You aren't wearing your funny collar, or that robe."

"I'm off duty," Father James said and then scooted out of the way as Kevin Michael returned.

"Here's the milk." He carried the gallon of whole milk in one hand and the quart of chocolate milk in the other. "Why can't we get a gallon of chocolate milk?"

"Because it's too expensive," Emmy said.

Father James looked at Kenny. Kenny shrugged.

"Should I take up a collection for you at mass?" Father James asked.

"Hush!" Emmy replied. "I know we can afford it, but it's just the way I am. Take me or leave me. Did you eat? I'm making blueberry pancakes," Emmy said.

"I might be able to choke down one or two. Do you have any fresh coffee? The girls and I are thirsty," Father James teased.

Emmy pulled her gray BMW X3 into the parking lot at Crest Ridge United Nazarene several minutes early.

"What year is this?" Father James asked.

"It's a 2011. Why?" Emmy unbuckled and hopped out of the SUV.

"I think the new ones might be a little faster."

"Oh, hush! I was only speeding a little," Emmy watched as the kids ran into the building.

"You were doing sixty-five in a forty-five zone."

"Was not," Emmy claimed.

Father James didn't answer.

"Well, it's a safe vehicle and there wasn't any traffic."

"None that could keep up at least," Father James said.

"You're just jealous because your old car couldn't go sixty-five if you were going down a mountain in Colorado." Emmy waved to one of the other mothers who had children in the program as she and Father James walked toward the old sanctuary building.

"I wouldn't feel safe in your car going that fast down a mountain," he said.

"Which one?"

"Either one," Father James said. "Especially not your sporty Civic."

"My Si is perfectly safe. It handles great, and it's not all that fast," Emmy responded.

"Maybe not with a normal driver, but you drive it like you're on a racetrack."

"Do not!" Emmy scoffed.

"Have you ever been to the SoHam Autobahn Club?" Father James asked as he held the door open.

"Kenny and I were there once for a special fundraiser. I didn't have a chance to drive on the track."

"You should check it out sometime. I bet you'd love it. You can drive like a maniac without getting a speeding ticket."

Emmy poked him in the side. "I've never gotten a speeding ticket in my life."

"Another of God's miracles," Father James said. He followed her to Noah's Ark, where the children would rehearse for the Christmas program, and took a seat in the back.

"Mind if I join you?" Pastor Tyler Hammond asked.

"Please do, Pastor." Father James patted the empty chair next to him. "Are your children involved in the program?"

Tyler sat down and pointed to the platform. "Natalie and Grayson have parts, but Phoebe is a little young. She will be two a week from tomorrow. Hard to believe she's that old already."

"Time flies. I've only known Emmy and the kids for a little over three years and they've grown up so much."

Tyler chuckled. "I know you mean the kids because Emmy hasn't grown up at all."

Father James slapped his knee. "I can't wait until the kids

12

are taller than her, and it won't be that far off."

Tyler and Father James sat and watched the kids in silence for a few minutes.

"I need to work on my message for tomorrow," Tyler said as he stood up. "Good to see you again."

"You, too, Tyler. Take care and I'll try not to let Emmy pester you too much."

"I appreciate that," Tyler said and then chuckled.

"Did you hear us sing?" Isabella asked Father James as they walked out to the car after practice.

"I did and you sound like angels," he answered.

"Do I look like a dork doing all the motions with the little kids?" Emmy asked.

Father James winked at the girls. "Yes, but I'm sure with a little more practice you will learn all the right moves."

"Stick it in your... ear," Emmy said as she tried to smack his arm but missed.

"Father James, did you know Mommy wrote those songs just for the Christmas program?" Isabella asked.

"I did hear that somewhere," he said. "Your mother is very talented."

"I'm hungry," Kevin Michael said as he picked up a rock from the parking lot. "Can we stop somewhere?"

"We have food at home, and don't you dare throw that rock," Emmy said. "There are too many cars around."

"I wasn't going to throw it at a car, Mom." He dropped the rock after Emmy frowned at him and pointed at the ground.

"And try to avoid some of the puddles, please," Emmy said too late.

"Stop it, you little twerp!" Heather shouted at her brother. "Mom, he splashed me."

Kevin Michael made a face at Heather and took off running. Heather gave chase.

Father James grinned as he watched. "Did you and Kenny act like that when you were kids?"

"Probably, but the situation was reversed. He's older than me." Emmy hit the button on her key fob to unlock the SUV.

13

"So you jumped in the puddle to splash him, huh?" Father James opened the rear door for Isabella. "Sounds like something a tomboy would do."

"Heather Rose! Kevin Michael Robert! Get over here this instant!" Emmy shouted.

"He's really in trouble now because Mom used all his names," Isabella told Father James as they climbed into their seats. "Me and Heather only have one middle name, but Kevin has two just like Daddy."

"Is that a longstanding tradition in the Colwell family?" Father James asked as Emmy got in and started the BMW.

"No, it started because Kenny's parents couldn't decide on his middle name so they gave him two. Allen with an E and Robert. There are lots of his relatives named Robert."

"After the famous Civil War general, right, Mommy?" Isabella asked.

"That's right, Isa. Robert T. Colwell was a confederate general." Emmy waited until Heather and Kevin Michael buckled up and took off through the parking lot for the trip back to the Bristol Ridge development where they lived.

Father James held on to the door handle as Emmy turned onto the four-lane street in front of the church and floored it.

"Are we going to race that police car?" Kevin Michael hollered.

Emmy swore under her breath and lifted off the accelerator just in time.

"You might have saved yourself a ticket, but your swearing will cost you three hail Mary's."

"I'm only doing five over the limit, and I didn't swear. I said shoot."

"Yeah, right," Father James said as he watched the squad car pull into the gas station on the corner. "You should think about a membership at the race track. You might get the speeding out of your system."

Emmy arrived home without being pulled over even though she broke the speed limit the entire way. She drove into the garage and everyone jumped out.

"What's for lunch," Heather asked racing her brother up the concrete steps.

"We have leftover meatloaf, cheesy potatoes and baked beans from last night," Emmy answered.

Father James stopped at the bottom of the steps leading into the mudroom. "You made all that yesterday and didn't invite me."

"Sorry. I forgot you like that stuff."

Kevin Michael turned around and grinned. "I like beans because they make you fart."

"You are so gross," Isabella said.

Kenny, Emmy and the kids sat in the breakfast nook for dinner that evening.

"Why didn't Father James stay? Doesn't he like pizza?" Kevin Michael asked as he took a bite of his pepperoni pizza.

"He had to get back for mass. They have church on Saturday night," Emmy explained. "And you have to eat your salad before you have more pizza."

He checked his salad. "But it's got cucumbers in it. I hate cucumbers."

"You don't have to eat them," Emmy said.

Just before the kids were about to leave the table, Kenny asked Emmy, "Are you sure you want to go back to school?"

The kids turned to look at her.

"You're too old to go to school," Kevin Michael said.

"I might go back to college and take some classes so I can become a teacher at your school," Emmy explained.

"You mean like a real teacher?" Heather asked.

"Yes, a real teacher like Mary and Sloane and Ms. Dalton and Mrs. Payne."

"What grade will you teach? Do I have to be in your class?" Kevin Michael asked as he took a small bite of a cucumber slice.

"I'm not sure what grade I would teach, but I probably wouldn't be your teacher."

"Mommy will have to go to school for at least a year before she's smart enough to be a teacher," Kenny said.

Emmy stuck out her tongue at him.

## Chapter Two

Kenny walked into the family room on Sunday afternoon and saw Emmy sitting on the couch. He walked up behind her and kissed the top of her head. "Why aren't you watching the game? Are the Bears losing?"

Emmy looked over her shoulder. "They played on Thanksgiving, remember? They beat the Packers in Green Bay."

"Right. I forgot," he said noticing her laptop. "What are you looking at? Have you been crying?"

"Kinda. I was reading this article about a baby boy who passed away last year. He only lived for forty-three days."

Kenny scooted around the couch and sat next to her. "What happened to him, Em?"

"His heart didn't work right and he had trouble breathing," Emmy said. "I feel so bad for his parents."

"What was his name? Does it say where he lived?" Kenny asked as he put an arm around her.

"He lived in Florida. His name was Gideon, but it doesn't give a last name."

"That's probably to protect the family's privacy."

"It says the parents would sit on a bench under an oak tree every morning to pray for their baby." Emmy closed her laptop and stood up. "Will you watch the kids for an hour or so?"

"Sure. Do you need some alone time?" Kenny asked.

"Remember how God told me to write that book?"

He nodded.

"I think God led me to this article for a reason. I think maybe I'm supposed to write a story about this family and the baby. Maybe just the baby," she said as she shrugged. "I'm not sure, but I want to use the den to pray about it. I'm not sure if anything will come of it, but I have to obey."

"I understand, Em. I'll make sure no one bothers you until you finish, or come out of the den at least." Kenny paused and then snapped his fingers. "The new guitar player's named Gideon. Is there any connection?"

Emmy shook her head. "This baby was born in Florida. The

16

article says the parents names have been changed. Gideon Logan from church didn't come to the States until the beginning of this year. He never mentioned being in Florida or having a son."

"He probably would have said something. Go do what you need. I'll take care of the kids."

Emmy took her laptop into the den. She made herself comfortable in her recliner and spent time praying and listening for an answer.

"All right, Lord. I'll give it a try," she whispered.

She opened up a blank document and typed in the title. "Gideon's Story," she said and then paused. "No, that's too plain. What else could I title it?" She tilted her head back and forth as she looked around the room. She saw Kenny's bible sitting on the desk. "Hmmm. How about Gideon's Truth?" She shook her head and looked outside. "The tree. I'll call it Gideon's Tree."

The simple change in the title sparked her creative muse. She typed for nearly ten minutes before she stopped to read what she had written.

"Wow! Did I really write this? I don't even remember adding this line."

She scanned the story and then began typing again. She worked for over an hour. She saved the document to a folder and then stopped to pray.

"I'm not sure what to do with this, Jesus, but I guess you'll let me know somehow."

She read through the document and corrected a few spelling and grammar mistakes. *I'll look at it later and tighten it up a bit.* She checked the document statistics. "Wow! That's the fastest 10,000 words I've ever written."

She used a thumb drive to make a backup and even sent it to her Dropbox account. Then she closed her laptop and left the den. She heard a commotion in the kitchen and walked in that direction.

"Mommy! Are you done writing your story?" Isabella asked. "Can we read it?"

"I'm finished for now. Maybe I'll let you read it later. Is anyone hungry? I am."

Kevin Michael looked at her and shook his head. "Dad made dinner for us because we thought you would never come out of the den. You were in there forever, Mom."

Emmy looked at the clock on the microwave. "Sorry, I didn't realize it was this late."

Kenny opened the fridge and pulled out a large Tupperware bowl. "We had enough stuff to make chili. Would you like some?"

"It was good, Mommy," Heather said. "It wasn't plain like Me-maw makes. It had some kick to it."

"Are there any crackers or shredded cheese left?" Emmy asked.

"We saved some for you," Kevin Michael said.

"Would you guys go play while I talk to your father?"

"Okay," Isabella said and then looked at Emmy. "Are you going to talk about grownup stuff? Is that why we have to leave the room?"

"I want to talk to your father about the story I wrote while I eat my chili."

Kenny poured the chili into a pot and turned on the stove.

Emmy sat at the island and looked at her kids. "On second thought stay here. Kevin Michael, would you get my laptop from the den and bring it here, please?"

"The black one?" he asked as he started to dash out of the kitchen.

"Yes, the one I use when I write stuff," Emmy said.

Kevin Michael raced to the den and returned in a few seconds. "Here you go, Mommy. Do you need your power cable, too?"

Emmy checked. "Nope, I'm good for now."

"Are you going to read us your new story?" Heather asked.

"What's it about," Isabella asked as she sat at the large island facing the stove.

Heather and Kevin Michael sat on opposite sides of Isabella.

"Is it another funny story like the one you wrote about Scout chasing that skunk in the woods?" Kevin Michael asked. "That one was funny even if Scout smelled horrible, and Uncle

18

Tony had to give her a bath with tomato soup."

"No, this is a different type of story. It's kinda sad." Emmy shook her head and looked at Kenny. "Should I read it?"

"I think you should," he said and then turned back to stir the chili.

Emmy took a deep breath. "This is a story about a baby boy who was born a little over a year ago."

"Do we know him? Is he walking now?" Heather asked.

Kenny held the large spoon in his hand as he turned around. "If you want Mommy to read the story, you need to sit still and listen. Don't interrupt her, okay?"

The kids agreed to listen.

"The baby was named Gideon, and his heart and lungs were... broken. He lived for forty-three days and then went to heaven to be with Jesus," Emmy explained. She heard the kids gasp, but they didn't interrupt her. "This is kinda like a story of what might have happened if Gideon had lived longer."

Emmy took a deep breath, looked at everyone and then began to read. The kids settled onto their barstools and soon the only sound in the kitchen was that of the gas burner hissing under the pot of chili. Emmy read for several minutes until she came to a natural place in the story to pause. She looked around the island and bit her lip as the tears she had been trying to stop overflowed and cascaded down her cheeks. "I'm sorry for making everyone cry," she said and then pointed at the stove. "Kenny, I think you're burning the chili."

He quickly turned around, shut off the burner and stirred the chili. "I think it will be all right." He sniffed it and took a bite. He turned around and nodded. "It's still okay."

"Should I read the rest of the story?" Emmy asked as she looked at the kids.

Kevin Michael rubbed his eyes. Isabella and Heather grabbed paper towels and blew their noses. Then the kids nodded.

Emmy read the rest of her story and then held out her arms.

The kids jumped down and raced around the island. They nearly knocked Emmy off of her stool as they all tried to hug her at the same time.

Emmy grabbed the island and held on. "I love you guys so much. I thank God everyday for the chance to be your mommy."

"Even on the days when we are bad, and you have to yell at us?" Kevin Michael asked.

"Especially on those days," Emmy said.

"I think the chili is ready," Kenny said as he dried his eyes with his handkerchief. "Should I make you a bowl?"

"Yes, please."

Kenny filled one of their colorful, ceramic soup bowls. "Could someone get the crackers and shredded cheese out, please?"

Isabella grabbed the cheese.

Kevin Michael walked into the pantry and brought out the oyster crackers. "Here you go, Mommy. You can eat all of them if you want."

"Thank you, guys."

Kenny walked around the island, placed the bowl of steaming hot chili in front of her along with a glass of water and kissed the top of her head.

"What are you going to do with your story, Mommy?" Heather asked. "Will it be a book like the one about Grandpa and the lions?"

"I'm not sure yet, sweetie," Emmy said as she added a handful of shredded cheese and a bunch of crackers to her chili. "I'll have to think about it."

"Ms. Dalton read us a story about Gideon from the Bible," Isabella said. "Maybe baby Gideon's parents named him for the Gideon in the Bible."

"I think they probably did," Emmy said as she blew on her chili. She took a bite and reached for the water. "It does have a kick to it. What did you put in it?" she asked Kenny.

"I found some jalapeno peppers in the fridge and added several. Did I add too many?"

"No, I think there were three of them in that spoonful."

"Water won't help. Drink some milk or add salt," Kenny suggested.

# Chapter Three

"Emmy, I told you not to bring anything," Diane Robertson said as Emmy handed her a large Tupperware bowl of taco salad. "We will have plenty of food."

"I brought it in case the kids want some. I know Carson and Caden like my taco salad."

"Hush. Will you help me with this veggie tray?" Diane asked. "Did I tell you the boys got a letter from their father?" Diane made the word father sound vulgar.

"I thought Craig was in jail. Is he out?" Emmy asked.

"He's not in jail." Diane made room in the large fridge for the taco salad.

"Where's he living?" Emmy asked while slicing a pepper.

"The return address was somewhere in Texas. You know he got married again, right?" Diane asked.

"Who would marry that creep?" Emmy asked.

Diane stared at her and frowned.

"Oh, come on. I didn't mean it like that. You didn't know any better when he knocked you up."

"Nice language, Emmy," Diane said.

Carson and Caden Garrett chose that moment to make an entrance.

Thirteen-year-old Carson asked, "Mom, can we have something to eat now? We're starving."

Nine-year-old Caden nodded in agreement. "Aunt Emmy, did you make some of your taco salad? It's always better than Mom's."

"I did, but you need to ask your mother if you can have some."

"Can we, Mom?" Carson asked.

Diane sneered and pointed to the fridge. "Don't eat it all. It might make you sick."

Emmy made a face at Diane and then asked, "Where is Brady? Has he said anything about turning fifty?"

"He's downstairs with the guys. They're watching football. He says this is just another birthday, but I think he's feeling his

21

age." Diane grabbed Carson's arm. "Put the bowl back in the fridge, please."

"He's in pretty good shape for his age," Emmy said.

"Don't tell him that. He went to the doctor for a checkup last week, and he weighs over 220 pounds. He's never been that heavy." Diane placed the veggie tray in the fridge. "I told the guys we would eat around three."

"I'm going downstairs," Kenny said. "Wanna watch some football, Em?"

"I'll come down to say hi to Brady and Mr. Robertson, but I'm not interested in college football."

Emmy followed Kenny to the finished basement. Kenny sat on an empty barstool next to John Randolph while Emmy walked up behind the couch that faced the large screen TV.

"Who's playing?" Emmy asked no one in particular. "Oh, happy birthday, Brady."

Andy Walker, the longtime manager of the band Fridays At Five, turned in his position on one of the recliners and answered, "Michigan State and Iowa."

"What are you doing here, cuz?" Emmy asked as she stood behind Mr. Robertson and massaged his shoulders. "You're not family."

"I happen to be Brady's next door neighbor in case you've forgotten. You never stop over to see me, and you don't bring the kids over anymore," Andy complained.

"Have a seat, Emmy," Tony Bertucci said from his position in one of the leather recliners that flanked the couch. "It's a close game. All tied at three at the end of the first quarter."

"How did they score three points?" Emmy asked with a straight face.

Andy started to answer but then shook a finger at her. "You know enough about football to be a coach. I'm not falling for your ignorance routine."

"I'm a girl. What do I know about football," Emmy said as she shrugged.

"Watch the game with us, Emmy. You can explain the different strategies to us," Tony said. "They're so confusing."

"No thanks. I just wanted to wish Brady a happy birthday. You guys can watch the game. I'll see if Diane needs any help," Emmy said and then headed back upstairs.

Kenny leaned back against the bar's granite countertop and asked John, "Do you miss playing football?"

John Randolph and Tony Bertucci met at Notre Dame. They shared a dorm room and played on the football team together. After college they both played professionally for the Chicago Bears before retiring.

"I miss the camaraderie, but not the bruises," John laughed. "Kristen is glad I'm retired, but I'm working longer hours with Bertucci and Keasling Construction. How about you? Do you miss being on tour?"

"I miss playing in front of people, but I like sleeping in my own bed every night," Kenny said. "I did spend a couple of weekends in Alabama playing guitar for BearFace. That's Jeremiah's band. I thoroughly enjoyed playing my guitar out of the spotlight. Are you going to coach anymore at North Park?"

"I've thought about coaching part-time, but both of my brothers are coaching at the college level, and they encouraged me to stick with the construction company."

"You definitely have more job security there," Kenny said.

John laughed. "It's good to be married to the boss's daughter."

"I didn't think Mr. Keasling was involved in the day-to-day stuff anymore."

John shook his head. "He's not. He was involved in the building of the new sanctuary for your church, but that was the last thing he really did. He's still the president of the company, but it's more of a... How should I say it?"

"It's just a title," Kenny said.

"Yes," John said.

The first half of the game ended with the score tied at six.

"There's beer in the fridge," Brady told his guests. "Water and pop, too."

Andy stood up. "Who needs a beer?"

Brady and his brother, Bennett, raised hands.

23

"Tony, you want one?" Andy asked.

"Sure, I'll take one," Tony answered.

The guys spent the halftime break checking out the display of Brady's photographs on the walls while sipping their beverages.

"Did you take all of these?" Kenny asked as he drank a bottle of water.

Brady answered in the affirmative and explained about his hobby and the gallery he operated.

"Do you still have time for your hobby since you have to travel to promote the new company?" Andy asked.

Brady and Bennett had started a new company in 2012 after their father, Bill Robertson, sold Robertson Industries, a hugely successful technology company, to a German conglomerate in 2010 for over 800 million dollars.

"I'm hoping I won't have to travel as much in 2016," Brady said. "We never expected Carson & Caden to become profitable as quickly as it has. I don't spend as much time at the gallery as I did the first couple of years after Dad sold the company. My cousin Jill Greenberg takes care of the place for me."

Kenny spotted a photograph of Emmy and asked, "When and where did you take this?"

Brady looked at the photograph and smiled. He checked the back of the enlargement. "It was taken in 2001. The spring if I remember correctly. I had just met Diane, and she and Emmy allowed me to photograph them. I took this at a park down the street from where they lived."

"So Em was twenty at the time," Kenny said.

Andy Walker stared at the photograph. "She doesn't look any older than sixteen. Seventeen tops."

Brady looked at a picture of Diane taken at the same time. *Diane might only be two and a half years older than Emmy, but she looks five to ten years older in this photograph. Now she looks at least ten years older. Maybe more.*

"Hey! Are you guys gonna watch the second half, or are you gonna stare at that picture of the brat?" Tony snickered. Though they were not blood related, Tony thought of Emmy as his little sister, and he teased her constantly.

24

The game ended with Michigan State winning by four points.

Emmy came downstairs and asked, "Is it over? Diane is ready to eat."

"Just ended," Tony said. "Should I carry you back upstairs like a sack of potatoes?"

She stared up at him and made a face. "I can manage on my own."

Tony stood over a foot taller than Emmy and outweighed her by about 120 pounds. He had dropped thirty pounds from his football weight of 250.

"Good! I don't want to hurt my back by carrying you," Tony said.

"I will escort you upstairs, Emmy," Mr. Robertson said.

"Thank you, Mr. Robertson. You are a true gentleman," Emmy said and then stuck out her tongue at Tony.

"Kenny, why do you put up with her?" Tony asked.

"The kids like having her around," Kenny teased.

An hour later Diane brought out the cake. Everyone, even the kids, gathered in the kitchen to sing "Happy Birthday" to Brady. Then Diane lit the two candles.

"Did you make a wish, Uncle Brady?" Isabella asked.

"I did, sweetie. Should I tell you what I wished for?"

"No!" Several of the kids hollered.

Heather explained to him, "If you tell anyone your wish, it won't come true."

"Well, I certainly want my wish to come true," he said and then blew out the candles.

Diane and Emmy cut the cake and scooped out the ice cream. After Brady and the kids got their dessert, Tony walked up to Emmy.

"I don't know if I should let you have any dessert," Emmy said.

"Why not?"

Emmy tapped her bottom lip as she thought of a good reason. "Because you're eating healthy stuff, and this might cause you to gain some weight."

25

Diane handed a slice of cake to Kenny. "Would you like ice cream?"

"Yes, please," he answered and then grinned at Emmy. "You better let him have some, Em, or else he might eat the whole cake."

Emmy rolled her eyes. "Fine! You can have a small slice and one little scoop of ice cream."

"You are too kind."

"Just don't come around asking for seconds if you know what's good for you," she said handing him a plate.

Fifteen minutes later Dotty Bertucci walked up to Emmy. "May I have another slice of the chocolate cake and two big scoops of ice cream, please?"

Emmy sliced the cake and started to scoop out the ice cream. She looked at Dotty, who was grinning. "Hey! Wait a minute. You never ask for seconds. Is this really for you, or is it for your father?"

"Papa Tony was afraid you wouldn't let him have anymore," Dotty said.

"I'll take this over to him, Dotty. I might let him eat it, or I might smash the cake in his face," Emmy said.

Dotty laughed. "Can we watch?"

"Sure, but I probably won't smash it in his face. That would be a waste of cake, and this is really pretty good." Emmy walked to where Tony waited with John and Mr. Robertson. "You should be ashamed of yourself," Emmy said as she frowned at Tony.

"Why?"

"Sending your eleven-year-old daughter instead of asking for seconds yourself."

"I thought you would let Dotty have it," Tony said. "You aren't going to smash it in my face, are you?"

"Not this time, but one of these days I will."

Tony stuck his finger in the frosting and then put some on the tip of Emmy's nose.

"You're such a creep." She wiped off the frosting, ate it and handed it to Tony.

"And you're such a brat," Tony teased back.

Isabella put her hands on her hips and looked up at Tony. "My mommy is not a brat. You better be nice to her."

Tony smiled at Isabella. "I'm not being mean to her when I call her a brat. She calls me a creep, and I call her a brat. It's just our way of being nice to each other, Isa."

"Then you guys are just weird," Isabella said rolling her eyes.

Later that night as Kenny was putting the girls in bed Isabella asked, "Do you think Mommy and Uncle Tony are weird?"

"Why would you ask that, Isa?"

"Because they always tease each other and call each other names. It seems weird."

Kenny laughed. "They do tease each other a lot, but it's just their way of expressing how much they love each other. They love each other like you love Heather and Kevin Michael."

Isabella thought about it for a moment. "I understand that Jesus says you need to love everyone, but Mommy doesn't tease Uncle Andy or Uncle John or anyone the way she teases Uncle Tony."

"That's true, but she and Father James tease each other."

"But he really is her brother. I just don't understand why adults act the way they do at times," Isabella said with a sigh.

"You know, sweetie, sometimes I don't understand it either," Kenny said and then kissed Isabella good night.

The next afternoon Emmy drove the kids back to the church to celebrate Phoebe Grace Hammond's second birthday. After playing games and eating cake and ice cream, Phoebe Grace began opening her gifts with a little help from her five-year-old brother, Grayson, and her eight-year-old sister, Natalie.

"Dany, did I mention I'm seriously thinking of taking some classes at North Park so I can teach school?" Emmy asked while adding Mrs. Grabavoy's name to the list of gift givers.

"No, you didn't. That's great. I'm leaving Hampshire Medical Group in January to start work on my doctorate."

"That's fantastic!" Emmy hugged Dany. "Will you guys be

27

all right on just Darian's salary with Aberdeen Investments?"

Dany grinned. "We will unless you and Kenny decide to raise our rent to what you should be charging us."

"We could always lower the rent if we need," Emmy whispered.

"Don't be silly! You're charging five hundred a month. You could easily get five times that much or more."

"We wouldn't think of raising your rent, Dany. The girls love having you guys live in the guesthouse. Maybe we can ride to North Park together," Emmy said.

"We might be able to do that," Dany replied.

Emmy bit her lip for a moment. "I have to admit I'm a little scared about going back to college. The classes will be tougher, and I'll have to get used to doing my own homework."

Dany grinned. "Maybe the girls could help you with your homework instead of you helping with theirs."

Liz frowned at Dany and Emmy. "Did you catch that last gift? If you're not going to pay attention, I'll do it myself."

"Sorry, Lizzie," Dany said. "We'll stop talking and do our job."

Phoebe finished opening her gifts and Emmy gave the list to Liz.

"Thanks, Emmy. I appreciate the help," Liz said.

"Kenny and I drove separately, so he can take the kids home. I could hang around and help clean up," Emmy said.

"Tyler, Darian and Larry will put all the tables and chairs away, but I could use help with the decorations."

"I can help with that," Emmy answered.

"I want to save the balloons," Liz said.

Thirty minutes later all the guests had departed except for family members and Emmy. The guys broke down the tables, loaded the chairs onto the long carts and put everything back into the storage closet. Emmy and the ladies took care of cleaning the kitchen and gathering up the trash.

"Darian, would you be a saint and take this out for us, please?" Emmy asked smiling up at him.

Darian took the trash out and then returned.

"I think we're finished," Tyler said.

Liz whispered in his ear and Tyler nodded. "It's okay with me."

Liz got everyone's attention. "We have an announcement to make."

Emmy's eyes sparkled. "Are you pregnant again?"

Liz smiled. "Yes, I am due sometime in August. We didn't want to announce it this morning, but we will next Sunday."

"Does that mean we can't tell anyone until then?"

Liz shook her head. "I know you can't keep quiet for that long, Em. We've told our parents, so I guess you can tell your friends. I wasn't going to post anything on Facebook until next Sunday."

Emmy hugged Liz. "I'm so happy for you. I get my baby fix every time you guys have a baby. Are you going to tell us the sex, or will you make us wait?"

"We'll tell our closest friends, but they have to keep it a secret."

Emmy's face fell.

"I'm teasing. You won't have to keep it a secret," Liz said. "When I knew I was pregnant, I told Tyler, and he didn't say 'Oh, no' like he did the last time. I told him I wanted to have six babies. Then he groaned."

"I wish I could have had six babies," Emmy said.

# Chapter Four

Monday morning the six members of the Bender Brothers Band along with their manager, Nelson Grapella, and their attorney met in a conference room with Max Kesson, the owner and founder of the Steward Music Group, and two attorneys representing the music label. The attorney for the band spent thirty minutes going over the proposed recording contract.

Micah Hurst acted as the spokesman for the band. "So we get to record two CDs over the next five years. The label will cover the expense of recording, but that will come out of our royalties, right?"

The attorney answered in the affirmative. He also informed the band the contract was for the band entity in whole not as individuals. He explained a few other legal details.

"What does that mean?" Quinten Matthews, who played keyboards for the band, asked.

"Basically, it means that it doesn't matter who is in the band as long as three of the original members are still active," the attorney explained. "It doesn't matter which three."

Nelson and the attorney talked to the guys for several minutes.

"We keep control of our music publishing and will own the master recordings, right?" Micah asked.

"That's correct," the attorney said. "The band is really licensing the recordings to the label for a period of ten years. It's a very good deal for an unknown band. The label will provide some promotion, which will come out of your royalties, and will be responsible for the distribution of the recording."

Bobby O'Connor mentioned the band's partnership agreement. "We are all equal partners in the band, but we won't equally share the mechanical royalties for writing the songs, however we will share the publishing income."

"We understand that the guys who write the songs will make more money," Quinten said.

The attorney explained the differences between mechanical royalties and performance royalties along with other details such as

over tomorrow and you could talk to them," Emmy said.

Kenny called Bobby and they agreed to meet the next morning at ten.

Kenny took the guys downstairs to his studio and asked, "Do you have a time period in mind?"

Micah answered, "We would like to get going as soon as possible. We want to record our original songs. We've got ten we think are pretty good."

Kenny replied, "I'm going back into the studio in January, and right now it's kinda busy with the holidays coming up."

"That's understandable," Micah said.

"Do you guys have time to play the songs? That would give me an idea of how long it might take to get the basic tracks recorded."

"We've got all day," Bobby said.

"Unfortunately, Adam Vicini will be using the studio this afternoon. He's finishing up some stuff for his solo project," Kenny said. "But we have a couple of hours."

The band set up quickly, and Kenny set some recording levels while they warmed up.

"I'm good to go," Kenny said when Emmy joined him in the control room.

Bobby counted off the song, and the band played for the next ninety minutes.

Kenny and Emmy left the control room and walked into the open studio where the band sat.

"What did you think?" Micah asked. "Our style is certainly different than your band."

"You guys sound good," Kenny said. "I'd like to be involved with your project. Give me some time to listen to what I recorded today, and let's see if we can come up with a time to get this done."

He shook hands with the guys as they gathered their gear and left.

"What do you really think?" Emmy asked.

"I really think they're talented. The lyrics could use some

33

work, but I love the way they jam together. It might be difficult to capture that in the studio, but I'll think about a way to do it."

Adam Vicini and Will Consoli arrived thirty minutes later. Adam needed to work on his vocal tracks, but all the backing tracks were finished. Emmy added some harmony to a couple songs.

Friday afternoon Adam, Will and Emmy listened to the eleven tracks.

"I could spend another six months making little changes and adding different layers, but I'm happy with the tracks," Adam said.

"They need to be mixed and mastered, and you should be finished," Will, who had worked with Fridays At Five on all of their recordings, said.

Emmy asked, "Do you have the artwork finished? I know the team at Steward Music has been working on it."

"We've got most of it finished. The booklet is done for the most part. I have to decide on the cover. I've got a couple of ideas."

"Did you ever decide on the title?" Emmy asked.

Adam shook his head. "I have a title in mind, but Juliana doesn't like it. She wants me to come up with something different."

"Spouses can be hard to please. Does Kinsey have any suggestions?" Emmy asked and then giggled.

"Em, she's not even three yet," Adam said about his daughter.

"Heather and Isabella keep coming up with titles for their first CD. They even draw pictures for the cover art."

"Who knows, Em. One of these days they might be recording artists like their parents," Adam said.

"They might be better suited to the life than me," Emmy replied.

# Chapter Five

"Mom, what time do we have to be at church?" Heather asked while standing in her parents' bedroom doorway. "We need to practice our songs again."

Emmy rolled over in bed and looked at the clock on the nightstand. "It's only six thirty. You don't need to be at church until nine. Why are you awake so early?"

Heather walked into the large room and sat on Emmy's side of the bed. "I woke up at six and couldn't go back to sleep."

Emmy patted a spot on the edge of the bed. "Do you need to cuddle?"

"Mom, I'm almost ten. I don't need cuddles anymore," Heather said but she climbed into bed next to her mother.

Emmy ran her fingers through Heather's long hair. "Are you nervous about today?"

"Maybe a little bit because I'm afraid the other kids will forget their lines and ruin everything. Isa and I know our parts and our songs. Eloise Frees knows her part, but Devin Lenagan didn't know all his lines and he plays Joseph. He will ruin everything, I just know it."

Emmy rubbed Heather's back and pulled her close. "He knew most of his lines, and I'm sure he will do just fine. You can't worry about this. It's not meant to be a professional performance."

"But you always tell us to do our best," Heather said.

Kenny turned onto his side, raised up and smiled at Heather. "I thought I heard one of my angels. Why are you in bed with us?"

"Oh, Daddy, I'm not a baby."

Kenny scooted over, patted a spot in the middle and pulled back the covers. "You're still my angel, and I need a cuddle."

Heather sighed, but she climbed over Emmy and pulled the covers up. "I didn't mean to wake you up."

"I'm going back to sleep," Emmy said. She turned onto her side and burrowed deep into the covers.

"Is something bothering you, Heather?" Kenny asked. He touched the tip of her nose and grinned.

35

Heather rested her head on Kenny's chest and whispered, "I'm just anxious about today."

Kenny squeezed her and kissed the top of her head. "It's all right to have some butterflies. I still get nervous before a show."

"Daddy, that's different," Heather said. "At our last practice I saw three boys laughing and picking their noses. Why do we have to have boys in the program?"

Kenny stifled a laugh and said, "If they do that today, it will only embarrass them and their parents."

"Uncle Tony will be mad if Ben picks his nose."

Later that morning, Kenny parked the Odyssey, and Emmy turned around to face the kids.

"What?" Heather asked.

"We need to meet in Noah's Ark to rehearse one last time."

"We know, Mom," Heather said rolling her eyes.

"I've had enough of your attitude, young lady," Emmy said. "Keep it up if you want to be grounded."

"Be careful and watch for cars," Kenny warned as the kids exited the van and began running toward the church. He looked at Emmy. "Should we take away her phone or her tablet?"

"Maybe we should restrict how often she can use her electronics. When I was a kid, Diane and I shared a landline," Emmy said.

Kenny chuckled and said, "Maybe you shouldn't tell them. It makes us seem ancient."

Emmy walked into Noah's Ark a few minutes later and sat beside Lindsey Frees.

"Are the kids ready for this?" Emmy asked.

Lindsey smiled as she watched her daughter, Eloise, talking to Heather and Isabella. "Eloise knows all her lines and she has helped the younger children learn the motions."

"Oh, Lindsey, I forgot about her birthday. I'm sorry," Emmy whispered.

Lindsey waved a hand. "It's okay. I can't believe she is nine already."

"Tell me about it," Emmy said. "My girls will be ten next month. I still think of them as babies."

Wade and Blaine Dickinson moved to the front of Noah's Ark. Blaine gestured for the children to settle down.

"We need to make the most of our time," she said. "I would like to go over all the songs first. Then we can go through the program from start to finish. Would my helpers join me up front, please?"

Lindsey turned to Emmy. "That means us."

Emmy stood and said, "I'm more nervous than the kids. I hope I don't screw up."

Lindsey laughed as they headed to the front. "I'm sure you will be fine."

Later in the sanctuary, Kristen waved to get Sloane's attention. "We saved some seats," Kristen said when Sloane and Tony got closer. "I thought Mama was coming, too."

Tony hooked a thumb over his shoulder. "She's talking to some people. Will I need my binoculars to see the kids?"

Sloane rolled her eyes. "We're only a few rows back."

Pastor Tyler opened the service a few minutes later with a prayer and some announcements.

"I won't take up anymore time because you are here to see the children," Tyler said. "Blaine, it's all yours."

The children marched into the sanctuary and took their places on the stage.

"I see you guys," Tony said waving back at Benjamin, Taylor and Coby. He whispered to Sloane, "Can you believe Peter and Dotty are too old to be in the program?"

"I can't believe Coby is old enough to be in the program," Sloane answered. "Noemi, Grace and Emmy's girls have the best parts in the play."

"Hey, who is that big kid trying to get the little ones situated on the stage?" Tony asked while pointing.

"Emmy is helping with the singing. Don't make fun of her. She's put a lot of effort into this."

"I did my part. I helped build the backdrop," Tony said. "That's important."

"Is that why the manger looks lopsided?" Sloane asked.

Tony tilted his head and stared. "It looks okay to me."

"Hush," Sloane said. "Blaine is ready to start and don't distract the boys."

The backing track started and Emmy helped the younger children with the motions from her position in the front row.

"The kids sound really good," Tony said.

"You are aware... Never mind." Sloane rolled her eyes.

"I know it's a track, but I can still hear the kids singing a little."

The younger children finished and sat down. Blaine waited until the platform was ready and introduced the skit. Devin knew all his lines, but Eloise forgot one of hers. Near the end of the program Heather and Isabella sang their song.

Mama Bertucci smiled and whispered to Sloane, "They are so talented."

Kristen turned around, smiled and said, "Emmy wrote that song specifically for this program."

Emmy wandered around the foyer after the service looking for her Bristol Ridge friends.

"Hey, Emmy!" Tony waved. "Are you looking for us?"

She dodged around some older people and made her way to Tony's side. "Don't you dare make fun of me."

Tony shrugged. "Now why would I do that?"

"I felt weird doing those motions."

"You looked all right to me," Tony said with a straight face.

Emmy glared at him but didn't say anything.

"The twins sounded amazing," Mama said. "I thoroughly enjoyed the entire program."

"Thanks, Mama, but I'm gonna get after Kevin Michael. Did you see how he and Ben stood there without singing. All they did was look around at the other kids."

"The boys aren't interested in performing," Sloane said.

"They could sing. I'll talk to you later. I need to find Kenny and his parents," Emmy said.

"I wonder if anyone got a video of that boy picking his nose?" Tony asked.

"Aren't you going to ride with me?" Patricia Colasanti asked Diane the next afternoon.

"No, Mom," Diane answered. "Emmy is going to meet you at Sunrise Garden."

"Is that the place with all those other old people?" Patricia asked.

"Yes, and you like living there."

"I think my shows will be on soon. I don't want to miss them."

"You can watch whatever you want." Diane observed the driver close the door to the med-car and pull away. *I'm grateful you are doing better, Mom, but all this going back and forth from the hospital to the nursing home and then to the memory care facility is taking its toll on me.*

Emmy paced in the Sunrise Garden lobby. Finally, her cell phone rang.

"Mom is on her way," Diane said. "You have to help her get settled into her apartment."

"I will, but I can't stay too long. I'm supposed to pick up the kids after school."

Diane shook her head. "Brady's home. He can pick them up. You have to stay with Mom."

"Fine!" Emmy sighed. "I'll stay for an hour, but I need to get home and make dinner. Where are you going? You didn't tell me."

"I have an appointment with my attorney if you must know," Diane answered.

"Why?" Emmy asked. She sat on a chair in the lobby to wait.

"None of your business, little sister."

Emmy made a face at her phone and asked, "You better tell me if something bad is going on. I need to know."

Diane rolled her eyes. "Craig is causing a stink. He wants more visitation rights, and I'm not willing to let him see the boys without supervision. You know he was arrested for passing bad checks, right?"

"You never told me," Emmy said. She jumped up and

39

walked around the corner. "When did this happen?"

"A month ago. He doesn't really want to see the boys. He just wants to aggravate me and cost me some money. He is such an..."

"Remember he is the reason you have your boys," Emmy interrupted.

"That's the only good thing Craig Garrett has ever done in his life," Diane replied. "I wish Carson and Caden didn't look so much like him."

The med-car arrived ten minutes later. Emmy and a care partner helped her mother get settled in her apartment.

"How do I turn on the TV?" Patricia asked after the care partner left.

Emmy found the remote. "See this green button?"

"Yes, I'm not blind."

"That turns it on and you change the channels by pressing this one," Emmy explained. "There are some residents who aren't allowed to have a TV. You need to take care of the TV by yourself and not bother your caregivers."

Patricia waved a hand. "Bah! I pay them enough money. They better do what I ask." She looked around the small apartment. "I don't think this is the same place. I used to live in a bigger apartment. There was a table and I used to play cards with my friends. Don't tell your father, but I made a bunch of money."

"It will be our secret, Mom," Emmy said. *I suppose it's a good thing you can't remember Daddy has been gone for almost ten years. I should stop by the cemetery soon.*

# Chapter Six

"Are you ready for me to pick you up?" Emmy asked Father James over the phone Wednesday afternoon. "I've got most of your special dinner ready to go in the oven."

"A special dinner, huh?" Father James asked. "Is it something I will like?"

"You said you wanted meatloaf, cheesy potatoes and baked beans for your sixtieth birthday, so that's what I'm making."

"I could drive over and save you the trip," he said.

"Have you looked outside lately? It's raining and trying to snow. Our driveway can get rather icy. I doubt if your old Civic would make it up the hill. I'll come and get you in about thirty minutes. You can spend the night here if you want, or else I'll take you home later."

"I'll be ready. Did you tell the kids I don't want any gifts?"

"I told them, and they ignored me. So you better not be a scrooge if they try to give you something," Emmy warned.

"I will be very gracious."

Emmy checked the oven and told Kenny to keep an eye on the food. Then she grabbed her purse, keys and coat and ran out to the garage. She started up her BMW X3 since it had four-wheel drive. She backed out, closed the garage door with the remote and started down the driveway. She slid to a stop at the bottom. "Wow! It's slipperier than I thought. I better watch my speed."

It took ten minutes longer than normal to arrive at the St. John's rectory where Father James lived. She pulled up in the driveway, parked and got out.

Father James saw her and stepped outside. "Be careful! I put some salt down earlier, but it's still slick in spots."

Emmy laughed as she slid along the sidewalk. "I can tell."

Father James shook his head and held the handrail as he walked down the concrete steps. He reached the sidewalk, let go of the rail and lost his footing. He tried to break his fall with his arm.

"Are you all right?" Emmy asked as she raced to his side. "Can you get up?"

He sat there for a moment and then held onto her arm as he

stood up. "I think I may have injured my wrist."

"Let me see. Does it hurt?" Emmy grabbed his arm and he winced in pain. "Sorry! I didn't mean to hurt you."

"I'll be all right," he said as he used his other hand to hold his injured arm.

Emmy looked into his eyes and could see his pain. "I'm taking you to the ER. You might have a broken arm. Stand here and I'll drive the car up the sidewalk."

"Don't be silly. I can walk to the car as long as you hang on to me," he said.

Emmy helped him to the car and buckled his seatbelt. "St. Bart's is only a few minutes away."

"Don't drive like a maniac, okay?"

"I'll get you there safely. I promise," Emmy said as she backed out and spun the SUV in a circle.

She arrived at the hospital, helped Father James out of the car and threw her keys at the parking valet. She grabbed a wheelchair, pushed her half-brother up the ramp into the building and approached the check-in desk.

"May I help you?"

"I think Father James has a broken arm," Emmy said.

The lady took Father James' information, and since the ER was unexpectedly slow, he was taken back to triage immediately.

"How did you fall, Father?" the nurse asked as she helped him remove his heavy winter coat.

"My own fault for not spreading enough salt on the sidewalk," he gritted his teeth to hide the pain as he answered.

"It's his sixtieth birthday, and I was taking him to my house for dinner," Emmy explained.

"Are you family?"

"Yes!" Emmy exclaimed. "Brother James is my father."

The nurse stared at her and then at Father James.

"She means I am her brother," he said and then chuckled. "I'm Father James from St. John's."

"I see," the nurse said with a smile as she felt his arm. "I'm sorry, but I think dinner will have to wait a while. We're going to take an x-ray to make sure, but I think you have a fracture."

"Should I come with you?" Emmy asked.

"You could wait here," the nurse said. "He won't be gone long, and I promise to take good care of him."

"I will be all right, Emmy. You don't need to worry," Father James said.

Emmy called Kenny and explained what happened. "Dinner might have to wait until tomorrow. I don't know how long this will take. They might want to keep him overnight. You could find something else for the kids to eat."

"Did he hit his head?" Kenny asked.

"No, but he is old."

Kenny chuckled. "I don't think they will admit him because of his age, Em. He's only sixty."

Fifteen minutes later the nurse wheeled Father James back.

"The doctor will take a look at the x-rays as soon as he can. We'll try to get you out of here as soon as possible," the nurse said.

"Does it still hurt?" Emmy asked.

He stared at her. "Did you ever break anything when you were a kid?"

"I broke lots of stuff," Emmy answered.

"I mean bones," he sighed.

"Oh! No, I don't remember ever breaking any bones. I skinned my knees a lot, and I got scrapes and cuts because I was a tomboy, but I never broke my arm."

Dr. Orestes Lawless pulled back the curtain and walked into the cubicle.

"I remember you," Emmy said. "You were the doctor who treated Mama Bertucci."

He smiled. "I remember Mrs. Bertucci. Are you her daughter?"

Emmy shook her head. "Not really, but kinda."

Dr. Lawless didn't bat an eye. "Father James, you have fractured your Radius, and you will need a cast."

"Couldn't you put a splint on it?" Father James asked.

"A cast will be better. I wouldn't want you to hurt it again. It won't take long." Dr. Lawless looked at Emmy again. "I think I remember you for some reason."

43

"She's married to Kenny Colwell the rock star," Father James said.

"Ah! Yes! You're a singer, too. I've seen your picture on my daughter's CD. Your CD, I mean," he added. "Someone will be with you soon, and you should be able to go home in an hour or so. I'll give you a script for pain."

After the doctor left, Emmy whispered, "An hour in hospital time usually means three hours in real time."

"Don't be so negative, Emmy."

"Did I ever tell you about the time Isabella broke her arm?"

"No, I don't think so. When was that?"

"She was three. She fell out of her bed because she was using it like a trampoline. I'll let her tell you about it. What about the time Tony broke his arm?"

"I haven't heard that story either. Did he break it playing football?" Father James asked the obvious question.

Emmy shook her head. "He was involved in an accident at school. Notre Dame." Emmy put a finger to her mouth as she tried to remember the year. "It was March of 2002. Tony's car was hit by a truck because of the icy roads. His car was totaled and he broke his left arm and suffered some cuts and bruises. At least it didn't happen during football season. Oh, there was one really good thing that happened."

"What might that have been?"

Emmy grinned. "That's when Kristen first met John Randolph. They fell in love right away."

"Yeah, right."

"Well, they kinda did," Emmy insisted. "And that was the night Richard Demarco made a pass at me."

Father James waited for Emmy to say more, but she just bit her lip. "Care to expound?"

Emmy took a deep breath. "This was when Kenny was seeing Becky. We weren't together."

Father James placed his hands together. "Go on."

"Richard was this older guy I knew from work. He's dead now, but he wasn't then. Duh!"

Father James raised his eyebrows but didn't interrupt.

"He liked me, and I saw him a few times, but I wasn't really interested in him as a... you know... someone I would want to date. Anyway, that night we went out to dinner or something. No! We went to a club and listened to The Notable Exceptions. He wouldn't dance with me, but Barry Newton did." Emmy rambled on as Father James listened silently. "We left and went back to my place. He said he wanted to watch a movie, but I think he really just wanted to make out and try to get me in bed. Anyway, the phone rang and it was Mama Bertucci. She told me about Tony's accident, so I threw Richard out of the house and told him never to call me again. I called Mama back and she told me he was hurt but not in danger. Then I called Kristen, and I think she came over. We left for South Bend the next morning and that's when she met John." Emmy paused to take a breath.

"This Richard is deceased?"

"Yes, he was killed in a plane crash," Emmy said and then bit her lip hard.

"Emmy, what is it?" Father James asked as he noticed Emmy's eyes fill with tears.

"I was going to be on that plane, but Mr. Robertson talked me out of it," she explained as she wiped her eyes.

Father James stared at her for a moment and then squeezed her hand with his good hand. "Thank God for Mr. Robertson and miracles."

This time an hour meant an hour. Father James's arm was placed in a cast, and they were able to leave.

"I'll get the car from the valet. Then we'll stop and check your prescription. I don't want you to be in a lot of pain."

"It doesn't hurt as much now as it did when I fell," he said.

"It might hurt more later."

The valet pulled up the car, and they stopped at the Walgreens. Emmy ran inside to get the prescription.

"Do you want one now?" she asked.

"Maybe with dinner. Are we still doing dinner?"

"As long as Kenny didn't let it burn," Emmy answered.

Heather, Isabella and Kevin Michael met Emmy and Father James in the kitchen.

"Did you really break your arm?" Heather asked.

"Do you have a cast?" Isabella asked.

"Did Mommy push you down?" Kevin Michael asked.

"I did not push him down. He slipped on some ice," Emmy said as she helped Father James remove his coat.

He held out his arm. "I have a cast. See?"

"Can we sign our names on it?" Heather asked.

"I would be happy for you to sign it."

Heather ran to get a Sharpie.

Isabella held Father James' other hand. "I bent my arm when I was three. I fell out of bed and the doctor put a purple cast on it. It hurt for a while, but it's all right now."

Heather returned and the kids signed their names.

"I hope it gets better real soon, Uncle James. Did Mommy make you fall down? You can tell me if she did," Kevin Michael asked again.

"I did not make him fall down, and why did you call him Uncle James? You don't usually."

"But he's your brother, so that means he's our uncle. A real uncle," Kevin Michael said. "Not like all our other uncles."

"Brady is our a real uncle because he's married to Aunt Diane," Isabella said.

"You can call me Uncle James or Father James. I don't mind either way."

Kenny walked into the kitchen. "Our dinner is in the oven. I put it back to keep it warm. Do you feel like eating, Father James?"

"I could use some meatloaf and cheesy potatoes..."

"Mommy made baked beans, too. They make you fart," Kevin Michael said with a grin.

After dinner Heather and Isabella sang for Father James.

"That was very good, girls," Father James said as he clapped. "You have inherited your mother's talent."

"Mom said you didn't want any presents, so we thought we would sing a song just for you," Isabella said.

"That was better than any other present ever," he said as he hugged them.

"Be careful of your arm," Emmy reminded him.

"It's all right. I took a pain pill."

After Emmy had gotten the kids in bed she came back downstairs and sat on the family room couch next to Father James.

"Are they down for the night?" he asked.

"They better be," she said. "They have school in the morning. Are you going to spend the night?"

"I packed an overnight bag, but in the excitement of falling and all I don't think it made it to the car."

Kenny heard them talking as he walked into the family room. "I don't think you're going home tonight, Father James. There's a thick sheet of ice on the driveway. It's not safe to go anywhere."

"I wonder if they will close the school for tomorrow?" Emmy asked.

"Well, it's a good thing I often sleep in my boxers. Do you happen to have a toothbrush I could borrow?" Father James asked.

"Oooh! Gross! Do you plan to use it and then give it back?" Emmy asked as she made a face.

"Perhaps you could save it for me in case I ever get stranded here again," he teased.

"There are new toothbrushes in the bathroom in the guest bedroom across the hall from Kevin Michael's room," Kenny mentioned. "Emmy stocks it with those travel samples of soap and shampoo and deodorant she steals from hotels."

"I do not steal that stuff. The hotels charge you for them so you might as well take it home," Emmy said.

"I could just wait until I get back to the rectory to brush my teeth and clean up."

"Oooh! Gross again," Emmy said making a face. "You can sleep in the nanny suite tonight. I haven't changed the sheets in the guest bedroom in ages."

"Hey, Em. Why don't you show your brother that box of family photos you got from Diane," Kenny suggested.

"What photos?" Father James asked.

Emmy rolled her eyes. "Diane found this shoebox of photos in Mom's closet at Sunrise Garden while she was in the hospital.

She assumed it contained shoes until she opened it."

"Are they family photos of you as a child?"

"Emmy's no older than ten in any of the photos, but there are a few of her grandparents and other family. There are some pictures of people no one knows," Kenny said.

"I'd love to see them, my child," Father James said using his formal, priestly voice.

"Fine! But I look awful in most of the pictures. I have this long hair that looks like it's never been washed or brushed out."

"I definitely want to see them."

"Not a chance."

"Please, Emmy. It's my birthday."

Emmy rolled her eyes but then got up and walked into the den to get the shoebox. She came back, sat next to her brother and took the top off of the old cardboard box. "I didn't know these existed. Mom and Dad never took many photo of us as kids. I'm guessing one of my grandmothers took most of the pictures."

"Are you forgetting that one of your grandmothers is also my grandmother?"

"That seems kinda weird, but it's true. Grandma Colasanti wouldn't have been very old when you were born. She was like seventy when I came along."

Father James pulled several photos from the box. He held one up and asked, "Is this you as a baby?"

"I think so, but it could be Diane," Emmy said after glancing at the picture.

Father James handed it to Kenny.

Kenny took one look and laughed. "That's not you or Diane. That's your mother. Look at the clothes of the person holding her. They look like they're from the forties."

"Let me see that!"

Kenny handed it to Emmy. She stared at it. "You're right. That must be Mom sitting on Grandma Isabel's lap."

"You look more like your mother than I would have thought," Kenny said. "You have the same nose and chin in your baby pictures."

"How do you know? Have you seen baby pictures of me?"

"I've seen a few. Not many." Kenny pulled out another photo. "I've seen this one before. Maybe a copy, but I've seen this." He handed the photo to Father James. "That's Emmy for sure. Diane's eyes are brown."

Father James stared at the picture. "You were a cute baby. Look at that face."

"Let me see," Emmy took the picture from her brother and looked at it. "I'm starting to cry! That's not a very good picture of me. Find a better one."

They pulled all the photos out of the box and sorted them into stacks.

"These are the ones of us as kids, and this pile is of people we don't know," Emmy said.

"Could some of these people be relatives of our father?"

"It's possible, but as far as I know Daddy's parents were the only ones who came to this country. I know Grandpa and Grandma Colasanti had older siblings in Italy. They're probably all gone by now, but this could be his aunts and uncles." Emmy stared at what had to be a copy of an old photograph.

"Is there anyone who might know?" Father James asked.

"It's possible Mom might recognize some of the people. It's weird how she can sometimes remember things from a long time ago and not be able to remember something that she ate earlier that day."

"We probably have distant cousins in Italy. It's possible some of their children or grandchildren emigrated to the States at some point," Father James said.

"You could do a search on one of those ancestry sites, Em," Kenny suggested.

"When would I find the time?" Emmy asked as she looked at the photo of her mother as a baby. "I'll show these to Mom before I start a search. Maybe she will know who they are."

Emmy woke up just before six and headed downstairs. She started the coffee, sat on one of the barstools at the kitchen island and then read her devotional book and her Bible before taking some time to pray. She didn't hear her brother enter the kitchen until he poured himself a cup of coffee.

"You're up early. Help yourself to some coffee."

He held up his cup and let her see it. "Thanks, I will. You're up early, too."

"I've found this is the only time I have to read my Bible and take some time to pray. You should try it sometime," she said and then grinned. "Warm me up, please."

He added some coffee to her cup. "I'm pretty sure I had to read it once in the online priest school I attended," he said and then took a long sip of coffee.

Kenny came downstairs in his boxers, poured a cup of coffee, took a sip and then noticed Father James. "Did you sleep all right?"

"I slept like a baby. I could get used to that mattress. It's a lot more comfortable than mine."

"I don't see any email about the school closing today," Emmy said. She checked the weather site. "According to this it's supposed to be in the lower forties today, and the temperature is already thirty-eight degrees."

"I guess the kids will have school after all."

"Could I get a ride home after you take the children to school?" Father James asked. "I should let someone know I'm still alive and mostly well."

"I can take you home. Do you want something to eat so you can take a pain pill. You probably shouldn't take them on an empty stomach," Emmy said.

"I'll take some gruel if it's not too much trouble."

Emmy rolled her eyes. "Would you like a piece of moldy bread to go along with your gruel?"

"Fine! How about steak and eggs?"

"You can have eggs and either bacon or sausage, but not both."

"I'll take bacon," Kenny said.

"I'll take sausage," Father James said simultaneously.

"Men! All right I'll make both," Emmy sighed.

# Chapter Seven

Emmy walked into the family room after putting the dishes and plates from lunch into the dishwasher. She saw Kenny sitting on the couch and noticed he had the Bears game on. She sat beside him. "What's the score?"

"The Bears are down by ten. The Vikings scored just before the end of the first half." He placed his arm around her shoulders and pulled her close. "I was going to take care of the dirty dishes."

"It's all right. I wanted to get it done. What are the kids doing?"

"The girls are upstairs with Dotty and Noemi. Kevin Michael and Ben went outside to play. I told him to bundle up," Kenny said.

"Does Sloane know the kids are over here?" Emmy asked. "I didn't have a chance to talk to her after church."

"Tony knows they're here. He dropped them off."

Emmy leaned back and closed her eyes.

"Do you need to take a nap?" Kenny asked as he kissed her ear and touched her side. "I could use a nap."

She opened her eyes and smacked his hand away. "Not while all the kids are here."

"Do you think that's why Tony brought Dotty, Noemi and Ben over here? Do you think they're taking a nap?"

"Not unless they sent the other three kids over to Kristen's or Diane's," Emmy said. "Hey! I just realized something."

"What?"

"The NFL season is almost over and I haven't watched an entire game all year," Emmy said.

"For real?" Kenny asked.

"I can't think of one. I couldn't tell you whether the Bears are having a good year or not. Do you know what their record is?"

"Not exactly, but I know they've lost more than they've won."

"So they won't be going to the Super Bowl, huh?"

Kenny grinned. "Not unless they buy tickets."

"You're a dork," Emmy said and then kissed him. "Maybe we can take a nap later."

"But I'm not sleepy," he said.

Their landline rang and Emmy got up to answer it.

"The kids are doing okay," she told Tony. "The girls are upstairs and Ben and Kevin Michael are outside."

"Then I'll leave them there for now," Tony said.

"I'll run them home when I get tired of them," Emmy said. "Hey! Are you watching the game?"

"No, Peter had it on for a while, but he turned it off."

"I started watching at halftime, but I realized something."

"What?" Tony asked.

"I haven't watched an entire game all season. I don't even know the Bears' record."

Tony chuckled. "It's not good. They won't make the playoffs."

"I used to watch every game. I would rush home from church and not eat until halftime. Now it doesn't seem to matter. Isn't it funny how our priorities change?"

"Ya think! Now we've got kids and don't have the time to sit and watch football all afternoon. I've been playing with Taylor Beckett and Coby. Peter is the only one who has an interest in sports. Did I tell you he made the basketball team?"

"No, you didn't."

"Of course, making the team at Crest Ridge Nazarene is easier than if he was going to Jamie McGee or Adolph Tockstein. The public school junior highs are so much bigger. The competition is much tougher."

"I'm glad he's taken an interest in sports. You do realize there are three other junior highs in SoHam now, right?"

"I know, and they are called middle schools now. The new high school should open next year, and there's even talk of a fourth one."

"I heard the school district wants to build one east of Roosevelt," Emmy said.

"Did you hear what they named the new one?" Tony asked and then chuckled.

52

"Yes, it's going to be Ronald Reagan High. That's where our kids will go if they don't have a high school at church by then."

"There's always St. Raymond's," Tony said. "They tried to get me to go there to play football."

"I'm glad you decided on Roosevelt. I might never have met you if you'd gone to St. Raymond's," Emmy said. "Does it bother you that the other kids aren't jocks like you were?"

"Not really. I mean it would be nice if the boys were, but I'm not one of those parents who's gonna force my kids into sports. I know that sounds like a cliché, but I mean it."

Emmy laughed. "What about the girls? What if Dotty or Noemi wanted to play basketball or volleyball? How would you feel about that?"

"Surprised. Sloane played basketball at Olivet, but she's never pushed the girls into sports."

"I forgot Sloane played ball in college," Emmy said.

"She was pretty good, but nothing special."

"What!? You don't think your wife is special?" Emmy teased.

"I meant as a basketball player, brat. Quit trying to twist my words around."

"Wait till I see Sloane. You're gonna be in big trouble," Emmy said. "I'll bring the kids back before dinner. I'm going to go see my mom, so I'll drop them off on the way."

Later, Emmy took the elevator up to the second floor of the memory care unit of Sunrise Garden. She carried the shoebox containing the photos, knocked on her mother's door and then entered.

Patricia Colasanti turned her attention from the TV to see who was there. "Is it time for my medicine?"

"No, Mom. It's just me. Emmy. How are you? Did you eat dinner already?" Emmy asked as she walked over and kissed the top of her mother's head.

"I had chicken and mashed potatoes for dinner. I was going to watch my show, but I don't think it's on now," Patricia said.

They talked about TV shows for a moment.

"Your show will be on at seven, Mom," Emmy said after

53

checking the programming guide on the TV.

"What's in the box? Are those my shoes?"

"No, Mom, it's not shoes. Diane found this in your closet. It's full of old photographs. Would you like to see them?"

Patricia looked at the TV and then at the shoebox. She shifted her attention back and forth two more times before making her choice. "Pictures of who?"

"Come and sit on the couch with me, and I'll show you. There are some people Diane and I don't recognize." Emmy patted the spot next to her.

Patricia took one last look at the TV, but then stood up and moved from her recliner to the couch.

Emmy took the top off of the shoebox and pulled out a stack of photos. She held one up for her mother to see. "Do you know these people?"

Patricia took the photo from Emmy and stared at it. "That's my parents with my sister Betty and me. That was taken in front of their house. I must have been about ten." Patricia handed the photo back to Emmy. "Show me more."

Emmy pulled out one of her as a baby.

Patricia stared at it, but then handed it back. "I'm not sure who that is. It might be one of my cousins."

Emmy bit her lip, held her tongue and pulled out another photo.

Patricia took it, looked at it and smiled. "This is my mother and father when they were just married."

"Who else is in the picture, Mom? They look a lot older than Grandma Isabel."

"That one is my grandfather Polmonari and that's my grandmother. Her name was Donatella and his name was Lazaro. I think her maiden name was Pecora, but I'm not sure how to spell it. All I remember about them is that they only spoke Italian."

*How on earth can you remember their names, but you forget my name.* "Do you know where they lived?" Emmy asked.

Patricia stared at the photo for a while longer. "I think they lived in New York City, but I have no idea where. I'm pretty sure they both died a long time ago."

Emmy pulled out a photo from another stack. "I think this might be Daddy as a boy. Can you tell? There's some writing on the back, but it's smudged. All I can make out is the name Milano."

Patricia looked at the photo and smiled. "I remember this picture. It was taken for school when he was in the fifth grade. His mother showed it to me after we got married."

"Do you remember anyone named Milano?" Emmy asked.

Patricia reached into the box, pulled out more photos and studied them. "That name doesn't ring a bell. Who are these girls?"

Emmy looked at the photo. "Don't you know, Mom?"

Patricia looked at the picture and then smiled. "Oh, that's me and Betty, but I don't know where it was taken."

Emmy bit her lip. *That's me and Diane in front of the house on Fifth Street.*

"I forgot I even had these pictures."

"You must have gotten them from Grandma Isabel and Grandma Mary over the years," Emmy said. "I can remember them taking pictures, but I don't remember you or Daddy taking any."

"I suppose we didn't have the money to do that," Patricia said and then looked at the TV. "Is it time for my show yet?"

"It should be on in a couple of minutes, Mom." Emmy gathered up the photos, replaced them in the shoebox and stood up. "I'm going home. I'll stop by and see you real soon."

"It was good to see you again, sweetie. You should bring your boyfriend over sometime."

"I will, Mom." Emmy kissed her mother and left.

# Chapter Eight

"Are you doing anything important, or do you have time to talk to me?" Emmy asked.

Rory Porter laughed as he took a seat in his secondhand recliner in the living room of his small apartment in Tampa, Florida. "Good afternoon to you, Olivia, and I always have time to talk to my best friend who almost never calls. I have to settle for an occasional email."

"The phone works both ways, Clarence," Emmy said using the middle name he detested. She walked into the den, closed the door and plopped into her leather recliner. "Don't tell me you are too busy with Rochelle to call me."

"Unfortunately, Rochelle is working today. Why aren't you watching football? This is New Year's Day."

"I've kinda lost interest. Did Santa come to your house?"

"He did! I've been a very good boy this year," Rory said as he turned down the TV volume.

"I don't want to hear about how good you've been," Emmy said while making a face.

"Yeah, sure. How is everyone in the land of ice and snow?"

"Shut up! I don't want to know how warm and sunny it is down there in the land of senior citizens."

"I prefer to think of it as the land of job security," Rory said and then laughed deeply.

"Someday physical therapists will be replaced by robots."

"I am an administrator not just a common therapist. I have skills."

Emmy glanced at the door to make sure no one could hear and said, "I know what kind of skills you have."

"Hey! You've never taken advantage of those skills."

Emmy leaned back and pressed the button to raise the footrest. She used one foot to scratch her calf and then pulled up her thick woolen socks. "Do you want to hear what I've been doing, or are we going to talk about... you know?"

"Tell me about your Christmas. Did the kids get tons of presents?" Rory fist pumped as Central Florida sacked the

Oklahoma quarterback causing a fumble.

Emmy rolled her eyes. "Kenny and I didn't buy them a lot of stuff, but his parents and Andy Walker did."

"Your mom?"

"She's back at Sunrise Garden," Emmy answered. "Kevin Michael still likes to get toys, but the twins are more into books and clothes. They have cell phones and other electronic stuff. We never had stuff like that when we were kids."

Rory snorted and said, "Duh! We didn't have any kind of technology, Em. We entertained ourselves by playing outside."

"Did you watch the video of the Christmas program?"

He nodded. "The girls sounded like angels, and at least Kevin didn't pick his nose like that other boy."

"I felt silly doing those motions, but you can't see me in the video."

"Why would you feel self-conscious? You dance all over the stage when you sing," he teased.

"That's different. What did you get Rochelle? Something special? How are the wedding plans going?"

"She says the plans are going okay. I don't have much say about that. She tells me what to do and I do it," he said while shrugging.

"You're a dork like Kenny. What did you buy her?"

"We bought a new bedroom set..."

"For your place? Turn on your computer and show me," Emmy insisted.

"It's at her apartment. That's where we will live after we get hitched."

"Turn on your computer anyway. I want to see you while we talk."

"Fine. Give me a minute to boot it up. I'm not interested in the game."

Emmy grabbed her laptop from the desk, returned to her recliner and waited. In a few minutes she heard the sound letting her know she had someone trying to Skype with her.

"What is that thing on your face?" she asked.

Rory rubbed his chin. "It's called a goatee. Do you like it?"

57

"It's a different look for you. Does Rochelle like it?"

"She does." Rory tilted his head as he stared at the computer screen. "What are you wearing?"

Emmy shrugged and glanced at her legs. "It's cold here, so I'm wearing leggings and a sweatshirt. Kenny bought these socks for me." She turned her laptop around and wiggled her feet. "They're thick wool and keep my toes warm."

"Yeah, it's been rather chilly here the last few days. I had to wear a light jacket because it was in the sixties," he teased.

"I hate you!" She set the laptop on her thighs and stretched her arms over her head. "Kenny took the kids to Tony's house. The guys are building an igloo. I hope it doesn't collapse on them."

"Does that sweatshirt belong to one of the girls?" he asked.

She lowered her arms and adjusted the tight-fitting shirt. "No, but it's a little small on me."

"Maybe you could buy a new one that fits better."

"They're expensive. Maybe you could buy one for me." She put a finger to her mouth and used an expression designed to get her way.

Rory laughed and shook his head. "That might have worked when we were kids, but not now."

"It was worth a try. Did I tell you about Kristen's party?"

"Not yet, but I have time to listen." He yawned to show his indifference.

"I can tell a fake yawn when I see one. So, Kristen always throws a New Year's Eve party at her house, right?"

"So I've heard. Did you get plastered?"

She frowned. "I had a glass of champagne. Not even a full glass."

"Did Kristen make everyone play charades?"

Emmy rolled her eyes. "For an hour. The guys are so lame at it, but they didn't protest as much this year. Tony didn't fuss like normal. Dany and Darian were there."

Rory tilted his head and looked puzzled.

"They live in the guesthouse."

Rory shrugged.

"Dany is Liz Hammond's younger sister. You should

58

remember Darian. He's Mary's brother."

Rory slapped his forehead. "Darian Michaelis. I remember now. Hard to believe he's all grown up already."

"Ya think! Dahlia's in college. She's eighteen and lives in Howe Hall."

"Is that at North Park College?" He carried his laptop into the kitchen and set in on the counter.

"Hey! Where am I? I can't see you," Emmy said.

"Hold your horses. I'm getting a tasty beverage from the fridge. I'd offer you one, but you're actually a couple thousand miles away." He twisted the cap off of a Sam Adams, picked up the computer, placed it on the island and sat on a barstool. "Can you see me now?"

"Tilt the screen back," she said.

"Better?"

"Yeah. We went skiing after Christmas. Did I tell you that already?"

Rory shook his head. "Where?"

"Somewhere in northern Wisconsin, or it might have been across the border in the UP. A small town called Brilliant Falls. Hardly big enough to be a town. The only thing there is the ski resort. The girls complained about being bored the whole three days."

"Don't they know how to ski?"

"Yeah, but if they weren't skiing, they complained. Kevin Michael tried to crash into them until I yelled at him. He's going to be a handful when he grows up."

"Is he bigger than his sisters?"

Emmy laughed and said, "He'll be bigger than me in a couple years, and don't give me any crap about everyone being bigger than me."

"Wouldn't dare," Rory replied as he grinned.

She made a face.

"You look so cute when you pout."

"You used to let me have my way when I pouted."

He took a long drink of his beer before answering, "You were a cute kid."

"Am I still cute?"

"Oh, for cripes sake. You know you're still cute."

"Thank you, Rory. You're sweet."

"And you're a spoiled brat. What's happening with your career? Any plans to record? How about Kenny's band? Are they still together? I haven't seen any new CDs for a few years."

"You should be a comedian instead of a world famous tambourine player," Emmy teased. "Does Tim Burine have any gigs lined up?"

He laughed. "He only plays with your band, you goof."

"Kenny and the guys have been working on a new CD, but they took a break for the holidays. Just between us, they were struggling to come up with decent tracks. He's going to work with my old band. They signed with Steward Music and are going to record in the basement."

"What about you?" Rory asked. He finished his beer and placed the bottle in the recycling bin.

"I've written some new songs, but we haven't started recording them yet. I doubt if I will have anything ready to release this year. Probably the middle of 2017 at the earliest. I'm more interested in writing my stories right now."

"How many books have you published?"

"Three, but I'm working an another one," she said without elaborating.

"Are you going to tell me what it's about?"

She bit her lip, but then answered, "It's about this couple who had a baby who didn't live very long. That's all I can tell you right now."

"Sounds serious."

"Yeah, it's not like the lion book, but it's not all doom and gloom. There are some funny things in it."

"Do you have a title?"

"Not yet, but I'm using *Gideon's Tree* for the time being. It will probably get changed."

"What else is new? Did Kenny buy another house in some exotic part of the world?"

She grinned and said, "No, we just have this one, the one in

60

Hawaii, the Swiss chalet." She paused and put a finger to her mouth then continued, "Of course there is Sheila's cottage in Surrey and the ranch in Australia."

Rory waved a hand. "Pfffft! Simple cottages. Nothing substantial."

"You have Kenny confused with Jeff and Dave. They're the ones who buy all the houses. Well, not Dave since the separation, but Jeff and Frances just sold another property in Timberline Heights. They love fixing up those big, old places."

"It's a shame you have to live in such a small house," Rory said sarcastically.

Emmy took a deep breath then sighed and said, "So true. We definitely need something with more space."

"I don't see how you can survive in only 10,000 square feet."

"It's not that big," she said. "Closer to 7,000."

"Poor baby!"

"You're worse than Father James. He teases me every chance he gets."

"Somehow I don't see you letting him get away with it."

"Oh, I give back as much as I take," she said. She stood up and set the laptop on the desk. "I need to stretch."

"If you have to go, I understand," he replied.

"No, don't go yet."

"You are still planning to sing at the wedding, right?"

She stretched her arms over her head and leaned from side to side while keeping her eyes on the computer. "We will be there. We've booked a suite at one of the Disney resorts. I used a code and got a discount."

"Rochelle said I need to pay you guys for singing."

Emmy shook her head. "Ain't gonna happen."

"Then I might hire the girls to sing. I'm sure they will take my money."

Emmy laughed. "You couldn't afford them. They drew up a contract on their computer. They want $50,000 for an appearance."

He rubbed his goatee. "Might be worth it."

"I get ten percent."

61

"Do you still clip coupons?"

"Are you calling me cheap?" she asked while leaning over backward.

"Will you stand still and talk to me? I don't need to see you working out."

She sighed and sat down at the desk.

"I'm not saying you're cheap."

"Then what?"

He tilted his head back and forth, then said, "Frugal."

"Stuff it, Rory. I can't stand paying more than I should."

He laughed and inspected a banana. "When we were kids, you would try to get Mr. Darby to give you free food."

"Sometimes I didn't have any money," she said and then bit her lip.

"I'm sorry, Em. I didn't mean to upset you."

"No big deal. There are millions of children who suffer more than I ever did. Billions." She spread her arms out wide."

"I'm sure you guys donate enough money to charity."

"All the money in the world wouldn't be enough."

"Did I mention Rochelle and I have been going to church pretty regularly?"

"What do you consider regular? There are some couples at church who only show up every other month. To me regular is every week."

"How about twice a month?" he asked.

"That's better than not at all, but it's what's inside that counts."

"Yes, Reverend Emily."

"I won't ever stop praying for you, Rory," she responded.

"I appreciate that." He checked the time on the computer. "I should let you go, Em. I need to make dinner."

"Okay, but you better call me more than once a year."

"You're a riot, Em. Say hi to the kids and Kenny for me. Tell them I miss them."

"You miss Kenny?"

He shook his head. "Take care, sweetie. I'll see you in June if not before."

# Chapter Nine

"What time are the guys supposed to start recording?" Emmy asked Kenny on Monday morning as she drank a cup of tea with honey.

Kenny hung his keys by the door. "They should start arriving around ten if they can get up the hill. Thanks for letting me use your car to take the kids to school. There's some snow and a little ice out there." He took off his coat and stocking cap and hung them up in the mudroom.

"I can understand why school started this week," Emmy said as she inspected an English muffin. "It's so they can get out earlier in the spring, but I don't think the girls were ready to go back. They wanted to use their cross-country skis some more."

"They will have enough opportunities to use them. I didn't realize how much they'd enjoy skiing," Kenny said as he walked over to the coffee pot. "No coffee?" he asked Emmy.

"I'm trying to cut down and drink more tea. It's pretty good. You should try some."

"I need some caffeine. I'll take a Dr Pepper instead. I'm going downstairs. Will should be here soon, and we need to get everything set up. We've only got this week to get everything recorded, so I don't want to waste any time."

All six members of the Bender Brothers Band arrived by nine thirty. They quickly set up their gear and Kenny entered the main studio room.

"I've been listening to the demos you recorded, and I would like to try something different," Kenny said.

"What?" Bobby O'Connor asked from his drum throne.

"We usually record drum tracks first and then add all the other instruments, but I want to try recording everything live. I think that might be the perfect way to capture your sound, and given our time constraints, it might be the quickest way. What do you say?"

Micah looked at Quinten and then at Freddy and Marshall. "It's worth a try, but how will you isolate the channels. Won't the drums bleed into all our mics?"

"I want to record everything other than the drums and the vocals using direct boxes," Kenny said.

"Even our guitars?" Freddy asked. "I get my tone from the amp."

Kenny and Will smiled and then Kenny said, "Wait until you hear the plug-ins. You won't be able to tell the difference. You can still use your pedal-board."

Fifteen minutes later Kenny let the guys know he and Will were ready to start recording. The band played a song, and afterward Kenny played it back for them.

"That sounds amazing," Micah said. "My vocal is rough, but the track sounds great."

"Other than one line in the second verse, I like the vocal," Kenny said. "I don't want to do a lot of overdubbing, but we can fix some things with the software."

"What did you do with my guitar track?" Freddy asked. "It sounds so warm."

Kenny explained the various plug-ins he and Will used.

Freddy shook his head. "I wouldn't have believed it possible, but my ears don't lie."

The band finished shortly after seven that evening.

"I can't believe we've got three tracks done," Quinten said. "I thought it would be a miracle if we got one track completed."

Micah nodded. "True, but those were the easy ones. We've got those songs nailed. We might struggle on the rest of them."

The band did struggle over the next three days, but with Kenny and Will guiding them they added five more tracks to the project. Friday morning they recorded the ninth track in one take.

"That sounded fantastic," Kenny told them through the talkback mic. "I loved that guitar solo, Freddy. We've got one more to go, and I feel confident we will finish it today."

Two hours later the band finished the tenth and final track.

"Let's take a little break, and then we can listen to the tracks," Kenny said. "We might need to punch in some vocals here and there, but for the most part, we're done."

The guys moved out of the studio and sat on couches in the

basement family room.

"Say, Kenny, who's going to do the mixing?" Bobby asked. "I know you're going back into the studio on Monday."

"Stuart Lederer is going to help. We're going to begin tomorrow, and I'll spend some time in the evenings next week. It shouldn't take too many hours to get a good mix. It's not like there are lots of tracks to mix."

After listening to the entire project in the correct track order, Kenny and Will had Micah overdub some vocals. Kenny had Freddy add another layer of lead guitar to two tracks.

"I think that's it, guys," Kenny said. "We'll get back together after the mixing is finished and see what you think."

Bobby patted Kenny on the back. "I think it sounds amazing for a rush job."

Kenny laughed. "We took a little more time to record the first Fridays At Five CD but not a whole lot longer."

"That one turned out pretty good, didn't it?" Micah said. "You guys sold a few copies."

Bobby laughed. "Yeah! A few million copies."

"Maybe we'll sell a few thousand," Quinten said.

All the guys in the band, except for Bobby and Miles, headed out to celebrate.

Bobby shook hands with Kenny and Will. "I appreciate what you did. Some guys would have tried to change how the band sounds. You understood our vision and knew how to get it on the CD. Thanks."

Will nodded.

Kenny smiled and said, "Glad we could help. In a way it worked out for the best that we only had a week to get it done."

Kenny made it upstairs just after nine and saw Emmy sitting on the couch in the family room.

She turned and looked at him. "Did you get it finished?"

He sat next to her and nodded. "We just have to mix it. It's a rather simple recording, but I think the public might be ready for something like this. They've got some really good songs. If this was the seventies, the college radio stations would be all over it."

"I hate to inform you, but the seventies are never coming

back," Emmy teased. She waved a hand and added, "Gone forever."

"How about the eighties?" he asked.

"Did you remember I'm letting Mary and Dahlia borrow the Odyssey tomorrow?"

"Shoot! I was supposed to take the seats out. Can I do it in the morning?"

"Sure," Emmy replied. "I still have trouble believing Dahlia is in college. She still acts a bit immaturely if you ask me."

"Maybe she could benefit from a year away from school," Kenny said. "It's kinda the opposite of me."

"How so?"

"I knew what I wanted to do with my life, but Mom and Dad wanted me to spend a year in college. Dahlia doesn't know what she wants to do, so she's wasting a year in college."

"How do you suggest she spend this year?" Emmy asked staring at Kenny.

"Don't look at me like that," he said.

"Like what?"

"You know. You stare at me like I don't have the sense of a rock," he said.

Emmy didn't change her expression.

"Some people take a year off to travel and see the world. Maybe Dahlia could spend time in Europe or something."

"Right! Dahlia in Europe by herself. She is spoiled. She relies on her mother for everything."

"She could travel with friends," Kenny suggested.

"Don't ever bring this up after the girls graduate from high school."

"That's a long way off," Kenny said.

Emmy looked at the photos above the fireplace. *It will happen sooner than we realize.*

66

## Chapter Ten

Monday morning Emmy parked her Civic Si in student lot D, grabbed her brand new purple backpack, got out, locked the car, stuffed her keys in the pocket of her comfortable jeans and began walking toward Lancashire Hall. She closed her eyes briefly as the bitterly cold wind whipped some snow crystals against her face and into the parts of her hair not covered by her stocking cap. She stopped on the sidewalk and looked up at the three-story, red-brick building. *I was twenty-four the last time here was and finishing up my degree. I felt just like any other student at that time. Now I'm thirty-five, and I feel a lot older than everyone.* She grinned as she saw another student struggling against the cold wind. *Maybe I'm not the only adult student. She looks over fifty.* Emmy took a deep breath, walked up the worn concrete steps, entered the building and tried to slip through the crowded hallway to her classroom halfway down the hall on the left. *They must have just polished these wooden floors. They look so shiny, but it won't last long with everyone tramping in the wet snow.* She almost made it into her classroom when her way was blocked by a dozen students. She looked up and listened to the two young ladies in front of her.

"I'm so glad all my classes are in Lancashire," one of the other students said to her companion. "Chapman Hall is too far away from Howe Hall."

The other student frowned as she removed her scarf. "You're so lucky. All of my afternoon classes are in Chapman. I'm going to freeze my butt off."

Emmy waited for a second and then scooted around the ladies and into the classroom. She chose a table close to the front, set her backpack on the table and sat down. She looked around the room and smiled at the other students. *Good! I'm not going to be the oldest person in this class.* She watched the two young ladies enter and walk to the back of the classroom. *I wonder if Howe Hall is still a female only dorm, or have all the dorms gone coed now.* Emmy smiled as another adult student took the other chair at the table.

"Is this seat taken?"

Emmy shook her head. "Go right ahead. I'm Emmy."

"Carissa Esposito. I hope this professor, or the assistant who actually teaches the class, doesn't bore us to death," she said. "I'm only taking this course because I need it to get my state teaching certificate. I've been teaching at a private school in Maryland for the last ten years."

"I'm taking it because I'm thinking about teaching at the school at our church," Emmy said.

"Trust me, honey. You need to get a job in a public school if you want to make any money at all. Not that you'll ever get rich as a teacher. The private schools don't pay squat. I'll never go back to a private school."

Emmy bit her lip. *I'm not thinking about becoming a teacher because of the money.*

Emmy walked out of Lancashire Hall in the early afternoon and heard her phone chirp. She checked it and texted a reply to Dany Michaelis. She walked to the four-foot high brick ledge and boosted herself onto it. From there she watched the other students as she kicked her feet back and forth and waited. *I sat here after my last final all those years ago. Oh, shoot! That was the day Sloane and Lindsey were involved in that accident and Kristen came to tell me. At least neither on them was seriously hurt.* Emmy waved as Carissa Esposito walked past. Carissa halfheartedly waved back but kept on going. *She probably thinks I'm some weirdo for sitting here.*

"Emmy! Emmy!"

Emmy turned back toward the entrance of Lancashire Hall, saw Dany and Dahlia walking toward her and jumped down.

"Emmy! What were you doing? How did you get up there?" Dany asked.

"I was waiting for you. How was your day?"

"Okay," Dahlia replied while watching the other students. "I gotta run. I'm meeting some friends for pizza."

"Are all your classes in Lancashire?" Dany asked.

Emmy pulled Dany to the side to let a two men walk by. The men smiled at Emmy, and she smiled back.

"Excuse us, ma'am," the taller one said.

"No problem," Emmy said. She waited until they entered the building and grabbed Dany's arm. "Did you hear what they called me?"

"Who?"

"Those two guys," Emmy answered.

"What did they call you?"

Emmy looked to make sure no one could hear and then whispered, "The one guy called me 'ma'am' like I was an old lady."

Dany put a hand to her mouth to stifle a laugh.

"It's not funny," Emmy said.

Dany tucked a strand of her hair behind her ear as she smiled at Emmy. "Is that the first time anyone's ever called you that?"

Emmy wrinkled her nose. "I suppose not, but it's the first time two good-looking guys like that have. Did they think I was a professor or something?"

"You do look younger than you are, but," Dany said then paused.

"I don't look like a college kid anymore, huh?"

Dany took a step back and inspected Emmy's attire. "Okay, you're small and you're wearing jeans and that disgusting army jacket or whatever it is."

"I should wear a nicer coat," Emmy said.

"You dress like a college kid, but... maybe you look like a graduate student."

"You're just being nice," Emmy said and then checked her phone. "Are you busy? I have an hour to kill before I have to pick up the kids. Wanna go over to the student union and grab a bite at the cafe?"

"I'm free. Darian won't be home until six. I promised to make dinner tonight. We've been eating too much prepared food from the store. I'm going to make something from scratch, but I haven't decided what."

They walked through the quad in the center of the campus and entered the student union. Emmy paid for the bottled water and blueberry muffins, and they sat at a table by the front windows.

69

"Do you have any suggestions for dinner?" Dany asked. "Something simple that won't take a long time."

"There's always pasta," Emmy said as two college guys walked past and smiled at her.

"I make too much pasta," Dany said. "How long did it take you to become a good cook? Did your mother teach you?"

Emmy laughed and then shook her head. "Mom never taught me how to boil water. Mama Bertucci gave me lessons when I was dating Tony. She even taught me after we stopped dating." Emmy watched as the two college guys returned.

"Excuse us for bothering you, but are you Emmy Colasanti?" one asked.

"Yes, I am," Emmy answered.

"Are you teaching a music class?" the other one asked.

"No, I'm taking some classes."

"Too bad. I was going to take your class. Pardon me for being bold, but I think you're pretty cute," he said and Emmy grinned for a second. "For an older lady," he added.

Dany put a hand to her mouth to stifle a laugh.

Emmy watched as the guys walked away and then faced Dany. "Don't say anything, Dany Michaelis. I guess that was God's way of putting me in my place. I should have realized I'm not a young college kid anymore."

"You aren't that old, Emmy. What year were you born?"

"1980 in July. Why?"

Dany shrugged then said, "Lizzie is only five years younger and you're only two years older than Larry. I don't consider him old even though he acts so serious all the time."

"That's because he's got an important job here at North Park. What is his actual title now?" Emmy asked.

"He's in charge of keeping the sidewalks clear in front of Old Main," Dany answered without cracking a smile.

"No he's not!" Emmy said. "He's like the comptroller or something."

"Yeah, but I still tease him."

"When are they going to have another baby? Lorraine has got to be five by now."

"Allie wants one more, but Larry is putting up a stink," Dany said.

Emmy sighed and said, "They should have another blueberry."

Dany tilted her head and stared at Emmy.

"Never mind." Emmy shrugged. "I just love babies."

Kenny walked into Steward Music Group's Studio Four just before ten the next morning. He shook hands with Will Consoli and Stuart Lederer.

"Are you guys ready to get this done?"

"I'm ready. I feel totally re-energized and we have some fresh material," Kenny said.

The rest of the guys arrived within five minutes.

Jeff Rawlings shook hands and slapped the guys on the back. "I'm ready to work. I didn't even look at my bass until last week." He flexed his fingers. "I'm good to go."

Dave Persching spent a few minutes getting his drum kit ready. Adam Vicini turned on his keyboards. Paul Joseph tuned a Fender Stratocaster. The guys moved into position and Kenny counted off the song.

"One two three four..."

All five members of the band began playing a different song.

Kenny waved a hand to get everyone to stop and then laughed. "Hey! What song are we playing, anyway?"

"Does it matter?" Jeff asked. "They all sound the same."

This time the guys felt loose and relaxed as compared to the last time in the studio when they felt under pressure.

"Let's do something easy to start just to get warmed up," Kenny said.

"How about Beethoven's Fourteenth Symphony in the key of D?" Adam suggested.

They guys stared at him.

"What? Don't you guys know that one? It goes like this." He played the intro to one of the band's early hits. "Catchy, huh?" Adam asked with a grin.

71

"Isn't that the 'Distances' intro?" Kenny asked. "Did we really steal that from Beethoven?"

"No, I think we borrowed it from Wolfie Mozart," Dave said.

The guys cracked up and eventually played a few songs to warm up and let the guys in the booth set some levels. They concentrated on two new songs and seven hours later had the basic tracks recorded.

"I think we need to set a deadline to have this thing finished," Jeff said.

Paul nodded. "I agree."

They discussed this for a couple of minutes and came to an agreement.

"So we call it finished by the end of May and go with what we have," Kenny said as he looked at the guys.

"Personally, I don't think it's going to take that long," Jeff said. "Today felt like recording did in the early days. We know the material and just play it. We didn't waste a lot of time time trying different arrangements and other crap. That's how we should record all the time."

The guys left the studio feeling more positive about the project than with their attempts the previous year.

# Chapter Eleven

"Did your class do anything special for your birthday?" Kenny asked as the kids climbed into the car after school.

Heather rolled her eyes. "Daddy! We're not little kids anymore. We're in fourth grade. We don't have birthday parties at school."

"Oh, excuse me," Kenny said. "I forgot how grown up you and Isa are now."

"Don't tease us, Daddy," Isabella said. "We may not be grownup, but we're not babies."

"I'm not a baby either," Kevin Michael hollered from the back row of the minivan.

Kenny looked in the rearview mirror and smiled. "I know you're not a baby because you didn't cry when you crashed your bike in the woods last week."

"It's a good thing I was wearing my helmet. I would have busted my head."

Heather turned around in her seat and grinned at her brother. "That wouldn't have mattered because you don't have a brain."

"I'm smarter than you," Kevin Michael said as he tried to grab Heather's long hair.

"Doubtful, but I'm not going to argue with you," Heather said. "Will Mommy be home in time to make dinner? She promised to make something special."

"She ran home during a break between classes and put together some lasagna," Kenny answered. "I have to put it in the oven when we get home. What else would you like for dinner?"

Heather looked at Isabella. "We will have to pick out a vegetable. How about cauliflower with cheese sauce?"

Isabella closed the book she was reading. "I like that. Maybe Daddy could make a salad, too."

"I can put together a salad," Kenny said as he turned onto Hough Street which would take them back to the gated Bristol Ridge neighborhood. "I don't like to brag, but I make a pretty good garden salad. I use a lot of different veggies..."

"Is anyone else coming over for dinner tonight?" Heather interrupted her father.

"Your grandparents are coming, and Uncle Andy said he would stop over," Kenny said. "I told them not to bring any presents, but they probably will."

"They will probably buy us some clothes. We can always use new clothes," Isabella said. "We don't need toys or dolls anymore."

"Dinner is ready," Emmy said as she walked into the family room later. "Kenny, will you ask Andy and Kevin Michael to come downstairs, please?"

Kenny got up from his recliner, walked out of the room and hollered up the stairs.

Emmy shook her head. "I could have done that."

"Do you need any help, Emmy?" Mrs. Colwell asked.

"No, Mom, everything is on the table. We're ready to eat as soon as everyone can take a seat." Emmy looked at her father-in-law.

"Girls, I think your mother wants us to stop watching our video and get ready to eat," Mr. Colwell said as he paused the DVD.

He and the girls got up from the couch and walked past Emmy into the dining room.

"Where did you get that old movie?" Emmy asked.

Mr. Colwell put an arm around Emmy's shoulders as they walked. "I found it in the storage area off of the third floor playroom. I took it to Hahn's Camera Shop, and they were able to convert all the footage to DVD. Do you remember me taking movies with my old camera?"

"Vaguely," Emmy answered.

"You were about the same age as the girls are now," he said. "And they look so much like you did. They have the same eyes and cheekbones as you."

Emmy grinned. "At least their hair isn't as curly as mine was. I should have kept mine a lot shorter than I did. It would have been so much easier to take care of."

"Why did you always have such long hair, Emmy?" Mrs.

Colwell asked. "I thought you liked it like that. It was always so soft."

"I guess I liked it, but looking back it would have been so much easier to manage if it was short like this." She ran a hand through her still thick hair. "Mom wouldn't let me get it cut short. She still thinks I should let it grow long."

A minute later Andy Walker appeared with Kevin Michael. "I hear we are ready to eat."

Emmy pointed to the two empty chairs. "We were about ready to start without you. Kenny, would you say the prayer, please?"

Kenny did.

Emmy dished out the lasagna as everyone passed a plate to her. The cauliflower and broccoli made it around the table. Kenny gave everyone some salad.

"How is the lasagna?" Emmy asked Mrs. Colwell.

"It's delicious. Did you do something different?"

"It's still basically Mama Bertucci's recipe, but I added a little more basil to the sauce," Emmy said.

"The sausage has some kick to it," Andy said.

"Since the kids are old enough, I use the hot Italian sausage more than I did before. Is it too spicy?"

"It's just right," Mrs. Colwell said.

Kevin Michael stared at his salad. He picked up part of it and showed it to his father. "Is this spinach?"

"Yes, why? Don't you like it?" Kenny asked.

"I hate spinach. It's yucky," Kevin Michael said as he placed the spinach on his plate.

"You've always eaten it before," Emmy said. "You even like it when it's cooked. I add bacon and onions to the spinach and you always eat it. What's different now?"

Kevin Michael looked through his salad for more spinach. "Jalen from school said that spinach is like lettuce and sometimes has worms in it."

Kenny frowned. "I always make sure the stuff I put in my salad is clean." He looked at his bowl of salad and moved it around with his fork. "There are no worms."

75

"Did you wash it with soap, Daddy?" Heather asked and then she and Isabella giggled.

"There are no worms in your salad, young man," Emmy said sternly. "If you want some birthday cake, you will eat your salad."

"You shouldn't believe everything other kids tell you at school," Andy said.

"But Jalen showed us a worm he said was on his spinach," Kevin Michael responded. "It was dead, but it was a real worm."

"It is possible for worms or bugs or other insects to get on some food, but not if you clean it thoroughly," Mr. Colwell said.

"Can we talk about something else, please?" Isabella asked as she inspected a bite of her salad and and then turned to her mother. "I liked watching old movies of you and Daddy. You did look like me and Heather."

"Did you recognize me?" Kenny asked.

Heather looked at Isabella and they both giggled for a moment.

"What is so funny?" Kenny asked.

"We could see your funny-looking ears and knew it was you, Daddy," Heather said. "You should have let your hair grow long enough to cover them up."

"Do I have funny-looking ears?" Kevin Michael asked as he looked at Andy and pulled on his own ears.

Andy laughed. "No, you're lucky. You have your mother's ears, but you have your father's nose."

Kevin Michael touched his nose. "Ian Plant said his father knows how to fix noses to make them look better. Can he fix my nose when I get older?"

"There's nothing wrong with your nose," Emmy said.

Kenny added, "Dr. Plant is a neurosurgeon. He operates on people with problems with their spine and nerves and stuff. He doesn't do plastic surgery on noses."

Kevin Michael rubbed his nose again. "If people have plastic noses, do they still get boogers?"

Everyone froze and no one spoke for several seconds.

Emmy put a hand to her mouth and started to laugh. Then

Kenny laughed and his parents began laughing. After everyone stopped laughing Emmy explained about plastic surgery.

"So their noses aren't plastic, huh?" Andy asked with a straight face.

Later that night Emmy said goodnight to Kevin Michael, moved a large firetruck from his bed, tucked the covers around him and kissed his cheek. She turned off the light, noticed the planets glowing on his ceiling, closed the door most of the way and walked into Heather and Isabella's bedroom.

"Mom, since we're ten now can we stay up an extra half hour?" Heather asked.

Emmy moved one of the dolls and sat on the edge of Heather's bed. She looked across the room at all the stuffed animals covering Isabella's bed. "I suppose you can stay up until nine thirty, but you have to be in your room and ready for bed. Teeth brushed. Prayers said and your clothes picked out for school."

"Okay, but we have to be allowed to stay up later than Kevin Michael. Some of our friends at school don't have to go to bed until ten o'clock," Heather said.

Isabella walked out of the bathroom. "I brushed my teeth, and I already know what I'm going to wear tomorrow. I put it on my dresser."

Emmy listened as the girls said their prayers. She was surprised when Heather mentioned Ian Plant.

"Okay, you can keep the lights on until nine thirty, but then it's time for bed," Emmy said. She kissed Isabella and then sat on Heather's bed again. "Is there something wrong with Ian Plant? Is he sick?"

"No, he's not sick," Heather said.

"You don't usually include him in your prayers. Why did you tonight?" Emmy asked as she picked up one of Heather's dolls.

"Do you promise not to get mad at me if I tell you why?" Heather whispered.

"I promise I will still love you."

Heather sat up and held one of her other dolls. "We were talking the other day after school when I had to go look for Kevin

Michael, and I let him kiss me."

Emmy tilted her head. "What do you mean?"

"He kissed me like boys kiss girls they like. I liked how it felt, so I said a prayer for him."

Emmy squeezed the doll tighter while she stared at Heather. "He's a couple of years older than you, sweetie."

"I know, but I did like the kiss," Heather said. "All the boys in our class are too gross, but Ian goes to a different school. Are you mad at me, Mom?"

"No, I'm not mad at you, but you probably shouldn't be kissing boys who are older than you. You shouldn't be kissing any boys until you're older," Emmy said. *I'm going to have to talk to your father about this.*

Isabella climbed under the covers on her bed. "I'm not going to kiss any boys until I'm in college."

Emmy moved across the room and sat on the edge of Isabella's bed. "You may want to kiss someone before then, but you don't have to think about it for a few years, Isa."

"Do you remember how old you were when you first kissed Daddy?" Isabella asked. "Gra said you were best friends when you were little. Does that mean I might kiss Zachary or Peter one day?"

"That doesn't mean you have to kiss anyone, Isa. Your father and I were best friends, and we fell in love when we got older. I'm pretty sure I was fourteen or fifteen when I first kissed him."

"Daddy said he kissed you in the carriage house on an old couch," Heather said. "Don't you remember it?"

"I remember the old couch and kissing your father there, but I don't remember the exact date."

"Didn't you keep a diary?" Heather asked. "I'm going to start writing in my diary."

"I didn't have a diary when I was that age. I have to talk to your father. I'll be back later to make sure you're asleep," Emmy said. She kissed both girls goodnight and slipped quietly downstairs.

"I'm going to make some hot chocolate. Would you like some?" Emmy asked Kenny as she walked into the kitchen.

"Sure. I'll take some. I'm getting the garbage ready," he answered.

Emmy made the hot chocolate and poured mugs for them. Kenny joined her at the island a few minutes later.

"I told the girls they could stay up until nine thirty from now on. Is that all right with you?" Emmy asked.

Kenny stirred his hot chocolate and took a sip. "It's okay with me as long as they don't stay up any later."

"Heather surprised me with something," Emmy said as she rested her chin in her hand and stared absently across the room.

"What? How did she surprise you?"

"Don't get upset, but she kissed Ian Plant, or he kissed her. Anyway, they kissed."

"For real? Does she know what kissing is?"

Emmy turned and stared at Kenny. "I think they know what kissing is. They see us kissing all the time."

"Why? Where? When?"

"Not sure, but it was recently. From what she said it was only one little kiss and I don't think it means much to her," Emmy said.

"She is much too young to kiss a boy. Isn't he older than her?" Kenny asked.

"I think he's in sixth grade. He's definitely older than Heather," Emmy said. "Do you remember our first kiss?"

"Sure! It was on the old couch in the carriage house." Kenny grinned and moved his eyebrows up and down.

"Do you remember how old I was?"

"You were almost sixteen, but not quite."

"Do you remember the date or anything like that?" Emmy asked.

"It was in the spring. I remember that much, but I don't remember the exact day. I remember how much I liked it," he said as he tried to kiss her cheek. "Don't you want me to kiss you now?"

"Maybe later. Are you sure we never kissed when we were little kids?"

Kenny stared at her for a moment. "I can't say for certain

79

whether we did or not, but I will always remember the first kiss in the carriage house. I think that inspired me to write 'Sweet Girl.'"

"I've always liked that song, and not just because you wrote it for me," Emmy said and then kissed him on the lips.

"You taste like marshmallows," he said. "I like it."

Just before midnight Emmy kissed Kenny and sighed.

"Are you all right, Em," Kenny asked while moving onto his back.

"I'm okay, but I was trying to be quiet," she said. She looked at Kenny. "Do you think Dave and Macy had a problem with sex? Is that why they separated?"

"Believe it or not, Em, but we don't talk about our personal life all that much. It's like any other job. We concentrate on the important stuff."

Emmy giggled and then touched his hair. "You need a trim, and I'm sure you talk about sex once in a while."

"Just because you discuss our sex life with all your friends doesn't mean I talk to Jeff or Adam or P.J. about it. Since the separation Dave doesn't talk about Macy at all."

"Does he talk about the kids?" Emmy asked. She got out of bed and walked into her bathroom.

Kenny followed and stood outside the door. "He talks about the kids."

"Could you close the door, please?"

He closed it most of the way. "He mentioned something about taking them to England in the summer."

Emmy dried her hands and they went back to bed.

"Frances called and wanted to talk about Dave, but I told her I didn't want to gossip."

"I think Frances and Amanda talk to each often quite often." Kenny slipped under the covers. "Probably more than you talk to Kristen, Diane and Sloane combined."

"We are so busy we don't have the time to gossip. I'll see you in the morning," she said and then kissed him. "I never want to be so busy we that we never have time for... you know."

He ran a finger along her spine. "I think it's important to make time for... you know."

80

# Chapter Twelve

Emmy walked out of the den and saw Kenny sitting in his recliner in the family room. She walked into the room, plopped down on the leather couch and sighed as she placed her feet on the coffee table.

Kenny glanced up from his magazine. "Did you finish your homework?" He chuckled as he noticed her thick, red wool socks. "Are your feet cold?"

She wiggled her toes. "The hardwood floors are cold. Do we have any hot chocolate, and where are the kids? It seems rather quiet."

He stood up. "I can make some hot chocolate, and the kids are around. The girls are upstairs, and I think Kevin Michael is playing with Ben and Taylor outside."

Emmy followed Kenny into the kitchen and looked out the window over the sink. "I don't see the boys."

Kenny filled the teapot with water, turned on the burner and moved behind Emmy. He wrapped his arms around her waist and kissed the top of her head. "They said something about building a new fort somewhere."

"I'm glad they like to play outside. Too many kids stay inside and play with their electronics all day," Emmy said.

"We used to play outside when we were kids," Kenny said as he kissed her ear.

"Yeah, unless you had to practice your guitar."

Kenny moved her hair and began kissing her neck. "You had to practice the piano, but you always complained about it."

She turned around and leaned against the sink. "What are you doing?"

He shrugged. "Nothing. Why?"

She grinned. "Are you trying to tell me you're horny?"

"Well, the kids are busy."

"Maybe, but now's not the right time. Where's the hot chocolate mix?"

Kenny sighed. "Fine. I'll get it." He checked the pantry and brought out two choices. "Dark or milk chocolate?"

"I'll take dark and some little marshmallows on top." She turned to stare out the window. "When are we gonna get enough snow to use the snowmobile again? I'd like to use it more often than we have."

Kenny filled two coffee mugs with the hot chocolate mix. "Sorry, but I can't control the weather. We could go back to Wisconsin. I'm sure they have enough snow up north."

"I don't want to take the kids out of school," Emmy said.

"Now is not a good time for me to go. We have to finish our recording soon. What about Tony? Is he busy at work? Maybe he could take a vacation."

"I can't go on vacation with just Tony, you goof."

"I meant him and Sloane. Mama can watch the kids. Peter is almost thirteen, and Dotty is more mature than other kids her age."

Emmy stared at him with her hands on her hips. "Are you forgetting something?"

Kenny tilted his head and then realized. "Sloane can't take time off because she's teaching school."

"Ya think," Emmy said and then rolled her eyes. "I suppose I could ask Tony, but I doubt if he would be interested."

"You could wait until it snows here," Kenny suggested.

The landline rang and Emmy checked to see who was calling. She picked up the phone. "We were just talking about you. Are your ears burning? Is that why you called?" She put a hand over the receiver and whispered to Kenny, "It's Tony."

"I kind of figured that," Kenny said. He turned off the burner and poured some hot water into the mugs.

"I was calling to see if Ben and Taylor are around. Sloane wants them to come home for lunch," Tony said. "What were you saying about me? Something nasty?"

Emmy leaned against the countertop. "Nothing bad. I want to go snowmobiling, and Kenny suggested I go to Wisconsin again since there's not enough snow here. He can't go, so he suggested I ask you. Are you busy at work? You do still go to work, right, or did they fire you?"

"Busy enough. Sloane can't take time off from school."

"I know that," Emmy said as she boosted herself onto the countertop.

Tony laughed. "So, you wanted to see if I could go by myself, huh?"

"I can't go by myself, and I can't think of anyone else who likes to go snowmobiling other than John, and I can't go away with him. That wouldn't be right. You're like my brother."

Kenny listened to Emmy's conversation and shook his head as he added some marshmallows to the hot chocolate and handed a mug to Emmy. "I'm gonna see if I can find the boys. I'll fix my hot chocolate when I get back" He left the kitchen and grabbed a coat.

"Are you talking about going up there for a day or longer?" Tony asked.

"It doesn't make much sense to go all that way for just a day."

"You're right about that," Tony said and paused. "I wish I could go, but sorry, Em."

Emmy took a sip of hot chocolate and then said, "I understand. It will snow here sooner or later. Kenny went outside to look for the boys. I'll send Ben and Taylor home."

"I'll talk to you later. See you in the morning," Tony said.

Kenny and the boys walked into the kitchen a few minutes later.

"Mom, we found a frozen rabbit," Kevin Michael said proudly.

"It had a hole in its side," Ben added.

"It didn't stink," Taylor said.

"Please tell me you didn't bring it home," Emmy said as she jumped down from the countertop.

"No, we left it there. Can I have some hot chocolate, too?"

"Yes, but Tony called and said Ben and Taylor need to go home."

"We'll see you later, Kevin," Ben said. "We can hunt for more dead rabbits."

Ben and Taylor left and raced each other to their home across the street. Kenny fixed some hot chocolate for Kevin Michael and they sat at the island to drink it.

"Mom, can Ben and Taylor come over after church tomorrow? We want to play in the woods again."

"It's all right with me if Sloane agrees," Emmy said. "I might join you because I'm bored staying inside all the time."

"You go to school. Don't they have recess there?" Kevin Michael asked seriously.

"Very funny," Emmy answered. "The only fresh air I get is walking from the parking lot to Lancashire Hall."

"You could join a gym," Kenny suggested.

Emmy shook her head. "They cost too much. I could use the trails around here and go for a run." She looked at Kenny. "Would you run with me or let me run on my own?"

"It's dark by the time I get home, and you can't go by yourself."

"Why not?"

"You could trip or fall down a hill and get hurt. How would we ever find you?" Kenny asked.

"I could take my cell phone and stick to the trails. This isn't like Maine or Canada."

"Might as well be. There's over 120 acres in Bristol Ridge and most of it is woods. You can't see any houses from the street except for Andy's and a couple of the houses off of Bristol Parkway. You could use the roads, Em."

"I'll go with you, Mommy. I can keep up if you run slow," Kevin Michael offered.

"I might just take you up on that," Emmy said as she looked out the window.

On the last Monday of February Emmy spotted Randy Braun talking to another professor as she left Lancashire Hall. She dashed along the snow-covered sidewalk and tapped his arm. "Do you have time to talk to me, Professor Braun?"

Randy ended his conversation, turned and smiled. "Normally, I ask students to make an appointment, but I suppose I could make an exception for you, young lady. Does this concern your failing effort in my class?"

Emmy grinned. "I've never come close to failing a class
84

and you know it. How have you been? How are the kids and Vanessa? How old is Maisie now?"

"Everyone is doing well, and Maisie is," he paused and tapped his fingers against the side of his jaw. "She was born in June so how old would she be?"

"Can't you count? You are a professor of mathematics, you goof," Emmy teased.

He figured out his daughter's age and told her. "How are your classes going? Do you want to grab some coffee and talk?"

"I've got time if you do. Are you allowed to socialize with students?" she asked.

"I suppose it would be all right since you aren't in any of my classes," Randy teased back.

They walked to the coffee shop in the student union, bought coffee and found seats at a table by the front windows.

"Catch me up on everything, Emmy," Randy said.

They talked about their kids for several minutes.

"So Heather really kissed this boy, huh?" Randy asked.

Emmy nodded. "She and Isa just turned ten last month. I can't believe how fast they're growing up. I'm going to have to talk to them about boys real soon."

"I'm glad I have three boys and Maisie is still a baby," Randy said. "Vanessa has years before she has to worry about that stuff."

*You will have to worry about her, too.* Emmy thought as she sipped her coffee. "We finally got to use our snowmobile again," Emmy mentioned. "We have trails around the neighborhood. Tony and John went with us. Do you ever get out to ski or anything anymore?"

"I haven't been skiing in several years. I don't have the time. Four kids and my job keep me busy. Are you still writing books or making CDs? I should know, but I'm out of the loop."

"Not right now. I'm concentrating on school. Oh, I wrote something a while back that I want to publish. It's a short story called *Gideon's Tree*, but I plan to expand it first," she said and explained about the story.

"That sounds interesting," Randy said.

85

"I really can't take the credit because God gave me the words to write. Do you understand what I mean?" Emmy asked.

"I understand. Sometimes I have that happen to me in my Sunday School class," he answered.

"You teach fifth and sixth graders, right?"

"More snow," Randy said as he glanced out the window. "Yes, and they can be very curious about stuff. Do you have any idea of what age children you would like to teach?"

Emmy grinned. "Younger than that. I could probably handle first or second graders, but not older ones. I will have my hands full with Heather and Isabella."

Randy stared silently at Emmy for a moment.

"Why are you looking at me like that? What are you thinking?" Emmy asked.

"Nothing."

She grabbed his hand and squeezed it. "Tell me, Randy."

"Okay. Do you remember when we were seeing a lot of each other before you got married? We weren't exactly dating, but we were doing stuff together. Volleyball at church. That concert we went to."

"I remember," she said.

"When you mentioned Heather kissing that boy it brought back a memory."

Emmy bit her lip. "You remember the night we kissed, huh?"

"I remember it, and how we felt."

"I'm sorry, but it didn't feel right, Randy."

He waved a hand. "No, I agree. I couldn't understand it at the time because you were so... desirable."

"You said I was sexy but in an innocent way or something like that. I don't remember exactly, but something along those lines."

"Yeah. It's kind of funny now because I could never think of kissing you even if you weren't married."

Emmy grinned. "Are you saying I'm no longer sexy or innocent?"

Randy laughed. "I'm sure Kenny thinks you are sexy, but I

86

think you're still pretty."

"But like a sister or something, huh?"

"Maybe a cousin or a sister-in-law," Randy said and then waited for a reply. "What are you thinking, Emmy?"

"I was thinking about Christopher," Emmy admitted.

Randy stared out the window again. "I could never understand why so many girls were interested in him."

Emmy giggled and then said, "Duh! He was so hot. You have to admit that. I'm not saying you weren't good-looking, but... you know."

"Yeah, I get that part, but why didn't girls realize he was only interested in one thing?"

Emmy shrugged. "I can't speak for anyone but myself, but I kinda had a thing for guys like him." She smacked his hand. "And don't you ever repeat that to a soul."

"You resisted his charms, Emmy. I know that for a fact."

"Yes, but it wasn't easy. If I hadn't become a Christian when I did, I might not have been able to resist."

"Oh, I talked to him last week. He and Maddy are doing great out in Pittsburgh. He got another promotion, and they're looking for a larger house."

"Good for them. I'd love to see Elena again. She must be a teenager by now."

"She turned thirteen last October, and she loves her younger brother and sister. Maddy said Elena wants to be a doctor."

"How is she doing with her... you know?"

"The Crohn's disease?"

Emmy nodded.

"She is on a special diet. In fact they all follow the diet. Maddy doesn't make anything that Elena can't eat."

"What can she eat?" Emmy asked.

Randy explained what he knew. "The hardest part would be not being able to eat chocolate. I can't survive without chocolate."

"I will keep her in my prayers," Emmy promised. "Have you seen or heard from Victoria recently?"

Randy shook his head. "Not for several years. The last I

heard she was living in Las Vegas and working at a hotel."

"Doesn't she ever see Elena?"

"Nope! And I hope she never does. She goes through men like... I don't know how to describe her. It's a good thing Christopher got full custody all those years ago."

"I will pray for Victoria, too," Emmy said.

"Why?" Randy shrugged. "She's hopeless."

"How can you say that, Randy?" Emmy asked. "Are you saying God can't change her life?"

"She would never accept Him."

"You should never underestimate the power of prayer. Did I ever tell you about Dawn Matuzak?" Emmy asked.

"The girl from Roosevelt who harassed you?" Randy asked.

Emmy nodded. "I used to hate her because of how she treated me, but guess what?"

"What?"

"She's now a Baptist minister and works as a prison chaplain."

"Get out! She was a bit... she was rather..."

"She slept around, and God changed her. There is no one God is willing to let go of. You know what I mean, right?"

"Dawn Matuzak is a preacher," Randy said as he shook his head. "I never would have believed that. She was as bad as Todd Delaney." Randy looked at Emmy and saw her eyes widen in reaction. "Shoot! I'm sorry, Emmy. I forgot about what happened to him."

"It's all right, but God could have changed him, too."

"I wish I had your faith, Emmy."

They were quiet for a moment and then Emmy smiled.

"What?" Randy asked.

"I know I don't look as young as I used to, but I have a funny story to tell you."

"I could use a funny story about now," Randy said.

"There's this guy in one of my classes. I'll call him Roger, but that's not his name. He's older than most students but younger than me. Anyway, we were talking after class one day, and he asked me out on a date. Can you believe it?"

Randy glanced at Emmy's ring. "Didn't he see that?"

"Oh, I just got it back from Watson's. The jewelry store. It needed to be cleaned."

"That's where Vanessa and I bought our rings. I know the place."

"It needed some work, so I wasn't wearing it for a while. Anyway, he asked me out to a dance and dinner."

"What did you say? Doesn't he know who you are?" Randy asked. "Does he live in a cave?"

Emmy smacked Randy's hand again. "Not everyone knows me, you goof. I don't go around telling everyone what I do."

"I bet ninety percent of the people at North Park College know you. Maybe even more."

"He didn't. He's an alien," Emmy said.

Randy interrupted with a laugh. "That explains it. Is he from Mars?"

"Not that kind of alien. He's from Kenya."

Randy stared at her.

"Oh, come on!" Emmy exclaimed as she exhaled. "Why would you think like that?"

"Sorry, I know it shouldn't matter, but I still have some prejudices. I'm not like you. You don't judge people the way most people do."

Emmy looked at her cell phone. "I should get going. I have to pick up the kids from school. It was good to talk to you, Randy. I mean Professor Braun."

Randy laughed. "You might have to call me Dr. Braun in a few years."

"That might be difficult to do," Emmy teased.

They hugged and Randy watched as she left.

## Chapter Thirteen

"Isabella, where is your sister?" Emmy asked while staring out the window by the kitchen sink. "I texted her five minutes ago to come home."

Isabella shrugged and grabbed a banana from the island. "She was riding her bike in the woods."

Emmy turned and stared at Isabella. "Why? She doesn't normally do that."

"You'll have to ask her," Isabella said. "I'm going upstairs to read."

"What are you reading now?" Emmy asked still staring out the window.

"The next Harry Potter book. You said I could."

"Okay," Emmy said. She pointed out the window. "There she is and why is that Plant boy with her?" Emmy watched and her eyes opened wide. "Heather Rose, you are so grounded!"

"Why is Heather grounded?" Kevin asked as he walked into the kitchen. "I'm starving. Are we ever going to eat lunch?"

"Eat a peach," Emmy said. "I'll fix lunch soon."

Kevin looked at the peaches on the island, but took an apple instead. "Is Heather in trouble for riding her bike with Ian again?"

"What?" Emmy asked. She set her jaw and turned to face Kevin. "What do you mean again?"

"They've been riding through the woods after school," he said and then grinned. "Is she in big trouble? Can I tell her?"

"No, you cannot tell her," Emmy said and then pointed. "Eat that in the family room."

Kevin froze in place. "For real?"

Emmy waved a hand. "No, I meant the breakfast nook. Where is your father? I need to talk to him."

"He's in the basement. Should I get him?"

"No, I'll go downstairs."

Emmy sighed and headed for the basement.

Kevin sat at the breakfast nook table and ate his apple. He grinned when he heard Heather walk into the mudroom. He tossed the core into the garbage and rushed to the mudroom door. "You are in big trouble," he said with a grin.

"Why? What for?" she asked.

Kevin shrugged. "Don't know, but Mom was watching you through the window. What did you and Ian do?"

"We were just riding our bikes," Heather said as she hung up her coat.

"Yeah, I think you did something more than that. Mom looked pretty mad. I bet you get grounded for a week. Ha ha!" He turned and raced away before she could smack him.

"Kenny, I need to talk to you," Emmy said as she entered the control room. "Are you busy?"

He turned around. "Not really. I was just listening to some old demos. What's up?"

Emmy let her shoulders slump and plopped onto the couch. "You'll never believe what I just saw."

Kenny waited for a moment, grinned when he realized she was not going to continue and asked, "Did you see a herd of barefoot elephants trampling through the woods?"

She stared at him then shook her head. "You're a dork."

"Tell me what happened." He moved next to her and put an arm around her shoulders.

"I saw Heather kiss that Plant boy. They were riding bikes in the woods and they came back and I saw them kiss by the deck. That is so wrong."

"By the deck, huh? I agree that is not right. They should be kissing... Where should they be kissing?" he asked with a grin.

She poked him in the side. "This is serious, and you're making jokes about it. She is only ten. She is way too young to kiss anyone but us."

"Are you sure they were kissing? Maybe they were whispering to each other."

Emmy stood up, rolled her eyes, twisted her head back and forth and sat back down. "I'm pretty sure I can tell when two people are kissing. I'm not blind, and I was not imagining this. It happened, and this isn't the first time."

"Okay, what should we do?"

"Well, obviously you have to ground her and take her bike away for at least a week."

Kenny smiled and said, "Should I paint it purple?"

"What?" Emmy asked.

"You know," he said and then squeezed her hand. "Like your father did when you were ten. Maybe then she will punch him in the belly like you did Barry Newton."

"You are no help. This is not like that at all. I never kissed a boy when I was ten. Why are you so dense when it comes to relationships?"

Kenny tilted his head. "Heather's ten. I doubt she even knows what a relationship is. She better not."

"I don't mean it like that, but that boy is older. He might try something."

"Ah! I get it now. How much older am I than you?" He tapped his jaw. "About three and a half years if my math is correct. Did I ever try anything when you were Heather's age?"

"Don't be silly. You never tried anything. We were best friends." She turned away.

He put a hand on her shoulder and tried to turn her back.

"Stop it."

"Are you afraid this boy is like Rory, and Heather will be like you?"

She turned back to Kenny and pushed him with both hands. He stumbled backward against the arm of the couch.

"Sorry. Are you okay?"

"I'm fine."

"I never kissed Rory, or any other boy until I was much older." *Not that I can remember.*

"I thought I was the first one to kiss you. Am I wrong?"

"No! You were the first," she said. "What should we do? What should I do since I doubt you will want to have the talk with them?"

"The talk?" he used air quotes. "Are we thinking about the same thing?"

"My mother never told me a thing about sex or babies or anything about boys," Emmy said. "I had to learn everything the

92

hard way." She looked at Kenny. "Stop grinning like that. I don't mean I learned about... Never mind. Will you back me up if I need to talk to them?"

He nodded. "Should I talk to Kevin Michael?"

"I think we can wait a couple years with him."

"Good, because I'm not sure I would know how to explain it."

Emmy shook her head. "You are such a dork. I will talk to them before they go to bed. Should we ground her?"

Kenny tilted his head as he thought. He grabbed Emmy's hands and said, "No, because I don't have any purple paint, and I don't want her to punch him in the belly."

She kicked his foot.

Later that night Emmy headed upstairs. She paused outside of the girls' bedroom. *Lord, give me the courage and wisdom to know what to say. I've never been in this situation. No one ever talked to me about this. Not my mother, I mean. I had to learn from friends and a little from Diane. They didn't teach it at school.* She knocked on the open door and stepped inside.

"It's not time for bed. We still have an hour," Heather said.

"I know, but I need to talk to you about something important."

"Mom, if it's about Ian kissing me, I won't do it again. I just wanted to see how it felt. The first time was just a quick one."

Emmy walked to Heather's bed and sat down. "Sit with me, please. Both of you."

The twins sat on either side of her.

She took a deep breath and said, "I know you're getting older and there is something you need to know."

"Mom, are you going to tell us how babies are made?" Heather asked.

"Well, I thought you might be curious," Emmy whispered.

Isabella patted Emmy's hand. "Mommy, we know how it happens."

"What do you know? Where did you learn about it?"

Heather and Isabella explained what they knew about the process as Emmy listened without speaking.

93

"Who told you all this?" Emmy asked after Heather stopped.

"Dotty had a health class, and she asked Sloane some questions. She explained it to us. We know what will happen in a few years," Heather said.

"You don't need to worry," Isabella assured Emmy. "We won't kiss any boys until we get married."

Emmy hugged them and said, "If you ever have any questions about boys or anything, you can always come to me and ask. I won't embarrass you."

Heather grinned and asked. "Do you think Daddy will talk to Kevin about this stuff when he gets older?"

Emmy laughed, shook her head and said, "I can't see your father ever talking about this stuff to your brother. He's such a dork."

Emmy and Kristen chatted about the kids while they strolled to their classroom for Sunday School.

"Maybe I should have you talk to Grace when the time comes," Kristen said. "I remember Mom talking to me, and how awkward it was. I've never felt so embarrassed."

Emmy paused outside one of the classrooms and asked, "How old were you?"

Kristen smiled and answered, "Twenty-one."

Emmy rolled her eyes and poked Kristen's side. "Tell me the truth."

"I was twelve and totally clueless. Except for Heather, I was the only girl on the Lombardi side of the family. She was five years older, so we weren't close. I had no one to tell me about things."

"What about on your dad's side. I know about Jenny and Julie. Are there any other girl cousins?" Emmy asked. "I know you've told me before, but does your father have any siblings?"

"Daddy is the oldest. Then there is Edward. He's Jenny and Julie's father. He moved to South Carolina after college and married Aunt Jean, but they divorced when Jenny and Julie were rather young. I rarely saw them when I was young. I don't think

94

I've seen those cousins since Jenny got married back in 2005."

Emmy waved to Pastor Williams and asked Kristen, "Doesn't your dad have a sister?"

Kristen nodded. "Aunt Martha. She married Pierre Quandt."

"Who's he?" Emmy asked. "Should I know him?"

"He was the Lieutenant Governor of Oregon for a few years, but was involved in some corruption scandal."

"How would I know that? I couldn't tell you who the Governor of Illinois is."

"Everette Pearcy," Kristen said. "And he's a Democrat."

"Whatever!"

"Anyway, Aunt Martha has three boys, and I haven't seen them in a dozen years or more." Kristen paused and asked, "What was your question?"

"Never mind," Emmy said. "We need to get to class, and I have to talk to Sloane."

Emmy talked to Sloane after the class and brought up her talk with the twins.

"Oh, Em, I didn't know Dotty would talk to your girls. I'm sorry if it caused a problem."

Emmy waved a hand as they walked down the hall. "It's no big deal. I was surprised Heather and Isa knew so much biological stuff. I sure didn't at their age."

"The school teaches it at a much earlier age now. Kids are exposed to so much. It makes sense to educate them early."

"Did Tony talk to Peter about stuff?" Emmy asked. "He's almost thirteen."

Sloane chuckled and said, "Are you kidding? Tony is afraid to talk about sex to me. I talked to Peter, and I suppose I will have to talk to the younger boys in a few years."

"Kenny is the same way. I'll have to talk to Kevin Michael."

Emmy was in the foyer after the second service when she felt a tap on her shoulder and turned around.

"Got a minute?" Bobby O'Connor asked.

"Sure. What's up, punk?" she asked.

"I'm not sure how many people know, but I thought you might want to hear this before it shows up on social media."

"Are you getting married again? I know you've been dating Shay Brennan."

Bobby shook his head. "Shay and I aren't that serious yet, but I'm hoping."

"She would be good for you. She's smart and much prettier than you deserve," Emmy teased. "I love her long hair. It reminds me of the way mine was before I chopped it off."

"Thanks a bunch. Anyway, Boyd and Bailey are splitting up. He's already moved out and she filed for divorce. Thought you might want to know."

Emmy stood still and looked up at Bobby. "You're not kidding, are you? That's why he's not on the worship team schedule."

He shook his head. "Boyd has actually joined the Bender Brothers Band."

"But he had a good job with the city. What happened?"

"It was a political thing. When the new mayor got elected, he started clearing out some people. Boyd didn't have the right connections," Bobby explained. "I should tell you I'm thinking of leaving the band."

"Why?"

Bobby took a deep breath and then said, "The guys are moving in a direction I'm not sure I can be a part of."

Emmy poked Bobby's arm. "You're a drummer. What difference does it make what kind of music you play. You just bang on the drums and keep time."

"Not what I mean, Em." He looked around. "There's Shay. I gotta run. Talk to you later. We're supposed to have dinner with her parents."

Emmy grinned and her eyes sparkled. "Sounds like it's getting serious, Bobby."

## Chapter Fourteen

"Why do we need to leave so early, Mom?" Heather asked. "I'm still tired."

"This is Easter Sunday, and there will be lots of people there today," Emmy explained.

"We don't have Sunday School because Pastor Tyler and Pastor Wade are making breakfast for us," Kevin said. "I'm going to eat a whole plate of biscuits and gravy."

"You better be careful not to stuff yourself," Kenny said. "Last time you had biscuits and gravy you got sick."

"Oh, yeah," Kevin said. "I threw up all over the breakfast table and Isa got sick, too."

"You are so gross, Kevin Michael. We should trade you for Noemi or Grace," Isabella said. "I'm not kidding. Mom, can we trade him for someone? Anyone. Maybe a dog or cat."

"We are not trading your brother for a sister or a pet," Emmy said.

Eventually, everyone made it to the Odyssey on time for the ride to church.

"I know this is Easter, but it's also the fourth Sunday of the month. Are the teens in charge of worship?" Kenny asked as he pulled out of Bristol Ridge.

"I think it's a combination," Emmy said leaning toward the middle to check Kenny's speed. "Some of the teens are scheduled, but Riordan and Sadie are leading like normal. The speed limit along here is forty-five. If you press harder on the gas pedal, we might get up to thirty."

Kenny checked the speedometer. "I'm doing just under forty-five. We will get there in time, Em."

She huffed to show her impatience. "Oh, I talked to Gideon last Sunday."

"How's he doing?" Kenny asked. He thought about the young man from the Philippines. "I haven't seen him lately."

"He said he turned down a chance to join Chris Stanfill's band. Stanfill is big time."

"I wonder how much he was offered."

"He didn't say, but I got the feeling it was a substantial offer," Emmy said. She watched traffic passing and said, "Have you guys ever thought about making him part of Fridays At Five?"

"I did mention it to Jeff. We couldn't make him a partner in the company, but we could hire him for the tours. Do you think he might be interested?"

"I'm sure he would love it. Would you still play your guitar if he was there?"

"Probably, but I wouldn't have to play as much," he answered.

"Do you want me to drive? That old man using a walker just passed us."

"I'm not listening to you, Em," Kenny said.

"Kids, wake up. We are finally here. It only took three hours," Emmy said after Kenny parked the minivan.

Kenny turned and stared at Emmy. She smiled and then stuck out her tongue.

"Mom, do we have to wait for you guys, or can we go eat?" Kevin asked.

"You can eat. I'll wait with your father," Emmy answered. "He's old and doesn't move that fast anymore."

"Keep it up, Em."

Emmy watched the kids race into the building. By the time she and Kenny made it to the large gym, there were long lines at each of the four food stations.

"Do you see them?" Emmy asked.

Kenny pointed. "They're over there with Sloane and her kids."

Tony walked up behind Emmy and pulled on her hair. "We're sitting in the back with Kristen. The kids have a table of their own. Some of the teens are babysitting."

Emmy turned around and pulled on Tony's tie. "Is this new? It almost looks fashionable."

"Sloane picked it out, so you can't blame me. Are you singing today?" Tony asked.

Emmy shook her head. "Nope! I only sing one Sunday a month. Usually the second one."

"I don't mean to inflate your ego, but I heard some people saying they miss listening to you. They said something about you adding energy to the worship time." Tony shrugged and added, "Of course, they might be senile."

"I can't believe it. That was close to being a compliment," Emmy said. "Let's get in line. Did you eat already?"

"Not yet. I thought I would wait until the lines are smaller..."

"And then take whatever is left," Emmy teased.

"Kenny, how do you put up with her after all these years?" Tony asked while holding out his hands.

"Only by the grace of God."

Emmy scooted around some people carrying food back to their tables and got in line behind Bobby O'Connor and Shay Brennan.

Bobby saw her and smiled. "I thought you would be here early so you could be the first in line."

Emmy laughed. "I made the mistake of letting Kenny drive." She touched Shay's shoulder and said, "I love this material. It feels so soft."

"Thank you, Emmy. Bobby bought it for me," Shay said as she smiled at Bobby. She looked at Emmy. "I love how your hair is curly and wavy even though it's shorter than mine. Do you do anything special with it? I've been using this natural conditioner. Bobby likes it."

Emmy touched her dark hair. "I don't do anything. It used to be as long as yours. Now I don't have to spend an hour brushing it."

"Do you ever straighten it?" Shay asked as she flipped her long hair over her shoulder.

"No, I've never thought about that. Where do you work, Shay?" Emmy asked. "Bobby might have told me, but I forgot."

"I teach English at Jamie McGee Middle School. Lindsey and Cam invited me to this church last year." She grabbed Bobby's arm and grinned. "I have them to thank for meeting this wonderful man."

Emmy's eyes opened wide as she looked at Shay and then

99

Bobby. *And you tried to tell me this isn't serious.* "He is something," Emmy said.

When Shay turned around to move forward in the line, Emmy poked Bobby in the arm.

He shrugged and smiled at Emmy. "What can I say? She likes me."

"I should tell her some stories about life on the road with you. She is obviously blinded by love at the moment."

"Any stories you tell her about me will implicate you, too, Em. You instigated a lot of the pranks we used to pull."

"I'll think of something to tell her."

"Where's Kenny?" Bobby asked while looking around.

"He's back there with Tony somewhere. I'm hungry and didn't want to wait for the end of the line." Emmy looked and spotted Tony. "Anything new with the band?"

Bobby shrugged. "I haven't been fired. We are off for a few days, and then we are doing a week in Texas. We're opening for Dixie Case. Do you ever talk to him anymore?"

Emmy bit her lip as she thought about the man who was part of her original touring band. "We've kinda lost contact."

"I know he went through rehab, Em."

"I hope he's clean and sober. Tell him I said hi, okay?"

Eventually, Tony and Kenny made it through the line and sat down across from Emmy, Kristen and Sloane.

"Is there anything left?" Emmy asked. "I didn't know these plates would hold that much weight."

Tony looked at his biscuits and gravy. "Peter eats more than this, brat."

"I saw you talking to Bobby and Shay. Any news?" Kenny asked. "Could I have the pepper, please?"

"They aren't engaged, but I bet he will propose soon," Emmy replied passing the salt and pepper to him.

"Did you want some eggs and hash browns with your ketchup, Em?" Tony asked.

Emmy rolled her eyes. "You are worse than Father James." She turned and asked Kristen, "Did John take Mama to mass at St. John's last night or this morning?"

"This morning," Kristen answered. "Zachary asked if he could go to church with his father."

"What did you tell him? He obviously didn't go because I see him with Peter and the boys."

Sloane glanced at her sons. "Peter asked Mama why she doesn't come to church with us."

"What did she say?" Emmy asked.

"She explained how she was raised in the Catholic church and that Jesus loves us no matter where we go."

"That sounds like an answer for the younger kids," Kristen said. "Peter is almost a teenager. He's going to want to start making his own decisions about church and stuff," Kristen said.

"Isabella asked Father James why he became a priest. I thought he would give her a smartaleck answer, but he didn't. He was serious and gave her some real answers."

"He only acts like a sarcastic priest with you, Em," Tony said.

"Are you getting anything out of the parenting class Pastor Tyler and Liz are teaching?" Kristen asked Sloane. "I read the book and I understand the concepts, but it's so difficult not to fall into old habits."

"I can see the difference in the way they deal with their children now. Do you remember the struggles they had with Zhy?"

"I was really surprised by some of the stories they told," Kristen said. "I know she had some issues, but I never would have guessed they were so serious. I can't imagine how John would react if Zach or Grace hit him."

"I've been thinking about the fear aspect of parenting. We try to get the kids to obey us using fear as a threat," Sloane said.

"I don't think I do that," Emmy said.

Tony laughed and added, "That's because they are almost as big as you, brat. You are about as intimidating as Moana."

Sloane stared at Tony. "FYI, Moana is a strong character."

"She's a cartoon. That's what I meant," Tony said.

"I know I treat the kids like I own them sometime," Sloane said. "I feel it's my responsibility to turn them into productive members of society."

"I try not to, but I feel I force my identity onto the twins," Emmy admitted.

Tony grinned and said, "Just because they look like you doesn't mean you forced your identity on them."

Sloane frowned at Tony. "Are you really that dense?"

"Sloane, you need to cut him some slack," Emmy said. "He has been hit in the head thousands of times. He's fortunate to remember his name."

"I need more grace in my life," Kristen said with a sigh. She looked at Tony and added, "I'm not talking about Grace Allison."

Tony shrugged. "I know what you mean. I still have a few functioning brain cells left."

Emmy swallowed a bite of hash browns, held up a finger to get everyone's attention and said, "I have a hard time accepting the fact that all our kids are born as sinners and are a danger to themselves."

The ladies talked about this for a moment as the men continued to eat.

Sloane said, "I liked the point about the law exposing sin, but doesn't have any power to save us from sin."

"That's where our faith in Jesus comes in, right?" Emmy asked.

Kristen nodded and said, "We have to realize it's the sin in our children that most often causes our anger toward them."

Emmy took a bite of eggs, chewed them fast and said, "I heard Zhy and her father moved back to Chicago. Is that true?"

Sloane looked at Kristen. They looked at Emmy.

"What? Do you know and can't tell me, or don't you know?"

"The last I heard was that he was living in the city, but had lost his job," Tony said. "I hope he found another one. He's changed so much from a few years ago."

"I will remember to pray for them," Emmy said.

Everyone stopped eating and looked at Emmy.

She glanced around. "I didn't mean right now. We can finish eating first."

102

"That's different," Kristen said. "You usually drop everything and pray immediately."

"Fine. I will pray silently. I don't want Tony to starve."

Do you have to be at Adam's press conference?" Emmy asked early Tuesday morning.

Kenny rolled over and looked at the clock on his nightstand. "I don't have to be there, but I thought I would take the kids to school and stop by the office. Since I'll be in the building, I might as well pop in."

"Do you like the CD cover?" Emmy scooted closer to Kenny and rested her chin on his chest. "I really like the music, but that cover kinda grosses me out."

"It's different, but it fits with the title."

Emmy ran a hand over his chest and asked, "Where did *The Medusa Protocol* come from? It's not the title of a song, and I didn't hear it in the lyrics."

"You should ask Adam. It's his project." Kenny smiled as Emmy moved her hand lower. "Are you in the mood?"

"We have some time. I don't hear the kids yet," she answered while biting her lip.

Ten minutes later Kenny heard a knock on the door.

"Mom! I'm hungry and we're out of milk. Can you get up and cook?" Kevin opened the door just as Emmy pulled the covers over her.

"There should be fresh milk by the garage. You are old enough to look by yourself," Emmy said.

Heather joined her brother in the doorway. She looked at her parent's bed and whispered, "Come on, Kevin. Mom and Dad are busy having sex right now."

Emmy sat up and held the sheet up. "We are not having sex."

Heather shrugged, turned around and pulled her brother along. "It's all right if you are, Mom. Carson said lots of old people still do it."

Emmy's eyes opened wide. She pushed Kenny away and said, "Did you hear what she called us?"

"Sorry, I was kinda busy. What did she say?"

"Never mind. Could you help me find my pajamas. They're somewhere under the sheet."

"Did you remember what today is?" Kenny asked while handing Emmy her pajama top.

She put her top on, grinned and said, "It's Tuesday. Big deal."

"It's a very special Tuesday," Kenny said holding her pajama bottoms.

She tried to grab them, but he moved them behind his back. "We did something on this day a few years ago. Don't you remember?"

She tilted her head back and forth. "I remember now. Today is the day we cleaned out the garage."

"That might be true, but I was thinking of something else. Something we did at the church."

"Can't think of anything. Did we sing a song together?" she asked. She reached behind him and snagged her bottoms. "Oh, are you talking about when we got married? I had almost forgotten about that. It's been so long ago."

"So you do remember, huh?"

"How could I forget marrying the dorkiest rock star in the world." She kissed him and put on her pajamas.

"Does this mean the honeymoon is over?" he asked.

"It is until tonight." She got out of bed and headed to the bathroom.

"I made reservations for dinner tonight."

"Anywhere special?"

"Darby's doesn't take reservations, so I booked a table at Ciao Bella. Is that all right with you?"

"It will have to suffice," she replied.


"Mr. Colwell, Ms. Colasanti, it is such a pleasure to see you tonight." Mr Sabatino bowed theatrically. "I have your table ready, and my wife has prepared a special treat for you."

"Did she make one of her famous chocolate cakes?" Emmy asked.

"She prepared it for this special anniversary."

Emmy's eyes sparkled as she asked, "What is so special about a thirteenth anniversary?"

Kenny nudged her. "I think Mr. Sabatino means that every anniversary is special."

"How long has Ciao Bella been open?" Emmy asked. "Do you think you will ever retire?"

He waved a hand in the air to encompass the restaurant. "We opened in 1980. Just a few months before you were born. Why would I ever retire? This is my life. If I retired, I would not see my friends."

"I hope you take a night off now and then," Emmy said.

"I seldom do, but I don't work as many hours these days. I let the younger Sabatinos do most of the work." He snapped his fingers and a hostess escorted Kenny and Emmy to their table.

"Do you know what you want, Em?" Kenny asked as he looked through the leather-bound menu.

"Can I order something expensive since it's our thirteenth anniversary?"

"I've only got fifty dollars with me."

"That's bull. I saw you put some hundreds in that old wallet of yours. Are you ever gonna let me buy you a new one?"

Kenny reached back and felt his wallet in the back pocket of his jeans. "You can buy me a new one for Christmas one of these years."

"Hey, guys. It's Emmy. I should take the call," Kenny said Thursday morning.

"Go ahead," Jeff said. "We should take five to listen to that track."

"Hi, Em. What's up?" Kenny asked.

"I'm sorry to bother you at the studio, but I need a favor. Could you pick up the kids after school?"

"I suppose so. Are you stuck at school?"

"I really need to finish this paper. Did you remember I need to be at rehearsal a bit early tonight? Riordan and Sadie are on vacation, and they asked me to lead worship this Sunday. I need to

105

make sure the songs are set."

"I remember. So, you won't be home until late this evening, huh?"

"We have leftover lasagna, and you could make a salad for dinner. There is garlic bread in the freezer," she reminded him.

"I can handle it. Dave needs to cut out early to take Madison to the doctor."

"What's wrong with her?" Emmy asked.

"Dave said she has some kind of rash that won't go away. Nothing too serious, but Macy is helping out at school. Some kind of book fair."

"So you will pick up the kids?"

"Yes."

"Thank you. I'll try to be home in time to put them to bed."

Emmy arrived at the church fifteen minutes early. She walked into the new sanctuary and saw Lois Crawford, the church secretary, in the foyer talking to Associate Pastor Darren Eaton and waved.

"Emmy, hold up a second," Darren shouted. He finished his conversation with Mrs. Crawford and walked over to Emmy.

"What's up?" Emmy asked looking up at Darren.

"Riordan asked me to remind you the order of service is on the computer."

"He doesn't want me to deviate from it, huh?" Emmy said rather sharply.

Darren looked surprised by her response. "He probably forgot you used to lead worship all the time. I don't think he meant it the way you assume."

Emmy looked down and kicked at a spot in the carpet. "Sorry, I shouldn't have snipped at you."

"It's all right, Emmy. I know you and the Schulenbergs aren't exactly best friends."

"They are okay."

"I know they were intimidated by you when they first started here."

"That was over two years ago, Pastor Darren. All of that is behind us. We get along fine now. I had a bad day at school. I've

106

been trying to finish a paper and I struggled with it today. I guess I took it out on you. Do you forgive me?" she asked and then bit her lip.

He looked down at Emmy, smiled and thought of the first time he met her.

"Why are you grinning at me like that?"

"I was thinking about when we met back in Columbus at my father's church."

"That was a long time ago before either of us was married," she said.

"Yes, and I remember how competitive you were at ping pong. I had to use my best game to beat you."

"I've always hated to lose," she said. "Do you remember anything else about that night?"

He smiled again. "I remember you flirted with me to get me to carry your merchandise inside the church."

"I was pretty bad, huh?"

"I didn't mind. I thought you were pretty cute for a young lady."

"If I recall correctly, I am a few months older than you."

"Possibly, but you look younger. You certainly did back then," he said.

Emmy shrugged. "Everywhere we went on that tour people thought I was still in high school."

"You surprised my father with how professional you were at such a young age."

"Ha! I couldn't make it through 'Yolanda's Song' without crying."

"Maybe so, but you were an amazing singer even then. You still are by the way."

"Thanks. What else do you remember about that night?"

"We ate pizza, played ping pong. I think we listened to some CDs in the teen room," he said.

"Is that all?" Emmy asked and then bit her lip.

"If you're thinking about what I think you are, it was a long time ago and only happened once."

"It was a nice kiss," she whispered.

"It was very brief. I do remember that, and we both felt awkward afterward." Darren glanced around to make sure no one could hear. "It was just a few months later that I felt the call to go into ministry. Before that I had planned to study medicine."

"I should get back to the music room. I want to make sure the music is ready."

"I'll talk to you later, Emmy. I'll be here to lock up later," he said and watched as she walked away.

She walked through the sanctuary to the music suite at the back of the building.

"Hi, Emmy. I guess we're the first ones here," Robby Collins said. "I guess Bobby is still on tour with the band, right?"

"They're somewhere in Colorado, I think. Thanks for filling in. Is Regina here?"

Robby chuckled and answered, "She's taking care of D'Andre."

"Is your son ready for a little brother or sister?" Emmy asked. "When is she due?"

"November tenth. D'Andre isn't sure he wants a baby in the house. He'd rather have a puppy."

Fifteen minutes later the entire worship team was ready to begin. Emmy went over the order of service and the team moved to the platform to rehearse

"You should be the worship leader," Kristina Liandro, one of the newest members of the team, said after Emmy showed her how to play the intro to one of the songs on the keyboard.

"Thanks, but I'm just filling in for Riordan and Sadie. It's their job to lead the team."

Kristina put an arm around Emmy and said, "That's only because you aren't here all the time. You're a better worship leader than them."

## Chapter Fifteen

Tyler Hammond took a seat in the conference room and looked at the church board members. "I want to thank you for taking time on a Saturday morning to be here. Some members of the team are working and a couple are out of town, but there are enough of us here to get started. I'm sure you all know by now that next April will be the fiftieth anniversary of the dedication of our church."

"It doesn't seem possible it's been that long ago," Roger Goldman said. "But I guess it has. I was ten when my parents started attending here. There aren't many original families left, but there are a few."

Tyler held up a booklet. "I found this in an old filing cabinet."

"What is it?" Lenore Toth asked.

"This is the official program from the dedication service. The date was April 16 1967. It has an order of service," he said and then chuckled. "Apparently the first two songs sung were 'Amazing Grace' and 'Victory In Jesus.' It's fitting we still sing them occasionally to this day."

"Could I see that, please?" William Griffith asked.

Tyler passed the booklet down the line.

William thumbed through it. "There are photos of the groundbreaking ceremony, and this teenager right here happens to be yours truly."

"Let me see that," Jim Rosek said. William handed it over and Jim stared at the photograph. "Well all righty then. It looks like you."

"My family attended South Hampshire First Nazarene, and my father was on the building committee," Mr. Griffith explained.

"Wait a second," Lenore said. All eyes turned to her and she asked, "Does that mean SoHam First is older than this church?"

Mr. Griffith nodded and said, "By thirty years or so. It used to be a much larger church. More people, I mean. It's the same building. The attendance has fluctuated widely over the years."

"I always assumed ours was the older church," Lenore said.

"Don't look at me," Tyler said and then chuckled. "I'm only thirty-one. I wasn't around when either church was organized."

Dylan Michaelis waited until the laughter died and asked, "Does this mean we should plan a celebration of some sort?"

"Several people have suggested it," Tyler said. "I realize it's a year away, but I feel we need to start planning now. We need to decide what kind of ceremony we want. We need to get it on the calendar. We should invite Dr. Schofield to be here."

Roger Goldman asked, "Would it be possible to have one of the General Superintendents lead the service?"

"We should ask Pastor Ausland to contact his friend. Dr. Borger is one of the General Superintendents."

"Before we get too far along in the discussion, I believe we need to form a committee, and appoint someone to supervise the organizing of the event. Do I have any volunteers?" Tyler asked.

At first no one raised a hand.

Marley Menconi looked around. "I haven't been on the board very long, but I would be willing to head up a committee. I think Joel would help me, but I would need more volunteers. I envision this as a two-day event. We could have an old-fashioned Singspiration Saturday evening with a special service Sunday."

"Should we invite former pastors?" Jim Rosek asked. "Are we still in contact with them?"

"I have the list of former pastors on my laptop," Tyler said. "We know Dr. Behren and Dr. Ausland, and I've heard a couple of these other names but not all."

"Could you read the list, please," Marley requested.

"Sure," Tyler said. "The first name is Lynford Jantz. He served from the beginning in April of '67 to August of 1975. Does anyone remember him?"

"I can picture him, but I don't remember much about him," Mr. Griffith said. "He was an older man, and I think he might have passed away shortly after he left, but I couldn't swear to that."

"The next name is Robert Sumner. He came in 1975 and left four years later. John Weaver replaced him and he left in January of 1982."

"I've never heard those names," Lenore said. "I've been here for twenty years."

The names were unfamiliar to the other board members.

"Dr. Ausland took over in March of '82 and served until Dr. Behren came in 2003." Tyler chuckled and added, "He came back and retired officially in 2015."

"We haven't had many senior pastors in fifty years," Mr. Griffith pointed out. "I remember when Dr. Ausland took over. My family was still attending SoHam First. After my first wife passed away, I lived in California for several years. When I moved back to SoHam, I started attending here. I don't know some of the early pastors, but it would be interesting to find out if they're still alive and where they might live."

Marley said, "I could look into that. If possible, I think we should invite all the former pastors. We could offer to pay for accommodations and perhaps their travel expenses."

After several more minutes of discussion, Tyler said, "I would entertain a motion to have Marley chair the committee and begin the planning."

"I so move," Jim Rosek said.

"I'll second it," Dylan Michaelis said raising a hand.

The motion passed unanimously.

"Marley, you are free to form a committee. The board will have to set a budget, but I'm sure you will have the funds to cover all expenses."

"The year will pass quickly," Mr. Griffith said. "My mother used to say the years pass more quickly the older we get. I believe her now."

Emmy arrived at the church early the next morning. She entered the new sanctuary and made her way to the music suite.

Pastor Tyler saw her and checked the time. "You're forty minutes early."

"I know, but I woke up at five and couldn't get back to sleep," Emmy said.

"Don't tell me you're nervous."

She looked up at him and nodded. "I haven't actually led

worship in over two years. Not since the Schulenbergs were hired. I hope I don't mess things up."

Tyler chuckled and said, "You can't mess things up any worse than the teen group did in February."

"You mean when the band started playing one song and the singers sang the wrong lyrics?"

Tyler nodded.

"That was kinda embarrassing," Emmy said. "I felt sorry for them. It wouldn't have happened if Pastor Jake hadn't been sick."

"I'll see you later, Emmy. Try to remember which songs to sing," he teased.

Emmy started the coffee and while it was brewing, she sat down and prayed out loud. She stopped and looked behind her when she heard someone enter.

"I'm sorry if I interrupted you," Gideon T. Logan said. "I see you've already started the coffee. That's usually my job even though I don't drink it."

"I was about finished," Emmy said as she stood up, walked to the table and poured herself a cup of coffee. "Did you hear what I was praying about?"

He shook his head and his long, jet-black, straight hair flipped back and forth. "I could tell you were praying, but I couldn't hear everything."

She bit her lip and said, "I was praying for help because I'm kinda scared about today."

Gideon opened a bottle of water and looked at Emmy. "Serious? Why would you be afraid?"

Emmy explained while staring at the tattoos on his arms.

"Okay, I can understand." He smiled and waved a hand. "You don't need to worry. The Holy Spirit will make sure you sing the right song."

"Very funny," she said and the grinned. "I should let you sing. You've got an amazing voice."

"Thank you. I did sing quite often back home in Quezon City."

"I've never been to the Philippines. What's it like?"

"Quezon is a suburb of Manila."

"Is it bigger than SoHam?" Emmy asked.

Gideon grinned and said, "Slightly. The population is probably over three million."

"That's not a suburb. That's like Chicago," Emmy said. "We should add you to the vocals here."

"Do you think the congregation would accept me?" he asked and took a sip of coffee.

"Why wouldn't they?" Emmy asked.

He touched his hair. "This and my ink. Not everyone is as accepting as you."

"Then they have a heart problem," she said. "Anybody who knows you, knows you have a gentle and spirit-filled heart." She turned around to walk away, but then quickly turned back spilling some coffee on the table and asked, "Did you ever have a son?"

Gideon coughed and almost spit out some coffee. "No, why would you ask?"

Emmy took a deep breath before answering," I read a newspaper article about a baby, and I wrote a story about it. The baby's name was Gideon." Emmy explained what happened to the child and noticed Gideon's eyes filled with tears.

"I'm sorry if I upset you," Emmy said putting her hand on his arm.

"It's okay. My brother lost a child, and I often think of him."

"It would break my heart if I ever lost a child," Emmy said.

It was close to eleven thirty when Emmy returned to the music room after finishing their part of the second service. Several members of the worship team followed her.

"Emmy, you were amazing," Liz said. "You didn't need to be nervous about leading worship."

Emmy hugged Liz and whispered, "I was so nervous. I thought I was going to be sick to my stomach."

"Like morning sickness?" Liz asked with a grin.

Emmy placed a hand on Liz's baby bump and shook her head. "No more blueberries for me."

Robby Collins high-fived her. "You still got it, Emmy.

You're a natural."

"I'm not a natural. I rely on God to sing every note," Emmy said. "And I really mean that. It's not just lip service."

Gideon stood silently behind the other team members and listened. Emmy finally saw him, walked up and hugged him. He wrapped his arms around her. They didn't say a word.

"I'm so glad you were here today," Kristina Liandro said to Adam Vicini. "I was totally lost on that last song. I stopped playing and didn't know which part to sing. I felt so foolish."

"You shouldn't be so hard on yourself, You do all right for someone who doesn't read music," Adam said. "I've had plenty of experience playing behind Emmy. I knew she would repeat that chorus twice and then allow a space for the music to kind of simmer."

"I'll never be as good as you," Kristina said as she turned away.

Adam looked to his left and saw Emmy and Gideon still hugging each other. He walked over and tapped her shoulder. "Are you okay, Em?"

She let go of Gideon, stood next to him and nodded. "I'm all right. I was so nervous about today, and Gideon got here early. He helped me get through my nervousness."

Adam grinned.

"Stop that." Emmy poked Adam's arm. "You know I sometimes get nervous before I sing. You've helped me get through some rough patches on the road." Emmy looked at Gideon and whispered, "Adam was in my band before he joined Fridays At Five. He was the poor guy who had to listen to me complain about stuff. That was before I understood complaining was sinful. Anyway, I leaned on him more than I should. He would always redirect me back to Jesus for the strength to know what to do."

Adam offered a hand, and Gideon shook it.

"I really love listening to you play," Adam said. "You have a great sound."

Emmy giggled and touched Gideon's arm. "Adam has to listen to Kenny play the guitar all the time. That's why it's such a pleasure for him to listen to a professional guitar player."

"I'll tell him you said so tomorrow, Emmy," Adam teased her back. "You should join us in the studio, Gideon."

"I appreciate the offer, but I have a day job."

Emmy said, "He works for the same company I did after high school. Coventry Shield Healthcare."

"You mean they're still in business after you worked for them," Adam teased.

Emmy made a face at him. "He lives in my apartment, too."

Adam, Gideon and Liz looked at her with an expression of surprise.

Emmy put a hand to her mouth. "I didn't mean it like that."

"I know what you meant, Em. Kenny told us the story a while back," Adam said. "You should see the look on your face."

"At least Gideon doesn't have to put up with the mean landlords I did."

"Were they mean to you because you partied all the time?" Robby asked.

"They would complain about me listening to music and would tell my mother every time I had a boy come over."

Adam and Robby looked down at Emmy.

"Shoot! That didn't come out right. I didn't have boys coming over all the time. Just at night."

"Emmy!" Liz exclaimed.

"After work!" Emmy responded as her childlike voice rose an octave. "Kenny and Tony would come over after work."

"Both of them?" Liz asked while grinning. She knew the story and was embarrassing Emmy on purpose.

"I'm not saying anything else. The more I say, the deeper in trouble I get." She zipped her mouth closed and threw the key over her shoulder.

"Simon, it's so good to see you again," Sadie Schulenberg said as she and Riordan walked into the control room of Steward Music Group's Studio Two.

"The pleasure is all mine," Simon responded holding out his arms for a hug.

Sadie put her arms around the diminutive man who was as

wide as he was tall. "How is Vera? Is she going to join you?"

"She will be here the last two weeks. I hope we will be able to add background vocals by then."

Riordan shook Simon's hand. "We are so grateful you are taking the time to produce this for us. I know a month in the studio is not a long time, but it's all we could afford."

"I have been listening to the demos, and I have some ideas already. Stuart is going to work with us, and we have Studio Two for the month. It's large enough to record the strings."

Riordan looked into the large room and spotted Stuart Lederer adjusting some microphones. "Mr. Lederer does a great job. We should thank Fridays At Five for letting us borrow him."

Thirty minutes later the musicians were ready to begin.

"This has been a very productive day," Simon said at four o'clock. "We will start again at nine in the morning."

"Are you sure you won't stay with us, Simon?" Sadie asked. "We have an extra room."

Simon waved dismissively. "I have a room at the Lincoln Hotel. That allows me the privacy I need to work on the charts for the orchestra. I hope to have all the basic tracks finished this week. The orchestra will be here all next week."

"How did you manage to schedule..."

"I called in a few favors. I wanted the best musicians in Chicago," Simon interrupted. "Vera's brother is my connection. He is one of the best bassoonists in the country."

"We will see you tomorrow, Simon. You have to promise to come over for dinner on the weekend," Sadie said.

"I will if you agree to make your homemade pizza. I haven't had one of those for too long."


"What did you want to talk about?" Riordan asked Ross and Heidi Knapp before rehearsal Thursday evening.

Ross closed the door and looked at his wife.

Heidi knew she would have to break the news. She took a deep breath, sighed and said, "We are leaving the worship team. Actually, we have bought a new house in Newcastle and found a new church. I'm sorry for the short notice."

Riordan looked at Sadie and then at Ross and Heidi. "I'm sorry to hear that. Not about the new house, but that you are leaving us."

"We wanted to tell you before everyone arrives," Heidi said.

"Would you like to tell the team yourself, or should Riordan and I inform them?" Sadie asked.

"We would like to tell them if that's all right," Heidi said.

Later, on their drive home, Riordan and Sadie discussed the news about the Knapps.

"We have plenty of singers to replace Heidi, but she does have a beautiful voice," Sadie said looking at the list of team members.

"Guitar players are more difficult to find," Riordan said. "Especially good bass players. Lots of guitar players can play the bass, but Ross was better than most. It's a shame his hand hurts so much. He was really good at lead guitar."

"You know there is one person in the church who is pretty good on guitar," Sadie said. "Oh, look! That new chicken place is finally open. Regina told me the chicken is better than any other place in town."

"You don't mean Kenny Colwell, do you?"

"He used to play when he wasn't on tour. We could ask Emmy if he might be interested."

"Should we see if Emmy will take over Heidi's place?" Riordan asked.

"I hate to ask. She's so busy all the time. Let me see if there's someone else interested. It's always good to add new members to the team," Sadie said as her cell phone chirped.

## Chapter Sixteen

"Do you like the dress I bought for the wedding?" Emmy asked Kenny. She held it in front of her. "Did you have a nice nap?"

"I needed it." He sat on the edge of the bed, stretched his arms over his head, tilted his head back and forth to remove the kinks in his neck, stared at the dress and said, "It looks rather short. I can see your legs."

"I thought you liked my legs," Emmy said while lowering the dress. "It almost comes down to my knees."

"Was it on sale?"

Emmy bit her lip.

"That means no." Kenny stood up, walked past Emmy into her closet. He waved both hands at the rack of clothes. "You have a whole walk-in closet full of dresses. Why did you buy another one? Couldn't you have worn one of these?" He grabbed one and showed it to her. "I like this one. The color looks great on you. It makes your blue eyes stand out."

"I can't wear that one anymore." She took the dress and put it back. "It was short on me ten years ago. I'm not young enough to wear it now."

"Then why do you keep it?"

"It's still a good dress. Isa or Heather might want to wear it when they're older," she said.

"Are you turning into your mother?" Kenny asked.

"Why would you say that?"

"I remember how you would complain because your mother made you wear Diane's hand-me-downs."

"That's different. Diane's dresses never fit me right. She was bigger." Emmy held her hands in front of her chest.

Kenny grinned.

"Stop that. We don't have time, and I already took a shower."

"The kids are with my parents," Kenny reminded her. "We are all alone in this big house." He stepped toward her. "You know you want me."

She giggled as she scooted out of the closet past him. He chased her toward the king-size bed.

"Don't you dare!" she squealed.

"I'm coming to kiss you," he said moving like the Frankenstein monster.

She lay on her back and put a hand over her eyes. "You don't scare me, you bad monster."

Kenny moved closer and stepped on a plastic firetruck. "Ow! I told Kevin Michael not to play in here." He hopped on one foot and fell onto the bed next to Emmy.

She turned on her side and touched his ear as he rubbed his foot. "The next time Dr. Frankenstein puts you together, would you ask for different ears?"

"Any other parts he should replace?"

"Just your ears," she said while grinning and pulling him on top of her.

An hour and a half later Kenny parked as close as he could to the entrance of the Barclay Country Club.

"I could have dropped you off, Em," he said.

She got out of the car and smoothed out her dress. "I don't mind walking. It's a beautiful day."

He ran around to her side and closed the door. "I would have opened it for you."

"That's so sweet. Are you being extra nice to me because of earlier?"

He smiled and held out his arms like the monster again.

She rolled her eyes. "Don't you dare act like that inside. I will disown you forever if you embarrass me."

"I will act like I normally do," he said putting an arm around her shoulders.

"Would it be possible for you to not act normally?"

"What do you mean?"

"Don't be a dork," she said with a grin.

"I'll give it my best shot."

"Do you have the card for Spencer and Mackenna?"

"In my pocket." He patted his suit jacket. "The card, our invitation and some cash."

119

"I haven't ever been to an actual wedding here," Emmy said. "Some receptions, but never the ceremony. I suppose it's here because Spencer and Mackenna don't attend a church."

They walked into the large foyer and saw a sign directing them to the right for the Barlow and Robertson wedding.

"Kenny, there's Mr. Robertson and Mona. I want to talk to them. Could you take my jacket to the check-in place, please."

"Certainly, what about your purse?"

"I'll keep it with me for now. I might have you run it back to the car later. If you wouldn't mind."

He helped Emmy remove her light jacket and smiled.

"Why are you looking at me like that?" Emmy asked while waving at Bill and Mona.

"I think that's a very simple but sexy little black dress."

"Thank you, m'lord."

Emmy threaded her way through the throng of people to where she had spotted Mr. Robertson only a moment earlier. *Where could they have gone?* She spun in a circle hoping to see them. She felt a tap on her shoulder and turned.

"About time you guys got here," Diane said. "Brady and I have been here for thirty minutes."

"We would have been here earlier, but something came up," Emmy said.

Brady thought he detected a slight blush on Emmy's face.

"I don't want to hear your excuses," Diane told her younger sister. "Who is watching your kids?"

"Kenny's parents. Yours?"

"Sloane and Mama Bertucci are taking care of them. I'd hate to be in that house tonight. There are like a dozen kids over there."

"Where did Mr. Robertson go?" Emmy asked glancing around the crowded foyer. "Did you see them, Kenny?"

Kenny rejoined his wife and glanced around. "Sorry, Em, but I don't see them."

"I think the photographer needed them," Brady said. "Diane and I are finished with photos for now. Bennett and Marissa are with Spencer, Mackenna and Abigail somewhere."

"Did Mackenna choose Abby to be her maid of honor?" Emmy asked.

Diane nodded. "There are almost twenty people in the wedding party. Not including the parents or anything. I've never seen so many bridesmaids and groomsmen."

"This is a big social event for not only SoHam but the entire state and country. The Barlow family is somehow related to the Barclays and you know how important they are."

"Mr. Robertson is pretty important, too," Emmy said. "Does that mean there will be celebrities here?"

"Marissa insisted every politician and businessman in the area be invited," Diane said.

"Have you seen Mackenna?" Emmy asked. "What color is her hair today? The last time I saw her she had purple highlights."

"I think she has some highlights in her hair, and she's wearing all her piercings," Diane said. "Marissa and Grandmother Hartley are probably having a fit, but Mackenna is a Barlow. Old money and social elite. That's important. Right, Brady?"

He answered, "It is to some people. I think we should be heading into the ballroom. The ceremony is supposed to start in thirty minutes."

"How soon is the reception supposed to start?" Emmy asked.

"Six o'clock. That means the ceremony won't be longer than forty minutes."

"Do you see any celebrities," Kenny?" Emmy asked.

He offered his arm and she put her hand on it. "Not yet, m'lady, but I'll point them out if I see any."

Diane nudged Emmy and whispered, "That man with the silver hair in front of us is a Senator from New York. See that couple over there?"

Emmy stood on her tiptoes and nodded.

"He's on the Supreme Court."

"For real?" Emmy asked. "Should I get his autograph?"

Kenny looked at Brady and made a circle around his ear. Brady smiled and nodded.

"Save me a seat, Brady. I see someone I need to talk to,"

Diane said. She hustled away and walked up to a man in a black suit standing by the wall. "Are you on duty, Rosco?" Diane asked.

"I am and it's a pleasure to see you again, Mrs. Robertson." He smiled but kept his attention focused on the room.

"Are there Secret Service agents here?" Diane asked.

"There are some important people here who have security details," he admitted.

"Emmy will be so excited, but I guess I shouldn't tell her, huh?"

Rosco shook his head just slightly.

Diane smiled and whispered, "You do look like Tommy Lee Jones, but more handsome."

Emmy looked at Diane when she sat down next to Brady. "Who were you talking to? He reminds of someone, but I can't think of the name. Is he a celebrity?"

"He's not exactly a famous celebrity, but he's a very important person," Diane said.

The ceremony began on time and lasted exactly forty minutes. The wedding party disappeared down the aisle and the crowd started filing out.

"Em, I'm so proud of you," Kenny said. "You didn't cry at all."

"I'm getting better at controlling my emotions, and I was kinda busy looking for celebrities."

Diane put her hands on Emmy's shoulders. "Brady said there won't be a reception line like at most weddings. We're supposed to head into the new ballroom. The Barclay family built a huge new ballroom when they learned about Mackenna's wedding. It's big enough to seat a thousand guests."

"I hope the food is good," Emmy said and then giggled.

Later, Kenny looked at Emmy and asked, "Aren't you going to eat your prime rib? It's really good."

"I've been too busy trying to spot VIPs to think about eating." She took a look around the ballroom and then sighed.

"What's wrong?" Diane asked.

"I know there are important people here, but they all just look like old men with white hair."

"I'm sorry Spencer and Mackenna didn't invite any movie stars or rock stars, Em," Diane said as she winked at Kenny.

"That's okay. There are lots of Spencer and Mackenna's friends here. I just want to be able to dance with some guys who don't need to use a cane."

Kenny shook his head. "I'm not going to dance very much, Em. Sorry."

"I know, and I know that's why you were being so nice earlier. You know I still love to dance at weddings. You won't mind if I dance with their friends, will you?"

"Not at all. I love watching you have fun."

"Are you going to drink your champagne, Em?" Diane asked.

"Isn't it for the toasts?"

"You can drink it now if you want. The waiters will refill your glass. There is an open bar. The Barlows are spending a large fortune for this affair."

"And I thought we spent a lot for our reception," Emmy said grinning at Kenny.

"Not even close to the cost of this one, Em," Kenny said.

Thirty minutes later Emmy turned to Kenny and whispered, "I want to talk to Mr. Robertson, but he's talking to that old guy."

"That old guy is Mr. Barlow. Mackenna's grandfather."

"Oh, how did the Barlows make their money?"

"I don't know," Kenny said.

Brady heard the questions and answered, "Banking. Back in the early 1800s in New York City."

"He's finished," Emmy said. "I'll be back."

She raced to Mr. Robertson's side.

"Good evening, Emmy. You look more beautiful than ever tonight."

She bit her lip for a moment. "Thank you, Mr. Robertson. Isn't it exciting to have all these VIPs here?"

He chuckled and said, "You don't have a clue who they are, do you?"

She shook her head. "Diane and Brady told me who some of them are. I don't even know who the SoHam mayor is."

"He's the man standing with the Governor," Mr. Robertson said while turning Emmy around.

She quickly spun back to face Mr. Robertson. "The real Governor?"

"Yes, sweetie. But just between you and me, I didn't vote for either of them."

"Where did Mona go? I saw her earlier."

"She is with Marissa and Abigail Hartley. Grandmother Abigail, not Abby."

"Now you have another granddaughter," Emmy said. "That makes three, right? Abby, Lily and now Mackenna."

"Yes, but I also have Heather and Isabella who I love just as much." He put an arm around Emmy and squeezed.

"You are so sweet. I love you so much. Will you dance with me later, please?"

He kissed the top of her head and nodded. "I wouldn't miss it for the world."

"We can wait for a slow song if you want."

"I can still do a waltz," he teased.

Two hours later Emmy sat down next to Kenny.

"Are you worn out, Em?" he asked. "Do you need something to drink?"

"I would like some water, please."

He poured her a glass.

"Were you watching me dance?" she asked after draining half the glass. She looked at her bare feet. "I lost my shoes somewhere."

"I have them. Diane brought them over for safekeeping," he said holding up a shoe. "You looked like you were having fun. Spencer and Mackenna's friends are having a blast." He glanced around the large ballroom. "It appears all the politicians and businessmen are having an important discussion at the other end of the room."

Emmy finished her water and stood up. "Mr. Robertson promised me a dance. I'm going to hold him to it." She walked straight to the table where Mr. Robertson sat, stood behind him and put her hands on his shoulders.

He turned and smiled. "Is it time for that dance, Emmy?"

"If you have the time."

"Bill, are you going to introduce me to this lovely young lady? Is she a granddaughter?" the man sitting next to Mr. Robertson asked.

Mr. Robertson stood up and put an arm around Emmy's waist. "This is my goddaughter, Emmy Colasanti-Colwell. Emmy, may I introduce you to the Honorable Benson Rutledge."

"It's a privilege to meet you, Emmy."

"Thank you, sir," Emmy said quietly. She looked at the other men around the table. *Holy crap! You guys are real important.*

"If you gentlemen will excuse me, I promised Emmy a dance or two." He placed a hand on Emmy's back, and they headed to the dance floor.

"Is he really what you said? Brady said he was on the Supreme Court."

"That he is, and we were discussing something very important," Mr. Robertson replied.

"Can you tell me, or is it top secret?"

"We were discussing the merits of two... franchises."

"Do you mean the CIA and the FBI or some other spies?"

"Not exactly," Mr. Robertson said. He chuckled and added, "Benson is a die hard Cub fan, and I have always supported the Cardinals."

Emmy looked at Mr. Robertson and rolled her eyes. "That's funny. I do believe we can dance to this song."

He glanced at her feet. "I will promise not to step on your... purple toes."

Emmy giggled and said, "I like the color purple."

"I know you do." He took her hand and they waltzed.

"You are pretty good, Mr. Robertson."

"Lily loved ballroom dancing. Mona tolerates it, but that's all right." He brought up his late wife's passion for dancing. "You won't remember, but Lily and I were watching you one evening. You were probably three. We played some music and danced in the living room. You watched and walked up to me with your

125

hands in the air. I leaned over, took your hands and you danced while standing on my shoes. When the song ended, you said something that reduced Lily and I to tears."

"What did I say? Was it something sweet and loving?"

He grinned and whispered, "You said you needed to go to the potty and needed help. You insisted I take you."

Emmy backed up a step and put a hand to her mouth. "Did I really?"

He nodded. "You told me how you were a big girl and didn't wear diapers anymore. Maybe you weren't quite three."

Emmy moved back into his arms and they continued to dance to a slower song.

"I hope that didn't embarrass you."

"It doesn't." She rested her head on his chest for the rest of the song.

"Thank you for the dances, Mr. Robertson. You should tell the judge he should know better than to root for the Cubs. They haven't won the World Series in a thousand years."

"I will pass that along, sweetie," he said. He hugged her and walked away.

"Em, it's after midnight," Kenny said later. "Are you close to wanting to go home?"

She put her feet in his lap. "Will you massage them for me? They are starting to ache."

"Certainly, m'lady."

She leaned back in the chair for a moment and closed her eyes. She opened them with a start, moved her feet to the floor and leaned close to Kenny. "I found out Mackenna is pregnant. She is due in October. Did you know that already?"

He shook his head. "I did not know."

"If we stay much longer, you will have to carry me to the car," she said as she slumped down in the chair.

He put his hands on her knees. "I could always get one of the security guys to carry you."

Emmy looked around. "Are they still here? Most of the big shots are gone."

"Mr. Robertson and Mona are still here. Do you want to

say good night? Then we can leave."

"Yes. Oh, there's Diane and Brady. I should tell them good night, too."

"Let's not take too long. We have church in the morning," Kenny said.

"Yeah, but I'm not singing. We can sleep in."

She took Kenny's hand and led him to the Robertsons. "Kenny is taking me home. He will have to put me in bed because I'm wiped out."

"Did you enjoy the reception, Emmy?" Mona asked. "I saw you dancing with Bill. I trust he didn't step on your toes."

"No, he didn't. That's just purple nail polish. Not bruises."

"Brady and I are leaving," Diane said. "Are you awake enough to drive, Kenny?"

"I am tired, but all I drank tonight was Dr Pepper."

"Diane, our driver is ready. He is waiting with the car," Brady said. "Dad, are you and Mona ready?"

Emmy hugged everyone while yawning.

"I'll get your jacket and here are your shoes. Your purse is in the car," Kenny said. He helped her with her jacket, and they headed outside.

Rosco held the limo door open for the Robertsons. Just as Mr. Robertson was about to get in the car, he spotted Kenny and Emmy, laughed and pointed. Rosco turned, saw them and smiled.

"I do believe our little angel is wiped out," Mr. Robertson said as he watched Kenny carrying her on his back.

"Em, you need to wake up. We need to leave for church in thirty minutes," Kenny said rubbing her back.

"Just five more minutes," she said rolling onto her back.

"That's what you said an hour ago."

She opened her eyes. "What time is it?"

He checked the clock. "Quarter to ten. We are missing Sunday School."

"Where are the kids?" Emmy asked jumping out of bed.

"With Gra and Me-maw."

"Do I have time to shower?" she asked while racing to her

127

bathroom. "I have to shower after last night."

"If you make it a quick one."

They arrived five minutes before the scheduled start of the second service.

"About time you got here," Tony said as Emmy sat next to him. "How late were you at the reception?"

"It was close to one when we got home." She poked his arm in a friendly way. "You should have seen all the VIPs. There were all kinds of big shots." She rattled off a few of the names.

"Did you get any autographs?"

"I thought about it. I danced with lots of Spencer's friends." She leaned closer and whispered in his ear. "One of them asked me to spend the night."

Tony pretended to look shocked. "No! Did you take him up on the offer?"

She smacked his arm harder this time. "Of course not. I went home with my dorky husband.

After the service Bobby O'Connor hurried to Emmy's side and asked, "Do you have time to talk?"

"I always have time for you, punk. What's up? Where's Shay?" Emmy glanced around.

"She left already. Can we go somewhere more private?"

"At the church, or do you want to come to the house. I could make lunch. Kenny has to pick up the kids later."

"Up to you, Em."

"Come to the house. Unless you have other plans," she said with a grin.

"Shay is going somewhere with her parents. I am all yours this afternoon."

"What will I do with you all afternoon? It's too cold outside. We haven't opened the pool yet."

"You do have a hot tub," he said.

Emmy pushed him away. "Stop looking at me like that. It makes you look like a dirty old man."

"I'm younger than you."

"I'll tell Kenny to go ahead and get the kids if you'll give me a ride."

128

Bobby pulled up to her garage thirty minutes later. "I would have paid for lunch, Em."

"That's all right. Kenny said he and the kids were going to eat at his parents. Mom made something special. The chopped salad will be enough for me."

They went inside and Bobby waited in the kitchen while Emmy changed into something more comfortable than her dress.

"We can eat at the breakfast table. Did you get something to drink?"

He held up a Coke. Emmy grabbed a bottle of water from the fridge and they sat down to eat. She prayed and then asked, "Now what is so important?"

"I'm leaving the band," he said while staring into her eyes. "Actually, I've already left."

"I don't really have a band at the moment." She waved her hands around. "But you can't leave me. I need you."

"Em, I'm leaving the Bender Brothers Band."

"Why? They're doing great. I heard the CD is coming out next month, and they have a summer tour booked. You're going to be a real rock star."

"That's just it, Em. Some of the guys are getting carried away with the rock star stuff," he said using air quotes.

"How? What are they doing? Who's acting like a rock star? What's going on?"

"If you slow down and give me a chance, I'll explain."

"Go ahead. I'll sit on my hands," she said and then zipped her mouth closed.

"You can eat your salad while I talk."

She nodded.

Bobby looked at the ceiling and then at Emmy. "Some of the guys are drinking too much, and I've seen some drugs around."

"Get out!" Emmy almost launched herself across the table. She ended up sitting on her knees with her feet tucked under her.

"It's getting to the point where I'm not comfortable being around the band. Miles is thinking about leaving, too."

"Did all this start after Boyd joined the band? I know he's struggling spiritually. Duh! That's why he's getting divorced."

129

"It started before that, but Boyd helped fuel the binge."

"Oh, Bobby, I'm so sorry. What are you going to do? Should I see if Andy Walker can talk to the guys at Prater-Saylor and book a tour for me?"

Bobby waved a hand as he took a sip of his Coke. "Not necessary. You don't need to support me."

"How are you paying the bills?" she asked, took another bite of salad and looked out the window. "Look! There are two cardinals."

"I see them. For the time being I'm working at DelSasso Sound. I'm giving lessons and I have some money stashed away. I'll be fine for a year or so."

Emmy leaned back in her chair. "I should have been praying harder for you guys."

Bobby shook his head. "This is not your fault, Em. The guys are making poor decisions. It's their choice."

"I still feel responsible."

"Trust me, Emmy. It's not your fault."

"I'm so glad Kenny never gave in to that crap. He was a lot younger when Fridays At Fire started touring." She waved a hand. "He might have done some stuff, but he didn't drink much, and he never used drugs. None of the guys did. They were dead set against anyone in the organization using any kind of drugs."

"What about the ladies?" Bobby asked.

She made a face at him. "He once told me he kissed a few hundred girls in the early days, but that was as far as it went."

"A few hundred?" Bobby asked.

"He was joking," she said. "I think."

# Chapter Seventeen

"Mommy! Your phone is ringing," Isabella hollered as she walked into Emmy's bathroom. "It might be Mary. Maybe she had the baby already."

Emmy peeked around the frosted-glass-block wall of the walk-in shower. "What did you say?"

"Your phone was ringing but it stopped," Isabella said. "It might have been Mary."

Emmy turned off the water and asked, "Can you hand it to me, please?"

Isabella waited until Emmy wrapped up in a towel and handed her the phone.

"Do you think she had the baby?" Isabella asked.

"It's possible." Emmy checked her messages and smiled.

"Heather! Come here!" Isabella shouted.

Heather dashed into the bedroom. "Where are you?"

"In the bathroom." Isabella stood in the doorway. "Mary had the baby. Mommy is trying to call Pastor Jonah."

Emmy held up the towel with one hand while talking to Jonah. "The girls are listening, so I'll put you on speaker."

"Mary and the baby are doing excellent according to the nurses. Emmy, she is so beautiful and absolutely perfect," Jonah beamed.

"I know Mary is perfect, but how about your daughter?" Emmy teased.

"You are so funny, Emmy. Let me give you the details. She arrived just after nine this morning. She has some good lungs."

"Does she have hair?" Isabella asked.

"Is she all red and wrinkly?" Heather asked.

Jonah laughed and said, "She has dark hair, chubby cheeks and all of her fingers and toes."

"Does she have two ears, eyes and noses?" Heather asked.

"Yes, I counted them."

The twins giggled.

"They fooled you, Jonah. You said she has two noses, and the girls are giggling."

131

"One nose," Jonah corrected.

"Is Mary sleeping?" Emmy asked.

"No, she's holding the baby."

"Pastor Jonah! Are you going to call her the baby all the time like Pastor Tyler called Phoebe?" Isabella asked with her hands on her hips. "Did you give her a real name?"

Jonah chuckled and answered, "She does have a real name. It's Baby Girl Galves."

"That's not her name," Heather said.

"Oh, you are right. Mary is staring at me and shaking her head. I suppose you want to know her name, huh?"

"That would be helpful, Jonah," Emmy said as she handed the phone to Isabella and tried to dry off.

"We had several picked out, but the winning name is... Drum roll, please!"

The girls patted the bathroom wall.

"Erin Karina!"

"That's a cool name," Isabella shouted.

"How do you spell it?" Heather asked.

Jonah looked at Mary and she spelled it.

"Did you hear that?"

"We heard," Emmy said. "What room is Mary in?"

"4012."

"I'm going to get dressed and rush right there," Emmy said.

"Can we go, too?" Isabella asked. "Please?"

"Do you mind if I bring the girls?"

Jonah looked at Mary and she nodded.

"Mary says yes."

"Come on, Heather! Let's let Mommy get dressed. We need to make a card for Mary and Erin."

Fifteen minutes later Emmy and the girls headed to St. Bart's. Emmy parked and the girls raced to the reception desk.

"How may I help you ladies?" the volunteer asked.

"Our nanny just had a baby and we're here to see them," Isabella explained.

"Hurry up, Mom," Heather said.

"And what would your nanny's name be?"

132

"It's Mary Galves now. G-A-L-V-E-S."

"Yes, I see it. She's in room 4012. Do you know how to get there?" the volunteer asked Emmy as she handed the visitor passes over.

"Yes, I've been there many times," Emmy answered.

The girls walked as fast as they could without running to the bank of elevators.

"Mom, you are so slow. We need to hurry," Heather said.

"Mary and Erin aren't going anywhere," Emmy said as they stepped into the elevator.

The doors opened on the fourth floor and the girls rushed out.

"Which way?" Heather asked.

Emmy led the way to room 4012 and knocked on the open door.

"Come on in," Jonah said.

The girls scooted past Emmy and slowly walked to the bed.

"Do you want to see Erin?" Mary asked.

The twins nodded emphatically. Mary patted a spot on the bed and the twins hopped up and stared at Erin.

"She's so tiny. I have dolls that are bigger," Heather said.

"We know how babies are born," Isabella said.

"You do?" Mary looked at Emmy.

Emmy shrugged and said, "They know a lot more at their age than I did."

Jonah sat on a chair in the corner and called his family.

"Did he call your parents?" Emmy asked.

"Right away. Ma and Da should be here soon. They don't drive as fast as you."

Mr. and Mrs. Michaelis arrived five minutes later.

"I want to hold my grandchild," Cora Michaelis said and took Erin, who was sleeping.

"I want to see her, too," Dylan Michaelis said. He stared at her and lightly touched Erin's hair. "Were our kids this tiny?"

"Mary and Dahlia were about the same weight. The boys were a bit heavier."

"Can we hold her?" Isabella asked.

"I suppose you can," Mary said.

Emmy shook her head. "You can hold her when she's a little bigger. I don't want her to catch anything from you."

Heather and Isabella settled for sitting on the bed and watching Erin sleep.

"Girls, we need to go and let Erin and Mary get some rest," Emmy said.

"Em, could I talk to you for a minute in private?" Mary asked.

"Okay," Emmy said. "Girls, I want you to wait in the hallway while I talk to Mary."

"Bye, Mary, we'll see you when you get home," Heather said.

Emmy waited until the girls were out of the room. "What's up?"

"I haven't been able to nurse Erin, and I'm worried."

Emmy held Mary's hand and squeezed it.

"I want to breast feed if I can," Mary said.

"I think I'll wait with the girls," Mr. Michaelis said. "Jonah, you want to join me?"

"Be right there," Jonah said.

"Oh, Da, you don't have to."

"It's all right. Jonah and I will keep the twins company while you talk about female stuff."

Emmy, Mary and her mother talked for a few minutes about possible reasons.

"These things take time," Mrs. Michaelis reassured Mary.

Emmy admitted, "My mother didn't nurse me or Diane, and we turned out all right." *I can't remember if I ever told Mary about my heart problem. I don't think it had anything to do with not being breast fed.*

"The formula they have nowadays is so much better than years ago. I don't think you need to worry. That's something God will take care of," Mrs. Michaelis said.

"I should go," Emmy said. "I will pray for you and Erin." Emmy leaned closer and kissed Erin and then kissed Mary's cheek. "Call me when you can."

134

"Thanks for coming, Em. Would you call Kristen and Sloane for me. I don't think Jonah thought to call them."

"Will do. Make sure he takes some photos for Facebook."


Emmy and Dany Michaelis walked out of Lancashire Hall the next Friday.

"I'm glad this semester is over," Emmy said. "I used to know how to budget my time for studying and everything, but now I am so busy. I hate to admit it, but I will be happy just to pass my courses."

"I'm sure you will do more than pass," Dany said.

"I don't mean to pry, but are you guys doing all right since you aren't working?" Emmy asked as she and Dany walked toward the parking lot.

"You don't need to worry about us, Em. We are doing just fine. Darian got a raise, and my parents are helping with college bills."

"Good. You can always talk to me if things get rough." Emmy unlocked her Civic and she and Dany headed home. Emmy dropped Dany off at the guesthouse.

"Thanks for the ride, Em. I can drive more often next semester," Dany offered.

Emmy grinned and said, "I appreciate the offer, but I've been in your Prius. Do you guys have plans for tomorrow night? We could get together for a cookout. Kenny wants to fire up the grill."

"I don't think we have plans. I'll talk to Darian and let you know," Dany said.

Emmy pulled into the garage and entered the house through the mudroom. She put her backpack on the kitchen island and plopped onto one of the barstools.

"Is that where your backpack belongs?" Heather asked with hands on her hips.

"No, but I am too tired to get up. Would you put it away for me, sweetie?"

Heather put the backpack away, came back and stood beside Emmy. "Is school getting too hard for you? Do you need

135

help with your homework?" Heather asked while rubbing Emmy's back.

"It's more difficult than before. Could you grab me a bottle of water, please?"

Heather pulled a bottle from the fridge and handed it to Emmy. "You should take a nap."

"I wish I could, but I have to get dinner ready. Is there anything special you would like?"

"If you are so tired, we could order pizza," Heather suggested.

"I like that idea. Could you find the menu from Kerry Lynn's Pizza and Pasta. It's by the desk."

Heather found the menu and looked it over. "I like their Supreme Pizza. Could we get breadsticks, too?"

"I suppose. Do you want to call in the order?"

"Mom! I can't do that. I'm just a kid."

"I know, but you and Isa are growing up so fast."

Later, everyone was sitting at the breakfast nook eating when Isabella asked, "Mommy, are you getting good grades at school. Do we need to see your report card?"

"I haven't gotten my final grades yet, but I am kinda worried. Maybe you should remember me when you say your prayers tonight."

"I will pray for you, Mom," Kevin Michael said while chewing on a breadstick. "I have to pray for my pet frog, too. I found him in the woods and put him in a box."

"I hope you didn't bring him in the house," Emmy said.

"Nope! I put him by the pool."

After the kids were in bed, Emmy went downstairs to the family room. She sat on the couch facing the TV on the wall.

"Did they complain about going to bed early?" Kenny asked.

"Not too much. Would you mind if I invite Father James for dinner tomorrow night?"

"Not at all. Are Darian and Dany coming?"

"Yes, but Mary called. She doesn't want to bring Erin over until she's older. She is afraid she might catch a cold."

"Do you think Mary is going to be overprotective of Erin?" Kenny paused the DVD and asked.

Emmy shrugged. "No idea. Was I like that when the girls were born?"

"The girls were born early. You needed to keep an eye on them."

Emmy pulled her cell phone from her back pocket and called her half-brother.

"Yes, may I help you?"

"Oh, shoot! Are you still at mass? Did I call too early?"

"I would say yes, but that would be a lie since we don't say mass on Friday night, and I'm trying to limit my lies to serious ones."

"You are a goof. Are you busy tomorrow evening? Kenny is grilling some steaks and stuff, and I haven't seen you in ages."

"I'll check my calendar, but I might be able to make it. Father Dennis is covering me tomorrow. We had a bet on the offering, and I won."

"I don't know which is worse." Emmy shook her head. "Telling a lie about betting, or actually betting on the offering."

"Should I bring anything?"

"We don't have any beer in the house. Bring your own if you want a tasty beverage."

"I gave up beer for Lent."

"You do realize Easter was the last Sunday in March, right?"

"Thank God! Now I can partake of my favorite beverage again."

"Come over anytime in the afternoon. I'll put you to work," Emmy said.

"Did I mention my arthritis is bothering me again?"

"You only have arthritis if I ask you to do something," Emmy said. "I won't ask you to chop firewood."

"Is anybody home?" Father James knocked on the mudroom door and walked into the kitchen holding a green bottle. "I'm sorry I'm late, but something came up."

137

Emmy poured the boiling water out of the potatoes and turned to look at him. "You're just in time to help with the potato salad and baked beans. What are you drinking?"

"I brought a tasty beverage for myself and whoever wishes to partake."

Emmy looked closer at the bottle and made a face. "I've had that brand before. I would rather drink stagnant water from the ditch."

"All the more for me," he replied.

"You can drink it all. I don't think Tony would even drink it."

"The house is rather quiet. Where is everyone?" Father James asked after patting Emmy on the back.

Emmy pointed out the window above the sink. "Kenny and Darian are getting the grill started."

"He does realize it's a gas grill, right?" Father James asked while looking at the men on the deck.

"He knows, and the kids are with Dany." Emmy set the potatoes on the island.

"I don't see them."

"They're playing in the woods. Kevin wanted to play Army and bribed his sisters to play."

"I hope he doesn't capture and torture them," Father James said. "How can I help?"

"Are you actually going to help me, or are you kidding?" Emmy asked while opening the fridge.

"I'm going to help by sitting on a barstool and listening to you complain about your week." He walked around the large, granite-topped island and sat on the middle barstool.

Emmy turned with hands on her hips and said, "I don't complain. We had a small group class at church about changing our attitudes, and we learned complaining is a sin."

"Okay, so how was school this week?"

Emmy sighed and waved a hand. "Don't get me started. One of my professors is an absolute bore. There's one guy who always tries to flirt with me, and my finals were a lot harder than I expected." She carried on for a couple of minutes.

138

Father James waited until she finished ranting and tilted his head. "What was the name of the book you studied?"

"Oh, hush," Emmy said with a sigh. "I'm doing the best I can."

"Maybe you should ask for His help and not try to do it on your own," Father James said with his hands in a prayerful position.

"Look who's talking. Are you going to lecture me now?"

"I don't think it will be necessary. Do you have a recipe for your potato salad?" he asked and took a long swig of his beverage.

Emmy walked into the pantry and came back with an onion. "I have one, but it's all up here." She pointed to her head and tossed the onion at Father James. "Could you peel that, please?"

He worked on the onion as Emmy sliced the potatoes. She finished and gathered everything she needed to mix into the potato salad.

"Are you going to put bacon and onions in the beans?" Father James asked a few minutes later.

Emmy nodded. "The kids like it that way, and do not encourage Kevin Michael when he says he likes beans because they give you gas."

"I wouldn't think of it." Father James watched Emmy prepare the beans for the oven. "I didn't know you put hot mustard in the beans."

"Just enough to give them a little bite." Emmy put the dish in the oven and set the timer.

Kenny walked into the kitchen a moment later. "Should we start grilling?"

She checked the timer. "The beans will be done in twenty-five minutes, so judge your time accordingly, oh great chef."

He opened the fridge and removed the platter of steaks, chicken breasts and hot dogs. He kissed her cheek, grinned and said, "I'm training Darian. He claims to have never used a grill before."

"Good luck with that. If you happen to spot Dany or the kids, let them know we are eating soon," Emmy said. She opened the fridge, grabbed a bottle of water, walked around the island and sat next to her half-brother.

"You could text Heather," Kenny suggested. "She never goes anywhere without her phone."

Thirty minutes later everyone sat at the breakfast nook table. Emmy prayed for the food, and they began eating.

"Mom, did I tell you I captured the enemy and won the battle?" Kevin asked while scooping beans onto his plate. "I love beans..."

"Don't you dare say because they make you fart," Heather said with a scowl.

Kevin grinned and replied, "I wasn't going to and now I don't have to."

"How is your steak, Dany?" Darian asked.

"It's almost perfect. Just a hint of pink in the middle," she answered. "Did you grill it, or did Kenny?"

"He kept an eye on everything, but I flipped the meat over when he told me to."

"I like burned hot dogs," Kevin said while squeezing the mustard bottle.

Father James took a bite of potato salad.

"What do you think?" Emmy asked.

"Not bad, but I have to say my mother made the best potato salad in all of Kansas."

"I like yours the best, Mommy," Isabella said.

"Thank you, Isa." Emmy turned to Father James. "Maybe one of these days your parents will come for a visit and she can make her famous potato salad."

"Well, as it so happens, they are coming to Illinois in December. They are going to spend two weeks with me."

Heather looked up at Father James and asked, "Will we get to meet your other parents?"

He smiled at the girls. "Yes. I have told them all about you, and they are excited about getting to know you."

"Can we ask them if you were good growing up?" Kevin asked.

"You can ask them anything you want," Father James

140

answered. "I have nothing to hide."

"We asked Grandma if Mommy ever needed to be spanked, and she said Mommy was sneaky," Heather said.

"That was a long time ago," Kenny said. "Eat your chicken before it gets cold."

Dany and Darian looked at Emmy.

Emmy shrugged and said, "I wasn't always an angel." She reached out and smacked Father James' hand. "Just wait! I'm going to learn all about your childhood. I bet you were a handful."

"Who are you listening to?" Emmy asked Tuesday afternoon. She walked up and tapped Kenny's shoulder when he didn't respond.

He spun around, removed his headphones and asked, "Did you say something?"

Emmy saw the CD on the mixing board and picked it up. "Did this just come out?"

"The official release is today, but I got a copy Friday. Do you want to listen?"

She sat next to him in one of the swiveling leather chairs. "Can you put it on the speakers?"

He made an adjustment and the music blared from the control room monitors.

"What do you think, Em?" he asked after the last track.

"I kinda like it. It's different than most bands I hear," she replied.

"That's because you never listen to southern rock. They remind me of the Allman Brothers Band with a bit of Marshall Tucker thrown in."

"Whatever. Do you think it will sell? What is the title?" She picked up the jewel case. "Hmmm. *Texas in the Moonlight*. Who came up with the title?"

"I think Micah suggested it," Kenny answered. "It wasn't Bobby."

"Will the Bender Brothers become overnight rock stars?"

Kenny shrugged. "It's a possibility."

The members of Fridays At Five sat in the control room of Studio Four and listened to tracks from their latest project.

"I think we have more decent tracks then we expected," Jeff said.

"True," P.J. said.

"But we have six or seven more tunes that we haven't even recorded," Dave said while twirling a drumstick. "I don't want to save them for another project. That might be years away."

Adam opened a folder and held up a chord sheet. "We have to record this one. It's the best thing you and P.J. have ever written."

"I am rather proud of that tune," Jeff said.

"What should we do?" Kenny asked. "Any suggestions?"

Dave stood up. "I know we've taken a long time for this project, but I want to take the kids to England this summer. They haven't been there for several years and Macy has agreed to it."

"Are you going to show them your ancestral castle?" Jeff asked.

"Probably, but they are more interested in staying in London."

"I wouldn't mind having the summer off," P.J. said. "Tommy will be starting college in the fall, and Timothy will be a junior. This could be the last chance to take a vacation as a family."

The guys discussed their options for several minutes.

"So, do we all agree to return to the studio in September after the kids are back in school?" Kenny asked.

Everyone agreed.

"All right. Everyone have a wonderful summer, and we'll figure out a day to get back to work."

Adam nudged P.J. and said, "I never would have dreamed Juliana and I would be able to take a whole summer off."

"It is a pretty nice perk," P.J. responded.

# Chapter Eighteen

"Uncle Rory, are you going swimming with us?" Isabella asked Tuesday afternoon.

"I took the afternoon off just so I could," Rory answered. "Where is your mother?"

"She's taking a shower," Isabella pointed. "She and Daddy have that room. Me and Heather are staying in that one, but we have to share with Kevin Michael. He can be so gross."

"Brothers can be like that," Rory agreed and looked around the suite. "Where is your father?"

"He took Kevin to Hollywood Studios again. We didn't want to go back."

"I thought I heard you," Emmy said as she walked out of the bedroom. "How are you? Are you getting excited about the wedding?"

Rory hugged Emmy and said, "That's this weekend, right? I almost forgot about it."

"Uncle Rory, you better not forget about getting married. That's why we flew to Florida," Isabella said with her hands on her hips.

"He's teasing you, Isa," Emmy said. "Did you bring your trunks? The girls are ready to go swimming."

"I'm wearing them," he answered.

"Can we go now, Mom?" Heather asked. "Isa and I have new bikinis. Do you like them?"

"They are very colorful," Rory answered.

Fifteen minutes later the girls were in the pool. Rory and Emmy sat under an umbrella at a table close to the pool sipping soft drinks.

"How has your vacation been, Emmy?" he asked.

"The kids are loving it. Even Kenny seems more relaxed than ever. We flew down Saturday in Mr. Robertson's jet, and we are heading home Sunday afternoon."

Rory watched the girls for a moment. "They are growing up so fast."

"Tell me!" Emmy said. "I had to buy new swimsuits

143

because their older ones didn't fit anymore if you get my drift."

"You were ten once, Em."

"Yeah, but I wasn't as... you know... developed as they are." Emmy used her hands for emphasis.

"They still look like you," Rory added.

"Did I tell you I had the talk with them?" she asked using air quotes.

Rory frowned as he looked at Emmy.

Emmy nodded. "Yeah, that talk. They know so much more than I did at that age."

"Is that good or bad?"

Emmy shrugged. "Not sure yet. I'm not worried about Isa, but Heather is another story."

She explained about Heather kissing a neighborhood boy.

"How old were you when you kissed Barry Newton?" Rory asked with a straight face.

Emmy poked his arm. "I never kissed Barry. You know that."

"Who did you kiss first? Was it that kid who lived across the street from us?" Rory asked.

"I don't remember who lived across from you. Who was it?"

"Rodrigo something or other. I can't remember his last name, but he turned out to be gay."

"Well, I never kissed him, so that's not why he's gay."

"Are we still on for dinner tomorrow?" Rory asked. "Rochelle is working tonight, but then she's off for two weeks. I think she's going somewhere."

"You're a goof. Where are you spending your honeymoon? You better tell me, or I will hire someone to look for you."

"We rented a house on Magen's Bay. That's on St. Thomas. You know... the Virgin Islands."

"If you're waiting for me to make fun of you, I'm not going to." She looked away but then stared at him.

"What?" he asked after seeing her staring.

"Have you guys... you know?"

"We've been looking for a house. Is that what you mean?"

144

he asked though he knew what she wanted to know.

"No," she answered.

"Rochelle would like a new car."

Emmy frowned at him. "Are you going to make me say it?"

"Say what?" he teased.

She smacked his arm again. "Have you guys been sleeping together?"

Rory laughed and touched her cheek. "You're blushing just like you did when you were a kid, and you asked me if I had slept with Rosalie Stevens. That's kinda sweet."

"Stuff it, Rory. Have you?"

He nodded. "Are you disappointed with me?"

"I guess not. You are engaged, and you're not kids. You better be faithful to her," she said.

"I will do everything in my power to do that."

"Maybe you should ask God to help you."

"I wonder what ever happened to Rosalie. Do you know?" Rory asked to change the subject.

"How would I know? She was Diane's age, and they moved away when I was a freshman."

"Do you remember hanging out after school and asking me?" he asked.

"Are you still talking about sleeping with her?"

"Do you remember?"

"I remember you were talking about making out with her trying to impress me," Emmy said and then pointed to the pool. "I told Heather not to talk to older boys, but look at her."

Rory looked. "Should I go over there and beat them up?"

"They look like they're twelve or thirteen. I doubt if you could handle them," she teased.

"I handled those guys for you, and I was trying to impress Diane not you."

"That's a load of crap! She shot you down, and you were trying to get in my pants."

Rory shook his head. "Bull! You were fourteen. You were such a tomboy. I remember you slugged that one kid for touching your butt when we played football."

145

"Why did you tell me about Rosalie if you weren't after me?" Emmy asked. She waved at Isabella and shouted, "Come here, please."

"I was your friend," Rory insisted.

"What do you need, Mommy?" Isabella asked dripping water everywhere. "Did you see me jump off the diving board?"

"I didn't see that, but I saw Heather talking to those boys. They are too old."

"They asked Heather how old she was. Then they went away. Are you going to swim, or are you just going to talk to Uncle Rory?"

"I might get in the pool later, but for now Rory and I are talking."

"Will you watch me dive?"

"Okay, we'll watch, Isa."

Rory gave Isabella a thumbs-up after watching her dive into the pool. "They still swim like fish."

"Rosalie was your first, right?"

"Geez, Em. Are we really going to discuss my sex life?"

"It doesn't embarrass me to talk about sex now," she teased.

"It sure did back then."

"Creep!" she smacked his arm again.

"What was that for?" He rubbed his arm. "I didn't do anything."

"I just remembered that time you showed me Owen's magazines. Like I would be interested in looking at naked women." She rolled her eyes.

"Hey! I didn't show you the magazines. You were at the house with Amy, and you guys walked into my room. You invaded my privacy. I should be mad at you."

"Those models were so fake," Emmy said. She stood up and removed her swimdress. "Are you ready to swim?"

He grinned.

"Stop looking at me like that. You've seen me in a bikini before."

"And you still look good, Em."

"Creep! Are you referring to the night out at Grafton's

146

place?" she asked. "That was my underwear, and you couldn't see anything."

"Mommy, watch me race Heather," Isabella said.

Emmy and Rory joined the throng of people in the pool.

"Should I dunk your mother under the water?" Rory asked the twins.

"Yes!" Heather shouted.

"Don't you dare, Clarence!" Emmy yelled.

"I'll be nice for now," Rory said with a wicked gleam in his eyes.

"Who's watching the kids?" Rory asked Emmy the next night as they waited to be seated for dinner.

"The hotel arranged for babysitters. We met them, and they seem trustworthy. They were an older couple. I think their names were Rosco and..."

"Teresa," Kenny said. "It wasn't the hotel that set it up. Mr. Robertson knows them and vouched for them. They are staying in our hotel."

"Rochelle, it's so good to actually meet you. Rory has told me so much about you," Emmy said. "And don't believe a word of what he says about me."

Rochelle smiled and tucked a strand of her brown hair behind an ear. "He hasn't told me anything negative about you, Olivia Porter."

Emmy turned to Rory and smacked his arm.

"Will you stop hitting me, Em. I've got a bruise from yesterday."

"Why did you tell her my secret name, Clarence?"

Rochelle looked at Kenny and they both laughed.

"Emmy has always teased Rory. She's known him almost as long as me."

"I want to learn more about how you guys grew up together. Rory has told me a few things, but I'm sure there is more," she said while watching Rory and Emmy making faces at each other.

An hour later Emmy finished her lobster tail and sighed.

"Are you stuffed, Em?" Kenny asked.

"I didn't realize I would get a gigantic lobster."

"My family is originally from Maine, and the lobsters there are better," Rochelle said.

"I've never been to Maine, but Pastor Tyler and Liz go there every year. One of them has family there," Emmy said. "I can't remember who though."

As they were leaving, Rochelle whispered to Emmy, "Thank you so much for agreeing to sing at the wedding. It means a lot to me, but it means even more to Rory."

"I wouldn't miss it for anything. I know Mrs. Porter will be here for the wedding," Emmy said and then paused.

"Oh, I thought Rory might have told you. My parents will be here. Did he mention I have three brothers and two younger sisters?"

Emmy shook her head. "I don't remember him saying anything about your siblings."

"You will meet everyone on Friday. My youngest brother is a fan."

"Of Fridays At Five?" Emmy asked.

"No, of you, silly. He flipped out when he learned you would be here."

Rory heard that part of the conversation, grinned at Emmy and said, "Her brother is a dork. That's why he likes your music."

Emmy stuck out her tongue and Rory tried to grab it. Kenny shook his head and headed outside.


"I suppose I should introduce everyone," Rochelle said at the church Friday evening. She introduced everyone and saved Emmy for last. She stood behind Emmy with her hands on her shoulders. "This is Rory's little friend from back in Illinois. He and Emily, or should I call you Olivia?"

Emmy whispered, "You should call me Emmy."

"Rory and Emmy have been friends for a long time."

A few minutes later Mrs. Porter walked up to Emmy and said, "It's so good to see you again, dear. It's been too long."

"It's good to see you again, Mrs. Porter. How have you

been?" Emmy asked. She thought about Rory's late sister Amy.

"Please, call me Elaine, dear," Mrs. Porter said. "You are old enough to call me by my name now."

Emmy nodded and waited until Mrs. Porter walked away. Then she looked up at Kenny. "I didn't know her name was Elaine."

"Really?" Kenny asked. "I think I knew. My parents probably called her that."

The rehearsal lasted forty-five minutes, and then everyone headed to Shakespeare's Pizza.

Kenny sat with Emmy in the back of the room. "What's on your mind, Em?"

"Nothing."

"Em, I know better. Tell me."

"Fine!" she exclaimed and said, "I never met Rory's first wife. I'm glad I didn't because I would have hated her for what she did, but I think I like Rochelle a lot. She is so mature, and that will be good for him."

"You are mature, too."

Emmy frowned at Kenny. "You're a dork."

"Are you thinking about years ago when you and Rory used to hang out together?"

"I suppose. I certainly wasn't very mature back then."

Just before she and Kenny were leaving, Emmy heard Mrs. Porter talking to Rochelle's mother. She looked around for Rory, saw him talking to one of Rochelle's brothers and hurried to his side.

"What's up, Em. You look like you've seen a ghost," Rory said as he put an arm around her waist.

"Can I talk to you in private, please?" she asked and then bit her lip.

"I'll talk to you tomorrow, Rory," Rochelle's brother said and walked away.

Emmy looked up at Rory. "Is it true your father is alive and lives in Australia? I overheard your mother talking to Mrs. Nash."

Rory sighed and pulled Emmy around the corner. "It's true."

149

She poked his side. "Why didn't you ever tell me? I always thought he was dead or something worse."

Rory chuckled and asked, "What would be worse?"

"Hush! You know what I mean."

He put his hands on her shoulders and looked deeply into her blue eyes. "I didn't know if he was alive or where he lived until a few months ago. Mom never talked about him, but I guess she heard from someone who knew them in the old days."

"Does he know you're getting married? Did you invite him?" Emmy asked. "Why did he leave in the first place?"

Rory shook his head and laughed. "Not a chance in hell, Em. He has never been a father to any of us."

"You should give him a chance. Why did he leave?" she asked again.

"Mom never said, but Owen found out about another woman. I guess Owen told Mom, or else she learned somehow and kicked him out. We never heard from him again. So, he doesn't deserve a chance to be a father now."

"He's still your father."

Rory took a deep breath.

"Well?"

"Em, I know you miss your father, and I know things were not always easy for you as a kid."

" I do miss Daddy, and I wish he was here to see the kids grow up, but he's not. You still have a father, and I think you should seek him out."

"I'm not going to promise you anything now, Em. I have too much on my mind, but maybe in a few years, I will consider it."

"Don't wait too long," she replied while walking away.

"Mom, Rochelle looks so beautiful," Isabella said as everyone watched Mr. Nash escort his oldest daughter down the aisle.

"Yes, she does, Isa," Emmy said. She reached out and held Kenny's hand. "I never thought he would ever get married."

"He had to find someone he liked better than you, Em,"

150

Kenny whispered. "That wasn't easy to do."

Moments later Kenny held Emmy's hand again. "Are you ready to sing?"

"I'm ready, but I wish you were singing with me," she answered.

"You will do fine. Try not to look at Rory and Rochelle."

Emmy sang "I Will Be True To You" and returned to her seat.

"Mommy, you sounded like an angel, and you didn't even cry," Isabella said.

"Thank you, sweetie. Is it all right if I cry later?"

Kenny squeezed her hand and nodded.

"Are you having fun?" Kenny asked later at the reception. He pointed to the dance floor. "The twins certainly are. I think they will be exhausted by the end of the night."

"You have to dance with me once," Emmy insisted.

"One dance, but it has to be a slow one."

"Should I talk to the DJ and put in a request. Maybe he has some old Fridays At Five songs on his computer," she teased.

Kenny made good on his promise and danced to the old Fridays At Five song "Hero For Hire."

"Thank you, Kenny," Emmy said as they headed back to their table.

"Your welcome, m'lady." He pointed to the other side of the room. "I do believe Rochelle's brothers want to dance."

Emmy danced with all three brothers.

Shortly after eleven Emmy felt a hand on her shoulder. She looked up and smiled.

"Where are Kenny and the kids?" Rory asked.

"They got tired and took a cab back to the hotel."

Rory smiled and whispered, "So, you are all mine for the rest of the night, huh?"

"I guess that depends on what you have planned. I think Rochelle might want to spend some time with you later," Emmy teased.

"How about a dance for starters," Rory asked holding out a hand.

"Where is Rochelle?" Emmy asked as they headed to the dance floor.

"She is with her mother and sisters. They were planning where to spend Christmas or something."

"Is Rochelle the last one to get married?" Emmy asked.

"Yes, but her oldest brother is divorced."

"How many grandkids are there?"

"Five," Rory answered. "And I don't expect that to change in the near future."

"You can always try," Emmy said.

Rory leaned close and whispered, "Oh, we are trying, Olivia."

"Hush, Clarence. I don't want to hear about your sex life."

"Am I holding you too close," Rory asked a moment later.

She lifted her face from his chest and whispered, "No, but... never mind."

"I can feel your heart beating, Em."

"Good. That means I'm not dead," she teased.

After two dances Rory pulled Emmy to an empty table against the wall.

"Do you need to leave soon, Em?"

"I can stay until midnight, but after that I turn into a pumpkin."

He tilted his head.

"No. I meant..."

"Oh, I get it now, Cinderella. Are you wearing glass slippers?" He looked at her feet and laughed. "I should have known. You're wearing sneakers."

She lifted her foot and put it on his knee. "They are new. Do you like?"

He touched her ankle. "Where did you find purple shoelaces?" He moved his hand higher and squeezed her calf.

"That's how they came." She stuck out her tongue.

"Put that back where it belongs before I cut it off."

"You liked it when you tried to shove yours down my throat."

"Never happened. You tried to kiss me like that."

152

He moved her foot and stared into her eyes for a moment.

"What?" she asked softly.

"Just because I love Rochelle doesn't mean I don't love you, Em. In a different way, I mean."

"I know you do, and I love you, too, Rory. You know I think of Tony as my brother, right?"

"I suppose so. Am I your brother, too?"

She shook her head and smiled. "I've never thought of you as a brother."

"You are still so wicked."

"We did a bunch of things when we were kids, didn't we?" She squeezed his hand and leaned against him.

"Yeah, we snuck around a few times. We swiped a few beers from your father."

"I haven't thought about that night at Grafton's for a long time. Somehow, it came back to me at the pool the other day."

"Do you remember much about that night?" he asked.

"I remember you drank too much. I only had one beer."

"I remember the pool," he said with a grin.

She elbowed his ribs. "At least I had my underwear on."

"So did I, and I remember yours was dark blue or something."

"Most likely it was purple, and I remember you trying to dunk me under the water. I should get back at you for that someday."

"It's not Christian to hold a grudge, Em," he said waving a finger at her.

"I wasn't close to being a Christian back then."

"Maybe not, but I think God protected you from some stuff."

"That's good. I doubt if I would be able to say that if I had to go through it all again." *I know for a fact I wouldn't.*

They looked at each other for a moment without speaking.

"Aw, I see Rochelle has returned. I should let you go, Em. I'll talk to you when we get back."

"Have fun on your honeymoon," she whispered while hugging him. "Make sure you get out of bed once in a while."

153

# Chapter Nineteen

"Are you busy, Emmy?" Father James asked. "Have you recovered from your vacation?"

She leaned against the kitchen counter and switched the phone to her other ear. "Kenny has, but I'm still tired. I stayed out too late the night of Rory's reception."

"Should I ask what you were doing?"

"It might not be wise to ask," she said while walking around the island and sitting on a barstool. "I didn't do anything too foolish. I did dance with Rochelle's brothers and one of them got a little fresh."

"Fresh? What does that mean in today's language?"

"He asked me if I ever fooled around. I told him to do something physically impossible."

"I don't want to know," he said. "Are you ready for some company?"

"Yes, and I have a list of questions to ask your parents. I want to know everything about you as a kid," she teased.

"I'm afraid you will find my past to be rather boring, and not nearly as exciting as your sordid childhood."

"I did not have a sordid childhood. I was a virgin on my wedding night," she said.

"Is that a technicality?" he asked.

"I wasn't totally inexperienced, but... Why am I even telling you this? You aren't hearing my confession."

"We should be there around one. I'm taking them to Darby's for lunch," he said.

"Darby's huh? Is there any way I could talk you into bringing me a chili dog?"

"Not a chance, little sister."

"Pretty please. I will be nice to you for a week," Emmy said.

"Nope!"

"You're the worst brother I've ever had. Could you at least buy a chocolate cake?" she pleaded.

"All right, but only because I'm being extra generous."

"Should I consider it my birthday present?" Emmy asked.

"You may, but when have I ever bought you anything for your birthday?" he asked.

"Certainly not when I was a child."

He chuckled and said, "Could that be because I didn't know you existed?"

"Lame excuse, but I'll buy it. See you when you get here with the chocolate cake," she said and ended the call.

"Was that Father James?" Kenny asked. He walked up behind Emmy and kissed the top of her head.

"They will be here around one."

"Are you getting excited about meeting his parents? I know they aren't his birth parents, but..."

She turned her head and stared at him. "He is my brother. We have the same father."

"I am aware of that fact. How do you think the kids will react?"

"I talked to them last night. They are curious, but aren't seeing it as a big deal."

Emmy paced the kitchen later and checked the time again. "It's ten after. Where are they?" she asked.

Kenny finished drying the dishes and put the towel on the oven handle. "Will you relax? They will be here when they get here."

"You are so smart. Why didn't I think of that?" she asked and then stuck out her tongue at him. She rolled her eyes. "Such a dork. Why did I ever marry you?"

He grabbed one of her belt loops and pulled her close. "Because you like how I kiss you." He had his hands on her hips and was kissing her neck when Heather and Isabella entered the room.

"Yuck! Can you get a room?" Heather said. "How soon will they be here?"

"They will be here when they get here," Kenny said.

Emmy scooted away and cupped a hand to her ear. "Did I hear something?"

"That was Kevin playing with a firetruck," Isabella said.

155

Ten minutes later Father James opened the mudroom door and hollered, "Anyone home? I have some chocolate cake, and I'm willing to share."

Emmy, Heather and Isabella raced into the kitchen and skidded to a stop by the island.

"About time you got here," Emmy said.

Kenny walked in and whispered, "I told you they would..."

Emmy elbowed him in the belly.

Father James set the cake on the island, turned back to his parents, smiled and faced Emmy. "I would like to introduce my parents. Josef and Helen Boyanov."

Emmy, Kenny and the twins stared at the white-haired couple. Josef and Helen stared back.

Finally, Josef scratched his head and asked, "Where is your sister, Mickel. I though you said she had twins, but I see three little girls who have to be triplets."

Heather and Isabella giggled.

Emmy glared at Father James. "Did you put him up to that?"

Josef laughed and approached Emmy. He held out his arms for a hug. "He said you would get a kick out of it."

"He's going to get a kick in the seat of his pants," Emmy said. She hugged Josef for a moment and then stood in front of Helen.

"You have your father's eyes. I can tell," Helen said.

Emmy hugged her also.

"Come on in and make yourself at home," Kenny said. "Oh, this is Heather Rose and Isabella Marie." He paused, tilted his head and asked, "Or is it the other way around?"

"Oh, Daddy, you know how to tell us apart," Isabella said as she walked up to Father James. "Why did they call you Mickel?"

He leaned down and touched Isabella's nose. "That is my real name. I chose to be called James when I became a priest."

Isabella and Heather looked at Emmy.

"Does that mean Pastor Tyler has a different name?" Heather asked.

Kenny shook his head. "No, Tyler is his only name. Let's sit in the family room."

Emmy grabbed Josef and Helen by the arm and said, "I have a thousand questions to ask about him." She turned her head toward her brother. "I know there has to be some dirt in his history. I need to use it to blackmail him."

Everyone headed to the family room. Kevin Michael raced down the stairs to join them.

"I was in the bathroom. I had some gas from the beans I ate for lunch," he said proudly.

"Don't pay any attention to him," Isabella said. "He likes to be gross."

"I brought chocolate cake," Father James said.

"So you said. We can have it later. First I have to ask your parents some questions. Please, sit with me on the couch," she said to Helen and Josef. Kenny and Father James used the recliners and the girls and Kevin Michael sat on the floor."

After asking about their trip and how they liked living in Kansas and other small talk, Emmy asked, "How old was he when you got him? And why did you keep him? He's obviously a dork."

Josef looked at the large TV on the wall and the stone fireplace on the opposite side of the room while Helen looked at the high ceiling.

"Em, are you really going to bombard them with questions?" Kenny asked.

Helen waved a hand. "I don't mind. I have some questions, too."

Emmy made a face at Kenny and Father James and held Helen's hand.

"He was two days old when we brought him home. We had made arrangements earlier, of course, to adopt him."

"Why did you name him Mickel?" Heather asked.

"That was my father's name," Josef said.

Heather and Isabella scooted closer to the couch.

"Did he cry a lot?" Isabella asked. "Kevin Michael cried all the time when he was a baby. He's better now, but he's still gross at times."

157

"I am not gross," Kevin insisted.

"He cried at times like all babies, but I would say he was an easy baby to raise."

"Did he get good grades in school?" Emmy asked. "I bet he didn't because he played football."

Josef laughed and answered, "He was class valedictorian."

"Get out! Was he the only kid in the class?" Emmy asked.

Father James chuckled and Emmy stuck out her tongue at him. Kenny covered his face with a hand and shook his head.

"He always got good grades, and he even helped other students."

"Why do you sound funny?" Kevin asked.

"Kevin Michael!" Emmy shouted.

"It's all right," Josef said. "We were born in Russia and came to this country when we were about your age. Our parents never spoke English at home, and we still have an accent."

"We know where Russia is," Heather said.

A few minutes later Emmy asked, "Did he ever have a girlfriend?"

Helen glanced at her son and he nodded.

"He did. In fact, he was engaged at one point."

"Get out!" Emmy exclaimed. "Are you yanking... are you kidding me?"

"It's true. He was a handsome young man, and could have married several young ladies," Helen said.

"We will have to talk about that in more detail later," Emmy said. "Who wants chocolate cake?"

The kids jumped to their feet and raced into the kitchen. The adults followed at a more sedate pace.

"We need plates and forks," Emmy said.

Moments later she handed a slice of cake to Helen and Josef. "We can eat in the dining room, and the children may eat in the breakfast nook."

"But, Mom," Heather whined. "We want to hear what you say."

"I need to talk to Father James and his parents about adult stuff."

158

Heather rolled her eyes, but she and Isabella and Kevin did as they were told. The adults retreated to the dining room to talk.

"This is good cake," Father James said.

Emmy glared at him.

"Well, it is," he said.

"You're only saying that to prolong the agony. I am going to find out about your past, so quit stalling."

Father James assumed a position of prayer and closed his eyes.

Emmy shook her head. "Not gonna matter."

Father James opened his eyes. "Go ahead. I have nothing to be ashamed of. God has forgiven me of all my sins. He remembers them no more."

"But I bet your parents do," Emmy said with a wicked grin.

"This really is good cake," Josef said. "It's moist and I love the frosting. I would ask for another slice, but it's too rich for my blood."

"You can have more later," Helen said.

"I know he played football, but did he play other sports," Emmy asked.

"He was on the wrestling team, but only because the football coach wanted his players to stay in shape," Josef said.

"I did not like sports, and did not encourage him to play, but football did pay for his education," Helen said.

Father James looked at Emmy.

"What?" she asked with a shrug.

"Stop stalling. You want to hear about my engagement, little sister, so just ask."

"Okay, tell me. What was her name?"

"Peggy Dvorak. I met her in college. She was my age, and we fell in love," Father James said.

"Is that it? There has to be more to the story."

"She was a lovely woman."

"Then why didn't you get married?" Emmy asked.

"If you must know, she broke off the engagement three months later, left school and moved to Vermont. She found another man and married him."

"Is that why you became a priest?" Emmy asked.

He shook his head. "No, it wasn't because of a woman. It was because God called me to serve him."

Emmy waited a moment and then asked, "How seriously engaged were you?"

Kenny sighed and shook his head. *Please don't go there, Em.*

"I don't understand the question," Father James said.

Emmy looked at Father James, then at his parents and finally back to her half-brother. "Did you have sex?" she asked quietly.

"Geez, Emmy!" Kenny slapped the table. "You can refuse to answer, Father James. She doesn't need to know. It's none of her business."

Father James held up a hand. "It's all right. We did sleep together, but there was no child if that's what you really want to know. I did not follow in our father's footsteps." He pushed back his chair, got up and walked out of the room.

Josef and Helen stared at each other. Kenny shrugged, sighed and shook his head. Emmy bit her lip.

"Way to go, Em," Kenny whispered.

"Crap! I shouldn't have been so nosy. I'll talk to him and apologize." Emmy found Father James standing in the middle of the den and approached slowly. "I'm sorry. You can hate me if you want. I was out of line."

He turned to face her and waved a hand. "I could never hate you. I'm not upset because of your nosiness. I guess it still hurts that she dumped me after all these years."

Emmy hugged her brother and put her head on his chest. "I'm sorry she hurt you, but I'm glad you got to know a little about love."

Chapter Twenty

Kenny walked into the kitchen Tuesday morning and saw Emmy sitting at the island with her chin in her palms staring at a bowl of oatmeal. He kissed her cheek and asked, "Is something bothering you? You look rather downcast."

"I guess I'm missing Helen and Josef. They left on Sunday, and I didn't have a chance to say goodbye."

"You saw them every day for a week, Em."

Emmy took a bite of oatmeal and made a face. She got up and dumped it into the garbage.

"They aren't your parents, m'lady," Kenny said.

"I know, but I still had questions to ask."

Kenny grinned and put his hands on her shoulders. She looked up at him.

"Don't look at me like that."

"Like what?" she asked.

He put a finger under her chin. "You use that sad face to get me to do something."

"I do not," she insisted.

Kenny laughed. "You have been doing it for thirty years."

"No way, dork," she said walking away with a grin. "I haven't know you for thirty years."

"You could always go to Kansas," Kenny said.

"Will you go with me, Toto?"

"What?"

"*Wizard of Oz*. It's a movie."

"Oh, I get it now."

She rolled her eyes and muttered, "Dork."

Later, Kenny walked into the laundry room with his laptop. "Have you checked your Amazon page today?"

"No, why?"

"There happens to be a new listing under your name."

She turned and grabbed his computer. "Is the book already available?"

"There is a new book titled *Gideon's Tree* available for purchase. Should I order one?"

She shrugged and said, "I don't know. What does the description say about it? It might not be worth whatever Amazon is charging."

"True, but I kinda like the author, and want to do whatever I can to support her," he whispered while putting a hand under her t-shirt.

"The kids are outside, and we could close the door," Emmy said as Kenny moved his hand higher.

"Mom! Where are you? Kevin Michael is being gross. He caught a snake and is trying to scare us," Heather yelled.

"I'll handle it," Kenny said. He kissed Emmy.

"Can I have a rain check?" she asked. She picked up the laptop, looked at her page and smiled. *I really like the cover. I hope a few people buy it.*

Kenny saw Heather getting a drink from the fridge. "Where is your brother?"

"Outside by the trail to Aunt Diane's house. He found a garter snake and tried to scare us."

"I thought you sounded scared when you ran inside."

"Not really. I needed a drink and didn't want to use the garden hose. I'm going outside. Can we go swimming later?"

"I don't see why not. It's going to be a hot one this afternoon," Kenny said while walking toward the laundry room. "I'm back," he said after closing the door.

Emmy's eyes sparkled as Kenny grinned wickedly.


"Em, I'm going to be gone for ten days," Kenny said Wednesday night as he got ready for bed. "Do you need me to do anything before I leave in the morning?"

She kept reading her book and shook her head. "Can't think of anything. Why?"

"Are you sure? What are you reading? Is that Annie O'Dell's book? What was it called? You read it before."

"Haven't you ever read a book more than once?" she asked feeling a hand on her thigh. "The title is *My Secret Life as a High School Private Eye.*"

"A few," he said. "Should we go downstairs?"

"Why? I'm in bed."

"Isn't there more laundry to do?"

"No, and you better not do that again."

"You weren't complaining yesterday," he said moving his hand again.

"Stop it. We've been married long enough for you to survive ten days without sex."

"Must be a really good book." Kenny flopped onto his back and sighed.

"What time do you have to leave in the morning?" she asked without taking her eyes off of the book.

"I need to be at the airport by ten."

"How are you getting there?"

"Andy is taking me. He has a meeting at the office, so he offered to drop me off."

"I might wake up early," she whispered.

"Oooh! I like that," he whispered back.

"Unless I stay up too late reading this interesting book," she said and then giggled.

Kenny opened his eyes in the morning and reached out for Emmy. *Ah! You're still in bed. I like that.* He turned onto his side, put a hand on her hip and gently shook it. "Are you awake, Em?"

"No, and I'm not in the mood," she replied shoving his hand away.

Kenny smiled because she often did that to make him work harder to get what he wanted. He touched her hip again and pulled up on the t-shirt she wore.

Again she shoved his hand away. "No, I really mean it. Not this morning." She turned onto her back and nudged his leg.

"Your foot is cold, and I'm not the only one who will have to go ten days without sex."

"I could go a whole year without it if I wanted to."

"Do you want to wait a year?" he asked scooting closer.

"Maybe six months," she said stretching her arms over her head.

"Six months is a long time."

"Three months."

She felt a hand on her belly and closed her eyes.

"One month maybe?" he asked.

"I can do two months. Easy as pie."

She felt the hand move lower.

"Ten days is a long time," he said.

"You're cheating," she said.

"Only with you."

She sighed and whispered, "Five."

"Five months? You said one before."

"No, not months. You have to give me five minutes at least." She pulled him on top.

"I can do five minutes. Easy as pie," he said and then kissed her.

Kenny landed outside Birmingham, Alabama, later that afternoon. He exited Mr. Robertson's Gulfstream and saw Jeremiah Tolla leaning against his car.

"You got my text," Kenny said.

"Yes, I would have gone into Birmingham otherwise. This is much easier."

Ten minutes later Jeremiah drove away.

"Any trouble on the flight?" Jeremiah asked.

"Smooth as silk," Kenny said motioning with his hand.

"The guys are willing to rehearse before tonight's gig."

"That might be a good idea. I haven't picked up a guitar for a couple of weeks. I might be a bit rusty," Kenny said. "How are you doing? How is Mia? Does she like living in the South?"

"We love it down here, and we are expecting."

Kenny turned and stared at Jeremiah. "Expecting as in pregnant expecting?"

Jeremiah nodded. "She's due in October."

"Congratulations," Kenny offered. "I will have to remember to tell Emmy."

"This is the last plate, Mommy" Isabella said handing it to Emmy.

"Thank you, Isa. You can play outside now if you want,"

164

Emmy said with a smile. She placed the plate in the dishwasher, straightened up and glanced out the window above the sink. Her smile dissipated and a frown began to take shape. "Heather Rose Colwell! You are in big trouble." Emmy shook her head, closed the dishwasher and raced to the mudroom.

Isabella followed her mother. "Are you going to play with us?"

"No!" Emmy hollered over her shoulder. "I'm going to yell at your sister."

"What did she do now?" Isabella asked trying to keep up.

Emmy dashed out of the garage and ran around the house and sprinted up the steps to the deck. "Heather Rose! Get in the house right now!" Emmy yelled and pointed. She stood with hands on hips and continued, "And you can go home!"

"Mom! We weren't doing anything," Heather said slowly.

"I saw you through the window. Get inside now!"

"You better go, Ian," Heather said. She turned and walked to the French door leading into the family room. She stopped and faced Emmy. "Mom..."

"Inside! Now!" Emmy hollered. She stared at Ian Plant.

"Bye, Heather. Text me soon." He waved at Heather, turned and looked at Emmy, then bolted down the stairs, stuffed his hands in his pockets and tried to walk away slowly.

"You sound really mad," Isabella said. "Are you going to yell at me?"

"Why? Did you kiss that Plant boy, too?"

Isabella shook her head. "No. I've never kissed a boy."

Emmy took a deep breath. She turned around and hugged Isabella. "I'm sorry for snapping at you. You're my good girl."

"Heather is good most of the time," Isabella said.

"Yes, she is, but sometimes she can be a little too much like I was at your age. You should stay outside while I talk to your sister."

"Okay, but try not to yell too much."

"I won't yell. I will talk to her using a calm, adult voice," Emmy said. She turned toward the house and yelled, "Heather Rose! We need to talk!"

Isabella looked up at Emmy and said, "Mom, I know you. You are going to yell. Please try to control your temper."

"I will control my temper. I am not like my mother." Emmy walked back into the house and saw Heather sitting in a recliner in the family room. "You are grounded for life and an extra year after that."

"Why? I didn't do anything."

"I saw you kiss that boy again. Is that nothing? You disobeyed me. Why?" Emmy stood in front of Heather. "Why can't you be like Isa?"

Heather kicked the footrest and yelled back, "Because I am not Isa. I'm Heather. We're different."

Emmy put a hand to her forehead, sighed and said, "You're right. I'm sorry. I know you are different. I shouldn't expect you to be the same even though you are identical. Can I sit with you and talk?"

"We can sit on the couch," Heather said.

"Mom! I'm hungry," Kevin yelled from the hallway. He appeared in the opening to the family room and hollered, "I am starving. I need a sandwich."

"Not now, Kevin Michael," Emmy said in a louder than normal voice. "I'm talking to your sister."

Kevin looked at his mother and then at Heather. Slowly a grin appeared. "Ha! Ha! You're in trouble again, Heather."

"Go! Fix your own sandwich," Emmy said pointing toward the kitchen. "And I will deal with you later."

"But I didn't do anything."

"Go away!" Heather yelled.

Kevin raced down the hallway and Emmy turned to Heather. She took a deep breath and closed her eyes.

"I'm sorry if I made you mad at me," Heather said. "I didn't know he was going to kiss me again."

Emmy opened her eyes and asked, "Is that the truth, or are you saying that hoping I won't punish you?"

"I really, really didn't know he was going to do that. We were just talking and he did it."

"Were you talking about kissing?" Emmy asked.

166

Heather shook her head. "No, we were talking about a movie we saw. Do you still have to ground me?"

"You are still grounded, but maybe not for life."

"How about for a day?"

Emmy grinned and said, "Are you like an attorney pleading a case before a judge?"

Heather made a face and answered, "No, I'm just a kid."

Emmy tapped her chin for a moment. "Okay, for now I want your phone..."

"Mom!"

"No phone for a week. Maybe not until your father gets home."

"But, Mom!"

"No phone and no computer for a week."

"What am I supposed to do? How will I survive?" Heather whined.

"You can do what your father and I did when we were kids."

"What did you do?"

"We played outside and made up our own games. We played football and climbed trees and stuff."

"I hate football!"

"You can still play outside," Emmy said.

"Can I watch TV?"

"You could read a book," Emmy suggested.

"How about three hours of TV at night. I can't play outside in the dark."

*Rory and I used to play outside in the dark. It can be a lot of fun.* "Two hours at the most," Emmy offered.

"Deal," Heather said and held out a hand.

Emmy shook her hand and laughed. "You are a better negotiator than I ever was."

"How about the phone?"

Emmy shook her head. "No way, and I am going to tell your father when he calls later." Emmy pointed outside. "Go! You can play outside."

"Can we use the pool?"

167

"Yes, but you have to wear a swimsuit," Emmy said without thinking.

Heather made a face and walked away. "I'm not going swimming in my clothes," she muttered to herself.

Kenny called later that afternoon, and Emmy explained about Heather and Ian.

"Did she give you her phone?" Kenny asked.

"I have her phone. She can't text anyone."

"Did you get both phones?"

Emmy paused. "Both?"

"Yeah, she still has that older phone. I'm not sure if it has service, but it might," Kenny said.

"It better not. I am not paying for service on a phone we don't use. That would be wasteful," Emmy said. "I better check our bill a little closer. Usually, I just look at the total, complain out loud and go ahead and pay it."

"She might try to trade something to Kevin and use his phone. She can be sneaky at times."

Emmy sighed then added, "Tell me about it. I'm afraid she will grow up and be like me."

"You or Diane?"

Emmy shook a finger at no one in particular. "Don't even go there. I dread the day she... never mind. How is the tour going? Are you having fun riding in an old bus?"

"It's not that bad. The air conditioning works most of the time, and we have a driver and two crew members."

"Do people recognize you?"

"Not every night, but they did last night. Your suggestion for a disguise is working."

"Sunglasses and a cowboy hat is not much of a disguise," Emmy said with a laugh. "Anything else going on? How are Mia and Jeremiah?"

"Doing good."

They talked for another ten minutes.

"I gotta go, Em. I'll be home soon."

"Do you miss me?" Emmy asked.

Kenny grinned and answered, "Oh, are you gone?"

Emmy shook her head. "Such a dork. I'm supposed to say that."

Five minutes after ending the call Kenny realized he forgot to mention Mia was expecting. *Oh, well. I'll tell her when I get home.*

Kenny walked into the kitchen shortly after two Sunday afternoon. "I'm home! Did anyone miss me?"

Kevin ran into the kitchen holding a police car in each hand. "I missed you, Daddy. Check out my new cars."

"They look cool. Where is everyone?" Kenny set his backpack on the island. "Where is your mother?" He looked at the police cars again. "Where did you get the new cars, buddy?"

"Heather gave them to me," he answered.

"What did you give her?"

"Nothing," Kevin said with a shrug.

"You didn't give her your phone by any chance, did you?"

Kevin shook his head. "No way! She's grounded for kissing that boy again. Mom took away her phone and computer. Heather has been reading books and helping clean the house."

"Really?" Kenny asked.

"Yeah! It's been real weird around here this week. Gotta go. Ben and I are playing bank robbers in his woods."

"See you later, buddy," Kenny said. "Em, are you home?" He waited for a response.

"Daddy! When did you get home?" Isabella asked.

"Just now. Where is your mother?"

Isabella pointed to the backyard. "She's in the pool. Father James and Uncle Tony are here. He threw Mommy in the pool, and she yelled at him."

"Who threw her in the pool?"

"Uncle Tony," Isabella said as she ran into the powder room and closed the door. "She called him a bad name."

Kenny shook his head and headed back outside to the pool.

"I hate you, Tony Bertucci, and I'm telling Kenny what you did when he gets home," Emmy shouted while standing on the edge of the pool.

169

"Tell me what?" Kenny opened the black, wrought iron gate and approached the pool.

Emmy turned to face him and said, "Tony threw me in the pool and my top..."

Kenny watched as Tony grabbed an ankle and Emmy flew backward into the pool before she could finish explaining.

Tony popped up, waved at Kenny and started to climb out of the pool. "When did you get back?"

"Just now." He watched as Emmy reappeared and tried to pull Tony back into the pool by climbing on his back. "Is she bothering you?"

"She's being a brat like normal," Tony answered as he shrugged Emmy off of his back, and she fell into the pool again.

Emmy swam to the other side, got out of the pool, pointed at Tony and yelled, "I am not being a brat! You are a creep, and I don't know why I even let you in my pool."

"Hi, Em. Did you miss me?" Kenny asked.

She bit her lip and asked, "Oh, were you gone?" She ran around the pool made a face at Tony, who was now sitting on the edge of the pool, and wrapped her arms around Kenny. "I did miss you, and he was mean to me."

Kenny kissed her and then asked, "What did he do? You looked like you were having fun."

"He threw me in the pool and my top came undone."

Kenny looked at Tony, who shrugged. He turned to look at Father James.

"Don't look at me. I've been sitting here minding my own business. It's not my responsibility to look after that child," he said and took a sip of his beverage. "Though I might add she was teasing him about looking a little flabby. I'm pretty sure she used that word."

Kenny looked down at Emmy. "Flabby?"

She bit her lip and tried not to look guilty. "Well, he has put on a few pounds around the middle."

"It was an accident, Kenny." Tony said.

"An accident? That's a load of bull! You tossed me in the pool, creep!"

170

Tony held out a hand. "I was walking along minding my own business when she ran toward me and jumped into my arms. It startled me and I tripped on... something."

"One of Kevin's toys, perhaps?" Kenny suggested.

"Yeah. That was it." Tony nodded and picked Emmy up again.

"Put me down, creepozoid!" Emmy yelled.

"So, here I was about to lose my balance and fall down. I could have landed on top of the brat and crushed her since I am so fat and flabby."

Emmy rolled her eyes. Kenny nodded.

"I instinctively realized I needed to do something to save her life, so I did what came naturally. I threw her into the pool to save her from a horrible death." He walked to the edge of the pool and pretended to trip over something.

"I hate you!" Emmy screamed as she flew through the air again.

Kenny put a hand on Tony's shoulder and waited for Emmy to surface.

She popped up, spit out some water, used both hands to flash a signal to the guys and swam to the side of the pool.

"I saw that, Emmy. You owe me twenty Hail Marys," Father James said calmly.

The guys squatted down and looked at her with concern.

"Are you all right, Em?" Kenny asked.

She splashed water at them and used her signal again.

"From what Tony said, it appears he acted out of concern for your safety, You should probably thank him for saving your life."

"I will if you help me out," she said holding up her hands.

The guys grabbed a hand and easily lifted her out of the water. She shook her head spraying water at them.

"Are you all right?" Kenny asked suppressing a smile.

"I hate you both," she shouted. She kicked Tony's shin. "Ow! That hurts." She hopped on one foot and tried to rub her other one.

"Ooops!" Tony said as he gently pushed her shoulder.

171

She didn't say a word as she toppled back into the pool.

"Should I rescue her since I'm already in my trunks?" Tony asked.

"She knows how to swim," Father James said. "She won't drown."

"How was your trip?" Tony asked as he and Kenny walked over to the table and joined Father James.

"I had a blast. Most of the time, no one knew who I was," Kenny said.

"How did you deal with the heat?"

"I stayed in air conditioning as much as possible."

Emmy swam to the end of the pool, put her elbows on the edge and hoisted herself partway out of the water. She stared at the guys without saying a word.

"Sounds like the smart thing to do," Tony said.

Father James glanced at Emmy, turned to the guys and said, "I do believe she is scowling at us. Could it be she is upset about something?"

Kenny and Tony shrugged.

"Do you need some help, little sister?"

"I am fine, but you guys might want to sleep with your eyes open tonight," she warned and then got out of the water.

Father James quoted some scripture.

"You can fix your own dinner tonight," she said. She ran her hands through her hair and sat beside Kenny.

"I missed you, Em."

She put a foot on his knee. "I missed you, too."

"I think I hear Sloane calling me," Tony said.

"I need another beverage," Father James said.

Emmy rolled her eyes. "Stop it! I'm not going to attack him until tonight. You don't have to leave."

"In that case, could you get us another tasty beverage?" Father James asked holding out his empty bottle.

172

# Chapter Twenty-One

"Are we going to watch the fireworks tonight?" Kevin asked at the breakfast table. "My eggs are runny."

"That's how you like them," Emmy said setting a plate of pancakes in front of Isabella.

Kenny looked up at Emmy. "Are we going?"

"Up to you, but there is a chance of storms later. It's been so hot while you were gone. The humidity must be two hundred percent."

"We had a bad storm a few days ago," Heather said. "Mom made us go to the basement."

Kenny looked at Emmy.

She shrugged and said, "It was an average thunderstorm. Lot's of rain, wind, hail and lightning. Just the usual. We didn't lose power."

"Was there any damage?"

"Ben and I looked in the woods, and we found some trees knocked over. It's great. We can use them to play Army."

"I didn't see anything close to the house. It would take a direct hit from a really bad tornado to knock this house down," Emmy said.

"Can I have another pancake?" Heather asked.

"What do you say?"

"Please, may I have one more pancake," Heather said and then sighed.

Though it rained rather hard later that afternoon, neither Kenny nor Emmy suspected anything out of the ordinary had happened until Kenny turned on the TV. He watched the news for a minute and hollered for Emmy to come and look.

"What's up? I was making some cookies."

Kenny pointed to the TV. "There was a tornado."

Emmy turned to look. "Where?"

"Here in SoHam."

"Get out! When?" Emmy asked as she wiped her hands on her jeans and sat on the couch. "Nothing happened here that I could tell."

173

"About two hours ago. It hit south of the river and apparently wiped out that trailer court on Morris St. Do we know anyone who lives there?" Kenny asked.

"Shoot!" Emmy bit her lip and pointed at the screen.

"It says at least three people were killed."

They continued to watch the news and learned the concert and fireworks had been canceled because of some damage to the stadium.

"That is so unreal," Emmy said. "It rained here for like ten minutes."

"I'm glad we didn't have a concert at the stadium this year. It would have been a daylong festival and the place would have been packed."

"Did he just say there were only five minor injuries at the stadium?" Emmy asked.

"I think so. Wow! It could have been a lot worse."

"I feel really bad for that family from the trailer park. They lost three young children," Emmy said holding back her tears.

Kenny put an arm around her. "We could find out more about the family and donate some money. They lost everything today."

"Yes, let's do that. I could call Denise at the paper. She will know if there's a way to help out."

"Okay, I talked to Denise and this is what I want to do," Emmy said to Kenny an hour later. "There is a way to contribute online. Is it all right if we donate some money?"

"Whatever you think is appropriate, Em," Kenny said.

She made an anonymous donation of twenty-five thousand dollars to the family.

"Em, are you ready to go?" Kenny asked. "The party is supposed to start at three and we should be there a little before that."

Emmy checked herself in her full-length closet mirror. "I guess I look all right. I would wear a dress, but it's supposed to be casual. These jeans will have to do." She walked downstairs and into the family room. "You guys behave for Andrea."

174

"We will, Mom," Heather said. "We're going to show Andrea our room."

Emmy walked into the kitchen where Andrea Plant was talking to Kenny. *Are you really seventeen? You look more like someone about to graduate from college.* "Hi, Andrea."

"Em, did you know Andrea's father is a neurosurgeon at St. Bart's, and her mother has her own accounting firm?" Kenny asked.

"Yes, Mona told me. Thank you for watching the kids. I hate to ask at the last minute, and I really appreciate it."

"It's all right, Emmy. I don't have a summer job, but I've watched Mrs. Robertson's kids. Conor and Lily are angels compared to my younger brothers and sister."

"Where will you be going to school in the fall?" Kenny asked.

"I will be a senior at the Barclay Academy, and I'm hoping to attend Yale," she answered.

"We won't be out too long," Emmy said. "Our numbers are on the fridge. Don't hesitate to call if you need, and don't let them pester you. They can entertain themselves. Oh, it's all right if Kevin Michael goes over to play with Ben or if Ben comes here."

Andrea nodded. "They shouldn't be any trouble."

Kenny drove to the Steward Music Group building and parked in the back.

"Are you surprised Mr. Kesson is retiring?" Emmy asked as they headed inside.

"Yes and no. He has hinted about it for a couple of years."

"How well do you know his son?" Emmy asked as Kenny opened the door for her.

"Klaus has worked here since college. He started at the bottom and has worked his way up. Mr. Kesson has two daughters, but they aren't involved in the company. You've met them at different events over the years. The party is upstairs."

"Are they married?" Emmy asked as they headed to the elevator.

"One of them is, and they both live in Los Angeles, or one of those cities around it. They both have kids."

They got off at the third floor and walked into the largest room in the building. At one time it had been used to warehouse the inventory, but had been remodeled for its current use.

"Are we late?" Emmy asked. "I didn't know this many people worked here."

Kenny looked around. "Not everyone works here, Em. I see some people from Prater-Saylor, and there are band members from all the artists on the label."

"About time you got here," a booming voice roared from behind.

Kenny and Emmy turned and saw Andy Walker with his business partner Charles La Rosse.

"We aren't late, cuz," Emmy said. She smiled at Charles and he hugged her with his good arm.

"It's good to see you, Emmy. Don't listen to Andy. He's been a bear all day."

"What's wrong with him?" Emmy asked.

"He has to see his throat doctor tomorrow and doesn't want to go. He's being a big baby about the whole thing."

"Where have you been, Charles?" Emmy asked. "We haven't seen you for since last September if I recall correctly."

"I spent a few months in Knoxville visiting my mother. After I got tired of staying there, I decided to take a trip."

"Em, do you want something to drink?" Kenny asked.

"I'll take a soft drink. Thanks, Kenny." Emmy turned back to Charles. "Where did you go?"

"I realized I have never been to two continents, so I booked a trip to Australia and spent two months down under. They have excellent beer by the way."

"I'll take your word for that," Emmy said.

"Then I started touring Africa. I can't count all the countries I visited, but I did see some large animals."

"Did you ride on an elephant?" Emmy asked.

Charles chuckled and answered, "No, but I did see a herd."

"When did you get back to the states? Are you staying with Andy? Did you sell the townhouse?"

"Geez, Em. Ease up on the cross examination," Kenny said

handing her a Coke.

"I haven't sold the townhouse, but there are renters. I got back three days ago, and have been bothering Andy ever since," he answered. "How are the kids? I bet they have grow since I saw them last."

"They are getting older by the minute."

Emmy continued to talk to Charles while Kenny and Andy joined Jeff Rawlings and Dave Persching.

"Did you hear what Klaus wants to do with the direction of the company?" Jeff asked.

Kenny shook his head.

Andy nodded. "If you're talking about the movie idea, yeah, I heard about it."

"What movie thing?" Kenny asked.

"Apparently, Klaus wants to break into Hollywood. He wants to open a movie production division," Jeff answered.

"Does his father know?"

"I'm not sure, but I don't like the idea," Dave said. "Movies can be a pretty risky business."

"Nice pun," Andy said. "I almost thought about laughing."

The owners of the Prater-Saylor Agency, Steve Prater and Greg Saylor, walked up and joined the conversation.

"Are you guys thinking about retirement?" Kenny asked the men he had known for over twenty years.

Greg looked at Steve and they both looked at Kenny.

"You are, aren't you?" Kenny said.

"Our wives have both retired. They taught at Robert T. Colwell for thirty-five years," Steve said.

"They taught Emmy and me," Kenny mentioned.

"We have been thinking about selling the agency. Steve wants to move to North Carolina, and I have a place in Arkansas," Greg said.

"I can't say I blame you for wanting to retire," Kenny said. "You guys have done a great job for us over the years."

"Kenny, you do know they throw darts at a map to determine our tours, right?" Andy asked.

"I wondered about that the first couple of years."

177

Klaus Kesson used a microphone to get everyone's attention. "We want to thank everyone for stopping by to wish Dad a fond farewell. He claims he is going on a world cruise for the next year, but he might miss the grandkids too much." Klaus waited for the laughter to subside.

"Must be nice," Emmy said.

"I'll share some biographical tidbits about my father. He was, and still is, the sole owner of Steward Music Group. He was born in southern Illinois, but his parents moved to the Chicagoland area when he was eleven. He found them a few years later." Again Klaus waited. "I know that's such a bad joke, but Dad tells it to people all the time, so I included it."

"No wonder you guys get along so well," Emmy said looking at Kenny.

"Why is that, Em?" he asked though he knew Emmy was going to zing him.

"Because you both have dorky senses of humor."

"If you say so," Kenny said.

"After college, he worked as an engineer for a radio station in Chicago. He eventually moved to South Hampshire and opened a small recording studio on Steward Avenue. He did that for a few years and decided to start his own record label. This was before the large corporations controlled everything. The company struggled in the beginning, but Dad kept it afloat. He had a huge hit with a group called What The Elephants Herd. That kept the company in the black for a couple years. I saw those guys play lots of times and I even sat in with them. I played the cowbell. They were not great musicians, but they sure knew how to entertain a crowd. I loved their name, too. Later Dad put out a CD by The Notable Exceptions, another SoHam band, before they broke up. Paul Joseph played guitar and sang lead for that band."

Emmy turned at smiled at Paul and his wife, Teresa.

Klaus paused to check his notes. "I think the fourth or fifth band he signed was a local group called Fridays At Five. Some of you might have heard of them." Klaus had to wait a little longer for the applause to stop this time. "Dad could see the potential in these guys, and as time has proven, he was right on the money. And boy

178

oh boy did the money start rolling in."

Emmy looked at Kenny and rolled her eyes. "That was the corniest line ever. Klaus might be a bigger dork than you." *I never thought that was possible.*

"Shush, Em. Klaus is going to be the boss now. You can't call him a dork."

Klaus concluded his speech a moment later and handed the microphone to his father.

Max Kesson looked around the room, clenched his jaw and fought hard to control his emotions. "It's not easy to say goodbye to you. There are many of you who have been with me almost from the beginning. I appreciate your support through the lean times."

Emmy bit her lip as she listened. Kenny put an arm around her shoulders.

"I'm not going to cry," she whispered.

"You can if you want."

The room was absolutely quiet except for Mr. Kesson. He elaborated a bit more about the formation of the company, his years in the Navy and how he met his wife in a Sunday School class when he was eleven.

"I never knew that," Emmy said.

"I want to thank God for the day I first listened to the guys we call F-A-F around here. I will admit I thought Fridays At Five was a lame name for a band in the beginning. I suggested a different name, which I can't remember now, but it takes a big man to admit his mistakes. The name kinda stuck."

Emmy looked up at Kenny, grinned and said, "I thought it was dorky, too."

"The immediate success of Fridays At Five enabled the company to give other, less commercial artists, an opportunity to find their niche. Other companies more concerned with only the bottom-line might have never signed some of the artists we thought deserved a chance."

"Does he mean me?" Emmy asked. "He was looking right at me."

Andy put a hand on her shoulder. "I think he meant the guys behind you, cuz."

179

Mr. Kesson laughed and added, "Now I'm not opposed to making money, so when some of those niche artists stated selling a lot of product, I bought a small yacht."

"Now he means you, Emmy," Andy said.

"Can we buy a yacht, Kenny?" Emmy asked.

"Why? It would never get used."

"I guess that's all I have to say. Thank you again for making this company the success it is, and for a bonus, everyone can have the rest of the day off."

Klaus took the microphone and added, "There is still plenty of cake, ice cream and some champagne left. Enjoy."

"Are we going to stick around?" Emmy asked Kenny.

"We don't have to. I've talked to everyone I wanted."

"Charles, you are welcome to come over for dinner. We have some steaks and I made some potato salad earlier."

"Hey! What about me?" Andy asked. "I'm family."

"Distant family," Emmy said. "I suppose you can come over, but you might have to share a steak with Kenny."

"I can bring my own, and I will even man the grill."

"I want to hear more about Australia and Africa. I've never been to either of those places. Kenny has, but not me," Emmy said.

"Should I tell Prater-Saylor to book a tour?" Andy asked. "They could have you doing one-night-stands all over the continent."

"I was thinking of a vacation," Emmy said and frowned at Andy. "Not a tour where I have to work."

Kenny rubbed his jaw. "That could be interesting."

# Chapter Twenty-Two

"Who were you talking to?" Emmy asked.

Kenny set his cell phone on the island, walked around and stood in front of Emmy. "Is that the last of the apple pie? I was talking to Mr. D'Antoni."

"Why?" Emmy asked and then took another bite of pie. "Do you want the last bite?"

"You can have it."

"There's nothing wrong with your car, is there?" Emmy asked. She took the last bite and set the plate in the sink. "It's not even twenty years old yet."

"Very funny, Em."

"So why did you call him, or did he call you?"

"I called him," Kenny answered and opened the fridge. "Do we have any lasagna left from yesterday?"

"No, did you forget Tony and Sloane were here for lunch? Tony ate the last of it while you were swimming with the kids. I could make you something. What would you like?"

"I'm not really hungry." He closed the fridge. "Do you think Andrea could watch the kids for two or three hours?"

"I don't know. You could call and ask. She liked talking to you the other day."

"She is a bright young lady," Kenny said.

"And she got a body that reminds me of Amber." Emmy made a motion that resembled an hourglass. "She must have to fight off the boys."

"I suppose you're right. We haven't seen Derrick or Amber in ages," Kenny said to change the subject.

"Not since the New Year's Eve party at Kristen's house."

"Could you call Andrea? I would feel like a stalker if I called her."

"I will if you tell me why we need her."

"Okay, I want to take a look at a new car," Kenny confessed.

"For real? Why? The Civics haven't changed. You would be throwing money away."

"I don't want another Civic," he said.

"What do you want? A CR-V like Rory's got?"

"No. I want to surprise you. Would you please call?"

Emmy called and Andrea agreed to watch the kids. Emmy told her they could use the pool.

"I'll watch the kids swim. Would it be all right if Brienna comes with me? She's the same age as the twins."

"It's okay with me if Brienna comes over," Emmy said emphasizing her name. *You better not bring Ian with you.*

Andrea and Brienna arrived thirty minutes later.

"I drove Dad's Porsche over here. I parked it away from the garage. Is that all right?" Andrea asked.

"I'm sure it won't be in the way," Kenny said trying not to stare at Andrea.

"It's fine where it is," Emmy said and poked Kenny in the side. "We should get going."

"We won't be out too long," Kenny said then he and Emmy left.

"You were talking to Mr. D'Antoni and you don't want a Honda," Emmy said. She thought for a moment. "I know you don't want a Buick or a GMC. Ross Knapp said the new GMCs are crap. He should know because he runs the service department there. Why were you talking to him? Are you going to tell me where we're going?"

"Mr. D'Antoni bought the Acura dealership."

Emmy smacked Kenny's arm. "Are you going to be a decadent rock star and buy one of those new sports cars? What are they called?"

"The name is NSX and they are too expensive."

"How much are they?"

"Over two hundred thousand, I think."

"Pfffft! A mere pittance," Emmy said waving a hand.

"No way, Em. I want to look at an Acura TLX."

"Get out! You do know they cost more than Hondas, right?"

"I am fully aware of the cost, Em. I did some research online."

"Did you bring the title? Are you going to trade in this car, or do we know anyone who needs a barely broken in Civic?"

"I tried to think of someone who might need it, but no one came to mind. I think I'll just trade it in, and the title is in the glove box."

They pulled into the dealership moments later and Kenny parked next to a red SUV.

"That looks nice," Emmy said.

"We already have an SUV and a minivan. I'm not buying another one."

"The TLX is a sedan, right?"

"Yes." Kenny opened the door and they walked inside. Kenny looked around and spotted Alan D'Antoni talking to another man.

"Are they fast?" Emmy asked.

"I don't know, Em. We will have to drive one and find out."

"Kenny, how are you?" Mr. D'Antoni offered a hand. "I was surprised to get your call. Is there something wrong with your Civic?"

"Not really, but I would like something a little larger."

"And faster," Emmy added with a grin.

"It's a pleasure to see you again, Ms. Colasanti. I hear you are a famous author now."

"I don't know about famous, but I have written some books."

After some small talk, Mr. D'Antoni introduced Roberto Emmanuel.

"It's a pleasure to meet you. How may I help you today?" he asked.

Emmy appraised the short Hispanic man and was instantly charmed by his smile.

"I would like to look at a TLX. I checked online and you have several in stock," Kenny said.

"We do. Should we take a seat at my desk, and I will check the inventory."

Roberto checked the inventory while asking some questions.

183

Emmy looked around the showroom. "Would you excuse me for a minute? I want to ask Mr. D'Antoni something."

"Go ahead, Em."

Emmy waved to Mr. D'Antoni and hurried to where he stood talking to one of the managers while Kenny and Roberto continued to talk.

"Do you have a question, Emmy?"

She looked back at Kenny for a second, then faced Mr. D'Antoni. "I know they are real expensive, but do you have any of those new sports cars?"

"You mean the NSX?"

Emmy nodded. "That's the one."

"I don't have any yet, but I will be getting one in a few weeks. They are rather rare at the moment. They just went on sale at the end of May. Is Kenny interested in one?"

"No, but I thought it would be fun to surprise him with one."

"That would indeed be a surprise, but knowing him, I don't think he would like driving it. Now you might like it, but are you really interested in spending that much money?"

"I guess not, but I thought I'd ask," Emmy said.

"Tell you what. When we get one in stock, I'll call you and you can take a look."

"Could I drive it?"

He tilted his head. "I don't know about that. I'm sorry but the people who buy cars in that price range usually want one with very few miles on the odometer."

"That's okay. Maybe one of these years Kenny will buy a supercar," Emmy said. She turned around and walked through the showroom checking the different cars.

"So, blue would be your first choice?" Roberto asked.

Kenny nodded. "Blue and fully loaded. The six cylinder model."

Roberto smiled and asked, "Are you ready for a test drive?"

Kenny looked around, spotted Emmy and waved. "I think we're ready."

"I'll pull the car up front."

184

A few minutes later Kenny and Emmy were sitting in front as Roberto explained the features.

"It's kinda strange not to have a transmission thing," Emmy said.

"That's the new nine speed," Roberto explained.

They returned to the dealership after a five minute test drive.

"What did you think?" Roberto asked while opening the dealership door.

"I liked it even though I wasn't driving," Emmy said.

Kenny grinned and said, "It's definitely faster than my Civic."

An hour later Kenny waved to Roberto and he and Emmy drove away in their new car.

"I still can't believe you bought a car that cost over forty thousand dollars. You better take good care of it," Emmy said.

"It wasn't that much. We got a decent price for the Civic."

Emmy grinned.

"What?" Kenny asked.

"Should we take our cars to the track and race them?"

He shook his head. "Not a chance. Besides, I would wipe you out by a mile. Wait till you drive this, Em. You'll realize it's a lot faster than your Si."

Kenny pulled into the garage, got out and checked his car.

"Are you looking for dust?" Emmy asked.

"I want to keep it clean," he answered.

"Let's see if the kids are swimming."

They walked around the house to the pool and heard some splashing. Emmy saw Andrea working on her tan and nudged Kenny.

"What?"

Take a look at Andrea. Does she remind you of anyone?"

Kenny stared for a moment. "She really fills out that bikini, huh?"

"Ya think! Not that there's much to her bikini." She looked up at Kenny and nudged him again. "You better quit staring now before you start drooling."

"I wasn't staring," he insisted.

"Whatever."

Isabella saw her parents, climbed out of the pool and ran to them. "Brienna can't swim as good as us, but she is having fun. Can we keep swimming?"

"Maybe for a few more minutes," Kenny answered.

Andrea heard Kenny and Emmy, opened her eyes, got up and walked over. "The kids weren't any trouble at all. I almost feel guilty about taking your money. I was able to work on my tan. Oh, Kevin decided to play with the boy across the road."

"That's fine. How much do we owe you?" Kenny asked.

Andrea answered and Kenny paid her.

"Do we have to leave now?" Brienna asked.

"We should go," Andrea answered.

Emmy saw the disappointment on Brienna's face. "We could run Brienna home later if it would be all right with your parents."

"Okay, but she needs to be home by five," Andrea said. "We are having company for dinner."

"We will make sure she gets home before then," Emmy said. She tugged on Kenny's arm and whispered, "We can go in the house if you can tear your eyes away from Andrea."

"I wasn't staring."

"If you say so,"

Andrea put on her shorts, got in her father's Porsche and drove away.

Emmy watched Andrea leave. *Must be nice to have a fancy sports car like that.*

"What are you doing, Em?" Kenny asked later. "Isabella and I just ran Brienna home. Isabella said they had a lot of fun swimming with her."

"Should we go away again?"

"Why?"

"So we could see if Andrea can babysit," Emmy answered drawing out the name.

"She's a kid, Em." He looked closer at Emmy's laptop. "Is that the same kind of car Andrea had?"

186

"I think it's her father's car."

"I know." Kenny scratched his chin. "Her parents have money. Do you think it's possible they bought Andrea a Porsche?"

"It's possible, but she said it was her father's car. You would remember that if you weren't so busy staring at her bikini," Emmy teased.

"Are you going to tease me all day?"

"Maybe," she said while grinning. "How much do you think the insurance would be on a Porsche Cayman?"

"I have no idea. Are you serious about looking at a new car?"

Emmy shrugged. "I don't know. When I bought the Si, I thought it was pretty fast, but it's not. It handles good, and it gets good gas mileage."

"But you need more speed, huh?"

"I was talking to Kristen, and she mentioned one of John's friends has a membership at the SoHam Autobahn Club."

"The place out by the track where they do the NASCAR races?" Kenny asked.

"Yeah, if we were members, I could drive without you worrying about me getting a ticket."

"We could look into it, I guess," Kenny said. He pointed at the laptop. "I like that color."

Emmy looked and changed the image. "I like yellow better than the blue, but both look good."

"Do you remember that Corvette I looked at when Tony bought his Envoy?"

"Vaguely."

"You could buy a used Corvette," he suggested.

"Do they make purple Corvettes?" she asked.

"I've never seen one, Em," he answered. "Oh, you were kidding."

"I'll do more research and decide if I'm serious about driving something sportier."

## Chapter Twenty-Three

"Emmy, I called Mr. Tockstein this morning," Kenny said as Emmy was drying off after her shower. "He will have everything set for the book signing. He hopes he has enough of your books."

"I'm sure he will," Emmy replied. "Denise and Ophelia should be there soon. They will make sure everything is ready." Emmy wrapped the towel around her and walked up to the bed. "Did he say anything about Annie's book? Does he think it's weird that we want to have the book signing thing together?"

"He didn't say anything about it being weird. It is rather unusual, but you guys are friends."

Emmy dropped the towel and faced Kenny with hands on her hips. "In case you haven't noticed, I am not a guy, and I don't think Annie is either."

Kenny grinned and took a step toward Emmy. "I apologize for referring to you as a guy. Obviously you are all woman."

She held him at arm's length. "You're a dork, and we do not have time for that. I need to get dressed, and we need to run the kids to your parents."

"I'll make sure the kids are ready. Do we have to bring anything? Books, I mean."

"I hope not because I don't have many copies of any of them," she replied.

"Do you remember what their son's name is?" Kenny asked.

"Keyshon Matthew, I think," Emmy said while getting dressed. "Yeah, it is. They named him after Mace Franklin's brother. He's a few years younger than Kevin Michael."

"They haven't had any other kids, have they?"

"Not that I know of," she answered. "Go! Make sure the kids are ready."

They dropped the kids at Kenny's parents and headed to downtown SoHam. Paul Tockstein's bookstore occupied an entire five-story building on Polk Street. Against all odds he managed to keep his brick and mortar store open and thriving. Kenny parked in the deck behind the store, and they walked across the street and entered through the rear door.

"Do you remember the first time you did this, Em? You were afraid no one would show up."

"I remember. There were enough customers to keep me busy for four hours, and they bought every book in stock."

"I think you sold out of CDs, too." Kenny walked toward the front of the store and spotted the owner talking to one of the cashiers. "Come on, Em. I see Mr. Tockstein."

Emmy scooted past Kenny and rushed up to Mr. Tockstein. "We're here. Where should we set up?"

Mr. Tockstein smiled and said, "If you don't call me Paul, I will not keep any of your books or CDs in stock."

"Okay, I will call you Paul."

He pointed to an open area. "I thought we could set up there and have the customers line up along the back of the front display."

Kenny walked up after looking around. "You've changed things up."

Paul shook Kenny's hand and responded, "I have to keep the place fresh. We needed an open area for events like this. We moved the coffee shop to the second floor. The upper three floors are all rows of shelving and bookcases."

"All the books on this floor are new, right?" Kenny asked.

"Yes, and actually, the first two floors are new product. We moved all the used books and whatever to the top two floors."

"What about your first editions and rare books?"

"We keep them on the third floor now. Some of the really valuable ones are kept downstairs. We installed a room designed to help with their preservation," Paul said.

"Have you cut back on the music section? I know CDs are not selling as well as years ago."

Paul nodded and pointed to the opposite wall. "I keep a limited numbers of titles. Local artists and independent bands. Don't tell Emmy, but her CDs still sell steadily."

"I won't tell her. It might inflate her ego, and I have to live with her."

189

Ten minutes later Denise Bartell and Ophelia Sturges walked in chatting away. Denise edited Emmy's and Annie's books while Ophelia worked as the literary agent for both authors.

"The vampire books are not selling as briskly," Denise said waving a hand.

Ophelia shook her head. "I disagree. *Melissa's Dream* is still selling."

Denise laughed and said, "If you want to call a few hundred copies a month as still selling. I see Emmy up front talking to Paul."

Ophelia brushed a strand of her flaming red hair out of her eyes and headed in that direction. "Good morning, Emmy. I'm sorry we are running a little late, but we needed to stop for coffee. Are you ready to work?"

"I am ready if anyone shows up."

Ophelia checked the front display. "I see we have all of your books in sight. I hope we run out of stock like last year."

"How is Annie's book doing?" Emmy asked.

Ophelia made a motion like a bird in flight. "Stores are having trouble keeping them in stock. Her first book is in its third printing, and this one had a much larger initial run. I like the title. *Marcella Spenser: C.I.A. Agent.* It flows nicely."

"I've read *My Secret Life as a High School Private Eye* three times," Emmy said. "Annie is a much better writer than me."

Denise removed her wide-brimmed burgundy hat, set it on the table, smiled and said, "I am going to have to quit working for the paper and concentrate on my own fiction. You and Annie are doing so well with your books."

"I thought you were working on a sequel," Emmy said.

"I am, but I need more hours in the day. I've lost two staff members this year to layoffs, and the kids are driving me up a wall." Denise rolled her eyes and waved her hand dramatically. "You'd think now that they're all out of college, they would be able to make decisions on their own. At least I only have two still living at home."

Paul and one of his employees joined the ladies. "This is Pam Kilander. She will be taking care of you today. Don't be shy about keeping her busy, Emmy."

"It's a pleasure to meet you, Emmy. May I call you Emmy?"

"Of course. This is Denise. She edits Annie's and my books, and this is Ophelia Sturges. She's our agent."

"It's a pleasure to meet you. Please let me know if you need anything," Pam said as she adjusted the name tag on her blue vest.

"We need some bottled water, and we will need more books on the table," Ophelia said.

"Right away!" Pam said. She spun around and flipped her long, blonde hair over her shoulder.

Denise checked the time. "Annie should be here shortly. She texted me and said she would be a few minutes late."

Ophelia checked the time. "Emmy, you have fifteen minutes to get ready."

"I will be back in a minute," she said and hurried to use the restroom.

"Denise, if it's all right with you, I'm going to make myself scarce," Kenny said. "I don't want to be a nuisance."

"I'll have Emmy text you when this is over," Denise said.

Emmy returned in time to give Kenny a kiss and a moment later Annie arrived.

"Annie, it's so good to see you," Emmy said racing up to her. She hugged Annie and smiled at Matt Sullivan. "How have you guys been? Is that your son?"

Annie nodded. "Can you believe he's almost five already. He's getting so big. He's bigger than most boys his age."

Matt smiled at Emmy and asked. "Is Kenny coming, or is he on tour?"

"He dropped me off, but couldn't stay. He'll be back when we're finished," Emmy answered. "Annie, do you mind if we share this table? It's pretty big, but if you'd rather have your own, I understand."

"I don't mind sharing. That way we can talk in case no one shows up."

Annie got settled and Matt took Keyshon upstairs to the coffee shop.

Pam smiled and asked, "Are you ladies ready? We're going to open the doors."

"Ready as I can be," Annie said.

Emmy nodded then bit her lip.

The traffic was steady for the two hours. Neither Annie nor Emmy had time to take a break.

"How have you been?" Emmy asked. "Are you working on another book?"

Annie moved her fingers around to prevent stiffness and answered, "I have an idea for one, but I haven't started a first draft. You?"

Emmy shook her head. "I really like writing, but I don't have an idea for another book yet. Will there be more Marcella Spenser stories?"

"Probably, but I've been considering a spin-off series. I might use the same location, but introduce new characters."

"Anything else happening? How are your father and grandfather doing?"

"Daddy retired from the force. He and Elisabeth built a home on Grandpa's farm. Did you know that already?"

"Yes, I heard he retired. He was a detective for a long time, right?"

Annie nodded. "Grandpa said he might stop by later. His hip has been bothering him, but he's doing pretty good for his age."

"He's the same age as my father would have been. They were born in 1937," Emmy said. "I've always thought it was weird that my father and your grandfather were the same age."

"It is unusual," Annie said. "I have something else to share. We haven't told too many people, but we're expecting our second. I'm due next February."

"That is so great!" Emmy shouted. She reached out and hugged Annie. "I hope you have a daughter."

"I would like a girl, but it doesn't matter as long as the baby is healthy. I know that's a cliché, but I really mean it. Keyshon said he wants a little brother."

"My girls fight with their brother, but they love each other."

Liam O'Dell arrived thirty minutes later and waited in line with the other customers. Annie signed a book for the lady in front of him and then asked, "Would you like an autograph, and who should I make it to?"

"If you and Matty would come and see me more often, you would remember my name," he answered. "Emily, it's good to see you again. Has my least favorite grandchild been pestering you?"

Emmy grinned and said, "I know Annie's your only grandchild, but I hear you have another great-grandchild on the way."

"Aye! It's taken them long enough for sure. I was afraid Keyshon would be an only child like Annie and her father."

"Grandpa, do you want a book or not?" Annie asked. "There are other people in line."

"I do want one. I'd like a copy of Emily's book," he teased.

Kenny returned shortly before two and joined Matt and Keyshon at the front of the store.

"Did you sell all your books, Em?" he asked.

"I still have a few left, but Annie sold all of hers."

"Did you buy a copy?" Kenny asked.

"We swapped copies," Annie said with a smile.

"She and Matt are expecting," Emmy said.

Kenny shook Matt's hand. "Congratulations."

"Thank you. We've been trying for over a year."

Emmy grinned and said, "We still like to try, too."

Kenny shook his head and put a hand to his forehead.


"Who were you talking to?" Kenny asked Tuesday morning. He opened the fridge and grabbed a bottle of water. "Where are the kids?"

"They're at Tony's. I convinced them to play over there," Emmy answered.

Kenny stared at her with a quizzical expression. "Em," he said slowly.

"Sloane and Mama are home and the kids will play outside."

"And?" Kenny asked with his palms out.

"I called the Porsche dealership in Newcastle and kinda made an appointment for eleven."

"To see what? Do they have any used cars?"

"They have three 2016 Cayman's in stock." She grabbed his water and took a drink. "It doesn't cost anything to look."

She pulled into the garage at two o'clock, slammed her car door shut, stomped up the stairs to the mudroom and slammed that door as well.

"Is it safe to follow you, Emmy?" Kenny asked while slowly opening the mudroom door.

Emmy sat on a barstool, picked up a banana and squeezed it. "I'm not mad at you."

Kenny sat beside her and took the banana away. "I think you choked it to death."

"Can you believe the rudeness of that salesman?" she pounded on the island. "I wouldn't buy a car from him if he paid me to buy it."

Kenny tried not to laugh.

"Well, I wouldn't."

"I didn't hear what he said to you when we first arrived. I saw him laughing though."

Emmy glared at Kenny.

"Don't bite my head off, Em.," Kenny said putting his hands up in surrender. "You did get to test drive the car."

"Yeah! After I proved I was old enough and knew how to drive. It wasn't even a stick." She lay her hands on the island and rested her head in them. "I did like how the car drove. It handled so amazing."

"We could find another dealer," Kenny suggested.

"I should have brought one of your CDs to show that jerk. Maybe then he would have believed we could afford the car."

Kenny touched the hole in her jeans and tried to tickle her knee.

She pushed his hand away. "Stop that. It shouldn't matter how a person looks. It's just a car."

"Yes, dear."

She made a face at him. "I suppose he would have fallen all

194

over us if I had worn a fancy dress with expensive bracelets and diamond earrings."

"There are other sports cars, Em. How about a Corvette or a Mazda Miata? They are chick cars. The Miata, I mean."

She scowled at him and made a fist.

"That's what Andy said. I kinda like how they look."

"If we look at one, you better bring your checkbook because I might buy it just to spite that arrogant Porsche salesman."

"That will show him," Kenny teased and was rewarded with a poke to his ribs.

"We could afford it, Em," Kenny said on the way home from Jacob Adams Chevrolet the next afternoon. "You said you liked the car, and they had a white one on the lot."

"I did like it, but it was too fast for me. I think I'd rather have a less powerful car that I have to rev up than something with too much horsepower. Do you know what I mean?"

"You like how you can push your Civic to the redline, huh?"

"Yeah! I can drive that car hard and not be going a thousand miles an hour. The Civic isn't likely to kill me either."

"We should look at a Miata. They don't have a lot of horsepower, but are supposed to be a blast to drive."

"Am I big enough to drive one?" she asked facetiously.

"You might have to sit on a pillow to see over the dashboard," he teased.

"I hate you!" She took a deep breath and looked at Kenny. "I'm sorry for wasting your time. I should learn to be satisfied with what I have."

"It's okay, sweetie. I did like driving the Corvette. Who knows? I might break down and buy one in a few years."

"Yeah, right! And pigs will soon be flying along with ducks and geese."

# Chapter Twenty-Four

"Last chance to go with me," Emmy said to Kenny.

He waved a hand. "You can go alone. I'll watch the kids."

"Is it because you don't want to be recognized?" Emmy asked grabbing her keys and small purse.

"Partly, but I'm too tired to fight the crowd."

"Plus the Bender Brothers Band isn't exactly your favorite band," she said.

"I like their music," he replied. He looked outside in time to see Kevin run and jump into the pool. "I did produce their CD."

"And despite that it has become a hit," she teased. "I'll try not to stay out too late, and I'll text you when I'm on my way home."

"Is Bobby going with you?"

"He texted earlier today. He said he would feel too uncomfortable being around the guys."

"I can understand that," Kenny said. "I respect him for not compromising his principles. Are you going to the show to spy on the guys?"

"I don't know what you mean," Emmy said.

"Come on, Em. You want to see if it's as bad as Bobby said."

"I am not. I just want to hear them live again."

"Okay, but if you see something you don't like, try not to preach at them. Life on the road can be..."

"I know what it's like. I promise not to be a stumbling block. Do I get a kiss before I go?"

Kenny kissed her lips for longer than she expected.

"Are you trying to convince me to stay home?"

He grinned.

"I promised the guys I would be there, but I hope you have some of those kisses left when I get back."

She arrived at the Spencer Auditorium early and pulled into the VIP lot. She gave her name to the security guard, and he pointed to a spot next to the building. She noticed a semitrailer with the Bender Brothers Band logo on the side and a bus parked

196

alongside. She passed through another security checkpoint, received an all-access pass and made her way to the green room.

"Yep! Same old cream-colored paint," she said rubbing a hand along the wall. She looked around and spotted Boyd Goldman a few feet away talking to Micah Hurst.

"Well, look who's here," Micah said as she approached.

Boyd took a quick drag from his cigarette, dropped it to the floor and turned around. "Hey, Emmy, how are you? Thanks for coming out. Are you alone?"

"It's just me. This place hasn't changed a bit, but I see you have upgraded your transportation."

Micah waved to someone holding a clipboard and smiled at Emmy. "We are leasing the bus, and we need the trailer for all our gear."

"The next time I see you guys, you might need two or three trucks and you might be flying to all your gigs." She looked around the crowded room. "Where are Freddie and Marshall? I see Christian talking to those ladies. I haven't met your new drummer. What is his name?"

Boyd pointed to a man with long, greasy-looking black hair wearing a leather jacket with the name of a motorcycle club on the back. "That's Gage Traylor. He's pretty good, Emmy. He fits our style better than Bobby."

"Is that a bottle of Jack Daniels in his hand?" Emmy asked.

Boyd looked at Micah.

Micah hesitated then answered, "It's an old Jack Daniels bottle, but he fills it with tea. He likes to maintain a party image."

Boyd said, "Freddie and Marshall are doing a radio interview. Do you want to listen to the opening act, Emmy?"

"Not really. Have you guys eaten?"

"We ate right after our soundcheck," Micah answered. "Emmy, we had to make a management change. Did you hear about it?"

"Of course I heard about it. Nelson Grapella is my manager, and Andy Walker is part of the family. What happened? Nelson wouldn't talk about it."

"We had a disagreement about the direction of the band. It

197

wasn't Nelson's fault," Micah said. "Will you be all right if we mingle, Emmy?"

"Sure, I will wander around. I might see someone I know," Emmy replied. Micah didn't catch the sarcasm in her answer.

"You are welcome to hang out on the stage, but we won't ask you to sing with us," Boyd said. He waited until Micah walked away and pulled Emmy aside. "I know you're pissed at me for breaking up with Bailey, but it wasn't all my fault."

"It's never just one person's fault, Boyd. When did you start smoking?"

"A while back. I didn't smoke when I was in your band."

"Did you drink?"

"Are you going to get on my case? I have a beer or two before a show. It's no big deal. You told us how you used to sneak a beer."

"That was before... never mind. I rarely drink anything now. We don't even have any wine in the house." She watched Gage for a moment. "Tea my butt."

"He keeps it under control."

"You guys are adults, so I can't force you to do anything, but I can pray for you. You know better, Boyd."

"Are you finished?" he asked angrily.

She looked up at him and bit her lip.

"I'm sorry, Emmy. You didn't deserve that. Thank you for still caring about us."

"I will always care about you and the other guys. You were in my band for several years, and we shared some good times on the road." She looked around and waved a hand. "We didn't need the alcohol to have a good time."

Boyd grinned and said, "No, we used Super Soakers. That was a different time, Emmy. We were all younger and more naive. Things are different now."

"That's the lamest excuse I've ever heard. You are only deceiving yourself if you believe that."

Emmy meandered through the crowd searching for a familiar face. She didn't find one. However, she found a cooler filled with beer. *I know some of the Fridays crew wanted beer on*

198

*the bus, but they never had it backstage and available before the show.* She eventually made her way to the side of the stage for the show. She saw Freddie and Marshall and did a double take. *Wow! You guys haven't had a haircut in ages, and those beards are like the old guys in that other band. Must be a Texas thing.* She listened to the band. *You guys sound pretty tight. You've come a long way from that first jam in our basement.* She decided to leave after Micah dropped an f-bomb midway through the show. She got home, climbed into bed with Kenny and nudged his hip.

He turned over and opened his eyes. "What time is it? How was the show?"

She snuggled next to him and he put an arm over her. "It was good, but I left early."

He felt her tremble and kissed her cheek. "You okay? Is there something wrong? Are you crying?"

"I'm sad and mad and upset with the guys."

Kenny sat up. "What happened?"

Emmy sat up facing Kenny, took a deep breath and began, "I got there and went into that big room backstage."

"I know the one you mean."

"You wouldn't believe these are the same guys who were in my band and on the worship team. The new drummer was drinking a bottle of whiskey. People were smoking and not just cigarettes. I could smell pot." She shook a finger at Kenny and then waved her hands around. "I know what it smells like even though I've never used it. Anyway, I talked to Boyd and Micah. Boyd really needs our prayers. They all do, but. Oh, Freddie and Marshall have real long hair now and these ugly beards. So does Micah. Long hair. He doesn't have a beard. The drummer looks like a member of Hell's Angels or some motorcycle gang. The band sounds pretty amazing." She paused for a moment and laughed. "Christian and Boyd are the only guys who look normal."

"Wait! What is normal, Em?" Kenny asked. He grabbed her hands. "Slow down and remember to breathe."

She frowned at him and said, "Christian and Boyd don't have long hair or beards. They didn't smell funny and were wearing clean jeans and shirts. They looked respectable and kinda

199

out of sync with the other guys. Boyd's playing bass since the band fired Miles. I can't remember if I told you that. Christian is even better than before. It wouldn't surprise me if some famous band hires him."

"We aren't looking for another guitar player," Kenny said.

"I didn't mean you guys. I meant someone like... I can't think of anyone right now, but you know what I mean, right?"

"Certainly, Em."

"I was listening to the band. Oh!" She smacked Kenny's arm. "Micah doesn't play his guitar on all the songs. Sometimes he wanders around the stage like he's the guy from The French Occupation of Quincy. I can't remember his name, but he strutted around like he was God's gift to women."

"Micah Hurst? Really?" Kenny asked.

"No! The guy from French Occupation. Why did they have such a long name?" Emmy asked and didn't let Kenny answer. "I was going to stay to the end, but changed my mind."

Kenny waited for her to continue. When she didn't, he asked, "What changed your mind?"

She sighed, rolled her eyes, plopped onto her back, stared at the ceiling and said, "Micah dropped an f-bomb."

"Is that all? You've used that word before."

Emmy sat up faster than the speed of light, poked Kenny's arm and yelled, "He said it right on stage like it was perfectly normal. I know I've used it, but it was because I was angry or upset or something, and I don't use that word anymore." She put a finger to her mouth. "I don't, do I?"

He shook his head. "I haven't heard you use it since that day Kevin said it, and you got after him."

"He said it in front of Tyler and Liz. I was so embarrassed I wanted to just die." She plopped onto her back again. "Oh, Kenny, I am so concerned for the guys. I don't think any of them are going to church at all. How could they change like that?"

"It doesn't happen overnight, Em." He moved closer and put a hand on her stomach. "There are lots of people who come to church for a while and then disappear. They move away, or find a different church, or..."

200

"Or decide they don't believe the way we do."

"Not all Christians believe exactly the same."

"I know that, but I think there has to be some common ground. Doesn't it say in the Bible that if you believe in Jesus, your life needs to be changed?"

"I believe so."

"So, if you accept Jesus and your life changes, why would you ever go back to living the way you did before? That doesn't make any sense. You would be risking your eternal soul. Unless you believe like that church that preaches once saved always saved." She turned onto her side and continued, "Am I being judgmental?"

"I don't think so. It sounds like some of the guys have lost their focus though."

"Ya think? If they were still in my band, I would fire them."

"That would fix everything," Kenny said.

"Are you being sarcastic?"

"A little. If you fired them, you wouldn't be able to keep an eye on them. They might join a secular band that didn't care what they did."

She made a face at him. "You think you're so smart."

"I don't know it all, but I do know one thing."

"What's that?"

He grinned and said, "I have funny ears." He kissed her and put a leg on top of her.

"You do have funny ears," she said after the kiss. "Do you think this will help me get to sleep?"

"Maybe in an hour," he whispered.

# Chapter Twenty-Five

"Kenny! Kenny! Where are you?" Emmy hollered as she raced down the hallway toward the family room.

Kenny dropped the TV remote, spit out the water he had been drinking and struggled to get up from his recliner. He succeeded and then stubbed a toe on the table. He quashed a mild expletive and yelled, "In the family room, Em. Are you all right?"

Emmy slid down the polished, hardwood floor in her white socks. She grabbed the wall and appeared in the wide, family room entrance holding up her phone. She saw Kenny hopping on one foot while trying to rub his toes. "Don't tell me. Did you run into the coffee table again?"

"You startled me. I thought maybe the house was on fire."

"The sprinkler system would come on, and you would be soaked." She suppressed a laugh.

"What's the emergency?" he asked.

Heather, Isabella and Kevin rushed into the room.

"Mommy, we heard you yell," Heather said. "Did Miss Liz have the baby?"

Emmy nodded and pointed to the couch. "Let's sit down, and I will share all the details."

"I know she had a boy," Isabella said. "Natalie told me. She wanted a baby sister."

Kevin sat on the edge of the table holding a cardboard box.

"What's in that box?" Emmy asked pointing at it. "It better not be alive."

Kevin shook his head. "It's some of my bugs, but I think they're all dead now."

"It was easier when all you collected were firetrucks and police cars," Emmy said looking at Kenny.

"I might still be a fireman, but I want to be a bug scientist first," Kevin said.

"Kevin Michael, you should leave your dead bugs outside."

"Tell us about the baby," Heather said.

Emmy checked her phone. "Okay, we all know it's a boy. His name is David Theodore. Tyler said that was his grandfather's name, but in reverse." Emmy motioned to indicate what she meant. "He is twenty-one inches long. He has some brown, fuzzy hair, and he weighed exactly eight pounds and two ounces. Poor Liz. He was a big one."

"Can we see the baby?" Heather asked.

"Maybe you should wait until they bring him home," Kenny said.

"But we're going on vacation Saturday," Heather said.

"Will Miss Liz come home before then?" Isabella asked.

Emmy looked at Kenny. "I'm not sure, but I want to see them. The girls are old enough to go with me."

Kenny shrugged and said, "If it's all right with Liz and Tyler, it's okay with me. Do you want to go, Kevin?"

Kevin looked inside his box and shook his head. "No, I have to find more bugs."

Emmy called Tyler a few minutes later.

"Liz says you can bring the girls. Dany was here, but she left ten minutes ago," he said.

"Are your in-laws there?" Emmy asked.

"No, they are in Hawaii. They won't be back for a week."

"We won't stay long, but I have to see the baby before we leave for Ireland."

Tyler chuckled and said, "Come on up. Room 4012."

"Who wants to go to the hospital?" Emmy asked.

Isabella squealed, "I do!"

Heather made a face. "Mom, you make it sound like we're going to Sainsbury's to go grocery shopping. We're going to see baby David. I hope they don't call him Theodore. That sounds like a name for an old person."

When Emmy and the girls arrived at room 4012, Tyler motioned for them to enter. "He's sleeping right now. Liz just fed him."

The girls approached slowly.

Liz smiled holding David in her arms. "You can look, but maybe you shouldn't hold him."

The twins moved close enough to see him.

Heather said, "He's so tiny, but Mommy said he's big."

203

Isabella looked at Emmy. "He doesn't look all red and wrinkled."

"Emmy, do you tell them all babies look like that?"

Emmy bit her lip for a second. "I might have mentioned something along that line. I told them some babies have a funny-shaped head, too."

"He looks normal," Heather said.

"Did we have lumpy heads?" Isabella asked.

"I don't remember," Emmy said. "I was kinda out of it after you were born."

"I've heard some stories about that day," Liz said. She glanced at the twins. "It was an exciting day."

"That's for sure," Emmy said. She stood behind the girls and smiled at David. "He looks just like Tyler."

"Does he really, Mommy?" Isabella asked.

"No, but I like to say that to fathers."

"Since this pregnancy was easier than the others, I told Tyler I want two more babies," Liz said while grinning at Tyler.

Emmy looked at him, too. "What was his reaction? I bet I know."

Liz rolled her eyes. "He groaned and shook his head."


"Thanks for taking us to the airport," Kenny said when they arrived at O'Hare Saturday morning.

"My pleasure," Tony said. "Now I can use your pool and raid the fridge without hearing anything from the brat."

"Uncle Tony, you promised you would stop calling Mommy a brat," Isabella said.

Tony lifted her and held her in front of him. "I'm sorry. I forgot, but I call her that with affection."

"We're going to stay in a castle, Uncle Tony," Kevin said. "I'm going to shoot arrows at anyone who tries to invade."

"I'm going to look for leprechauns," Heather said. "I'm going to steal their pot of gold."

Tony set Isabella down and ruffled Kevin's hair. "Try not to hurt anyone." He helped Kenny unload the van.

"I left some lasagna in the fridge," Emmy said. "Make sure

you eat it and don't forget the mail. Are you still willing to pick us up?"

"I have your itinerary on my computer," Tony answered.

"Two weeks from today at six o'clock."

"In the morning?"

"No, you creep. In the evening. I wouldn't make you pick us up that early."

"Have a safe trip and enjoy the scenery and don't spend all your time in..."

She smacked his arm. "We're not on our honeymoon."

"I was going to say don't spend all your time in a pub. Guinness is too strong for a weak drinker like you."

"I'll keep that in mind. Tell Mama I'll post some photos on Facebook. She can have Sloane show them to her."

"Mama, do you have time to look at Emmy's posts? She has some interesting photos," Sloane asked Sunday afternoon a week later.

"I can take a moment after I put this load in the washer," Mama said carrying a plastic tub. "And before you get on my case, these are my dirty clothes."

"I know you are still doing laundry for the kids. Peter and Dotty will be old enough to do their own soon," Sloane said.

"I don't mind helping out. It makes me feel useful."

Sloane followed Mama into the laundry room. "You keep busy volunteering at St. Bart's, and you have your group at church. You are always finding ways to help people. You are just as busy as when you were younger."

"I'm only seventy-two, and I feel better than I have for years. I only wish I didn't have to take so many pills," Mama said with a smile. "I am so grateful I still have my mind. I feel so sorry for Emmy's mother. She's only two years older than me. She could live to be a hundred like her mother." Mama loaded the washer and followed Sloane to the kitchen.

Sloane set her laptop on the island and opened her Facebook account. "Emmy posted photos of everything they're doing. This is the airport in Dublin."

Ten minutes later Mama took a closer look at one of the photos. "They really stayed in this place on their honeymoon?"

"That's what she says. It doesn't look anything like I imagined. I pictured some Tudor-styled house in the country, but this is right in town," Sloane said.

"Do you and Kristen post as many photos of the kids on your Facebook accounts?" Mama asked.

Sloane shook her head. "Probably not."

"I would be worried about their privacy. I don't think it's good for anyone to be able to see these photos."

"I don't think just anyone can see these. Emmy probably uses the privacy setting." Sloane explained some of the security settings to her mother-in-law.

"I still wouldn't post too many pictures."


"Mom, you don't have to come with us to school," Carson Garrett said. "Brady knows where to drop me off, and you have to stay here with Lily and Conor."

"Okay, but I want to hear about your first day of high school when you get home," Diane said as she held his shoulders. *I can't believe I have one child in high school and my youngest isn't even in preschool yet.*

Caden looked up at his older brother. "Will you take me to a football game?"

"I guess so, but I didn't think you liked football," Carson answered.

"I like to hear the band play," Caden said.

Carson stared at his brother for a moment and then pushed him on the shoulder. "You want to check out the girls."

"Do not," Caden insisted but his face turned red.

"Are we ready?" Brady Robertson asked. "I remember my first day of high school like it was yesterday."

Diane laughed.

"Okay, maybe like it was only a few decades ago." He kissed Diane and adjusted his tie. "Does this go with this shirt?"

Diane readjusted the tie. "You look like an investment banker for SoHam National."

206

"Has Bennett said anything about us choosing St. Raymond's for Carson?" Brady asked.

Bennett Robertson served as the headmaster for The Barclay Academy: a prestigious private school located closer to Bristol Ridge than the older Catholic school.

"He hasn't said anything, but Marissa made a snide remark about St. Raymond's not having up-to-date facilities."

"Should I go on out to the car so you can talk?" Carson asked.

"No, this concerns you," Diane said. "If you don't like St. Raymond's, we could always send you to Roosevelt High. That's where I went."

"My father attended Roosevelt, too," Brady mentioned.

"Aunt Emmy went there and so did both of our parents, but I don't think either of them graduated," Diane said.

"I think I will like St. Raymond's. At least I don't know any of the teachers or the principal," Carson said.


Sloane walked outside, stood on the deck and watched Tony and the boys tossing a football around. She waved and got his attention.

Tony tossed the ball to Peter and pointed. "I need to see what your mother needs." He walked to the deck and looked up. "Ben is getting pretty good at catching the ball."

"I noticed and Coby is better than Taylor and he's bigger than most seven-year-old boys," Sloane said. She waved to the four boys and shook her head as Ben and Coby tackled Peter. "Peter might be bigger than most thirteen-year-old boys, but he's not very physical."

"What's up?"

"You told me to remind you about the airport. Emmy will not be pleased if they have to wait for you."

"If it was just Emmy, I would make her wait, but I should get there early for Kenny and the kids." He turned just in time to catch the football. "Nice pass, Ben, but you shouldn't throw it at anyone who's not looking."

"Sorry, Dad. I was trying to throw it to Mom," Ben said.

207

An hour later Tony leaned against a column in O'Hare's International Terminal. He checked the arrival board again and glanced at his watch. He was about ready to walk to the other exit when he heard a familiar voice.

"Uncle Tony," Kevin Michael yelled. "I want to live in a castle when I get older."

Tony smiled and watched Kenny pushing a cart loaded with luggage. Kevin, Heather and Isabella rushed through the crowd to join Tony.

"I want to hear all about your trip," Tony said. He waited until Emmy was close enough to hear and asked, "Did your mother and father have fun?"

Emmy made a face and tried to smack Tony, but he moved. "We did a lot of sightseeing this time."

"Sloane showed me some photos." Tony took over pushing the cart.

Ten minutes later Tony looked into the rearview mirror and asked, "What did you like best about Ireland?"

The kids shouted answers simultaneously.

"I liked the peace and quiet of Ireland, but we did spend several days in London," Emmy said.

"I want to live in King Henry's castle," Kevin said.

The girls rolled their eyes.

"He forgot all about bugs," Kenny whispered. "Now he wants to be a knight and go on a Crusade."


Emmy checked on the kids Monday morning and found them still sleeping. She began singing in the girls' room.

Isabella finally opened her eyes. "Mommy, do you have to sing that baby song? What time is it?"

"It's time for you to wake up and get ready for school. This is your first day of fifth grade, and Mrs. Patton will not want you to be late," Emmy said. She sat on the edge of Isabella's bed and spotted Doll Kitty on top of the dresser. I remember when you wouldn't sleep without Doll Kitty beside you.

Kevin Michael walked into the room rubbing his eyes. "Mom, do I have to go to school? I'm still sleepy from jet logging."

"Get out of our room!" Heather yelled. "Go away! Boys are not allowed in here."

Emmy hugged Kevin. "Yes, you have to go to school, and it's jet lag. It has nothing to do with logs."

"Is Mrs. Payne going to be my teacher?" he asked.

"Yes, and you will like her. Your sisters were in her class, and they loved her."

Isabella sat up and said, "She's not scary like some black people I know."

Emmy took a deep breath. "I never said Pastor Williams was scary. He looks intimidating is all I said."

"Do we know Mrs. Patton?" Heather asked getting out of bed. "Is she Faith's mother?"

"Yes, and I think Faith will be in your class." Emmy shrugged and said, "Maybe, I don't know for sure."

"Why can't we wear normal clothes to school?" Heather asked. "Ian made fun of me because I have to wear that stupid uniform."

"It's not a stupid uniform, and we do not use that word in this house," Emmy said. "Kevin Michael, come with me. You need a shower, and the girls need to get dressed."

He looked at his sisters, grinned and said, "Are they going to wear their train bras?"

Heather threw a pillow at him and yelled, "They are not train bras, you creep! Mom! Make him go away."

"How do you know about training bras?" Emmy asked.

"Ben makes fun of Dotty because she has to wear one," Kevin admitted.

"You go swimming with your sisters all the time. You've never made fun of their swimsuits before."

Kevin shrugged and said, "I didn't think about that. It's just fun to tease them."

"Brothers are absolutely horrid," Heather said.

"I am not!" Kevin replied and looked at his mother. "What does that mean?"

"It means I love you very much. Now scoot and take a shower. Do you need help?"

209

"Mom! I don't need your help to take a shower anymore. I'm big enough to do it myself."

"You don't need to be shy," Emmy said. "I changed your diapers, remember?"

Heather and Isabella laughed.

Kevin turned red. "Mom! I don't wear diapers. I'm a big kid now."

"Yes, you are. Get ready. I need to talk to your sisters."

Kevin made a face at his sisters before running out of their room. He raced to his bedroom, which was next to the twins' room.

Emmy looked at the girls and whispered, "Don't let his teasing bother you. He doesn't really understand why you need to wear bras now."

"Mom! We need to wear them because Dotty told us we do," Heather said. "We don't want other girls in our class to make fun of us."

"When I was your age, I didn't need to wear one, either. I think I might have been in sixth or seventh grade before I started wearing one."

"Mom, please don't tell us when you started your period."

Emmy stared at Heather without speaking.

"Oh, Mommy, we hear you complaining when you get yours," Isabella said.

"I'm going to get dressed. I'll meet you downstairs. Don't take too long to get ready." Emmy left and headed back to her bedroom.

"Are the kids awake?" Kenny asked.

"Yes, and your son is teasing his sisters about training bras."

"My son?"

"Yes, and do I complain when I get my period? I know I'm not real regular, and I did get my tubes tied. I don't know if that makes them worse or not, but the girls know about getting your period. How can this be happening? They are still babies."

Kenny scratched his ear, shrugged and said, "I don't suppose locking them in the closet is an option, huh?"

210

# Chapter Twenty-Six

"Where should I put this?" Tony asked as he walked into the kitchen late Monday morning.

"What is it?" Emmy asked. She pulled a second pan of cheesy potatoes from the oven, inspected them and then placed them on top of the stove. She turned to face Tony.

He looked at her and laughed. "Did you puke on your shirt?"

"Stop it! I've been working all morning, and I spilled sauce on my shirt."

"This is Mama's potato salad. She said you requested it," Tony said.

"I did because hers is so much better than mine. Why didn't you put it in the fridge in the garage?"

"Duh! Because it's full of beverages."

"You can put it in this fridge if there's room."

Tony set the large bowl on the island and opened the wide stainless steel fridge. "Is this new?" He moved a container of leftovers and made room for the potato salad.

"The compressor or something broke on the old one. Nothing lasts like it should." She opened the oven and checked the baked beans. "Five more minutes."

"Five more minutes what? Who are you talking to?"

"The baked beans need five more minutes," she said wiping some sweat from her forehead.

"You talk to the beans, huh?"

"Shut up, you creep. Are you letting the kids come over early to swim?"

"Do you mind?"

Emmy shrugged and answered, "What's a few more? There are going to be about twenty kids here and about that many adults. Maybe more. Will you and John keep an eye on the pool?"

"Sure. Can I throw you in the water?"

"I might let you if the humidity gets any worse. I don't remember a Labor Day in the nineties." Emmy fanned her face with a hand and pushed some of her wet hair away from her face.

"I heard Ben is becoming quite the jock."

"He's taken an interest in football," Tony said picking up an apple from the wicker basket on the island. "Next year he might start playing organized ball. He's got a strong arm."

"Did you start playing so young?"

"I was younger," Tony said. "I better get back. I'll bring the kids soon. Do you need any extra tables? Mama told me to ask."

"We might need an extra one for the food. Could you bring that white plastic one you stole from the church, please?"

"I did not steal it from the church. They bought new ones when the new sanctuary was finished and sold some of the older ones. I paid twenty bucks for it."

"Yeah. Whatever. I think we have enough picnic tables."

"Do you even know how many tables you have scattered around the estate?" Tony asked with emphasis on estate.

"I've never counted them. The Quezada brothers keep building more for Kenny. I had Alberto and Luis move some of them from the woods up closer to the deck."

"Alberto told me he hired another crew. I guess the business is doing all right."

Emmy grinned at Tony.

He rolled his eyes. "Go ahead. Make fun of the name."

"Maybe they should change it," Emmy said.

"To what?"

Emmy put a finger to her mouth then said, "Three Bears Landscaping. Like in Goldilocks."

"You're a real riot, brat. Two Bears Landscaping has developed into a recognizable and trusted brand identity."

"Yeah, thanks to the hard work of the Quezadas. You and John didn't have a clue when you started it. All you knew how to do was mow yards and rake leaves."

Tony turned and walked away. "Leaving now. We'll be back later, and you are definitely getting tossed in the pool at some point."

"Talk is cheap," Emmy said. But I'll probably wear a bikini under my clothes just in case."

212

"Emmy, are you ready for us to start grilling?" Kenny asked thirty minutes later.

"I think everyone is here other than Derrick and Amber. I still haven't heard from them." She looked out the kitchen window and saw the kids running around the pool. "Yeah, go ahead and get started. I'll ask Kristen about Derrick."

"I'll let Andy know we're good to go," Kenny said. He took a platter of meat from the fridge and headed outside.

Kristen walked into the kitchen and sat at the island. "Do you need any help?"

"No, everything is done, and Peter and Carson are carrying the food outside," Emmy answered. "Oh, I haven't heard from Derrick or Amber. Do you know if they're coming?"

"They aren't coming. They're in Phoenix right now. I thought I told you already," Kristen said.

"If you did, I forgot. Why are they in Arizona? Isn't it hot down there?"

"Amber's parents aren't doing too well. They have Parkinson's. I think she needed to see them."

"That sucks. I should pray for them," Emmy said. She pulled the potato salad out of the fridge.

"Are you taking classes this semester?" Kristen asked. "I talked to Randy Braun last Sunday. He is going to be a full professor soon."

Emmy hesitated but then answered, "I liked the classes I took last semester, but I've kinda lost interest. I'm not sure I could ever be a teacher, and that's the only reason I was taking classes."

"Anything else, Aunt Emmy?" Carson asked as he dashed into the room.

Emmy handed him the potato salad. "That's everything."

"I don't blame you, Em. I could never be a teacher. I don't have enough patience to deal with Zach and Grace at times. I could never teach other children," Kristen said.

Emmy and Kristen followed Carson outside. Emmy walked up to Kenny and Andy. She put her hands around Kenny's waist.

"This is the last of the chicken breasts, Em," Kenny said. "Everything else is on the table."

213

"If you help Tony and John corral the kids, I'll ask Pastor Paul to pray and we can eat."

Fifteen minutes later Emmy sat next to Lynette Jefferson. "I can't believe how grown up your girls are."

"Heather and Isabella are growing up fast, too. They were babies when we moved to Iowa."

"I need to talk to you later if you can stay," Emmy whispered.

Lynette smiled.

Emmy shook her head. "I'm not having men trouble like the old days. I want to ask about female stuff. The girls are... you know."

"I understand. We'll talk later. This is good potato salad. Did you make it?"

"Mama Bertucci made it. Do you remember when I asked for your recipe?"

Lynette shrugged and answered, "Not really."

"Doesn't matter."

"Mom, can we go swimming if we're done eating?" Kevin asked. He held out his plate to prove he had eaten everything.

"You need to wait thirty minutes," Emmy said. Kevin dashed away and Emmy turned to Lynette. "I have become my mother in too many ways."

"It happens to all of us," Lynette said and then laughed.

After putting the leftovers away and cleaning the kitchen Emmy and Lynette sat on the deck and watched the kids playing in the pool.

"What did you want to ask?" Lynette said.

Emmy glanced around to make sure no one could hear. "Okay, the girls will be eleven in January. They want to wear training bras even though they don't need to."

Lynette chuckled and said, "My girls were the same way. Some of their friends started wearing them, so Ruth and Esther wanted them, too."

Emmy bit her lip for a second and then asked, "How did you handle it when they started their periods? How old were they?"

214

"Let's see," Lynette said and thought about it. "I'm pretty sure they had just turned twelve, and they both started within a few days of each other."

"Twelve!" Emmy groaned. "I'm not ready for that."

"It's gonna happen, so you might as well resign yourself to it. I talked to them beforehand, so they knew it would happen. They had some older friends who talked about it."

"I talked to them a while back, and found out they know more than I suspected. They certainly know more at their age than I did. I was clueless at ten," Emmy admitted. "I caught Heather kissing a boy, so I figured I needed to talk to them. They took a health class at school, so they know the basics."

"My girls are homeschooled, so I was able to deal with the birds and the bees when they were ready," Lynette said.

"Kevin Michael teases them about stuff, but he has no idea why he does it. He hears other boys doing it and thinks it's cool."

Lynette smiled and said, "It's nice to talk to you about things the way we did years ago."

"I'm so glad you guys moved back to SoHam," Emmy said. "How are things at church?"

"Better. It took a while, but the finances are in better shape. The attendance is climbing. We're never going to be too large. We don't have the facilities, and there's no money in the budget for expanding. Paul keeps busy. He needs a secretary."

"Some people are more comfortable in a smaller church."

An hour after the guests left, the skies darkened, the wind blew and the rain started.

"Kenny, do you think we should move the tables off the deck?" Emmy asked.

He looked outside. "I don't think the wind is strong enough to blow them away."

"I was more concerned about them blowing against the house. They might break the windows."

"They would have to smash the railing and the benches to reach the house. I would worry more about some of the big trees getting blown down."

"Is that hail?" Emmy asked.

215

They looked through the family room windows and saw hailstones collecting on the deck.

"I remember running out in a storm at Tony's house and grabbing a bunch of them."

"That was at your birthday party. I remember you telling me about it. You ran outside and got soaked and Mama got on your case. I would have liked to see that."

"I could go outside now," she said.

"You could, but it wouldn't be too wise. The wind is picking up."

They watched the storm for several minutes. Then it passed through the area.

"Should we check for damage?" Emmy asked.

"We could go for a walk. Should we take the kids?" Kenny asked.

"No, I'll tell them to stay here. We won't be gone long."

They walked through Bristol Ridge but didn't see anything more than a few downed tree limbs.

"Mom, can I go play in the woods with Ben and Taylor?" Kevin asked the next day after school. "We want to see if the wind blew down any trees. We can play on them."

"Okay, but be careful. I don't want you to get hurt."

"We won't," he answered. "Come on, guys! We can play and make a new fort."

Emmy watched the boys scamper into the woods, walked into the family room and saw Kenny playing one of his acoustic guitars. "Is that a new song?"

"Yeah, I've been working on it. What do you think?" He sang the first verse.

"Not bad. It's better than some of those other songs you guys were working on."

"Some of them were pretty weak, huh?"

"You could say that. Are you ready to get back to work?" she asked.

"We're meeting at ten in the morning. I'm ready to start recording again."

She sat on the couch beside him. "I know you get bored if you aren't doing something, but it's been nice to have you home. I kinda miss you when you're touring."

He set the guitar down, grinned and tried to pull her closer.

"I don't miss you that much," she said with a sparkle in her eyes.

"I'm going to take the kids to school and then head to the studio," Kenny said the next morning. "I want to run through a few ideas with Will and Stuart."

"Will you be home for dinner?" Emmy asked. "We've got leftovers from the party."

"Tony didn't eat them?" Kenny asked.

"He wanted to take some home, but Sloane wouldn't let him. She said we should be allowed to eat them."

"He did eat two steaks."

"He's cut back. He used to eat three large steaks and never gain any weight."

"He can't do that now, or else he would... Never mind."

Emmy grinned. "You were going to say he would get as heavy as Sloane, weren't you?"

"Yeah, but I shouldn't say anything. You might gain a pound or two one of these years," he teased.

"I'm a few pounds heavier than when we got married, and my hips are wider."

"You still look pretty sexy to me," he said.

"Remind me tonight after the kids are in bed. I might show you how sexy I can be."

"Great! How am I supposed to concentrate on recording if I'm thinking about that?" he asked.

"Should I send some sexy photos to your phone?"

"Better not. The guys might decide to steal my phone. I should be home for dinner. Whatever you make is fine."

"Fried bologna it is," she teased.

Just before noon Klaus Kesson stopped by Studio Four. He listened to the band for a few minutes. When they took a break he asked, "How are things going? Do you have a time frame in mind for finishing this project? I would like to release a new Fridays At Five project before the end of the year. The company could use a boost to the bottom line."

Kenny nudged Jeff. "Mr. Kesson would never think of asking that."

Jeff shook his head and said, "I have a feeling things are going to be different around here now."

Since none of the other guys answered Klaus, Dave did. "We've got six tracks ready, and I think we can make good progress on another four or five. I can't guarantee it, but we might finish soon."

"All right!" Klaus said. "I'll let you guys get back to work. I have a meeting in Hollywood tomorrow. I'm taking the family out there for a vacation. We probably won't be back until December."

Jeff whispered, "That's great. Take all the time you need."


Kristen heard her cell phone, saw it was Derrick calling and answered, "Are you guys home now? How are Amber's parents doing?"

"We got home yesterday. They're doing better, but that's relative. They aren't going to improve."

"I'm sorry to hear that. I've only seen them a few times, but they are nice," Kristen said.

"I have some news, and I don't know how you will react," he said.

"Tell me. I won't get upset."

"We are selling the house and moving to Phoenix."

"No! You can't move away," she said. "I will... I mean the kids will miss you. You're the only real uncle they ever see. Amber's brother never leaves South Africa anymore."

"I'm afraid it's a done deal, Kristen. Amber needs to be closer to her parents."

"What about your law practice? What about Amber's? Will you start over in Phoenix?"

"I am taking a position with a Phoenix firm. I'll actually be making more money. Enough to let Amber stop working. At least while her parents are alive," he said.

"Shoot! This sucks. Did you tell Mom and Dad?"

"I told them yesterday."

"Did you already put the house on the market? Maybe you could keep it and buy a townhouse in Phoenix. You need a place to stay when you visit SoHam."

"We thought about that, but neither of us want to deal with renting it."

"But it's home."

"Krissy, you haven't lived there since you got married. How long ago was that?"

"2004," she answered. "I suppose I'll get over it, but maybe it won't sell."

Derrick laughed then asked, "Are you and Emmy planning to sabotage the house? Are you going to blow it up or something?"

"Probably not, but I can't guarantee she won't try something."

"It won't sell overnight, but Amber is heading back to Phoenix this weekend. Oh, if there's any furniture you want, come and get it. We're not taking it to Phoenix, and I don't want to put it in storage."

"I can't think of anything. Mom took the dining room table already." Kristen thought about the house where she and Derrick grew up. "I don't suppose you would consider selling it to us for a mere pittance? We could let Zach live there when he gets married."

"Zach is ten. He won't be getting married for a couple of years," Derrick teased.

"Yeah, it will take some time for me to adjust to someone else living there."

"If you talk to Emmy, make sure you tell her the news."

"I will. She won't be happy you guys are moving even though we seldom see you."

# Chapter Twenty-Seven

"What are you doing out here?" Diane asked as she walked up the steps to the deck at Emmy's house Saturday afternoon. "I rang the bell and waited, but no one answered. Where is everyone?"

"Kenny dropped the girls at his parents, and he and Kevin Michael went to a football game with Tony and Ben. I'm sitting out here because I like the fall colors. I didn't hear your car."

Diane smiled and said, "I walked over here. Are you surprised?"

"Yeah. What's up?" Emmy asked.

"I want to start exercising. I need to lose a few pounds," Diane answered. "Some of us are not the same size as when we were twelve."

"Oh, hush. You still look good, and I have gained some weight, too."

"How many ounces?"

"Have you talked to Mom lately? Or gone to see her?"

"I was there yesterday. She's not getting any better, Em. I wouldn't recommend taking the kids anymore. Any change in her routine upsets her."

"I feel guilty because I seldom see her. I never call her anymore."

"Don't feel guilty. She doesn't answer the phone, and she can't remember what she was doing ten minutes ago. You could visit every hour and she wouldn't remember."

"Do you ever worry about that happening to us when we get old?" Emmy asked.

Diane shook her head. "I've got too many things on my mind to worry about what might happen years from now. Oh, before I forget, Mackenna had the baby last night."

"I didn't know. Did they name her what they were planning? You told me the name but I forgot it. I know you said their mothers didn't like the name."

"Whitley Marie," Diane said with a grin. "Marissa and Crystal were furious, but Spencer and Mackenna didn't care."

"Who's Crystal?' Emmy asked.

"Mackenna's mother. She has been staying in SoHam, but she lives somewhere in Pennsylvania. She's about as bad as Marissa. They try to control everything."

"You should try to get along with her. She is your sister-in-law," Emmy said.

"Only by marriage."

"What does that mean? Do you know something?" Emmy asked with renewed interest.

Diane waved a hand. "Nothing like that. Bennett would never divorce Marissa. She would take everything he owns and suck him dry."

"Did I tell you Dave from the band is separated?"

"You might have. That's a shame." Diane listened to some geese flying overhead. "Is there a lake close?"

Emmy pointed north. "There's a retention pond in that subdivision past Bristol Ridge. That's the closest one I know about."

"That's not real close."

"I think there might be a small pond at the back of one of the houses on Bristol Parkway. Kenny knows because he uses the trails to go mountain biking."

Diane stared at Emmy and asked, "You look worried about something. What's going on?"

Emmy waited a few seconds then answered, "I told you Heather kissed that boy, right?"

"Yeah, but I thought he kissed her."

"Whatever! They kissed, and she's too young."

"For crying out loud, Em. She was just curious. That doesn't mean anything."

"It must mean something," Emmy insisted.

"Are you worried she will turn out like me?" Diane asked.

Emmy frowned and crossed her arms over her chest.

"You don't have to worry about that. She is smarter than me."

Emmy rolled her eyes. "You're smart. You just didn't like to say no."

"Lily will grow up one of these days," Diane said.

Emmy snorted and said, "She's four. You have a little time. The twins are almost eleven! They will be wanting to date before I know it."

"You're right, Em. They will be bringing boys home to spend the night in a few weeks. You might be a grandmother before you turn... How old are you? Eighteen?"

Emmy made a face. "You are so funny. At least they can't sneak out of their bedroom windows like I did."

Diane looked over her shoulder at the large house and asked, "Do they still like sharing a room? What will you do if they want separate bedrooms?"

"We will move Kevin across the hall and the girls can have their own rooms. We might do that pretty soon. We aren't using the nanny suite at all, but I still have to clean it."

Diane rolled her eyes and sighed. "You can hire a maid. You still act like you're as poor as Mom and Dad."

"They could have lived a better life if Daddy hadn't spent so much money at Miller's Bar."

"Did you hear it burned down?"

"No! When?"

"A couple months ago. Arson, I think."

"Too bad that didn't happen forty years ago," Emmy said.

"Hah! It wouldn't have mattered. Dad would have found a different bar. There used to be a dozen of them within walking distance from Fifth Street."

They heard a car pull up and park by the garage.

"You expecting company?" Diane asked.

"Father James is coming for dinner. That's probably him. He likes to eat early." Emmy went inside and brought him outside.

"Hello, Diane. It's good to see you."

"You, too, James. How have you been? Break anything lately?"

He looked at his arm and flexed it. "Not lately. One interesting thing about breaking my arm. I can now tell if it's going to rain. I feel it in my bones," he joked.

"Don't give up your day job," Emmy said.

"How are the kids?" he asked Diane. "I don't see them as often as I do Emmy's."

"Yeah, that's for sure. They're doing well. The older boys are getting taller. Lily and Conor get along good. She lets him play with her toys."

"Kenny will be home after the game," Emmy said. "I told the girls they could spend the night with Gra and Me-maw."

"That's all right. Is Kevin still collecting bugs?" Father James asked.

"Yeah. Thanks so much for getting him started with that."

Father James shrugged and said, "He was into critters before I suggested anything."

"Carson found a dead deer last week," Diane said. "He said it was gross."

"Where?" Emmy asked.

"Somewhere in the woods behind Tony's house. Peter and Ben were exploring. Carson said they walked all the way to the edge of Bristol Ridge. Did you know there's a wall separating us from whatever that part of town is called?"

"It's called Cumberland West. Did I tell you I had to help Kevin with a school project about SoHam? He had to fill in a map of the city and the towns around it."

Father James and Diane shrugged.

"Anyway, I learned a lot about the city."

"And I suppose you're gonna tell us everything you learned," Diane said.

"Aren't you interested in where we live?" Emmy asked.

"Not as much as you," Diane said.

"I'm interested," Father James said. "I'm not native to SoHam."

"I'm going home. I'll talk to you later, Em. Good to see you again, James," Diane said as she left.

"Still want to hear about SoHam?" Emmy asked.

"Sure, I could use a nap."

"Fine! I'm telling you anyway. According to the latest info, there are over two hundred thousand people in SoHam. It's the third largest city in the state. West Bartlett is bigger, but not by

223

much." She pointed to the north. "Past Bristol Ridge is Carney Woods. It's a fairly new development that extends all the way to the western branch of the Britton River. There's a golf course along the river."

"How interesting, Emily."

"Crest Ridge is to the west and SoHam butts up against New Linden to the east," she said.

"How special."

Emmy was determined not to let his disinterest deter her from her story.

"There isn't anything keeping SoHam from expanding to the south. It might even surround Crest Ridge one of these days. It already runs into Melrose Grove to the north. There used to be open land between the towns, but not anymore. Melrose Grove is where Robertson Industries is, or used to be."

Father James closed his eyes and pretended to snore.

"If you want dinner, you will listen to me."

"I'm listening, child. Pray continue."

"Stuff it! You don't care. Do you even know how many parishes are in SoHam and Crest Ridge?"

"No, but I'm sure you do."

"Too many! There are only two Nazarene churches in a city of over two hundred thousand. Ridiculous!"

"Are you planning to start a new one?"

"No, but... Oh, never mind. What do you want for dinner?"

"How about venison or something native to SoHam?"

"Morning, Pastor Tyler, is something wrong with David or Liz? You never call. You always text or send emails."

Tyler chuckled and answered, "Liz and the baby are fine. I was going to send an email, but Liz said I should talk to people more often."

Emmy walked into the family room and sat on the couch. "I'm guilty of texting too often now. I didn't use to be like that, but it's so much easier."

"I have a couple things on my mind. Darren and I met with Riordan. Oh, are you aware their new CD was released today?"

"I was not aware. Thanks for informing me," she said.

"I'm not rubbing it in, Emmy. I know you've been working on a new project."

"I'm not jealous or anything. I'll probably buy a copy, but I won't ask them to autograph it for me."

"If it makes you feel better, Liz wants another copy of *Gideon's Tree*. She wants to give it to one of the neighbors. Will you autograph one for Liz? She will pay you," Tyler said.

"I'll bring one to church, but she doesn't have to buy it."

"Emmy, you need to stop giving your books away. People should know you work hard to write them, and your time is worth something."

"Okay, she owes me a dollar," Emmy said. She moved onto her back, lifted her knees and stared at the ceiling. "Is David sleeping through the night yet?"

"He sleeps in four hour shifts."

"Do you ever wake up when he cries at night?"

Tyler smiled and said, "Nope! I would sleep through a tornado. Once I'm out, I'm out."

"Kenny is getting more like that. He used to be a light sleeper, and would wake up every time I bumped against him. I kinda move all over the bed," she explained.

"So I've heard. Anyway, Riordan popped into my office while I was talking with Darren. He and Sadie are going to be on tour for most of November. Would you be willing to lead worship? I would ask Regina, but she will be close to having the baby. We could pay you."

"Don't you even think of offering me money," Emmy said. "I'll sub for them. Do I have to choose the songs?"

"I can assist you. I usually give Riordan my themes a month in advance. Of course, sometimes my messages change at the last moment, but most of the time the songs are still applicable."

Emmy sat up. "I kinda miss leading worship, and I'll gladly help out. They aren't doing a concert in SoHam, are they?"

"I think most of the tour is in California and along the coast. Should we book them for a concert here? We could probably sell lots of tickets," Tyler said.

"Oh, stop it. You're teasing me."

After dinner a week later Emmy checked her email, saw a message from Jeremiah Tolla, read it and rolled her eyes. She went downstairs, found Kenny in the control room of his studio. She tapped his shoulder. He turned around in his chair and smiled.

She motioned for him to remove the headphones and when he did, she said, "I got an email from Pastor Jeremiah. Would you like to know what it said?"

"Sure," he answered.

She kicked his chair, folded her arms across her chest and said, "He and Mia had a baby boy yesterday."

"Really? How are they doing?"

"Fine, according to Jeremiah," Emmy answered while scowling.

"What did they name him?" Kenny asked while scooting his chair away from Emmy.

"Jackson Mark Tolla."

Kenny rubbed his chin and then tugged on his ear. He lowered his face, shrugged and looked up at Emmy. "I have a sneaking suspicion I might have forgotten to tell you she was expecting. Am I correct?"

"Yes, you dork! How could you forget to tell me? Are there any other expectant mothers I should know about?"

He sucked in his breath through clenched teeth. "I can't think of anyone. Am I in deep trouble?"

"I'll think about it," she said turning around and walking away.

"Sorry, Em. I'll try to do better next time."

"You know I love babies to death," she said over her shoulder.

# Chapter Twenty-Eight

"Tony, would you have time to talk after the service," Pastor Tyler asked in the hallway after Sunday School. "I need to ask something. It won't take too long."

"Sure, should I wait in the foyer, or should I meet you in your office?" Tony asked.

"We could meet in the Coffee Corner after the crowd thins out. I would ask you now, but I need to go over the order of service with Darren. There's been a slight change."

"No problem. Sloane can take the kids home, and I could catch a ride from Emmy or Kristen."

"See you later," Tyler said and hurried down the hall.

Emmy tapped Tony's arm and asked, "What did Pastor Tyler need? Are you in trouble?"

Tony shrugged and answered, "Not that I know of, but he needs to talk to me about something. Can you give me a ride home?"

"I suppose, but it will cost you."

"How much? Where's Kenny?"

"Oh, he came to the early service. He's taking the kids to a birthday party for one of the kids of one of the guys on the road crew," Emmy said waving her hands around.

"Yeah, I totally understood that," Tony said and then shook his head.

"Let me think about it, and I'll get back to you. Save me a seat. I need to talk to Kristen about her brother," Emmy made brother sound vulgar.

"I'll save you a seat, but you have to sit in the back," Tony said, but Emmy didn't hear.

Emmy scurried through the crowd and hollered, "Krissy! Stop, Krissy! I need to talk to you."

Kristen stopped and turned around.

"Excuse me, Mrs. Perez," Emmy said. "I didn't mean to bump into you."

"It's all right. Are you singing today, dear?" the older lady asked.

"No, my team sang last week," Emmy answered.

"I missed it. My son had to work, and I couldn't get a ride," Mrs. Perez said. "I can't drive anymore because my eyes don't work as good as they once did."

Emmy waved at Kristen to wait. "I'm sorry, Mrs. Perez. We should do something about that. I really need to run."

"I understand. I hope I can be here the next time you sing. You have such a lovely voice."

"Thank you," Emmy said and hurried away.

"What's on your mind, Em? Is it about Derrick?" Kristen asked.

"Yes, but we can talk while we walk."

They moved along with the crowd, walked downstairs and out of the educational building into the large foyer of the new sanctuary.

"It's a good thing they designed the new building to have access to the old foyer. That way we don't have to go outside," Emmy said and pointed. "It's pouring."

"It's still a long walk from our class. I'm glad they don't ring a bell like in school," Kristen said.

Emmy grinned. "Yeah, we would get busted for being in the hallway after class started."

"Are you busy the last Saturday this month? I think that's the only day everyone will be free for a going-away party."

Emmy shrugged as they flowed with the crowd. "I can't think of anything, but I'll check my calendar later."

"It won't be a big deal, but I want to have some friends over to say goodbye."

"I can't believe they're really moving away. I will miss them even though we hardly ever get together."

Forty minutes after the second service ended Pastor Tyler walked toward Tony and Emmy. "I apologize for taking so long, but I like to greet people."

"It's all right. We weren't planning to watch the Bears," Emmy said. "They suck this year. They've only won one game so far. Should I wait outside?" Emmy asked Tony.

"Actually, Emmy. I could talk to you, too."

Tony grinned at Emmy. "I guess you're in trouble, too."

She nudged his arm. "Hush, I didn't do anything."

"Let's sit at that table." Tyler chuckled and led the way.

Tony and Emmy sat across from him at one of the tall, round tables.

"That was a good message," Tony said.

Emmy grinned and asked, "Did Andy ask a bunch of questions? He was asking me about the passage in Romans you used last week."

"He often asks good questions," Tyler said and smiled at Emmy. "I appreciate that. It means he's listening."

"I listen," Emmy protested.

"I'm not implying you don't," Tyler said. "Okay, I'll get right to the point. Church elections will be coming up, and the church board is looking for some new people to serve. Fresh blood and new ideas. I met briefly with the nominating committee to come up with suggestions of people with leadership skills."

"And you came up with him?" Emmy jerked her thumb toward Tony.

"Actually, your name came up, too, Emmy."

Tony laughed.

Emmy stared at Tyler with shock. "Me? Are you kidding? I don't know anything about church business."

Tony nodded. "True. She is clueless."

"Am not!" Emmy insisted.

"Immature," Tony said.

"You can walk home," she replied.

"I think you would both be excellent choices to serve in leadership roles. The committee will meet in early November to finalize the nominations. I wanted you to have time to think about this. You don't need to decide until later, but I'm almost certain you will be nominated to serve in some capacity."

"This is quite unexpected, Pastor Tyler," Tony said. He looked at Emmy. "I know I will do some serious thinking and praying about this."

Emmy frowned at him, but didn't say anything.

"All right. I'll talk to you later. I hope the Bears win unless they're playing the Lions. I'm still hoping the Lions make it to a Super Bowl in my lifetime," Tyler said as he stood up.

"Good luck with that," Emmy teased. She waited until Tyler was walking away and poked Tony's arm. "Why would anyone think I could be a church leader, and why did you call me immature?"

"You have grown up a little," Tony said.

Emmy stood up and pulled her keys from her purse. "You're only saying that so I will take you home. You wanna drive? I brought Kenny's Acura."

"Sure. All I ever get to drive is a minivan," Tony said.

They walked to the exit.

"Should we wait a minute?" Emmy asked. "It's still raining."

"Are you afraid of getting wet, Em?" Tony asked. "Where did you park?"

"Over there. About five rows back," she answered while pointing.

"I could bring the car up for you," Tony said.

"Really? You would do that for me."

He shook his head, laughed and said, "No way, brat. If I have to get soaked, so do you."

"Why do I even like you? Come on! I won't melt and neither will you."

They ran to the car. Emmy shrieked as she landed in a puddle.

"How do I open the door?" Tony asked while standing by the driver's door.

"Just put your hand in the door handle. There's a sensor, you creep," she shouted. "Hurry up! I'm getting soaked."

Tony grinned and opened the door. Emmy jumped in and smacked his arm. Tony pushed the button to start the car.

"Are you sure you can handle this? It's more powerful than your old Sienna."

"It still smells like a new car. Doesn't Kenny ever drive it?" he asked.

"Not as much as he thought he would. He's been riding

230

with Andy to the studio. Andy bought a Subaru Outback and gave his old Envoy to that charity that finds cars for people who can't afford one."

Tony revved the car a few times. "Sounds pretty smooth."

"It's a six-cylinder engine, and it's faster than my Civic."

"I'll take it easy," Tony said. He slammed the transmission into drive and mashed the accelerator pedal to the floor.

Emmy held onto the seat bolsters. "You're paying for the ticket if you get pulled over."

"I just wanted to test the traction. It does all right on wet streets," he said while slowing down to a reasonable speed. "What should I tell Pastor Tyler? I've never thought about being on the church board."

"I wouldn't worry about it. The committee will regain their senses and realize it would be a huge mistake to nominate you," she said.

"You're a real riot, brat. What will you do if they nominate you?"

"I would be willing to serve on some minor committee, but certainly not on the church board. You were right about one thing. I would be clueless in that situation."

Tony stopped for a red light. "It's not the time commitment that would bother me."

"What then?"

"Beer."

"What about it?" she asked and pointed. "I'm pretty sure that's as green as..."

"I see it," he roared through the intersection. "Would I have to give up all forms of alcohol?"

"Yes, and you would have to stop taking drugs. No more heroin or cocaine," she teased.

"I'm serious. Do you think anyone on the board drinks beer?"

She shrugged and said, "I'm not sure who all is on the board."

"I know John won't come to our church because of the alcohol thing," Tony said.

"I'm sure there are people in the church who have an occasional drink, but I understand the church's stand. I know there's scripture that says it's wrong to get drunk."

"I have always liked a beer or two, but I can honestly say I've never been drunk," he said and then looked at Emmy.

"I wasn't totally smashed that day with Kristen. I had a couple margaritas on an empty stomach. That's all, and I prayed for God to forgive me, and it's never happened again."

By the time they pulled into Tony's driveway, the rain had stopped.

"Thanks for the ride, and letting me drive Kenny's car," Tony said as he got out and Emmy switched places.

"Don't tell him I let you drive. He doesn't know I took his car."

"What's it worth to you?"

"I'll think of something," she answered. "Just between you and me, I think you would make a good board member."

"Really?" he asked waiting for a smart remark.

"I really do," she said nodding her head.

"Thanks, Em. I'll have to think about it."

"Of course, I'm clueless and immature so what do I know?" She laughed and drove away.

After lunch Tony told Sloane about Tyler's idea.

"How often does the board meet? I think the board back in my home church met every month or maybe more often. Can you fit that into your schedule?"

"I think so," he answered.

"I'm not sure. I think they usually meet on Monday nights. Would you be willing to give up Monday Night Football?"

"Yeah, I think so."

"You better do a lot of thinking about this," Sloane said. "If I had to give you my endorsement, I'm not sure I would. I want you home to help with the kids."

"Well, I don't have to decide right now, and I might not even get nominated. Pastor Tyler was just trying to see how I felt about it."

Near the end of the monthly board meeting the next evening, Pastor Tyler held up a piece of paper. "I don't think this will be a surprise to any of you, since Jake told the teens last Wednesday. He has officially resigned. Pastor Jonah and Mary have agreed to take over the teens on a temporary basis. Jake and Maddy are moving back to Ohio. Well, back for Jake. He has taken a position with Mount Vernon Nazarene University. This will allow him to be closer to his family. Let me read this because it goes into more detail."

"When are they leaving?" Lenore Toth asked after Tyler finished reading.

"Unfortunately, the last Sunday of this month will be their final one with us. Jake is already in Ohio, but he will be back for the last week. The teens will be in complete charge of both services that Sunday."

"Do we have anyone in mind to replace them?" Roger Goldman asked.

Tyler chuckled, smiled and held up another piece of paper. "I'm glad you asked. I mentioned Jake's resignation to Dr. Schofield a few days ago, and he told me about this couple. Daryl and Brenda Wiley. They are originally from the Indianapolis area, but have been serving in Kansas City for two years. They are both Olivet graduates. Daryl was two years ahead of me at Olivet, and Brenda is the same age as Liz. Liz and Brenda lived in Williams Hall for a year, and knew each other slightly. They have a son and a daughter. They come highly recommended and would be available to start at the beginning of January."

"We do need to interview them, right?" Carol Wisnewski asked. "Is this a position you could hire someone for without board approval?"

"I'm not sure, but I have made it a practice not to hire new staff without board approval." Tyler passed out copies of Daryl's resume. "You can read this on the resume, so I'm not sure why I'm telling you."

Dylan Michaelis quickly read the resume and said, "I'm in favor of bringing them in for an interview. They certainly have the experience." He glanced at the resume again. "I don't see anything about playing a guitar. Who would take over the teen musicians?"

"I haven't thought that far ahead, but we do have Riordan on staff. We could let him figure that out."

The members of Fridays At Five arrived at the studio Thursday morning at ten for another day of recording. They drank coffee and chatted for a moment.

"Before we get started, I need to tell you guys something," Dave Persching said. He glanced at the other band members, took a deep breath and said, "Macy has filed for divorce. I got served yesterday morning. I didn't want to mention it yesterday because I wanted to talk to Macy first."

"Crap! That sucks," Jeff said. He spilled some coffee on the carpet and swore.

"It's been coming for a few years. We did what we could for the kids. Counseling. Whatever." Dave shrugged. "I will not contest it, and last night we began sorting out the property stuff. We both agree we do not want this to be an instance where the lawyers drag it out and charge up a fortune."

Jeff looked at Kenny and shook his head. "I'm sorry it has to come to this, Dave. I know you guys have seen a counselor."

"We have, and it didn't resolve the issues," Dave said without elaborating.

"I really feel bad for the kids," Kenny said. "You have five beautiful children."

"Yes, and telling them was the hardest thing we've ever done. The older ones understand because they have friends whose parents have gone through divorces, but Madison doesn't know why I don't live at home. She's almost six now."

"You will be paying child support and probably alimony for the next dozen years or even longer," Jeff said. "Is it worth it? Can't you guys keep trying?"

"I'm not the one who filed, Jeff. If it was my decision, I would stay separated and see how it works out."

"So Macy wants it to be done, huh?" Adam asked.

"She wants to get on with her life. Without me," he added.

"I hate to even ask, but is there... you know?" Jeff asked.

234

"I'm not seeing anyone," Dave asserted. "I can't say one way or the other about Macy, and I'm not going to let that be a factor. I would be happy for her if she finds someone down the road."

"Should we push the recording back until this is all settled?" Kenny asked.

Dave shook his head. "I don't think this will affect the band. It might make things a little tricky for the wives, but I'm sure they will deal with it."

P.J. stood up and said, "We should consider ourselves fortunate because most bands, or other businesses, fare much worse. Three of the guys who were part of The Notable Exceptions have gone through nasty divorces. Calbert has been married three times."

Kenny patted Dave on the back. "We are here for you in whatever capacity you need. All married couples struggle at times. Emmy and I had a rough patch ourselves, but we survived."

"Will you be able to keep your Porsche?" Jeff asked.

Dave laughed and answered, "Yes. Macy has no interest in what she calls my old cars. She does want the house in California."

# Chapter Twenty-Nine

"I really appreciate you watching the kids tonight, Andrea," Emmy said. "I know it's a Saturday night and you probably had plans."

"It's all right, Emmy. I would have been spending the night at home," Andrea replied.

"We won't be out too late, and we'll be just across the road." Emmy showed Andrea a whiteboard by the kitchen desk. "Kristen's number is here, and so is my cell phone. If they give you any trouble, don't hesitate to call."

"Mom!" Heather whined. "We aren't going to do anything as long as Kevin leaves us alone. Can we stay up later tonight?"

"You have to be in bed at your regular time. Tomorrow is Sunday," Emmy answered. She turned to Andrea. "The lights need to be out by ten. That's giving them a little extra time."

"We will have fun," Andrea said.

"Emmy, should I wear a tie?" Kenny asked. He walked into the kitchen holding two ties. "And which one looks better?"

Emmy looked at Kenny, but then shifted her attention to Andrea and rolled her eyes. "He loves to be a dork."

"I think the red tie would look better, Mr. Colwell," Andrea said. "No one wears green ties anymore."

"Thank you, Andrea. I thought so, too."

"If no one else is wearing a tie, will you take it off?" Emmy asked.

"I think all the men will be dressed up," Kenny said.

"Wanna put some money on it?"

"What are you going to wear, Em?" he asked staring at her faded jeans. *Those are getting a bit tight in the derriere.*

"This is what you get," she used her hands for emphasis. "It's just an intimate party. It's not a formal ball."

"Are we driving?" Kenny asked.

"We should unless you plan on drinking."

Andrea turned to the kids and waved her hands. "Shoo! Run upstairs, and I will be there as soon as your parents leave."

The girls dashed away. Kevin hugged his mother and father

236

before following his sisters.

"We can take my car," Kenny said. "It might be a bit cool when we're ready to come home."

"Call us if you need," Emmy reminded Andrea.

They drove across the street and up John and Kristen's long driveway.

"Should we have gotten a card or a going-away gift?" Kenny asked.

"I have a card, and I signed our names," Emmy answered patting the pocket of her army jacket.

"I really wish you would burn that thing."

"Why? This is a new coat. I found it at Once Upon a Child."

"Did you really?" Kenny asked as he turned off the car and got out.

Emmy got out and closed the door. "No! I thought that would sound better than saying I got it at the Goodwill store. I took some of the girls' old clothes there and saw this for five bucks."

"Did you at least wash it first?"

"Yes, but it didn't smell funky."

"Thank heaven for small favors."

John opened the front door and offered to take their jackets.

"Thanks, John, but I want to wear mine for a while. It's nearly new and I want everyone to see it," Emmy said. She looked at John and grabbed his blue tie. "Why are you dressed up?"

John shrugged and answered, "All the guys are dressed up. Didn't Kristen tell you it was not super casual?"

"Crap! I feel underdressed now." She removed her jacket and handed it to John. She turned and saw Kenny grinning at her.

"Oh, wipe that stupid grin off your face. Did you know everyone was dressing up and didn't tell me just to embarrass me?"

"Maybe," he said keeping the grin. He stopped grinning and admitted, "No, but I like to wear a tie."

"Have fun sleeping on the couch tonight," she spat and walked into the living room. *Great! This is just great. Every lady here is either wearing a dress or something nicer than these jeans. At least I'm not wearing a t-shirt.*

Kristen walked up to Emmy. "Em, didn't you get my email?"

"Obviously not." She turned, walked back to Kenny and held out her hand. "Give me the keys. I'm going home to change."

Derrick walked up behind her, touched her shoulder and said, "Don't do that. I think you look comfortable which is more than I can say for everyone else. Amber made me wear a tie and a sport coat. I feel like I'm taking a deposition."

Emmy turned to face Derrick. "I would rather be dressed comfortably than wearing a dress like that lady. Who is she, anyway?"

Derrick glanced over his shoulder, saw who Emmy meant and whispered, "I take it you've never met Pavel and Shandra Ramel. They live next to Bennett's property and across the street from the Plants."

"I don't really know anyone from that part of Bristol Ridge. Did Kristen invite everyone who lives here?"

"Not everyone, but she knows the Ramels and invited them. They are both doctors."

"Are all the families out here doctors and big shots in business?" Emmy asked.

"They all have money," Derrick said. "Amber and I couldn't afford to live here."

Emmy took a deep breath. "I don't care. I'm wearing my jeans. If they don't like it, too bad."

"I like your jeans, Em," Derrick whispered. "They fit... never mind."

She grinned at him. "They are tight in the butt. Is that why you like them?"

"I better find Amber," Derrick said and walked away.

"Nice talk, Em," Kenny said. "Do you want the keys or not?"

She shook her head. "Nope! I'm sticking with my tight jeans." She walked up to the Ramels, who were now talking with Kristen and her mother.

Karla Keasling saw Emmy and checked her out. "Shandra, Pavel, have you met Kristen's friend?"

238

"I don't believe so," Shandra said, holding out a hand and introducing herself and her husband.

"Do you live in the area?" Shandra asked looking at Emmy's faded jeans.

Emmy hesitated. *Should I tell her the truth, or should I say I live in the Mayfield neighborhood where all the poor people live and I'm Kristen's cleaning lady? Shoot! I better not lie.* "Kenny and I live across the road."

Pavel's eyes lit up. "Are you married to our controversial, neighborhood rock star?"

*Rock star, my butt! And why do you think he's controversial? He's about as controversial as Dr. Ausland.* "That would be me," Emmy said. "I'm his..."

Kristen bumped Emmy's hip. "She and Kenny have been married for... How long has it been, Emily?"

"Forever and a day," Emmy answered.

"Would you excuse us, please?" Kristen asked. "I need to show Emily my new computer."

Emmy scowled as Kristen dragged her by the arm into the butler's pantry.

"What were you going to say to the Ramels? And why are you in such a pissy mood? Did you and Kenny have a fight? Are you trying to ruin the party?"

"No, we didn't have a fight and I'm not trying to ruin your party. It would have been nice for someone to tell me it wasn't super casual." She used air quotes.

"Is this a private party, or can anyone join?" Tony asked.

Emmy and Kristen turned to him and said, "Go away!"

He held up his hands in surrender. "My bad. Mama asked me to find a large platter."

Emmy reached out and grabbed Tony's arm. "Wait a second. Do you think these jeans are too tight and too faded?"

Tony looked down as Emmy turned in a circle. "Is this a trick question? Will I be in trouble no matter how I answer?"

"Yes," Kristen said.

"No," Emmy responded.

Tony looked back and forth at them, shrugged and said, "I

239

plead the fifth amendment, or ignorance, or whatever I need to plead not to get smacked by either one of you."

"Nice tie," Emmy said and then pushed him away. She turned to Kristen. "Why would I care... Oh, never mind. That was just an excuse. I don't care if your mother or your fancy friends think I'm dressed like one of the help. At least I'll be comfortable."

"If I had any help at the party, they would be in uniform," Kristen said.

"Crap!" Emmy said and looked at the floor. "I'm sorry for being in a foul mood. Should I run home and change? I do have nicer jeans."

"Are you feeling all right, Em?" Kristen asked.

"It's not that time if that's what you're asking. I guess I'm kinda upset because Derrick and Amber are moving so far away."

"I am not exactly thrilled about it, but Amber does want to be closer to her parents. I can understand her point," Kristen said pulling a large platter from the cabinet. "I will cover for you if you want to run home and change. You have plenty of nice dresses. You wear them on tour and don't complain."

"That's because it's kinda expected. It's like my job, so I have to dress appropriately. And I can't wear a dress tonight," she added.

"Why not? I'm wearing one," Kristen said while smoothing out the front of her dress.

"Because I haven't shaved my legs in over a week. I look like a bear."

"Too much info, Em. I should take this to Mama. I don't know why she needs it. Come with me."

Emmy followed Kristen through the kitchen into the formal dining room. Emmy saw Mama talking to Mr. Robertson and Mona.

"Tony said you needed this," Kristen said handing the platter to her aunt.

"Thanks, dear. I brought some finger food with me, but forgot a platter." Mama took the platter and set it on the table. "You look very nice tonight, Kristen." She turned, looked at Emmy, who was trying to hide behind a chair, and sighed.

240

"I thought it was supposed to be casual," Emmy said. "I'll go home and change. The neighbors must think I'm homeless."

Mona walked around the table, put an arm around Emmy's shoulders and whispered, "To be honest, I would rather be dressed as you are than wearing these dress pants. This material feels so artificial."

"Thanks, Mona, but I feel weird and embarrassed."

Mr. Robertson smiled at Emmy but didn't say anything.

"Bill, do you think Emmy should change clothes?" Mona asked.

Emmy moved away from the chair to let him see her faded jeans.

He put a hand to his chin and inspected her. He motioned for her to turn around.

Emmy rolled her eyes and said, "I know they're tight. It's kinda hard to put them on, but once they're on they feel so good."

"There aren't any holes in the knees or... anywhere else that I can see. I don't see any reason you should change. In fact, I'm taking off this tie and jacket. We can be casual together."

Emmy hugged him and said, "Thank you. No one will say anything about how you look."

"Should we tell everyone there is food in here?" Mama asked.

"Yes," Kristen said. "I want everyone to feel free to mingle. I told John the guys can't watch TV and hide in the family room or downstairs. They have to be social tonight."

An hour later Emmy opened the fridge looking for a bottle of water.

Derrick walked in and saw her. "What do you need, Em? I could use a beer."

Emmy handed Derrick a bottle of Sam Adams and grabbed a water for herself.

"I would like a beer, but it might go right to my head. I haven't had one in ages."

"Thanks, Em," Derrick twisted off the top and took a drink. He leaned against the island and smiled at her.

Emmy leaned against the counter facing him, took an even

longer drink and bit her lip.

Derrick studied her for a moment. "It's better for Amber."

"I know. I guess I'm kinda upset because I feel we've kinda neglected you guys. We've hardly seen each other the last couple years."

"You are busy with the family and your career. I enjoyed your last book, by the way. Amber has been so concerned about her parents, she's neglected other aspects of our life."

Emmy stopped biting her lip and slowly grinned.

Derrick shook his head but then nodded.

"Poor baby," Emmy teased.

For a moment they stared at each other while sipping their drinks.

"Do you remember the night we met?" Emmy finally asked. "Officially met, I mean."

Derrick set his beer on the island behind him and smiled. "I have a vague memory of a petite young lady running into me and then Kristen introducing you a bit later."

"I did look like a kid back then even though I was sixteen," she said.

"I don't remember the exact color, but you were wearing a dress. A stylish one, I believe."

"Hah! It was old and probably too short on me, but I didn't have many choices at the time. You probably liked it because of my legs."

"Kristen and I gave you a ride home later that night."

"Yeah, Rory never made it to the dance. I would have walked home, but you guys didn't let me."

"You and Kristen became best friends right away," Derrick said.

"Yeah, it's kinda funny now. You guys were like the exact opposite of my family. Socially and economically, I mean, but you acted like normal kids."

"Grandpa Lombardi made sure of that. He taught all of us that a person's character was a lot more important than how much cash you had in your wallet."

"I remember him. I was dating Tony when he died."

242

Derrick smiled.

Emmy gazed at him. *You still look like a movie star. You're more handsome than Kenny or Tony or anyone else I ever dated.*

"What are you thinking, Em?" he asked.

"I'll tell you if you promise to keep it a secret."

He held up a hand. "I swear, your honor."

"You're a goof, Derrick. When was the last time you entered a courtroom?"

"Last week, but what were you going to tell me?"

"Do you remember the girl you were dating when we met?"

Derrick nodded. "Clarissa Morgan. Her family lived in the Barclay Estates a couple of blocks west of us."

"Do you know where she lives now?" Emmy asked.

"Somewhere in Connecticut, I believe. Mom still talks to Mrs. Morgan. She said Clarissa married some guy in politics. Her third marriage, by the way."

Emmy glanced at the floor for a second, then looked up at Derrick. "You were sleeping with her at the time."

"That was a long time ago, Em. We all make mistakes."

"We had fun on our dates. Did you ever think of them as dates? We were more like friends," she said, grinned and added, "But without benefits."

"There were some benefits," he said.

She moved closer, put a hand on his hip, laughed and said, "You said kissing me was like kissing a sister or a cousin or something like that."

He rubbed his jaw. "I did say something along those lines, but if I recall, you felt the same way. It wasn't all on my part."

"We probably didn't give it a real chance to become more romantic. You dated other girls after you dumped Clarissa. I didn't really date anyone. Kenny was gone for so long. I didn't know Tony yet."

"There were guys who wanted to date you," he said.

"Bull! The only guys interested in me were the ones who thought I would be easy like Diane. They just wanted sex." She stared at him and saw his expression change. "Did you hear those stories?"

243

"I heard rumors about you, but once I got to know you, I knew they were false."

"Did you hope they were true when you first met me? Is that why you asked me out?"

"To be perfectly honest, I was curious. Hey! You were one of the prettiest girls in the school." He shrugged and added, "Why wouldn't I have been interested?"

"Then I ruined it by being a tomboy who wasn't any good at kissing," Emmy said with a smile.

"You were too young for a serious relationship, Em." He tapped the countertop for a moment while looking at the ceiling. He looked back at Emmy and continued, "Plus, I think you were in love with Kenny at the time even if neither of you knew it."

"He always told me to see other guys because he was gone so much."

"Oh, so the only reason you hung out with me was because Kenny wanted you to, huh?"

Emmy smiled. "You have always been easy on the eyes if that's still an expression that makes sense."

Derrick laughed. "You too, Em. You were always sexy even if you didn't know it."

"Then why didn't you like kissing me?"

"Must have been God intervening. He made kissing you less appealing for some reason."

"Good thing. If that first kiss had been more exciting or arousing, then who knows where it would have led."

"You know where it would have led, Em."

"Yeah, we would have ended up in bed and eventually broken up after you got tired of me. I would have been another Clarissa. Oh, what was that bimbo's name you took to Barry and Linda's wedding? I think she had red hair and a real annoying laugh."

Derrick shook his head, sighed and said, "You would have to bring her up."

"What was her name? Didn't she have lots of freckles?" Emmy asked while grinning. "She was a total airhead compared to Amber." She poked Derrick in the stomach. "You're embarrassed because the only reason you dated her was for sex. You were so bad."

"Her name was Haley and she drove me nuts."

"Even in bed?" Emmy asked.

"She talked all the time and that quirky laugh was intolerable. Luckily, she found someone else and dumped me."

"Yeah, how lucky for you," Emmy teased.

"Fine! I admit I made some ill-advised choices in my youth."

"Like me?"

"How do you mean that?"

"Was it a bad choice because we never... you know?"

"Are you trying to embarrass me?"

"Maybe," she said and then backed up. "I thank God for protecting me even before I knew Him. I don't have any history to be ashamed of except for kissing a few boys."

"Not even Rory?" he asked. "There were rumors about the two of you going to wild parties and sneaking around."

Emmy shrugged and took a sip of water before answering, "Some of those were true, but we weren't sexually involved."

Derrick waited for more.

"He thought I was too young. He had a thing for Diane, but she shot him down. He got married in June. He and his wife, Rochelle, live in Florida."

"That's right. Kristen told me."

"Rory and I would do stuff, but not like you. He was almost like a big brother in some ways. He looked out for me and protected me from some things."

"Do I want to know?"

She shook her head. "I need to have some secrets."

"I should find Amber. She probably thinks I'm lost."

"I should find Kenny. We have church in the morning." She looked up at Derrick and bit her lip. "I will miss you, but I understand why you're moving."

He put his arms around her and hugged her. "We could move back one of these days."

245

"Did you notice how many teens were crying after the service?" Kenny asked on the way home.

"I didn't think the service was that bad," Emmy said with a straight face.

Kenny shook his head. "No, I think they were sad because today was Jake and Maddy's last Sunday." He looked at Emmy. "You're yanking my chain, huh?"

"Ya think?" She looked over her shoulder at the kids. "You shouldn't use that phrase in front of them. They think it means something naughty."

"Does it?" he asked.

She looked at him for a moment. "Now you're being facetious."

"I thought the teen band sounded pretty good. I didn't know there were so many in the group."

"I don't think there's usually so many, but all the college kids came home for today." She paused and tried to remember how many musicians were on the stage. "If you count Pastor Jake, there were ten musicians. I thought the Ladlow kids did a great job."

"The brother and sister who play keyboards, right?" Kenny asked.

"Yes, and they play other instruments, too."

"David Belanger sounds pretty good. I've heard his father sing. David must have inherited his talent from his mother," Kenny said.

"I thought P.J.'s son did a great job on guitar, but did the other guy make a couple mistakes?"

"He hit a couple of wrong chords, but not too many people could tell," Kenny said. "The kid on bass and the drummer..."

"His name is Luke, but I don't know the bass player's name," Emmy said.

"They were pretty tight."

"I enjoyed how they had a discussion instead of Jake preaching. They set up chairs and read some scripture and talked about how it applied to them. They are pretty wise."

246

"What are we having for lunch?" Kenny asked. "Do we need to pick something up?"

Kevin heard the question and hollered, "I need nuggets and fries."

"Not today," Emmy answered. "I thought we could have salmon patties, mac and cheese and peas. How does that sound?"

"Are you making the mac and cheese like Uncle Andy does?" Heather asked.

"I have the boxed kind. How does Andy make it?" Emmy asked.

"He doesn't use a box mix. He makes it from scratch," Isabella said. "His is better than the box stuff."

Emmy sighed as Kenny braked for a yellow light. *I hoped you checked behind us. I would have gone through the light. It was still yellow when you stopped.* "Maybe we can invite him over some other day, but we don't have time today."

"Can we have sardines instead?" Heather asked.

"No way! Yuck! I hate sardines," Kevin shouted. "What are sardines, Mom? Are they those little fish things in a can?"

"Yes, and you usually like them. You didn't like the ones your father bought that time because he bought the ones packed in some weird mustard sauce."

"Hey! That only happened once, and it was because they were mixed together on the shelf," Kenny said in his defense. He slowly accelerated through the intersection.

"I need to use up the salmon," Emmy said. "What did you think of the service today?"

Kevin answered immediately, "I liked it because it didn't last forever."

"We did get out a few minutes early," Kenny said.

"Yes, but it's taking us twice as long to get home," Emmy said. "I should have driven my car instead of taking the Odyssey."

"It's too crowded in your little car, Mommy," Isabella said.

"I meant the BMW not my Civic."

"I like the minivan better because we don't have to sit in the same row as Kevin," Heather said.

"I like sitting in the back. It's easier to watch for police cars," Kevin said. "And I can hide my bugs back here."

"You better not have any bugs with you," Isabella yelled. "Mom, he tried to put a bug in my hair yesterday."

"That's not very nice, Kevin Michael," Emmy said.

"I didn't really, and it was dead anyway."

The next evening Pastor Tyler met with the five people making up the nominating committee.

"I have a list of all the positions we need to fill, and a ballot from last year. I printed an updated membership list. This is a list of active members."

"Do all the positions require church membership?" Sofia Talford asked. "I'm sorry if I should already know this, but I've never served on this committee before. I wonder why you even chose me."

"I tried to choose people from different age groups. That way a broader section of the church is represented," Tyler said. He looked around the table. "I think we have a good representation."

"How do we start?" Dylan Michaelis asked.

"I suggest we take a look at the membership roll and make a list of people you think are qualified to be church leaders. Don't think about specific positions, but only think of people with leadership skills."

Tyler allowed ten minutes for this and then opened a discussion. Many of the people came up with the same names.

"How about Mrs. Toth?" Sofia asked.

"She is already on the school board," Tyler answered. "She says that keeps her plenty busy and has requested not to serve on both boards this coming year."

After thirty minutes the committee had enough names to ensure all the positions had enough candidates. Tyler explained that not everyone would be willing to serve.

"Are there some people on our list who get nominated every year and always say no?" Arlene Connors asked.

Tyler looked at the longtime member of the church and nodded. "Unfortunately, many people who would make excellent leaders are not willing to accept the responsibility."

Sofia raised a hand.

"You can speak freely, Sofia," Tyler said with a chuckle.

"I know someone we haven't mentioned tonight, but we did the first time we met."

"Who?" Roger Goldman asked.

Robby Collins, the fifth member of the group, smiled and said, "I bet I know who. You're thinking about Emmy Colasanti, right?"

"I was. I think she would be perfect for the SDMI council. She's not a Sunday School teacher, but she would certainly have fresh ideas."

"I believe we can add her name to our list," Tyler said. "I talked to someone else who you might not have considered."

Roger Goldman scanned the list of members. "Who?"

Tyler and Robby laughed.

"You sound like an owl, Roger," Dylan explained.

"Tony Bertucci. Now before you say anything, I know there are certain Christian standards to be met, and there is one area where Tony might struggle." Pastor Tyler paused and looked at each person at the table. "Years ago I don't believe anyone who consumed alcohol would have even been considered for a position on the board."

"Times have changed," Dylan Michaelis said. "If we took a survey, I believe we would find that most of the people in the church would not see anything wrong with an occasional glass of wine or even a beer now and then."

"Tony has never hidden the fact he likes an occasional beer," Tyler said. "That aside, he has grown considerably in his faith. Like many of our congregation, he comes from a Catholic background. His mother is a devout Catholic."

"I've noticed that as well," Roger said. "In the past I've always assumed he would be too busy with his career. Now that he's retired from football, I can't remember the last time I didn't see him here on Sunday. He's even talked to the teenage boys a few times. He commands a lot of respect."

"He is rather intimidating," Arlene said.

"I have no problem adding him to the list," Robby said.

Twenty minutes later Tyler closed the meeting with a prayer. "I will send a letter to all the nominees. We know some will refuse, but I think we have enough names to have real elections for every committee and position."

"Tony, do you have time to talk?" Pastor Tyler asked after the Wednesday's Family Night service.

"Sure, Sloane and the kids won't be ready to leave yet. Is this about the letter I received?"

"Yes. I have some concern about..."

"Beer," Tony said. "I was talking to Emmy about that. I do like a beer once in a while. I don't drink nearly as much as when I was younger. In fact, I doubt there is any in the house right now."

"I'm not foolish enough to believe that everyone in the church is a teetotaler, but we have run into issues in the past with people in leadership positions who have struggled with alcohol or other addictions."

"I wouldn't consider myself addicted to alcohol by any stretch," Tony said. "I knew Emmy's father pretty well, and he certainly struggled at times. Sloane has never approved of having beer in the house, and she's never had a drink. No, I take that back. She and Lindsey did have some champagne at a wedding reception."

Tyler smiled and asked, "What would your response be if the Holy Spirit told you to give up all alcohol?"

Tony rubbed his jaw as he thought about this. "I would have to obey what the Spirit was telling me. If I didn't that would be a sin like any other sin. I could do it," Tony said and then laughed. "I think Emmy could do it, too." Tony waved a hand. "I shouldn't be talking about Emmy. This is about me."

"I know she and Kenny keep beer in the garage. Father James insists."

"John and I take advantage of it at times," Tony said.

"Before you make a decision, take time to pray about this. The Holy Spirit will guide your answer."

Pastor Tyler smiled and walked away.

Emmy approached Tony. "You in trouble again, creep?"

250

"No, we were discussing you. You are in deep... mud."

"I got a letter about being on the SDMI board. I had to ask Kristen about it. I still call it Sunday School."

"How are you going to answer?"

Emmy shrugged and said, "I prayed and told Tyler I would be willing to have my name on the ballot. I don't expect to be elected, but who knows?"

"If I did get voted onto the board, do you think I should give up beer?"

"Is that what you guys were discussing?" She waved a hand. "Sorry, none of my business."

"Yeah, it kinda was. I'm pretty sure I could give up beer. I might have to quit going to John's house."

"No way I'm going to keep Father James from stocking the fridge in the garage with his favorite beverage," Emmy said. "He would get pissed at me. I can't remember the last time I even had a beer. Must have been in the early summer."

"Before I even think about it, I need to get Sloane's approval. She's concerned about the time commitment."

"I think she should be proud they nominated you," Emmy said. "Gotta run. I'll talk to you later."

On the way home Tony brought up the nomination to Sloane.

"I've been thinking about it, and I did pray," Sloane said.

"Did you make a decision?" Tony asked.

"You can tell Pastor Tyler yes. I talked to Mrs. Michaelis, and she said her husband has been on the board for years. She said he considers it a privilege to serve."

"I'll let Pastor Tyler know, but this is nothing to worry about. I doubt if I have much of a chance to be elected."

# Chapter Thirty-One

Bobby O'Connor handed his customer the bag of drumsticks, the receipt and his change. "Take care, Jahmir, and keep working on your timing. See you next week." Bobby smiled as his sixty-something-year-old student left DelSasso Sound. "It's never too late to learn new skills," Bobby whispered to the young cashier next to him.

"Does he have any talent at all?" the cashier asked.

"He has troubled clapping with two hands," Bobby answered.

The cashier looked at her hands and then flipped her blonde hair over her shoulder. "I get it now."

Bobby heard his phone chirp, checked the message and decided to reply with a call.

"Did you get my text?" Emmy asked. "Can you help me out? I'll owe you."

"You better believe it, Emmy. Why can't Robby be there tonight?"

"Because he's at the hospital," she answered.

"What happened? Is he okay?" Bobby asked.

"He's fine, you goof. Regina had the baby a couple hours ago. I'm pretty sure Robby won't have time to rehearse."

"Shoot! I forgot about that. What did they have?"

"They had a baby girl, and I'm not sure I'm pronouncing this right, but her name is Nahanni Ruby."

"I'm pretty sure that's how you pronounce Ruby," Bobby teased.

Emmy rolled her eyes. "That's what Kenny said when I told him the name. You guys are both dorks. Will you help me?"

"Sure. I don't have any lessons tonight. Do you have the songs picked out? Any new ones?"

"Of course I have the songs ready. What difference would it make? You play the same pattern for everyone anyway."

"I do change the time signature, Em."

"They're all the same. I'd play the drums myself, but Riordan and Sadie are gone, and I need to sing."

"You can play the drums, and I will sing. How about that?"

"Not a chance. See you at six thirty."

"How did rehearsal go?" Kenny asked later that night. "Any trouble?"

Emmy plopped onto the couch and put her feet on the table. "No issues. I would have been home earlier, but we were having fun jamming."

"Who was there? Did Bobby fill in for Robby?" Kenny asked. He moved from the recliner and sat next to her.

She moved onto her back and put her feet on his legs. "I'll tell you if you rub my feet."

He grinned as he pushed her feet away. "No chance. I don't want to know that bad."

"My feet don't smell, do they?"

He grabbed a foot and began massaging it. "Not sure, and I don't want to get close enough to find out."

"Bobby was there. He wanted to sing, but I didn't let him. Oooh! That feels good. Don't stop," she said. She closed her eyes and scooted back a bit. "Adam and Kristina were both there to play keyboards. Adam gave her some suggestions about how to be just part of the band. Sometimes she plays too much."

Kenny nodded as he continued. "Who else was there?"

"Gideon and Paul played guitar and Mason played bass. Do my other foot, please."

"Your wish is my command, m'lady," he responded knowing it would get a reaction.

"Dork," she replied. "Liz was there and Adam helped with vocals. We needed him since Riordan wasn't there. Some songs need a male lead."

Kenny moved a hand to the back of her knee.

"Don't you dare tickle me," she said. "You can massage my calf." She flipped over and continued talking. "Kristina has a good voice, but sometimes she gets a bit loud."

"I've noticed that. She can be heard even without using a microphone." Kenny moved a hand farther up the back of her leg.

"What are you doing?" she asked without moving his hand.

"I thought you might need a full-body massage."

253

"You just want to rub my..."

"Mom!" Heather yelled as she sprinted into the family room. "Will you make Kevin leave us alone? Tell him to stay in his own room."

"I'll handle it, Em. Stay where you are, and I will return as soon as I can," Kenny said. He patted her bottom as he stood up.

"Tell them it's time to get ready for bed."

Kenny returned in five minutes. "They want you to tuck them in."

Emmy got up and kissed Kenny. "Poor baby. Maybe you can finish the massage later."

The worship band finished their set for the second service Sunday and left the stage. Liz walked beside Emmy into the music suite.

"Did we do all right?" Emmy asked. "I wasn't sure if we should sing that chorus another time or not."

"If you hadn't kept the song going, I think Tyler would have had the congregation sing it a cappella," Liz answered. "You know when to extend a song and when to cut it short. Riordan tries to follow how he plans a song without allowing for changes on the fly."

"Are you saying he and Sadie are more professional than me?"

"Not at all. It's not a matter of being professional," Liz answered using air quotes. "We are here to worship not give a performance."

"I'm glad because sometimes I feel the Holy Spirit telling me to sing something a bit differently than how we might have rehearsed it, but I'm always afraid I will mess everything up."

"Riordan and Sadie will be gone the rest of the month. You have two more Sundays to screw up," Liz teased.

Emmy nudged Liz. "Thanks for the vote of confidence. I should make you sing with me every week."

"No can do. I have to work in the nursery," Liz said.

"You could hold David and still sing," Emmy suggested.

"Have you seen my phone, Kenny? I thought I heard it," Emmy hollered Monday night while watching the Giants play the Bengals.

Kenny saw her phone on the kitchen island and brought it to her. "Anything else you desire, m'lady?"

"You didn't finish my massage," she said while grinning.

"Maybe if the Giants win," he replied.

She sat up and checked her texts. "Liz texted." Emmy read the entire text. "She says the board hired that new couple to be the youth pastors."

"Both of them?" Kenny asked as he sat next to her.

"You know what I mean. Jake was the official youth pastor, but Maddy helped just as much."

"What are their names?" Kenny reached down and grabbed a foot.

Emmy pulled her foot away. "Daryl and Brenda Wiley. They're from Indianapolis."

Kenny rubbed his jaw and said, "Wiley. Wiley. Where have I heard that name?"

"From the cartoon, you goof. Wile E. Coyote and the Road Runner."

"Yeah! That's where I heard it." He looked at her and grinned.

She poked him in the side. "I will make you sleep on the couch if you say 'beep beep.'"

"How about one beep?" he asked pushing her onto her back.


"Why do I even watch the Bears? They suck big time," Emmy said. "They had the lead at halftime and blew it."

"The Giants are pretty good this year. They will probably make the playoffs," Kenny said.

"The Bears aren't making the playoffs. They've only won two games all year."

"We don't have to watch the games, Em. The kids are with my parents. We could do something else," Kenny said.

"Will you stop moving your eyebrows like that. You aren't

Groucho Marx, and I'm not in the mood."

"What could I do to get you in the mood?" he asked while still doing his Groucho thing.

"You could shave, and while you're doing that, my legs feel kinda hairy."

Kenny stood up. "I am not shaving your legs for you. I'm going to make a pizza. You hungry?"

"I'll eat some." She flipped the channel to see who was playing the later game. "Hey! I just thought of something."

What?"

"We should invite Paul and Lynette to dinner. We haven't seen them in like forever."

"They were here Labor Day," Kenny said.

"Like I said. We haven't seen them in forever. I'm going to call her, and see if they can do dinner soon."

"Do you mean tonight? Should I wait on the pizza?" Kenny asked from the hallway.

"Yeah. I'll see if they have plans for tonight."

Emmy called and invited them to dinner that night.

"Oh, Emmy, we'd love to come over for dinner, but tonight is popcorn-at-the-parsonage night," Lynette said.

"What is that?"

"Once a month we invite everyone over to hang out and socialize. It's a chance for people to get to know each other in a more relaxed setting," Lynette explained.

"Do many people show up?"

"We usually have twenty or so. One time we had thirty, but that was in the summer. Good thing because thirty people inside would be a bit crowded."

"Do you guys have an open night in the next couple weeks?" Emmy asked.

"The weeknights are pretty busy. We have church on Wednesday, and Paul started a men's group that meets Tuesday nights. The girls have events at school. Did I tell you they have parts in the school play?"

"Not that I remember," Emmy answered. "When is it?"

"Next Friday and Saturday. You should come. Their parts

256

are small, but the play is funny."

"We can try to make it. I haven't been to a school play since I graduated from Roosevelt. That seems like a hundred years ago."

"I had a part in the plays at Crest Ridge Central all four years," Lynette said. "I had the female lead my senior year."

"I never got involved in any extracurricular activities at Roosevelt," Emmy said. "I hope my kids are more involved in whatever school they attend."

"Never?" Lynette asked.

"I went to football and basketball games. Does hanging out with Rory count?"

"I don't think so, Emmy."

Lynette checked the calendar, and they agreed to get together for dinner the first Saturday in December.

"We can talk later, and figure out what to eat," Emmy said. "The girls are welcome to come."

"I will tell them, but they often have to work on Saturday."

"Where are they working?" Emmy asked. "I keep forgetting they are sixteen already."

"They work part-time at the Burger Bob's down the street. It's close enough they can walk."

"Please tell them they are welcome if they aren't working," Emmy said. "I worked at Darby's when I turned sixteen. I worked as many shifts as I could. I needed the money."

# Chapter Thirty-Two

"Gideon, are you all right?" Vijay Patel, one of his coworkers at Coventry Shield Healthcare asked Tuesday morning. "You look rather pale for someone with your complexion."

"It's nothing. I'm sure I will feel better soon," Gideon said.

"Nothing, my butt! You better sit down," Vijay insisted. "I'm going to see if I can get one of the doctors to look at you. We do have doctors here, right?" he joked.

When Gideon didn't respond, Vijay raced away and returned a moment later with one of the doctors.

"Does your chest hurt?" the doctor asked while listening through his stethoscope.

Gideon nodded.

The doctor turned to Vijay and whispered, "Call 9-1-1. I want Gideon to go to St. Bart's."

Three hours later Gideon opened his eyes and saw a nurse standing next to the bed adjusting a machine.

She looked down at him, smiled and said, "Good! You are awake. My name is Genna, and I'm taking care of you. Do you know where you are?"

Gideon looked around and nodded. "In a hospital, but I'm not sure where."

"This is St. Bart's in SoHam. I can tell you are Filipino. So am I. Do you know what day this is?"

"Is it still Tuesday?"

"Yes, it is. Good job." Genna checked the numbers on the machine monitoring his vitals. "You were having chest pains, so your doctor sent you to us. You are doing better now, but we're going to keep you for a day or two to make sure. You've already had some tests, and a cardiologist will be coming soon to talk to you."

"I'm thirsty," Gideon said weakly.

"I will get you some ice water." Genna recorded his vitals on the computer and left the room.

Gideon closed his eyes and prayed silently. He was moving his lips when Genna returned. She placed the water on the stand

258

next to the bed and waited.

Gideon opened his eyes.

"Can you sit up a bit?" Genna asked as she raised the bed slowly. "Were you praying? You looked like it." She held the water to his mouth. "Take slow sips."

He took three sips. "I was praying."

"I've seen you at church," Genna said with a broad smile. "I go to Crest Ridge United Nazarene, too. Sometimes I have to work, but if I'm not on duty, I go to church. Take another sip for me, please."

He did and then sat back. "Have we met at church?"

"Maybe not formally, but I know all of the Filipinos. We might have talked as a group." Genna adjusted his cover. "Are you warm enough?"

He nodded.

"I ordered some soup broth for you because I didn't know if you would be hungry or not. I will heat it in the microwave when ever you want."

"I'm not hungry now," Gideon replied in Tagalog without realizing it.

Genna replied using the familiar language spoken by most Filipinos, and they talked for several minutes until a man in a white coat entered.

"Hello, I am Dr. Ocampo, and I am your cardiologist." He smiled at Genna and spoke to her in Tagalog.

"I can understand you," Gideon said.

Dr. Ocampo had Gideon sit up and listened to his heart. "You are doing better, but the tests show you had an issue with your heart..." He explained trying not to use too technical of terms.

"I've always known my heart was not real strong," Gideon said.

"It is rather large for your size and age. I do not like to be a pessimist, but you might need a new one when you get older," Dr. Ocampo said. "We are going to keep you here for a day or two to run more tests. I will be back in the morning."

Gideon nodded.

Genna walked out with Dr. Ocampo. "I am not sure he has

259

any family in this country, Ramon, but I will let our pastor know he is here."

"I'm sure you will take good care of him," Dr. Ocampo said. "You always do."

Emmy gathered the worship team in the music suite Thursday evening. After everyone had taken a seat, she moved to the podium and said, "I haven't often worked with this group, and I see some unfamiliar faces, so I want to introduce myself. I'm Emmy Colasanti-Colwell, and I'm covering while Riordan and Sadie are on a short tour."

She looked at Tommy Joseph, who she had known since he was a child and smiled. She had the members of the teen group introduce themselves and noticed some new faces among the tech crew. She repeated the introduction process with them.

"I guess I'm last," a lady, who appeared to be in her middle forties, said. "My name is Genna Ademilola, and I'm fairly new to the tech team. I work at St. Bart's in the CICU, and I work with the computers. I do the lyrics and slideshows and video clips."

"It's nice to meet everyone," Emmy said. "I'm glad to see new faces in the group. I want to go over the songs in here before we move to the stage."

Emmy spent the next twenty minutes going over details of the songs and the technical aspects.

"If there are no more questions, let's head to the sanctuary," Emmy said.

Genna raised a hand and said, "This isn't about the songs, and I know we prayed at the start of the meeting, but I forgot someone. Could we take a moment to pray again? I'm so sorry for my forgetfulness."

"Certainly," Emmy said. "Would you lead us, or would you like me to?"

"I will pray," Genna said.

Emmy listened and thought about how difficult it would be for her to learn a new language.

"So, dear Lord, I would ask you to be with Gideon as he recovers from this..."

Emmy's eyes opened and she stared at Genna. *Did she say Gideon? Could she mean our Gideon?*

Genna continued, "We know You can heal his heart and allow him to have a long life. We thank You for all your blessings to us. In Your precious name, I pray." Genna opened her eyes and smiled, "That is all. I'm sorry to have interrupted, but I promised I would pray for Gideon."

As the group left the room to head into the sanctuary, Emmy walked up to Genna and said, "I know someone named Gideon who plays guitar. Surely, it can't be the same person."

Genna nodded. "Yes, he plays guitar and has long, dark hair. He is from the same area of the Philippines as my family."

Emmy rapidly blinked her eyes and asked, "What happened to him?"

"I'm not supposed to tell anyone. He had a mild heart attack," Genna whispered.

Emmy froze. She bit her lip as tears flowed down her cheeks.

"I'm so sorry if I upset you." Genna guided Emmy to a chair and sat next to her.

"He was all right on Sunday. What happened?" Emmy asked.

Genna saw a box of tissues by the podium, got them and handed one one to Emmy. "It happened at work." Genna explained everything she could reveal without compromising Gideon's privacy. "He was released this afternoon. Are you close?" Genna asked.

Emmy nodded. "He lives where I used to, and he played with my band the last time I did a concert. I had no idea he was even in the hospital. Why didn't we know? Does his mother know? I think she lives in Los Angeles now."

"Yes, she does, and she knows. Gideon gave me her number, and I called her. She flew into SoHam, and will stay with Gideon until he is well. I met her yesterday. She is even tinier than you." Genna hugged Emmy and used a tissue to dry her eyes. "I am so sorry I upset you, but I did not know you knew each other."

Eighteen-year-old Tommy Joseph walked into the room

261

and saw Emmy with Genna. "Are you okay, Emmy? We're waiting."

"Miss Colasanti needs a moment, young man," Genna said using her nurse's tone.

"It's okay, Genna. I've known Tommy for a long time, and he's always called me Emmy. I'll be there in a minute." Emmy stood up, looked at Tommy and held out her arms.

Tommy walked up to Emmy and hugged her. At close to six feet tall, he towered above her. "Should I call Uncle Kenny or something?"

"No, I will be all right." Emmy explained why she was crying.

"That sucks! I know Gideon. He's taught me some awesome riffs."

"I will tell everyone you will be right there," Genna said. "Then I will go upstairs and make sure the lyrics are in the computer."

"Thank you, Genna," Emmy said. "We will be right there."

Emmy waited until Genna left the room and looked up at Tommy. "Your father must be so proud of you. You have grown into a fine young man."

Tommy shrugged and stared at the floor.

"I'm not trying to embarrass you. You and Timothy are like family. All the Fridays At Five children are like family," Emmy said. "I'm so glad you are part of the worship team. Maybe one of these days your father will switch churches and get more serious about his relationship with Jesus. Not that I'm judging him," she added.

"Mom and Dad have come to a few services here, but they say this is too big for them. They are more comfortable in their smaller church."

Emmy was home by nine thirty and found Kenny upstairs putting the kids to bed. She kissed the kids good night and then went back downstairs with him.

"How was rehearsal, Em?" he asked at the bottom of the stairs. He looked at her and held out his arms. "I know that look." He held her close and let her cry. He handed her his handkerchief

262

when she finished and sat beside her.

She sat on the stairs, leaned against him, wiped her nose and explained everything.

"Why didn't we get an email from Pastor Tyler? We should have known about Gideon."

"It's possible Tyler doesn't know. They are on vacation this week, and he did say he wouldn't be checking his messages until Saturday."

"Even so, someone at the church needs to be responsible." She stood up and handed Kenny the handkerchief.

He looked at it, made a face and put it back in his pocket. "I'm sure it was just a miscommunication, Em."

"It's a good thing Genna was his nurse."

Kenny nodded but then asked, "Who is Genna?"

Emmy explained.

"I think I know who she is. She has an accent, right?"

"She is Filipino," Emmy said. "I should apologize to Tyler for getting mad at him because it was his fault Gideon was in the hospital."

Kenny stared at her.

"I mean it wasn't Tyler's fault. Did I say the opposite?"

"Yes, but I knew what you meant."

# Chapter Thirty-Three

"Lynette! I told you you didn't have to bring anything," Emmy said Saturday evening as Paul and Lynette arrived for dinner.

"Don't worry, Em, it's just a berry pie for dessert. Paul insisted we bring something, and he bought this because it's his favorite." Lynette handed it to Emmy.

"You can hang up your coats in here," Emmy said pointing to empty hooks in the mudroom.

Heather and Isabella stood in the doorway.

Lynette saw the looks on their faces and shrugged. "I'm sorry, girls, but Ruth and Esther are working tonight."

Isabella sighed and walked away.

Heather put her hands on her hips and said, "I wanted to show them a new story I wrote about having a twin sister."

"You can show it to me," Lynette said. "I would love to read it. A friend of mine once wrote a book about having two sets of twins."

"We still have that book," Emmy said. She turned to Heather and added, "It's called *Twins Again!*, and it's in your room."

"We've read that book," Heather said with a smile. "Do you really know Janae Wenger?"

Lynette smiled and replied, "Yes, I know her very well. We're close friends. We attended Wheaton College together, and we shared an apartment one year."

Emmy tilted her head. "I don't think I ever knew that. Oh, come on in. Dinner should be ready in twenty minutes."

"You didn't know I roomed with Janae or that I went to Wheaton?" Lynette asked. "Her name was Janae Marshall back then. Wenger is her married name."

"I can't remember if I knew you went to Wheaton. I think I always assumed you went to North Park for some reason," Emmy said as she set the berry pie on the island.

"I did go to North Park for a year, but then I finished at Wheaton."

"That must be it," Emmy said. She pushed a button on the intercom. "Kenny, they're here. Would you and Kevin come upstairs, please?"

"Something smells good," Paul said.

"It's the cheesy potatoes," Heather said. "Mom made two pans in case she burned one of them."

"It dinner ready?" Kevin hollered as he burst through the basement door and into the hallway. "I'm starving, and I want some baked beans because they make you fart."

Lynette looked at Emmy and smiled.

"He's all boy," Emmy said and frowned at Kevin. "Go wash your hands, and if you mention farts at the table, I will throw two police cars in the garbage."

"Can I pick the cars?" he asked.

"No!" Emmy pointed to the powder room.

"I'm sorry if the meatloaf is a bit dry," Emmy said later after she took a slice. "I used a different recipe."

"It's all right, Em," Kenny said. "Especially if you put lots of ketchup on it."

"The beans are real good, Mom," Kevin said. He looked at his mother and then at Paul and Lynette. "Beans give me gas sometimes."

"Kevin Michael!" Emmy exclaimed.

"Mom, I didn't say anything about farting," he insisted with a straight face.

After dinner the kids went upstairs so the adults could talk in the family room. Kenny lit the fireplace and sat beside Emmy.

"How are things going at your church?" Emmy asked.

Paul rubbed the arms of the leather recliner and answered, "There have been a few families leave, but there are new families coming. We have seen a few people who might have been attending Crest Ridge, but not many. Overall, our attendance has grown by about fifteen this year."

"I heard the city council has given the green light for that new truckstop. Will that affect the church?" Kenny asked.

"There has been some concern about it. In fact, the entire area around us is becoming more commercial. There are no new housing developments planned," Paul said.

Lynette added, "The board has discussed the possibility of selling the property and finding a new location."

"Really? How can you sell a church? Who would buy it?" Emmy asked.

"It happens, Emmy," Lynette said. "Sometimes other churches will buy a church property. There was a school that bought a church in New Linden."

"Nothing concrete has been decided yet," Paul said. "It might never happen."

"Have the girls thought about college yet?" Emmy asked to change the subject.

"They say they want to go to Olivet, but they might change their minds," Lynette said.

"More than likely they will attend Paul Frank the first year. Maybe two years," Paul said.

Emmy looked at Kenny. "You spent a year at the junior college, right?"

"Yes, but only because my parents insisted."

"Do you think it was worthwhile, or would a four-year college be better?" Emmy asked.

"It was so long ago, Em. I don't remember much about that year," he answered.

Emmy poked him in the ribs and rolled her eyes.

"Olivet offers financial aid," Paul said. "That's the only way we could afford to send them."

Lynette got up to look at the family photos on the fireplace mantle. "I remember when your twins were born. They were so little, and look at them now."

"Yeah, they'll be taller than you pretty soon, Emmy," Paul said.

"They were only a year old when we moved to Iowa," Lynette said. She picked up a photo and showed it to Emmy. "This looks like your father, but I don't think it is."

"That's Father James. You know who he is, and you know my father wasn't a priest."

"The collar did give it away," Lynette said with a grin.

266

They talked about family and the growth of SoHam for a few minutes.

"Is anyone ready for dessert and coffee?" Emmy asked.

They moved to the breakfast nook.

"I heard the Schulenbergs are in California for a tour," Lynette said. "Oh, black is fine with me."

Emmy poured the coffee and sat next to Lynette. "They are, or were. They should be back by next Sunday. I have been leading the worship team. Robby and Regina would be in charge, but she just had a baby. I've been helping with the Christmas program. We're doing an even bigger production this year."

"It must be nice to have so many talented people to fill in," Paul said.

Lynette frowned at him and Kenny caught the look.

"I didn't say that to brag," Emmy said.

"Crest Ridge is certainly the exception among Nazarene churches. If we keep growing, we might turn into a megachurch," Kenny said. "Not everyone likes churches that large."

"I've always thought SoHam needs one or two more Nazarene churches," Lynette said. She took a sip of coffee and added, "It's not like we're in competition with each other."

"There are over 200,000 people within the city limits. I'm sure a large percentage of that number does not have a home church," Paul said. He took a bite of pie, smiled and said, "This tastes almost as good as homemade."

Lynette made a face at him. "I made pumpkin pies for Thanksgiving." She looked at Emmy and admitted, "I don't bake very often. It's not one of my gifts."

Later Kenny and Emmy walked outside with Paul and Lynette.

Paul looked up at the sky. "The stars are more visible here than where we live."

"We need to get together more often," Emmy said as she hugged Lynette. "I will need your advice when the girls are older."

"I'm just a phone call away," Lynette said.

"I hope that's close enough," Emmy replied.

"Are you busy tonight?" Father James asked. "I got home this afternoon and thought I might stop by to see the kids."

"Be quiet!" Emmy told the kids. "Father James is on the phone, and I can't hear him if you are yelling."

The kids settled down and Emmy answered, "I just picked them up from school. You could come over for dinner. We're having leftover spaghetti from last night. Kenny should be home by six."

"Sounds good to me. I'll pick up some bread," he replied.

"Where have you been?" she asked.

"I'll explain when I get there."

Father James arrived just after Kenny. He walked into the kitchen to find them kissing and coughed to get their attention.

"Oh, hush," Emmy said. "He just got home a minute ago, and it's okay if I kiss him."

Father James set the garlic bread on the island. "Where are the kids?"

"I told them to clean their rooms before dinner," Emmy said. "Would you prefer a vegetable or a salad?"

"A salad, please."

Kenny asked, "Do I have time to shower?"

"You have time. Check the bedrooms while you're up there," Emmy said. "Oh, check Kevin's closet, too. Sometimes he throws everything in there."

"Will do," Kenny answered.

Emmy turned on the oven and asked Father James, "Where have you been? I didn't know you were gone."

He sat on one of the barstools on the opposite side of the island. "I've been in Kansas all week."

"Why?" Emmy asked as she opened the fridge and pulled out the spaghetti.

"I was visiting my parents," he replied.

Emmy grabbed what she needed to make a garden salad, set the stuff on the counter and faced her half-brother. "And how are they doing?"

Father James inspected the lights in the ceiling. "You need a new bulb."

"There are new ones in the laundry room. Why are you being evasive? Answer my question."

"My mother is doing all right."

"And your father?" Emmy asked with hands on her hips. "You better spill it or I will call them myself."

"My father suffered a mild stoke last Saturday. He was in the hospital for a few days, but he's home now and doing better."

Emmy stared at him and frowned. "Why didn't you tell me?"

He shrugged. "They are my parents."

"That's a bunch of... baloney! They may not be my family, but they are family."

"That doesn't make any sense."

Emmy pulled a pot from the cabinet and dumped the spaghetti into it. "You know what I mean," she said over her shoulder. She turned on a burner on low, walked around the island and sat next to him. "You should have told me."

"I thought about it, but I knew you would worry. You've got enough on your plate without fretting about my parents."

"I might not have fretted about them, but I could have been praying for them. Why did it happen?"

"High blood pressure and stress according to his doctor. He adjusted the medication."

"Will he be all right?"

"His right arm and leg won't be the same, but he can still walk. He just needs a cane and has to go slow. His speech wasn't really affected." Father James pointed to the stove. "Are you going to stir that?"

"I'll heat up the spaghetti and throw the bread in the oven if you put a salad together." She walked back to the stove.

"I thought it was Kenny's job to make the salad. I hear he used to be quite good at it."

"You can chop up stuff and slice the tomatoes. Don't forget to wash everything."

He slid off the barstool, walked around the island and hugged her. "Thank you for being concerned."

"Yeah, I care about you for some reason." She stirred the

269

spaghetti, unwrapped the garlic bread and set it on a baking sheet. "The kids are in the Christmas program this Sunday. I know you can't be there, but I can get a DVD for you."

"Are the girls singing again?"

Emmy pulled a large knife from a drawer and handed it to him. "They are doing two songs by themselves and have parts in the skit. Would you slice the veggies, please, and try not to cut yourself."

"Bread or salad?" he asked. "I can't multitask like you."

"Fine! I'll do everything," she answered shaking her head. "How old is your father?"

"They are both eighty-four. Until now he's been in great shape. For his age, I mean. Mom is doing all right, but it will cause her more stress to take care of him."

Emmy stopped chopping a bell pepper and looked at Father James.

"Why are you staring at me like that?"

"Are you going to move back to Kansas to help with your parents?" she asked.

"We did talk about that," he answered.

"What did you decide?" She put the bread in the oven.

"They told me to stay here. They know how much the kids mean to me."

"What about me?" she asked waving the knife.

"I'm not answering until you put that down."

She set the knife on the island.

"I'm not going anywhere for now. If my father gets worse, I may considering going to Kansas, but it wouldn't be a permanent move."

"I would understand if you moved back. You probably consider Kansas your home more than SoHam," Emmy said. She picked up the knife and finished chopping the pepper.

"Can I help with anything?" Kenny asked.

"You timed that just right," Emmy said stirring the spaghetti and turning up the heat. "Everything is almost finished."

Kenny smiled at Father James and high-fived him.

# Chapter Thirty-Four

"Hi, this is Emmy. We used to be friends, and I'm calling to ask something very important. Why do you hate me?"

Rory Porter laughed and turned off the TV. "What did you say your name was? Eleanor? Elaine?"

"You know my name, you creep. Why haven't you called me in forever? I haven't gotten an email in two months, and that was a lame Christmas card. You didn't even sign it. Rochelle did." Emmy tried to sound angry as she sat in her recliner in the den. "Did Rochelle order you not to be my friend anymore?"

"Wait a second," Rory said. "I think I recognize your voice. Are you the little kid who used to live down the street and follow me around the neighborhood and pester me all the time?"

"Ha! Ha! You are funnier than that guy who smashes watermelons. I'm serious. Why haven't I heard from you? Is everything all right down there in the land of old people?"

"Things are going great here in Tampa, and not everyone who lives here is retired," he said. "How was your Christmas? Everyone okay?"

"It was a good Christmas. The normal stuff. We went to church and then over the see Kenny's parents. They bought too much stuff for the kids like always. The kids were in the program at church. It was a combined program for the kids in the school, too. Kenny and the guys have finished recording their CD, I think. He and the kids are still sleeping. Is Rochelle home. Will she get mad at you for talking to me?" Emmy shifted her position and took a breath. "Why aren't you at work? Who's taking care of the old people?"

"Are you finished? Can I get a word in now?"

"Please do. I want to hear your excuse for not talking to your best friend in the whole world."

"I have no excuse," he said.

"Thought so," she replied. "When are you coming to SoHam? I came down there to see you last. It's your turn now."

"You came down here for a vacation."

"And to sing at your wedding. How was the honeymoon?"

"The best sex of my life," he teased.

"That's because we never... never mind. What's new?"

"Well, I am off today. That's why I'm not at work and stuck talking to you, Olivia. The sun is shining and it's..."

"I don't want to know."

"What would you like to know?" he asked and then chuckled. "I'm not telling you about my sex life."

"Good! Poor Rochelle has to put up with you. Is she pregnant yet? You're not getting any younger."

"She is not, and we have discussed the pros and cons of starting a family."

"What cons could there be?" she asked.

"Well, we could have a daughter who might turn out like you," he teased.

"Can you see me pointing a finger at you?"

"Be nice, Em. How are the kids? The girls will be ten in January, right?"

"No!" She sat up in the recliner. "They will be eleven! Can you believe it? They are growing up way too fast. Pretty soon they will start having periods."

"Way too much information, Olivia."

"They are wearing bras now," she said knowing it would embarrass him.

"TMI. Do you have any snow on the ground?"

"No, it's been too warm. We've had more rain than snow. We should sell the snowmobile since we never get to use it."

"How are Diane and the boys?"

"Doing good. Carson is in high school."

"No way! For real?"

"He's going to St. Raymond's. Caden is gaining confidence. He's not as shy as before. Lily and Conor are adorable. She's four and he's three. They aren't babies anymore, but are so much fun."

"You still love babies, huh?"

"Yeah, but there are plenty of them at church. Liz and Tyler had another one in August. His name is David, and he's so cute. I get my blueberry fix with him."

"Blueberry fix?"

272

"Baby fix, you goof. Never mind. It's a long story. How old are you now?"

"You know how old I am, and Rochelle turned forty in April."

"Wait! What is that sound?" Emmy asked.

"What are you talking about?"

"Oh, I heard a biological clock ticking," she replied.

"Real funny, Olivia. How is your mother?"

"Mom is... well... she's doing all right for someone in her condition. How is your mother doing? Did she decide to move in with you guys?"

"She is okay, and she's living in Georgia. Close enough to visit once in a while, but not close enough to pop in anytime of day if you get my drift."

"Understood. Kenny's parents learned pretty quickly to call first."

Rory laughed. "Did they catch you running around the house naked?"

"Wouldn't you like to know," she said while scooting around in the chair. "When are you coming up to see me? See the kids, I mean. They miss you. I don't want to see you."

"We could fly up in the spring if the kids really want to see us."

"The church is celebrating it's fiftieth anniversary in April. You guys could come up for that," she suggested.

"Yeah, that sounds like fun," he answered.

"Don't be sarcastic. It's a big deal. There will be a concert Saturday night and a special service Sunday."

"We'll see."

"Creep! You should be going to church. It won't kill you."

"Rochelle likes your books. Are you going to keep writing? Are you still going to record new songs? Not that I ever listen to your CDs. I like Killer Zombie Breath and Vengeance Puppies."

"Are you making that up? Are those real bands?"

"They're local groups. I've never seen them, but I saw the names on a poster."

"I'm glad she likes the books and yes and yes. The CD

won't come out until next year, I think."

"You think?"

"Okay, it won't come out until next year. We aren't spending a lot of time on it right now. Most of the time I know what I want to call my CDs, but I don't have a clue about this one. Any suggestions."

"Nope! I don't come up with titles. I just play the tambourine for special friends."

"So I'm special, huh?" she said. "Crap! I shouldn't have said that. Go ahead and give me your best shot."

"I've always thought you were special, Em. You know that."

She waited and when he didn't say anything else, she said, "That's sweet. You still love me."

"Just like I love puppies and kittens and baby alligators," he said.

"Baby alligators?"

"Yeah, they're cute when they're little, and then you flush them down the toilet."

"You're such a creep. Why do I even like you?"

"Because of my charming personality, good looks and overall desirability," he said. "I am the sexiest man in Tampa."

"You wish," she said. "But I guess that could be true. You're probably the only man in the state who doesn't use Viagra." She stood up, walked out of the den and into the bathroom. "What did you buy Rochelle for Christmas? Don't tell me you bought her some clothes."

"She likes jewelry, so I bought this bracelet she really liked and a diamond necklace that cost a small fortune. Did you get something for Kenny?"

"Not really. We didn't buy gifts for each other this year. No money."

"What a liar!" Rory listened for a second. "Did you just flush the toilet?"

"No," she insisted.

"What did I hear?"

"How should I know?"

"Why do I hear the faucet running? I can't believe it. You used the bathroom while talking to me. You are as gross as Kevin Michael."

"You can't see me. We're not faceting or whatever." She checked her face in the mirror and walked out into the hallway.

"Who are you talking to, Em?" Kenny asked.

"Some creep in Florida who never calls me," she answered and held out the phone.

"Hi, Rory. I'm sorry she called you a creep." He shook his head at Emmy and pointed a finger. "I'll talk to you later, young lady."

Emmy grinned at him and put a finger to her mouth.

"What did he mean by that?" Rory asked.

"He was probably referring to what I'm wearing," she replied.

"Do I dare ask?"

"No," she said while walking toward the kitchen. "Okay, you can ask, but I might not answer."

"Would you get arrested if you were walking down the street right now?"

"In what part of the world?"

"Never mind. I don't want to know."

"Did you go anywhere yesterday?" she asked. "We popped over to Tony's because Marco and Nancy are here. Oh, Derrick and Amber are home for a few days. I saw Derrick and he gave me a hug. He still looks as handsome as ever. Amber is so lucky." Emmy grinned at Kenny. "I married a man with funny ears."

"We stayed home. We're getting together with Rochelle's family for New Year's. Let me know when that church anniversary thing is. We might make an effort to see the kids and Kenny."

"Don't go out of your way. I better let you go. Kenny is holding up a coffee cup and pretending to drink out of it."

"Doesn't he know how to make his own coffee?" Rory asked.

"He does, but he's lazy at times." She nodded at Kenny and held up a finger. "Tell Rochelle I said hello, and I'm sorry she had to spend her honeymoon with you."

275

"I will. Please give Kenny my condolences. I know how difficult it can be to live with you."

"No you don't! We've never lived together."

"I didn't mean it like that, Olivia. I promise to call you more often next year."

"Ha! If you call me twice that will be more often. Take care and try not to get sunburned." She ended the call and sighed.

Kenny looked at her and said, "I know how to make coffee. I was asking if you wanted some by using charades."

"Thank you, but I'm good, m'lord."

"Yes, you are," he answered with a grin.

"I bet that was the smallest crowd we've had all year," Emmy said on the way home from church New Year's Day. "I'm surprised Pastor Tyler didn't cancel everything."

"It wasn't the best first impression to make on the new youth pastor," Kenny said. "What's their names? I forgot."

"Daryl and Brenda Wiley," Emmy answered.

"Oh, right," Kenny said with a grin. "Like the coyote."

"Such a dork," Emmy said rolling her eyes. "You are so predictable. Are we going to watch football this afternoon?"

"Do you know who's playing?" Kenny asked.

"Not that it matters because they suck this year, but the Bears are playing the Vikings in Minnesota."

"It sure is different now that Tony and John have retired from football. Are we going to watch it anyway?" Kenny asked.

She shrugged and said, "Maybe. Did Pastor Tyler mention the church elections at all today?"

"He announced they are next week. Why?"

"I was just wondering. Do you think anyone will vote for me? I doubt if many of the members know who I am."

"Em, everyone knows you," Kenny said. "You've been leading worship for twenty years."

She reached across the front console and smacked his arm. "I have not!"

"I didn't mean exactly twenty years, but you've been doing it a long time."

276

"Yeah, but not so much lately. Years ago the church only had one worship team, and we would sing every week. Now I'm only scheduled one Sunday a month."

"Do you want to do a last minute email campaign?" he asked.

"Don't make fun of me. I guess if God wants me on the Sunday School board, I will get enough votes."

"If it will make you feel better, I could bribe some people."

"Ha! Ha! Keep it up and you'll be making your own lunch."

"What are we having for lunch, Mommy?" Isabella asked from the second row of the Odyssey.

"I was going to make soup and sandwiches," Emmy replied.

Kenny stared at her. "I could make soup and sandwiches. Open a can. Slap some mayonnaise on a slice of bread. How hard is that?"

"I'm making homemade potato and leek soup with grilled cheese sandwiches."

"Yuck!" Kevin Michael hollered. "Is that the soup I don't like?"

"You ate two big bowls the last time I made it," Emmy said. "You like it. It has bacon in it.

He rubbed his belly, smiled and said, "I love bacon. Bacon tastes great on anything. Can I have bacon on my grilled cheese sandwich?"

"That sounds gross," Heather said. "I don't want bacon on mine."

"I used all the bacon for the soup," Emmy said. "You will have to eat a regular sandwich."

At the end of the second service the following Sunday, Pastor Tyler made an announcement. "If you are interested and can't wait until next week to hear the results of the election, the results will be posted in the welcome center and outside the church office. I will be sending emails to all those elected concerning our next meeting."

"Hey, brat, do you think you got elected?" Tony asked on

277

the way out of the sanctuary. "Actually, you've got a better chance than me. Everyone knows you."

"It doesn't matter to me. If I get elected, I will do my best to serve, and if I don't I will support the people who did," she replied.

Tony surveyed the large crowd. "Let's go around that way to the church office. There won't be a huge mob there."

"Kenny, will you corral the kids while I go with Tony, please?" Emmy asked.

"Sure, Em. I hope you won."

Tony led the way through the throng of people and they found the results posted on the glass wall of the church's main office. Emmy scanned the results for the church board. She smacked Tony's arm. "Look! You got elected!"

Tony looked closely at the results. "Wow! Imagine that. I did get elected. I never would have believed it was possible." Where are the results for the SDMI board?"

They scanned the results for the various elections.

"Who is Hilary Cox? She got elected to be the NMI president. I don't know her. Is that the missionary society?" she asked.

Tony nodded. "I don't know her either."

They found the results for the SDMI board and read them. Tony looked down at Emmy and put a hand on her back. "Sorry, Em. I thought you would get elected for sure."

"It's all right," she said. "According to this, I didn't get many votes."

"I voted for you, Em," Tony said. "Ten times."

"You're a doofus." She grinned at him and said, "I can think of one good thing about not getting elected."

"What's that, brat?"

"It means you will have to give up your beer, and I don't."

"You rarely have a beer anymore," he said.

On the way home Emmy told Kenny about the election results.

"I'm sorry you didn't get elected, Em. Are you disappointed?"

She looked at him. "Would it make me sound egotistical if I admitted I was?"

"I don't think so. If it makes you feel any better, I voted for you."

"Thanks, Kenny. How many times did you vote?" she asked remembering Tony's remark.

"Just once," he answered. "Why? You can only vote one time. This isn't Chicago or Florida."

She shrugged and said, "Just something Tony said. No biggie. I'll get over it. I will bug Tony, and make him tell me everything that happens at the board meetings. I wonder if the members ever get in arguments."

"I'm sure they don't agree on everything," Kenny said.

"I've never thought much about board meetings and stuff like that, but I guess the church needs to make business decisions like any other organization."


"Can you believe the difference a few years makes?" Emmy asked Kristen as they watched the twins open presents.

"Well, for one thing it's a lot quieter in here without a bouncy house," Kristen said. She looked around the gym, then at Emmy and laughed. "You're disappointed because you like to jump around like the kids."

Emmy frowned at her longtime friend. "I'm too old for bouncy houses."

"So true," Kristen agreed. "At least you admit it now. Why did you schedule the party for a Friday night? More people would come on a Saturday."

"Today is their actual birthday, and the gym was already booked for tomorrow," Emmy replied. "Now that the kids are older, could I make a suggestion?"

"Sure, Em. What is it?" Kristen asked.

"I don't think the girls would mind if we have a big party for them, Zachary and Noemi. Their birthdays are within a month of each other. We could even include Caden. His birthday is in April," Emmy said. She glared at Kevin Michael who was making faces at his sisters.

"I like that idea, Em, but Caden's birthday is two months later than Noemi's. You might as well have one big party for all the kids in Bristol Ridge," Kristen said as her daughter walked up to her. "Are you having a good time, Gracie?"

"Yes, but when are we going to eat? I'm hungry." Grace sat on her mother's lap.

"Scoot down. You're hurting my leg, and you wouldn't be hungry if you had eaten your dinner," Kristen answered.

"But I hate pork chops and sauerkraut. It smells yucky," Grace replied.

"I won't make it again," Kristen said. "We will have the cake after Heather and Isabella finish."

Emmy looked at Kristen. "Pork chops and sauerkraut?"

"I thought I would try it. I bought it at Sainsbury's. All I had to do was heat it up, and I didn't burn the pork chops," Kristen said.

"You are a better cook than when we lived together," Emmy said. "You couldn't have gotten any worse. You couldn't make instant oatmeal."

Kristen shrugged. "We survived. I still buy a lot of prepared meals. I rarely make anything from scratch like Mama does."

"Who has time? I am so busy even without being on tour. I work as a taxi driver in the morning and afternoon. I work on my songs and try to clean the house. I have to get up early to read my Bible and pray." Emmy waved her hands as she talked. "Don't get me started on social media. I never should have started a website."

"You don't have to do anything with it, do you?"

Emmy threw her hands in the air, sighed and said, "I have to answer the emails and reply to the comments."

"You should hire someone to handle it. Couldn't you combine all your stuff with Kenny's office? He doesn't have to answer fan mail, does he?" Kristen asked.

"No, the office takes care of that. He is so pampered. All he has to do is write songs and play his guitar and sing."

"I meant to ask earlier, but were you disappointed Tony got elected and you didn't?" Kristen asked. "I voted for you if that makes any difference."

"Not anymore. I'm over it. At least I can bug him if I want to know what's going on in the church. I feel bad because I've been going there for years and I didn't recognize all the names on the ballot," Emmy said.

"Neither did I. Maybe they should introduce everyone before the election," Kristen suggested.

"Yeah! They could have all the candidates have a debate like real politicians," Emmy teased.

"So how was your first board meeting?" Emmy asked Tuesday night. "Are your kids in bed? Do you have time to talk?"

"Sloane is getting the younger ones in bed. I have time, but I really can't discuss anything from the meeting," Tony said.

"Why not?"

"It's classified, and you don't have the proper security clearance," he teased.

"You're a creep. Did you have to get sworn in or anything?"

He chuckled and answered, "It's not like becoming a senator or a judge, brat. There were three of us who are new to the board."

"Did they put you in charge of anything important like emptying the trash?"

"I am the head of the tables and chairs action team," he replied.

"For real? Is there such a team?"

"Not really. The maintenance crew takes care of that."

"So you aren't in charge of anything?" she asked.

"Not really. Mr. Goldman is in charge of the finance team, and..." Tony talked about the various ministry teams for a couple of minutes.

"Did you guys give Tyler a raise?"

"I'm sorry, but I cannot divulge that information."

"It's all right. I'll ask Liz. How long did the meeting last? What can you tell me about? Did you hear any good gossip?" she asked and then giggled.

"We were done by nine. Pastor Tyler said the meetings don't normally last more than two hours, but this one was longer because of the anniversary weekend coming up."

"Did you talk about that at all?"

"Yeah. Joel and Marley Menconi are in charge of the planning. Hang on a sec. I need to give Coby and Taylor good night hugs."

"Aren't they a little old for that? Do you still tuck them in?" Emmy asked.

"They use hugs as stall tactics so they can stay up a few more minutes." Tony hugged his youngest sons and resumed the call. "Hey! Did you know the church has only had six senior pastors in fifty years?"

"I didn't. Pastor Ausland was there when I first came to the church."

"There were three before him. Two of them live in Florida and the other in Ohio, I think. The one in Ohio is really old and pretty sick according to what Marley said. She wasn't sure any of those men would be here for the anniversary."

"But Pastor Herb and Dr. Behren will be here, right?" she asked.

"They plan to."

"You're a big help," she said sarcastically. "Is it still going to be a special service, or will it be like a regular Sunday? Are they still going to have a concert?"

"It will be different, and they are planning a concert Saturday evening. Riordan and Sadie are in charge of putting that together. They might ask you to sing."

"I will if I'm not on tour. I better go. I hear Kevin Michael whining. Talk to you later."

# Chapter Thirty-Five

"Daddy, are you awake?" Kevin Michael asked from the side of the bed.

Kenny opened his eyes and yawned. "I'm starting to wake up, buddy. How are you this morning?"

"I'm hungry. Mom said we have to be nicer to you now because you are old."

Kenny reached to the other side of the bed, but it was empty. "She said that, huh?"

Kevin nodded and turned to watch his sisters walk up to the bed.

"Daddy, are you all right?" Isabella asked.

"I'm fine, sweetie."

"Mommy said you are an old man now. Are you as old as Gra?" Heather asked. She climbed onto the bed and sat next to her father.

Kenny sat up and looked at his children. "Did your mother tell you to say all this stuff?"

Kevin scratched his head. Isabella looked out a window. Heather fluffed up Emmy's pillow.

"Not talking, huh?" Kenny grabbed Isabella, pulled her onto the bed and tickled her sides.

"Daddy! Stop it," Isabella squealed.

Kevin grinned and said, "Mommy told us to tease you because you are forty years old now. She said that's really old."

Kenny stopped tickling Isabella, and she sat by his feet.

"Mommy's making breakfast. We're supposed to keep you in bed until she brings it upstairs," Heather said.

"What is she making?" Kenny asked.

"She called it a fry-up. It smells good," Kevin replied.

A second later Emmy appeared in the doorway. "I was going to serve you breakfast in bed, but would it be all right if you come downstairs? We could all eat in the breakfast nook."

"I can come downstairs," Kenny said.

"Kevin, will you give this to your father, please? He might need some help walking." Emmy pushed a walker into the room.

"This is a new, lightweight, titanium model. It should make it easier for you to carry it up and down the stairs. You will need it until we can install an elevator."

Kenny sat on the edge of the bed and frowned at Emmy. "Did you borrow that from your mother?"

"Maybe," she answered. "Come on, kids. Let the old man use the bathroom and throw some clothes on."

"Do we have to get dressed?" Kevin asked.

"No, we can eat in our jammies," Emmy answered. She looked at Kenny. "The fry-up will be done in ten minutes. Will that give you enough time?"

"I'll try my best."

"Come on, kids. Let's give Daddy some privacy so he can get his old body ready for the day," Emmy said.

"This old body worked okay last night," Kenny said with a smile.

Emmy shrugged, turned to leave and said, "You weren't nearly as old last night."

Kenny walked into the kitchen five minutes later. He stood behind Emmy and leaned over. "I love the smell of a fry-up." He moved her hair and kissed her neck while moving the other hand lower.

"Stop it. I could bottle the smell and wear it as a perfume."

"Daddy, we have a card and one present for you," Isabella said. "You can open it now if you want. We only bought one present because Mommy said you haven't been all that nice this year."

The kids giggled because Kenny swatted Emmy.

"I've been very good. I haven't been on tour all year."

Emmy snorted and said, "It's only January."

"Come and open it, Daddy," Kevin insisted.

Kenny opened the card first and read it. "That is very nice, and you all signed it. Thank you."

"Open the box," Kevin said.

Kenny picked it up and lightly shook it. "It doesn't rattle and it doesn't feel real heavy. It must not be a brick."

Emmy rolled her eyes. The girls giggled. Kevin grinned.

"Will you open it already," Emmy said. "The fry-up will be done in a minute."

Kenny tore off the wrapping paper. "It's from Amazon. What could it be?"

"It's not clothes," Heather said. "Mommy said we should buy you new underwear."

Kenny looked at Emmy.

"You need new boxers, but I will order some later."

"Do you need a hint?" Isabella asked.

Kenny lifted the box again. "It feels heavier than a CD."

"It's not music, but you can look at the pictures," Kevin said.

"Kevin! You are giving it away," Heather shouted. "Let Daddy guess."

"I think it's a picture of my adorable family," Kenny said. He used a knife to cut the tape and tore open the package. He removed the packing material and lifted up the present. "It's a book."

"What book?" Isabella asked while grinning. "Is it one of Mommy's books?"

"No, this is a surprise." He held up the book to show them the cover. "It's *Fly the W: The Chicago Cubs' Historic 2016 Championship Season*. What a surprise!"

"Do you like your present?" Kevin asked. "The Cubs play baseball, but Mommy says they aren't very good."

"How did you ever think of this?" he asked Emmy.

"You made such a fuss about them winning the World Series, and I saw this online. I thought it would be a great addition to your collection of sports memorabilia," she said and then turned off the stove.

"But I don't have a collection," he said opening the book.

"Now you have the start of one," Emmy said.

"Thank you very much for my gift," Kenny hugged the kids. He looked at Emmy and made a face.

"Don't you dare," she said.

He slowly walked toward her with his arms stretched out in front of him. "You belong to me."

285

"Kids, help me," Emmy hollered as she put a hand to her forehead in dramatic fashion. "There's a monster after me. Whatever shall I do?"

"You should run away," Kevin suggested. "I'll get my lightsaber and chop the monster's arms off."

"It's too late," Emmy wept sorrowfully fluttering a paper towel. "I am doomed."

The girls giggled as Kenny did his best impersonation of the Frankenstein monster and grabbed Emmy. He picked her up and set her on the island. He grunted several times and then said, "You shall be my prisoner."

Emmy did her best to impersonate a silent movie damsel-in-distress.

"Mommy, climb over the island, and we will save you," Kevin said.

"It's no use," Emmy said putting the back of her hand to her forehead. "Save yourselves, my adorable children."

Kenny couldn't keep a straight face any longer. He began to laugh and then hugged Emmy. "Maybe we can finish playing monster tonight," he whispered.

"Maybe," she said and then bit her lip.

"Mom, I think breakfast is ready," Heather said pointing to the stove. "You and Daddy can finish kissing each other after we eat."

That evening Emmy picked out a dress from her closet, held it in front of her and showed it to Kenny. "How about this one?"

He looked at the red, sleeveless dress. "You might freeze. Don't you have clean jeans and a nice top to wear?"

"We're going to Ciao Bella," she said. "I want to dress up. It's not everyday my husband turns forty."

"Does that mean I have to wear a coat and tie?" he asked.

"Isn't that what you planned to wear?" she asked.

"Well, yeah." He shrugged.

"How cold is it?"

"It's in the teens and kinda windy," he answered.

Emmy tapped a finger on her chin. "It's Tuesday. That

means we might find a parking place less than a mile from the restaurant."

"Em, they have a parking lot now. It's right next door."

"Should I wear a dress?"

"You could, but wouldn't you be more comfortable in jeans?"

"Fine! You've talked me into it. I was going to wear my sexiest dress, but you blew it."

"You could wear those really tight-fitting jeans," he said with a grin.

"What time did you tell Andrea we would be home?" she asked pulling out some jeans from her closet.

"I told her ten. Why?"

"No reason," she said with a sly smile.

"Em," he said slowly. "I know that look."

"I was thinking we could take the Odyssey and check out that spot along Fifth Street. You know the one?"

He thought about it for longer than she thought he should.

"You are such a dork," she said shaking her head.

"Oh! I get it now. You want to go parking and make out like you used to do with..."

"I never did that with... Who were you thinking?" she asked biting her lip again.

He stared at her for a moment. He tilted his head and scratched his ear. "How many guesses do I get?"

"You might need twenty or more."

"That many, huh?"

"Oh, at least. There were so many guys. It's difficult to remember them all. I should have tattooed their names on my..."

"I should swat your you-know-what," he said.

She giggled and wiggled her you know what at him. "Are you jealous?"

He shrugged and said, "Not a bit. You told me Derrick said kissing you was like kissing his sister."

She stuck out her tongue at him.

"We could stay at the carriage house tonight," Kenny suggested. "We haven't spent the night there in a few months."

287

"Not tonight, but I kinda already made arrangements for Tony and Sloane to watch the kids this Saturday."

Kenny grinned wickedly. "Oooh! I like that idea. We can spend the night and pretend it's our wedding night again."

She put her hands on her hips and frowned.

"What?" he asked while shrugging.

"You want me to fall asleep before we can do anything, huh?"

He smiled and said, "I did get to undress you before you fell asleep."

They arrived at Ciao Bella, parked in a reserved spot and walked inside. Mr. Sabatino hugged Emmy and kissed her cheeks. He shook Kenny's hand and proudly escorted them to his best table.

"Florentina has prepared a special meal for you this evening. I have a bottle of wine I have been saving for a very special occasion, and it should compliment your meal perfectly," he said with a wave of his hand and a smack of his lips. "As always, if you need anything at all, please ask and it shall be granted."

Emmy smiled and said, "Mr. Sabatino, you are the perfect host. I hope you never retire. Ciao Bella would never be the same."

An hour later Emmy patted her stomach and looked at Kenny. "Are you as full as me?"

He finished his glass of wine, smiled and asked, "How can you be full? You only ate half of your ravioli."

"I ate all my dessert, and I'm saving the ravioli for tomorrow."

Mr. Sabatino stopped by their table. "Did you enjoy the ravioli? Florentina used a special filling just for you."

"I loved the combination. I could taste the spinach and one of the raviolis was filled with salmon."

"We wish you many more happy birthdays," he said to Kenny.

"Mr. Sabatino, why is it that you didn't make everyone sing 'Happy Birthday' to Kenny, but if I come here on my birthday, you have the whole staff sing and it embarrasses me."

"I think you answered your own question, Em," Kenny said.

"You guys are so mean to me," Emmy said but then she smiled.

Kenny helped her put on her coat, and they waved goodbye to Mr. Sabatino. He shook hands with Kenny and hugged Emmy one more time.

"It's not really all that cold," Emmy said as they walked to the car.

Kenny opened the doors and she slipped inside.

She glanced at the back seat and turned to Kenny. "There's not a lot of room back there."

He started the car and glanced over his shoulder. "You're right. Too bad we didn't bring your BMW." He pulled out of the parking lot and headed home.

"You're no fun anymore. Ever since you turned forty, you don't want to fool around."

"I've only been forty for less than twenty-four hours, Em. Give me a chance to get adjusted to my old age," he said moving his eyebrows up and down.

"You're a dork," she said but then giggled. "Will I get a prize if I say the magic word? Is that how Groucho pronounced it? Word I mean."

"Close enough, m'lady."


"How many people did you invite, Emmy?" Liz Hammond asked as she helped Emmy hang a banner on the gym wall.

"I can't remember how many people I invited, but I got responses from close to two hundred," Emmy answered. "The guys at Steward Music had a party for him at the studio yesterday. This one is for church friends and family."

"That end needs to be higher," Tony said pointing at Emmy's end of the banner.

"You have to fix it, creep. I can't reach any higher unless I get a bigger ladder."

Tony put his hands around her waist, lifted her up and set her on the floor. "I'll fix it, brat."

289

She watched, tilted her head and said, "A couple inches higher."

Tony adjusted the happy birthday banner.

"No, that's too high. Just a bit lower."

He moved it again.

"No, it's..."

"That's as close as it's gonna be," Tony said. "If you want it to be perfect down to the sixteenth of an inch, do it yourself."

"And here I thought you were a construction engineer," Emmy said shaking her head. "Don't you know how much a sixteenth of an inch can throw off a building?"

"I'll throw you off a building if you keep it up," Tony teased.

"If you keep threatening me, you can't have any birthday cake," Emmy said. She pointed to the table where the cake was sitting.

Tony checked out the cake, laughed and asked, "Did you make that yourself?"

"The girls helped decorate it. Can you tell what it is?"

Tony looked at the cake again. "It's a guitar. Why?"

"What kind of guitar?" Emmy asked.

"A cake guitar," he answered.

"No, you goof." She smacked his arm. "It's a specific kind of guitar."

Tony looked closer. "It says Fender on it."

"You're getting warmer."

"I give up. What kind of Fender guitar is it?"

"It's the first Telecaster he ever bought," she said.

Tony shook his head. "How on earth is anyone supposed to know that?"

"He was holding it on the back cover of their first CD," Emmy answered and walked away.

Tony looked at Liz.

She shrugged and said, "I knew it was a Telecaster." Then she laughed and walked away.

Tony sighed and shrugged.

Forty minutes later Liz and Kristen brought out the large

sheet cake Emmy had purchased from Sainsbury's.

"We need to get everyone's attention," Kristen said to Liz and Emmy.

"I know the perfect way," Emmy said.

"Liz, you better cover your ears," Kristen said covering her own. "This will be loud."

Emmy put her fingers to her mouth and whistled.

All movement and talking ceased immediately.

"I think you've got their attention, Krissy," Emmy said.

"We need to sing 'Happy Birthday' and then we will serve the cake," Kristen announced.

They sang and Kristen and Liz began cutting the cake.

"Would you like chocolate or white cake?" Liz asked Kenny, who was first in line.

"Chocolate, please," he answered.

"Chocolate for me, too," Emmy said.

Kenny pointed to the guitar cake. "Aren't we going to eat that one?"

Emmy shook her head. "We're taking that one with us to the carriage house. We can have some tonight and eat the rest for breakfast."

"Will we have time to eat some cake?" Kenny asked.

Kristen grinned and whispered to Liz, "Not if Emmy has her way."


Emmy opened her eyes and stretched her arms over her head. She turned on her side and looked at Kenny. "Why are you grinning like that?"

"Because you look so good," he said.

She pulled the sheet up higher. "Stop it! What time is it? Do we have time?"

"It's seven thirty. Give or take. Are you sure you want to get out of bed?"

She scooted closer. "Can you give me a reason to stay in bed?"

He kissed her and gave her a reason.

"Are you sure you have the strength and endurance?" she

291

asked after breaking off the kiss. "You aren't as young as you once were."

"Geez, Em! I'm only forty. I'm not ready for the nursing home."

"What time is it now?" she asked later.

He checked the clock on the nightstand. "Almost eight thirty." He grinned and whispered, "I still have some..."

"You don't need to brag," she said throwing off the sheet. "Can you make some breakfast while I shower and get dressed?"

"I thought we were going to have cake for breakfast."

"There might be a little left, but we used most of it last night," she said with a grin.

"It wasn't my idea to smear it all over... you know."

"True, but you didn't object, m'lord."

# Chapter Thirty-Six

"Before we start rehearsing, I would like to introduce two new members of the team," Riordan said Thursday night. "Some of you may have seen them in church, but maybe haven't had a chance to meet them. Ryan and Rebecca, could you stand, please?"

The young couple stood and waved shyly to everyone before sitting back down.

"Is it all right if I share some background info about you guys?" Riordan asked.

"You may," Rebecca said.

"Okay," Riordan said and then checked his notes. "Ryan and Rebecca grew up in New Linden, and have been married for seven months. They attended Faith Bible Church with their families and have recently moved to the west side of Crest Ridge." Riordan looked at Ryan. "They heard about our church from some friends and decided to give us a try since we are much closer than Faith Bible."

Emmy whispered to Bobby O'Connor, "That's the church Kenny's parents attend. I bet they know their families."

Riordan continued, "Ryan has a degree in education from North Park College and is currently teaching at Robert T. Colwell elementary school in SoHam."

"Oh, my God," Emmy whispered. "That's where Kenny and I went."

"I know, Em. Listen to Riordan," Bobby said.

"Rebecca graduated from Morgan Bible Institute in Chicago with a degree in worship arts and works part-time at the Sunrise Garden assisted living facility," Riordan said.

Emmy poked Bobby's arm. "That's where Mom lived."

Bobby rubbed his arm and nodded. "I know, Em."

"Ryan is a percussionist and Rebecca plays piano and other keyboards. This might just be the perfect time to begin using the grand piano that's been in storage. I took the liberty of having the maintenance crew move it onto the stage." Riordan took a few more minutes to go over the songs and arrangements for the coming Sunday services.

"Unless there are some questions, let's move to the stage, and I promise not to keep everyone any longer than necessary."

The team finished rehearsing forty minutes later.

"Liz, do you have a minute?" Emmy asked as they headed back to the music suite to grab their coats.

"Sure. What's up, Emmy?"

"I'm not positive, but I'm pretty sure Kenny's parents know Rebecca's and Ryan's families."

"Why do you think so?" Liz asked.

Emmy explained her reasons.

"Let's ask them," Liz suggested and pulled a reluctant Emmy to where Ryan and Rebecca were talking to Bobby.

"Speak of the devil," Bobby said grinning at Emmy.

Emmy made a face at Bobby.

"I was telling Ryan and Rebecca that Kenny's parents still attend Faith Bible," Bobby said.

"This is wild," Rebecca said holding onto Ryan's arm. "Our parents have known the Colwells all our lives. Well, almost all our lives. Our families first came to Faith Bible when Ryan and I were five. We grew up together. I mean we've attended church together since then. My family lived in Hampshire Park, and Ryan lived in New Linden. His father was the worship pastor at Faith Bible for several years."

"Emmy and Kenny grew up together, too," Bobby said. "Well, Kenny grew up. Emmy's still a kid."

Emmy poked him in the side. "A friend of mine grew up in Hampshire Park. His name is Bertucci, and they lived on Crystal Drive," Emmy said.

"Crystal Drive is only a few streets away from where we lived," Rebecca said.

"Kenny and Emmy lived on Fifth Street which is close to where you teach," Bobby said.

"Did you attend Colwell School?" Ryan asked.

"We did," Emmy said. "Did Bobby tell you the school is named for Kenny's grandfather?"

"No! Really?" Rebecca asked.

Ryan tapped his chin with a finger. "There's a photo of Mr.

Colwell in the hallway outside the main office. I never made the connection."

"You sounded pretty amazing on the piano," Liz said.

Rebecca rolled her eyes and patted the bun in her brown hair. "I was just trying to fit in. I've played all of those songs before."

"Even 'Never Been Unloved?'" Liz asked. "That's one of Emmy's newer songs."

"I know," Rebecca said. "Ryan and I were on the worship team at Faith Bible, and we did several of your songs. I wish I had the talent to be a songwriter."

"Riordan mentioned you have a degree in worship arts," Liz said.

"I do, and one of these days I hope to put it to use."

"I'm sure we can find a way to utilize your gifts," Liz said.

"You have so many talented people in the church. I'm just hoping to be a part of the team," Rebecca said.

"Em, did you hear that Ryan plays the drums?" Bobby asked.

Emmy grinned and said, "That's great! We've had to put up with this doofus trying to play drums for like forever. It will be such a relief to finally have a drummer who can keep time and play in more time signatures than..."

"Hey! I can play in any time signature you can think of," Bobby insisted.

"If you say so," Emmy teased. "It was nice to meet you, but I need to get home. I promised the girls I would listen to a story they wrote for school."

"It was a pleasure to meet you, too, Emmy," Rebecca said.

Emmy hurried home, listened to the stories, said good night to the kids and went downstairs to talk to Kenny.

"How was practice, Em?" Kenny asked.

Emmy sat next to him on the couch. "Good. There was a new couple there tonight. Their families attend Faith Bible. Do the names Deighton and Taylor ring a bell?"

"Sounds like a law firm," he joked.

Emmy rolled her eyes.

Kenny put down his *Billboard* and rubbed his jaw. "I bet my parents know them, but I'm not sure I do. Remember, I haven't gone to church there for a long time."

"Are you saying we've been married for ages?"

"Yes! I mean no. What do you want me to say?"

"Nothing. Rebecca and Ryan are twenty-five, so they would have been children when you were going there."

"I kinda remember hearing Dad talk about a worship leader named Deighton," Kenny said.

"That would be Ryan's father."

"Small world, huh?"


"Hey, Em, I was going to call you earlier, but I forgot. Jeff ordered lunch from the Hungry Lion today and had one of the secretaries pick it up," Kenny said the next afternoon.

Emmy shrugged and stared at her phone. "So. Big deal. Is that why you're calling? I'm doing laundry while the kids are busy with homework."

"Yes and no," Kenny said. "She said there were tons of pink balloons inside..."

"Oh, my God!" Emmy yelled. She slammed the dryer door and started it. "Annie had the baby."

"Yeah, that's kinda what I thought," Kenny said.

"I have to let you go. I need to check Facebook. Matt probably posted it. Why didn't you call me earlier?"

"Sorry, we got busy going over details of the summer tour and I forgot. I should be home by five. I'll talk to you then."

Emmy ended the call, hurried out of the laundry room, raced down the hallway and into the family room. She saw her laptop on the couch and turned it on. A minute later she was checking Facebook.

"Alanna Catherine. That's such a pretty name."

"Mom, I need help," Isabella said walking into the room with her math book. "What were you saying about a pretty name?"

"Do you remember Annie O'Dell? She had a baby girl today, and her name is Alanna Catherine."

"I remember her. She's married to Matt Sullivan, right?"

296

"She is married to Mr. Sullivan," Emmy said. "You are too young to call him Matt."

"They're the couple you thought would never get married," Isabella said.

"Well, they were together for a long time before they actually got married."

Isabella sat beside Emmy on the couch. "Are you going to run to the hospital to see the baby?"

"Probably not. Annie and I are friends, but I don't want to bother her."

"Good. You can help me with my homework. I have trouble understanding algebra," Isabella said.

"Algebra!" Emmy shouted. "I didn't have that until I was in high school."

"I'm kidding, Mommy," Isabella said. "We won't have that until next year."

"When is Daddy getting home?" Heather asked while walking into the room. "He is supposed to buy me some valentine cards to give to my friends."

"He should be home soon. Are you going to give one to Ian?" Emmy asked. "I saw you riding your bike with him."

"Mom! We were just riding our bikes. I wasn't planning to send him a Valentine's Day card."

Emmy was in the laundry room later when she heard someone pull into the garage.

"Em, where are you?" Kenny hollered as he hung up his coat in the mudroom a moment later.

"I'm in here," Emmy said. "I'm finishing the laundry."

He turned around, walked over and stood in the laundry room doorway. "The summer tour is booked, and tickets are going on sale the same day the new CD is released."

"When is that?" she asked folding a bath towel.

"The last Tuesday of the month. I think it's the twenty-eighth. This isn't a leap year, is it?"

She looked over her shoulder and answered, "No, last year was. This is 2017. It can't be a leap year. It's an odd number."

"I knew that."

"Did you talk to Gideon?"

"Yes, he came to the office, and we offered him a position for the tour," Kenny said.

"Well, did he take it?" Emmy asked. She handed Kenny a basket of clean, folded clothes. "These are yours. You can put them away."

Kenny shook his head as he looked at the clothes. "You paired up my socks. Thank you, sweetie."

"You're welcome. What did Gideon say?"

"He thought the stress would be too hard on his heart."

"I was afraid of that. It's only been a few months since he was in the hospital."

"Have you given any thought to who you want in your band for the Fourth of July show?"

Emmy held up a t-shirt. "This is so old."

"You only wear that to bed," he said inspecting the faded lettering. "This is from a tour in 2002. I think you can toss it out."

"I'll add it to the box of rags, and I thought I would ask Bobby to help me put a group together." She added more clothes to the washer and then sat on the countertop. "Could you open that cabinet and get that box for me, please?"

He retrieved the rag box for her. "He is available since he left the Bender Brothers Band."

"I thought I could use most of the same guys I did for last year's show." She put her hands under her thighs, took a deep breath and stared at Kenny.

"What?" he asked looking up from the rag box.

"I know you miss performing live, but last year I only did one show, and it might be the same for this year. I just realized I don't miss it at all. I like writing songs, and I love singing at church, but I don't miss the tours."

"No, no," he said shaking a finger at her. "It's the traveling you don't miss, Em. You still love performing."

"You aren't saying I think singing at church is a performance, are you?" she asked jumping down and almost landing on his foot. "You better not be."

He waved a hand. "No, I know better. I think you would

298

love to tour if it didn't involve travel."

"Have you invented a transporter thing?"

He laughed and answered, "No, I don't have a beam-me-up-Scotty machine."

"Too bad. I hope Gideon is able to play on the Fourth. That way I will have the best guitarist in the area in my band."

"Are you saying I need to practice more often?"

"It wouldn't hurt. You aren't getting any younger, and there are new guitar slingers coming along every year."

"I've never claimed to be the best guitarist around."

"That's good because I heard Kevin Michael playing that small guitar of his, and he sounded pretty amazing."

"So, you're saying I'm probably not even the best guitar player in my own house, huh?"

She patted his back as she walked past. "Don't worry. You're still the second best in my book."

"Which book? Do you mean that literally, or was it a figure of speech?" he asked following her out of the room.

"Yes," she said.

"You used to like listening to me play." Kenny scratched his ear. "If you need me, I'll be in the studio. I need to practice."


"Kenny, did you remember I have to fill in for Regina and Robby tonight? They are going to be out of town Sunday, and she asked me to sing."

"I remember, Em. Are you going to sing Regina's part or Robby's?" he asked with a grin.

"You're so funny. I'll be home as soon as I can. Oh, I need to talk to Gideon about the Fourth of July."

"If Robby can't be there Sunday, who's playing the drums?" Kenny asked.

"Ryan is going to play. He's the new guy who teaches at your grandfather's school."

"Right. Let me know what Gideon says. If he can't play, maybe I could." *Shoot! I shouldn't have said that. She's going to come up with some smart reply.*

"Thanks for volunteering, but I would hate to put you in a

299

position where you have to play with us amateurs," she said.

He stared at her for a moment. "You guys aren't amateurs."

"I know, but I thought I would say that instead of you're not good enough to be in my band," she teased.

"Real funny, Em," he said.

Emmy grabbed Gideon's arm after rehearsal and asked, "Got a minute?"

"Yes," he answered.

"I know you turned down Kenny."

Gideon nodded and brushed his long, silky hair away from his eyes.

"I understand why, but would you be willing to play for me on the Fourth? You did last year, and it was amazing."

"I hate to make a promise right now, Emmy," he replied.

"Is it because of your heart issues?" she asked softly.

"Yes. If I agree, I would have to get an okay from my cardiologist."

"I'm willing to wait for an answer." Emmy noticed a new tattoo on his arm. "Does that have some significance?"

"The acorn?"

"Yes," Emmy said. "I like it."

Gideon took a deep breath. "Do you remember me telling you about my brother?"

Emmy thought about it for a moment. "You said he had a son who passed away."

"Yes, he was a brave little boy, and my brother used the acorn as a symbol of his son's strength and courage."

"That's so touching," she said blinking away some tears.

"Thank you, Emmy. I will talk to my doctor, and if he agrees, I will play in your band."

"I really appreciate it." She watched Gideon walk away. *I need to remember the acorn and write a story about it.*

After the press conference to debut their new CD, *New Priorities*, the members of Fridays At Five gathered in their office on the second floor of the Steward Music Group building.

"This is going to be a busy summer," Dave said looking at

the tour schedule. "There aren't many nights off."

"We did have to arrange the tour when the kids are out of school," Jeff said.

"I talked to Gideon about joining us, but he can't because of health issues," Kenny said. "I only know of one other musician who knows the material well enough." He looked at P.J.

Adam saw the look and snapped his fingers. "That's right! Tommy can play all the old songs. He could learn the new material easy enough. What do you say?"

P.J. rubbed his jaw. "He does need a summer job. His mother has been on his case about that."

"He sat in on that gig you did last year with the Notable Exceptions," Kenny said. "Would he be interested?"

"I can ask him, but I'm not sure Teresa would allow him to tour with a decadent rock band all summer."

Kenny sighed. "Yeah, I can understand that. We do have a reputation as rock and roll rebels."

"Is that why we don't schedule any shows on Sundays?" Dave asked.

After the guys stopped laughing, P.J. said, "I'll talk to Teresa and Tommy."

Kenny stopped at Darby's to pick up lunch on his way home.

"Did you get any fries?" Emmy asked as she looked through the bag. "All is see are hot dogs and a hamburger."

"That's because I have the fries," Father James said.

"I hope you plan to share them," Emmy said with her hands on her hips.

"I will. That's the Christian thing to do, little sister."

"How many did you eat on the way here?" Emmy asked while getting the ketchup from the fridge.

"Only a few, but don't worry. They fell out of your bag."

"That figures." She looked at Kenny. "How did the press conference go? Did you guys talk about hiring someone for the tour?"

"P.J. is going to see if Tommy can fill in."

"Really?" Emmy asked as she took a chili cheese dog from

301

the bag. "Don't you think he's a bit young?"

"He's as old as I was when we did our first tour," Kenny said and then took a bite of his burger.

Emmy wiped Kenny's chin. "No way! That can't be. You were a lot older than Tommy."

Kenny shook his head. "He's nineteen. He had a birthday in January."

"Does Teresa know about this?" Emmy asked.

"P.J. is going to talk to her about it today. I think she will agree since his father will be along."

"You better hope so," Emmy said covering her fries with ketchup. She looked at Father James and asked, "If you had a son would you allow him to travel with a rock band?"

Father James took a sip of root beer before answering, "Our father let you sing with the band when you were a lot younger."

"I never went on tour with them. There's a big difference. I know Tommy's good on guitar, but how will he handle the social stuff?"

"What stuff?" Kenny asked.

"There are always a lot of people on the edges of the tour if you know what I mean. That's a big temptation for someone his age."

"I think he's mature enough to handle it."

"Were you?" Emmy asked staring at Kenny.

"Do I need to leave?" Father James asked. "I don't want to get in the middle if you're going to fight."

"We are not going to argue," Kenny assured him. "And to answer your question, Em, you know I was."

"Just making sure." She stuffed some fries into her mouth and said, "Actually, I was thinking about asking him to play with my band."

"He could probably play with both bands, Em. First, we have to find out if Teresa will allow him to tour."

# Chapter Thirty-Seven

"Well, what do you think?" Kenny turned his chair around to face Emmy in the control room of his basement studio. "Are you happy with the mix?"

"Did you really arrange the strings for that last track?" she asked from her position on the couch.

"I had some help, but it was mostly me," he replied turning back to the mixing console.

"I hate to admit it, but you're getting pretty good at this producing gig," she said getting up and standing behind him. "I might have to start paying you."

"I thought I was getting paid, Em," he said while grinning.

She ran her fingers through his hair. "I mean real money. You've got a few gray hairs, and you need a trim."

"I know, but I haven't had time. Maybe you should learn to cut my hair."

"No way! The last time I trimmed Kevin Michael's hair he complained so much I ended up taking him to the barber to fix it."

"Uh, we really need a title for this CD, Em. We can't keep calling it the 'new one.'"

"I know, and I've been trying to come up with one. I'll keep working on it. I'm sure something will pop into my head. I'm going to fix some lunch. You hungry for anything in particular?"

"Do we have any leftovers from last night?" he asked. "I only had one helping."

Emmy made a face and shook her head. "I threw that stuff away. The kids didn't like it and made me promise never to make it again. How about soup and a salad?"

"Works for me. I'll be up as soon as I save everything," he said.


"Hey, Emmy, did you buy tickets to see the Bender Brothers Band?" Bobby asked after church Wednesday night.

"No, did you?" she replied while putting on her coat. "When are they going to be in the area?"

"I'm not sure. I didn't check out the website."

"Kenny told me they are using almost all of the Fridays At Five crew at least until summer. I'm glad those guys are working," Emmy said. "Do you have time to talk about the Fourth of July show?"

"I suppose. You want to buy me some coffee?"

"Why should I buy? You're the one with a job," she said.

"Yeah, right. Like I make a ton of money."

"Fine! I'll buy, but I have to let Kenny know where I am." She texted him and he answered right away. "Okay, I can buy. You want some food or is coffee enough?"

"I wouldn't turn down a pizza," Bobby said.

"All right, but it's coming out of your salary."

They stopped at Kerry Lynn's Pizza and Pasta and ordered a medium pepperoni. They sat at a corner table and talked about his job while they waited for their pizza.

"Do you have any idea who you want to use?" Bobby asked after the pizza arrived.

"I was thinking I would use the same guys who did last year's show, but then I thought about something else." Emmy took a sip of Dr Pepper.

"What?"

"Okay, I'm going to have a new CD out this year, and Klaus Kesson will insist I do a short tour to support it."

"Do you know when it will be released?" Bobby asked taking two slices of pizza.

"Probably not until May or June. I don't even have a title, so that means no artwork either."

"Duh," he said.

"So, if I do some shows on the weekend, I will need some players who can travel."

"Makes sense."

"I have you under contract, so you have to be my drummer whenever I need one."

"Is that in the small print I never read?" he asked.

"Yeah. I've talked to Gideon, and he will play if his health allows. Paul Mahnari agreed, but I need a bass player. I have no idea where Miles Goossens or Jackson Brewster are these days."

"You could ask Mason Williams," Bobby suggested.

"I thought of him. I like the way he plays. It's funkier than the other guys."

"Do you want that last piece?"

Emmy waved a hand. "No, you can eat it. Two pieces were enough for me."

"How about Robby and Regina? Have you asked them?"

"No, and don't talk with your mouth full," Emmy said. "You're as bad as Kevin Michael. I don't think they will be willing to travel because of the baby."

"I could sing harmony," he offered.

"Yeah, but I still need a female to sing the lower parts."

He held up a finger, finished chewing and swallowed his pizza. "I thought of someone. Two people actually, who would be a good fit."

"Who? Do you want another pitcher of pop?"

"No, I'm good."

Emmy put her hand over the pitcher to let the waitress know they were finished.

"Susan Lemmert and Tariq Jones. She can sing the lower parts, and Tariq would be an awesome addition."

"Isn't he still in high school?" Emmy asked as she looked at the check. She dug some money out of her purse. "You can leave the tip."

"How much?"

"Five if you want to be cheap. No more than eight."

"He's a senior, and I think Susan will finish college this year. Maybe not, but if you only do shows on Friday and Saturday, she might work out."

"Good idea, Bobby. Having Mason and Tariq in the band would add some color," she said with a grin.

"Tell me you didn't say that."

"You know it doesn't matter to me. I still need a keyboard player, and don't say Cameron. He told me last year he wouldn't do it again."

"Why not?"

She shrugged. "He claims it was too much pressure."

Bobby added the tip and put his wallet back. "How about the Ladlow kids, or the new piano player? She's really good."

"She is, but I'm not sure how much experience she has with programming."

"Yeah, and the Ladlows don't seem all that eager to play."

"There is someone who would be perfect, but I'm not sure he would do it," Emmy said as she grabbed Bobby's hand.

"Who? Are you thinking about Chase?"

"Oooh! He would be perfect, too, but I was thinking of Jeremy Lenhart."

"For real? Jeremy from Fridays At Five? I thought he was like retired or something."

"He left the band because of his daughter's health, but she's doing better, and this would only be a few shows. I think I'll ask Kenny."

"Did Jeremy ever do a solo album?"

"Not a real one, but he did an instrumental thing. He would be perfect. He certainly has the experience."

"Well. Let me know what he says. I'll talk to some of the other people and get back to you. Thanks for the pizza, Emmy. I gotta run."

"You're welcome, Bobby. I'll talk to you later."

"Hi, Frances. What's up?" Emmy asked later in the month.

"Did Kenny already tell you?" Frances asked.

Emmy shrugged. "Tell me what?" *If this is more gossip, I'm going to hang up.*

"Dave and Macy's divorce is final."

"How do you know?" Emmy turned down the radio. "Kenny hasn't said anything."

"I talked to Macy, and she told me. She told me some of the details. It's costing Dave a small fortune."

"I don't understand why they couldn't work things out. They have five kids to think about."

"Maybe I shouldn't say anything, but I've always wondered if Dave is Madison's father," Frances said softly.

"What!?" Emmy screamed into the phone. "Why on earth

would you say that, or even think that. That's ridiculous!"

"Then why would Macy insist on the name Madison? All the other kids have names that start with D. Makes you wonder, huh?"

"Maybe they just ran out of D names, Frances," Emmy yelled. "You better not repeat what you told me because there's no way it can be true."

"I won't repeat it, but I will always have doubts," Frances said.

"I'm hanging up now," Emmy said. She ended the call and stomped down the hallway into the kitchen and saw Kenny. "That was Frances on the phone..."

Kenny listened to Emmy vent and put his hands on her shoulders. "Dave called me this morning, but he didn't want everyone to know."

"What about Madison?" Emmy looked up at him. "Could it be true?"

Kenny frowned and shook his head. "No way, Em. Madison looks more like Dave than all the other kids."

"I am so mad at Frances I could just spit. I should drive over there and give her a piece of... What? Why are you laughing?"

"Because I love the way your eyes sparkle when you get mad. I could kiss you."

"You can try, but it won't..."

"Do you feel better now, m'lady?" he asked a moment later.

She pushed him away. "Oh, hush. You know I can't stay mad when you kiss me like that."


"I will be there in five minutes. You're coming with me," Diane shouted into her phone Monday morning.

"Why? What are you talking about? Where are you going? I just got home from taking the kids to school," Emmy answered.

"We are going to St. Bart's," Diane yelled. "I'm taking the kids to Mona's and picking you up."

"Okay, but tell me why? You're scaring me, Diane."

"Sorry." Diane took a deep breath and said, "I got a call

307

from Sunrise Garden. Mom had a stroke or a seizure or something and they called an ambulance."

"A seizure! Why would she have a seizure? Was it a stroke?" Emmy asked.

"How would I know?" Diane yelled. "I'm not a doctor. Just be ready."

They arrived at St. Bart's, inquired about their mother and were taken back to a room in the ER.

"What happened? Where is she?" Diane asked.

The nurse explained, "She is rather confused, but her vital signs are stable. It doesn't appear to have been a heart attack, but the doctor has ordered some tests including neuroimaging. She will be taken upstairs as soon as possible."

"She's going to be admitted, right?" Diane asked.

"Yes, most likely she will be here for a couple of days. Maybe more."

"Can we see her?" Emmy asked.

"Yes, but please don't be alarmed if she has trouble talking to you," the nurse said.

They walked around the corner and saw their mother.

"Mom! What happened?" Emmy asked. "Can you talk to us?"

"I don't know what happened. I was eating breakfast, and I felt dizzy," Patricia said.

Diane stared at the nurse. "She sounds pretty normal now."

"Keep talking to her," the nurse said.

"Mom, do you know where you are?" Diane asked.

Patricia looked around the small room and touched the gurney. She pointed to the cabinets along one wall. "Did I get moved to a different apartment? Where is my TV?"

"You're in St. Bart's, Mom," Emmy said.

"Well, I don't want to be here. I want to watch my shows. Can you take me home? I have to finish the laundry."

"We will take care of the laundry, Mom. You don't need to worry about it," Diane said.

"Make sure you keep the whites separate from the colors." Patricia pointed at Emmy and said, "She mixed them together and ruined some shirts. I had to throw them away."

Emmy looked at Diane. "I was like ten or eleven when I did that. I didn't know any better."


"Now that we've approved the minutes and reports, we need to discuss the fiftieth anniversary weekend," Pastor Tyler said. "Joel, would you like to bring us up to date?"

Joel Menconi cleared his throat and began, "First of all I would like to thank the people in charge of the various committees. They have done the bulk of the work. Riordan and Sadie have an order of service for the Saturday night concert. The catering company has been notified, and we will be giving them a final order in less than two weeks..."

Tony listened to the report and made some notes because he knew Emmy would call him that night.

"Do we have a motion to adjourn?" Pastor Tyler asked shortly after eight thirty.

The motion was seconded and Tyler closed the meeting with a prayer. Tony drove home, helped get the kids to bed and sat on the couch with his cell phone handy.

"I knew it," he said when his phone rang five minutes later.

"What did you know?" Sloane asked looking up from the table.

"It's Emmy. She will want to know what went on tonight."

"Are you allowed to tell her?"

"I can tell her most stuff," he said and answered the phone. "What's up, brat?"

"I know your kids are in bed because Heather was talking to Dotty, and she said you were turning off the lights, so tell me about the meeting."

Tony looked at Sloane and smiled. She rolled her eyes and continued grading papers.

"All right. I took notes. We started at exactly 6:34, and Pastor Tyler prayed. We had a short devotional and then read the minutes from last month..."

"I don't need a minute-by-minute account of the boring reports. I want to know the good stuff."

"What good stuff?" he asked knowing it would push a button.

"The anniversary weekend, you creepozoid! You know what I meant," she said. "Did they say anything about Chase and Yvonne being here? What about Pastor Behren? Are they coming?"

"Let me check the notes I smuggled out of the conference room." He made a show of rustling some paper. "You know I could get arrested for smuggling church secrets out of the building. You aren't a spy for a Baptist or Catholic church, are you?"

She sighed and said, "Yes, Father James is paying me a ton of money for church secrets. Tell me."

"Okay, it says here that Chase declined because he knew you would be here."

"If there was still a cord attached to your phone, I would strangle you with it," she warned.

"You know they are coming. Have you talked to Riordan about the Saturday concert?"

"Yeah, Sadie asked if I would be available to sing, and I said I was."

Tony checked his notes again. "They booked hotel rooms for any former staff members coming in from out of town. They have a plan for the potluck and are going to order a ton of food."

"I hope that will be enough for you," she teased.

"Anything else you want to know? If not, I'm going to make myself a sandwich. I didn't have time to eat after work. I'm lucky I had a Snickers bar with me."

# Chapter Thirty-Eight

On the first Tuesday of April Emmy booted up her laptop and pulled up the website she had found the previous week. *Do I really want to spend fifty bucks on this. What if I don't learn anything? Tony and Andy will make fun of me if they find out I wasted the money.* She was ready to close the site, but hesitated. *Lord, it's only money, and if this is a waste, I'll donate extra to the school.* She decided to spend the money on ItalianHeritage.Com. She began her search with the Sandusky side of the family. She quickly found information about her grandfather Jim Sandusky and his parents, Charles Sandusky and Blanche Rozzi. But there the trail grew cold.

"What are you doing, Em?" Kenny asked looking over her shoulder.

She explained and said, "Shoot! I thought this would be the easy part because they lived in the States."

"Maybe they were illegal immigrants, or maybe they changed their family name because they were criminals or in witness protection."

Emmy made a face at Kenny. "Very funny. You're lucky because you can trace your family back to the middle ages."

"Not quite that far," Kenny said as he chuckled.

She spent the entire afternoon trying other sites to learn more about the Sandusky or Rozzi family without any success.

"I give up. I can't find anything," Emmy said.

"Maybe you should try the other side of the family. You already know your great-great grandfather's name. Pietro Jacovelli. And you know where he lived. Maybe you'll have more luck there."

"I'll try tomorrow. I have to get dinner ready now."

The next day Emmy traced the Polmonari side of the family, and after several hours of research was able to trace her lineage back to her great-great grandparents. She showed the results to Kenny.

"Good! At least you have some names," Kenny said.

"Polmonari, Polcari, Donte Pecora and Maria Mione. You can sure tell my ancestors were all Italian, huh?"

"I think your grandfather Sandusky was the only non-Italian in your family."

"I'm getting better at this. Tomorrow I'm going to try Daddy's side of the family."

On Thursday Emmy had even better results.

"Kenny, look at this!" She carried her laptop into the family room and plopped down on the couch beside him.

"What did you learn?"

"We already knew that Pietro Jacovelli was my great-great grandfather, right?"

Kenny nodded.

"Well, his wife's name was Isabella Faiola and they had eight children. One of them was Giulio Jacovelli, my great-grandfather, and he married Luciano Carosi and they had six kids and one of them was named Isabella."

"That's amazing," Kenny said.

Emmy looked at him and her eyes sparkled.

"Okay, I can tell you've got more to tell me. Spill it, Em."

"This is kinda weird, but I started researching the Colasanti side and came across something rather surprising."

"What? Are you related to someone famous?" Kenny asked.

"No, but I came across the name Milano and that led me to another name."

"What name?" he asked after she didn't say anything for a moment.

"Bertucci."

"Get out! For real?"

"Yes. I'm going to call Mama and see if she's busy," Emmy said.

"There's no way it's the same Bertucci family, Em. That would be too much of a coincidence," Kenny said.

Emmy called and told Mama she needed to ask her something important. Mama said to come right over.

312

"I'll be back as soon as I can," Emmy said as she raced out of the house.

She drove across the street and found Mama in the kitchen.

"What do you need to ask me, sweetie?" Mama wiped her hands with a towel. "I'm making two pans of lasagna for dinner."

Emmy explained what she had been doing.

"Anyway, I was tracing the Colasanti name and came across the name Milano. My great-grandmother's maiden name was Milano. Her father's name was Stefano. I kinda went back and forth and learned that Stefano had a bunch of kids. One was Maria, but she had a brother named Salvatore. I searched Salvatore Milano and he had some kids. He had a daughter Dorotea Mariana and she married a Pietro Bertucci. Do you think he could be related to Tony's father?"

"Tony's grandfather was named Peter, or Pietro, but Bertucci is a common name," Mama said.

"Oh, I was wondering if it could be the same person," Emmy said and then sighed.

Mama looked at Emmy and saw her disappointment. "There is one way to check."

"What's that?" Emmy asked.

"I have an old Bertucci family Bible in my closet. I haven't looked at it in years because it's rather fragile, but we could take a peek. I seem to remember a list of births and marriages and other information. Of course, most of it's written in Italian."

"But we could read the names, right?" Emmy's eyes began to sparkle.

"You're probably right, Emmy. Let's go back to my bedroom and take a look."

Emmy followed Mama through the kitchen to her mother-in-law suite and helped her retrieve the old Bible from the top shelf of the closet.

"It's in this dusty old box," Mama said.

Emmy watched as Mama removed the lid and lifted out the old Bible. She unwrapped the cloth that protected it.

"Do you have any idea how old this is?" Emmy asked.

"It was printed in the 1890s."

"Oh," Emmy sighed. "The Stefano Milano I found was born in 1840, so this Bible probably isn't old enough to have anything about him."

Mama carefully opened the large Bible. "It's in Italian, dear." Mama opened a few more pages and then turned to the back of the Bible. "This is where the names are written."

Mama and Emmy looked through the names together.

"I'm pretty sure this belonged to my mother-in-law," Mama said. "Yes! Here is her name. Dorotea Milano and she was born in 1904. She married Pietro Bertucci in... I can't tell because it's smudged."

Emmy checked her laptop. "The year is the same as what I found."

"Let's see. It appears that Dorotea and Pietro had seven children, but two of them died as infants. There are five other names and the last one is Peter Renato which is Tony's father."

"But that doesn't prove the Milanos I found are the same people, does it?" Emmy sighed.

"I'm afraid it doesn't, dear. The names are so common." Mama opened a few more pages and was about to close the Bible when she came across a yellowed envelope. "I don't remember this."

"Can we open it and see what's inside?" Emmy's eyes pleaded with Mama.

"Okay, but we have to be careful."

Mama took the contents out of the unsealed envelope. "There are two papers here, Emmy. Let's see if we can read them."

Mama unfolded the first page and scanned it.

"What is it?" Emmy asked.

"It's a list of names."

"Whose names?"

"Well, it starts with Stefano Milano and Maria Lubrano who were born in 1840 and 1841."

"Just like the ones I found," Emmy said as her eyes sparkled.

Mama checked for more names. "Stefano and Maria had six children. The oldest was Maria."

314

"Did everyone name their daughters Maria in those days?" Emmy asked.

"It was quite common for the oldest daughter to be named Maria. Everyone was Catholic," Mama explained. "The youngest son was..." Mama looked at Emmy and grinned. "Salvatore." Mama turned the page over and read more.

"When were they born, Mama?" Emmy asked.

Mama checked. "Maria was born in 1869, and Salvatore in 1879. They both passed away in 1944."

"That fits perfectly with what I found," Emmy squealed.

Mama read some more. "Okay, this is very important."

"What did you find?"

"There is a list of Salvatore's kids, and some years when they passed away." Mama continued to read and then stopped suddenly. She looked at Emmy. "What is your great-grandfather's name and when was he born?"

Emmy checked her laptop. "His name was Guiseppi and he was born in 1865 in Naples. He died in 1910. Why?"

Mama put an arm around Emmy's shoulders and squeezed her. "That matches exactly. I think your great-grandfather married the sister of Tony's great-grandfather."

"What does that mean?" Emmy asked.

Mama tilted her head back and forth. "I don't know exactly, but it would appear you are distant cousins."

"No way!" Emmy shouted. "For real?"

"I think it would be too great a coincidence for it to be otherwise. The dates match, and we have this written record."

Emmy wrapped her arms around Mama Bertucci and hugged her tightly.

Mama patted Emmy's back and whispered, "I always knew there was a reason I loved you so much."

Emmy broke off the hug and wiped her eyes. "Let's look it up on Wikipedia."

Emmy opened Wikipedia on her laptop as Mama carefully replace the papers in the envelope and then back in the Bible. "Good thing I know the password for the network over here." Emmy typed in 'cousins' and, after a short search, they found a

315

chart that explained familial relationships.

"I guess you and Tony are third cousins," Mama said after they studied the chart.

"I have to tell him. Is he home yet?"

"Let's go see," Mama said.

She led the way into the kitchen, and they saw Tony sitting at the table drinking a Dr Pepper.

He looked up and saw Emmy. "Hey, brat. What are you doing here?"

She walked over, stood behind him, smacked the back of his head and then put her hands on his shoulders.

"What was that for?" he rubbed his head.

"We have some interesting news, son," Mama said.

"What? Are you guys moving away?" Tony turned in his chair to look at Emmy. "Please, tell me you're moving."

"No! We're not moving, you creep."

"Too bad. So what's the big news?"

Emmy sat in the chair next to Tony. "I've been doing some research into my family this week, and Mama and I found something... interesting."

"Like what? Are you related to Mussolini or some other creep?" He took a drink of his pop.

"Some other creep," Emmy said and then sighed. "You and I are third cousins."

"Very funny," Tony said and then took another drink.

"It's true, Tony," Mama said.

Tony spit out his pop and coughed several times. "That's impossible! I can't be related to her."

"I'm afraid you are, cousin," Emmy said and then giggled.

Tony stared at Emmy and then looked at his mother. "Mama, is she pulling my leg? Please tell me she is."

"I can't do that. It seems that you share a set of great-great grandparents, and that makes you third cousins."

"And it's not because someone married someone. We are related by blood," Emmy said.

"If you go back far enough, we're all related," Tony said.

"Nice try, bucko. Face it. We're blood cousins."

316

Tony and Emmy stared at each other for a moment.

"Shoot!" Tony said.

"Crap!" Emmy swore.

They looked at Mama and then back at each other.

"I will let you two figure this out," Mama said and then left the kitchen.

Emmy bit her lip.

Tony scratched his jaw. "Are you thinking what I'm thinking?"

"Maybe. Are you thinking about when we... kinda... you know... uh, we got carried away all those years ago."

"And then I proposed to you. What if you had said yes. Would that even be legal?"

"I think it's only first cousins that can't get legally married," Emmy said as she crossed her arms over her chest. "Some royal families marry cousins and stuff."

"Does Kenny know?" Tony asked.

"No, Mama and I just found out," Emmy answered.

"I meant the other thing," Tony said.

"He knows you proposed, silly. He bought the ring from you, remember?"

Tony shook his head.

"Oh, that," Emmy said and then sighed. "Kristen knows all the details, but I don't think Kenny does." *That would be kinda like him sharing all the details of his time with Becky. Except we didn't quite... whatever.*

"I guess now you don't have to think of me as your adopted brother," Tony said and managed a weak smile.

"You're still a creep," Emmy said as she punched his arm. "I better go home and let this info digest. I'm not sure if I'm going to like being related to you or not."

"Yeah, I hear ya," Tony said.

Emmy started to smack the back of his head again, but stopped and kissed the top of his head instead. "I'll talk to you later." She walked back out to her car. She started it, but then sat there for a moment. *Geez! I hope I never find out that Rory and I are related. That would be too much.*

317

# Chapter Thirty-Nine

Heather walked into her parents' bedroom and asked, "Mom, why can't me and Isa sing a song tonight? We've been practicing. We could sing with you and Daddy."

Emmy walked out of her closet and held up two dresses. "Which one?" she asked Kenny and then turned to Heather. "I explained this before. Tonight is just a time for adults to sing."

Heather spun around and stomped out.

"The red one might be a bit too flashy for tonight," Kenny said.

Emmy walked back into the closet, hung up the red dress and inspected the white dress with small red roses. "This one is shorter."

"It's not that short. You've worn it before. You could wear some leggings, too."

"Okay. What time do we need to be at the church?"

"If you want to rehearse your songs again, you should be there by five. It's supposed to start at six."

"We rehearsed everything last night," she said. "It wouldn't be the end of the world if I didn't do a soundcheck tonight. Are your parents going to meet us there?"

"Yes, and they volunteered to bring the kids home if we want to hang around after the concert."

"Perfect!" Emmy exclaimed. "I'm sure there will be lots of people I want to talk to."

Later, only a minute after six, Pastor Tyler ended a conversation with Dr. Schofield, glanced at Emmy and whispered, "Are you ready? It's time."

She nodded. "Do I look nervous?"

Tyler chucked and answered, "You look kinda like you always do. Are you always nervous before you sing all by yourself with no musicians and close to a thousand people staring at you?"

"You're a big help," she answered, but then took a deep breath and smiled. "I'm as ready as I'm going to be."

Pastor Tyler walked onto the platform. He waited until the crowd settled down and began, "I want to thank everyone for

318

coming." He prayed to open the service and said, "I think it was over a year ago I was going through one of the filing cabinets in the main office, and I came across this program." He held it up and a camera zoomed it on it and projected it onto the large video screens. He looked to his right and turned the program right-side-up. "Sorry about that. Anyway, this is the program from the dedication ceremony fifty years ago. April 16, 1967, to be exact. Liz warned me that would sound dorky, but..." He shrugged. "I said it anyway. I should have listened to Liz." He opened the program, which was several pages long, and said, "The first song in the order of service that morning was 'Amazing Grace,' and I thought it would be a fitting way to open this service..."

*That's my cue.* Emmy thought. She stood up and climbed the steps onto the platform. *Lord, please give me strength not to screw this up.*

Tyler continued, "Would you please stand and join Emmy Colasanti-Colwell in singing."

Emmy waited a few seconds to allow the crowd to rise and began...

Ninety minutes later Riordan walked to the center of the platform. "For the final song of the evening, I would like as many of the worship team members who can to join us on the stage. If you ever sang with the Crest Ridge worship team, please join us."

"If you can't climb the stairs, you could stand in front of the platform," Sadie said.

Emmy whispered to Liz as several people walked to the front of the auditorium, "What song are we singing? I forgot."

Liz turned her head and looked at Emmy. "Are you serious?"

"Kinda, sorta. Riordan said he might change it."

"He might have wanted a different song, but Tyler insisted on this one."

Emmy bit her lip.

Liz smiled and put an arm around Emmy's waist. "Did I ever tell you we had one of my friends sing this at our wedding?"

"For real?"

319

Liz nodded.

"If you don't know all the words, follow along on the screens as we sing 'I Will Be True To You.'"

Kenny moved past Regina and Robby Collins and stood next to Emmy. He took her hand in his and smiled at her. "They're singing your song, m'lady."

She squeezed his hand and wiped away a tear with the other.

"Hey, Emmy, I hate to admit it, but the Schulenbergs put together a pretty good program," Tony said. "You guys are staying for the desserts, right?"

"Yes, we told the kids we could stay until nine," Emmy answered.

Tony looked at the crowd leaving the sanctuary. "It's a good thing we got here early. I don't think they could have jammed more people in here." He nudged Emmy and pointed. "I see your in-laws talking to Mr. and Mrs. Robertson."

"It did look pretty full," Kenny said.

"Mommy, you did a good job and you didn't even cry when you sang that napkin song," Isabella said while hugging Emmy.

"I would have if I had looked at the big screens. I didn't know we still had that video available."

"Chase saved it in the computer archives. He asked if I thought you would mind if they played it. I told him better to ask forgiveness later than permission beforehand," Kenny said.

"Daddy, can we go to the gym and get some cake?" Heather asked. "We want to get in line before everyone else does."

"You can go," Kenny said.

"I will make sure they behave," Carson promised. "You sounded better than anyone, Aunt Emmy."

Emmy looked up at her nephew and smiled. "I'm glad your mother and Brady brought you here instead of just making you ride with us. Do you know where they are?"

Carson pointed toward the back of the sanctuary. "Somewhere back there. Grandma and Grandpa Robertson came, too, but I'm not sure if they will stay for cake and stuff."

"I'm just pleased they came. Go ahead and get in line and make sure your cousins don't get too out of line." She spotted Chase and Yvonne Hillman talking to Riordan and Sadie. "I need to yell at someone. Be right back."

Chase saw Emmy approaching and whispered to his wife, "Don't look now, but I think you're in trouble."

Yvonne saw Emmy weaving her way through the crowd, smiled and answered, "Not me. It was totally your idea to play that video."

"Chase Hillman! You are in such deep trouble you might never get out of it. Why did you make me sing that song, and where did you find that old video. I looked like a child." She frowned at Chase for a second but then hugged him. She turned to Yvonne. "It's so good to see you guys."

"Why am I in trouble?" Chase asked. "You made it through without crying, and FYI you still look like a child."

"I will take that as a weird compliment," she said. "I have to talk to you more before you head back to Toledo. I want to know how everyone is doing?"

"We are here for a few days, Em. Maybe we can get together for lunch," Chase said.

"I will hold you to that."

Emmy spent close to thirty minutes talking to people before she and Kenny headed to the large gym. They were in line behind Tony and Sloane when she felt a tap on her shoulder.

"Excuse me, but is this the line to get dessert?"

She spun around, smiled and said, "It is, but I'm not sure there will be any left. Tony is ahead of us." She stood on tiptoes and hugged Rory Porter. "When did you get here? Why didn't you let me know you were coming? You should have told me."

"We were hoping to surprise you, and I guess we succeeded," he said squeezing her.

Emmy let go and grabbed Rochelle's hand. "It's good to see you, too. Did you guys enjoy the concert? Tell me the truth."

"It was better than a visit to the dentist," Rory teased.

Kenny shook Rory's hand and asked, "Did you have any trouble finding the place?"

321

"I haven't been gone that long," Rory answered. "And the code worked okay."

"What are you talking about?" Emmy asked. "What code, and what place was Rory looking for?"

"Our place, Em. Rory let me know they were coming a few days ago, and I told him they could stay in the nanny suite rather than find a hotel. You don't mind, do you?"

Emmy poked Kenny in the side. "You stinker! You knew they were coming and didn't tell me. I hate you both."

Rory grinned at Emmy and said, "We must have arrived at the house just after you guys left. We would have arrived earlier, but the flight was a bit late getting to Chicago."

"How did you get here from the airport?" Emmy asked. "You flew into Midway, right?"

"Yes, and Kenny arranged for a ride to your place. He even let us borrow his car to get to the church."

"I'm so glad you guys came." She hugged him again. "How long can you stay?"

"We fly back next Saturday. We can find a hotel if you don't want to put up with us for a whole week," Rory said.

Emmy grinned and her eyes sparkled as she said, "I'll try to tolerate your presence for a few days."

"We thought about sneaking Tim Burine onto the stage for one of your songs, but decided against it," Kenny said.

"That would have been priceless," Emmy said clapping her hands together. "Why didn't you?"

Kenny shrugged and answered, "I wasn't sure how you would react. I didn't want to embarrass you."

"I probably would have laughed so hard I would cry, so maybe it's a good thing you didn't."

Emmy turned around and poked Tony in the back. "Hey! Did you see who made it up from Florida."

Tony turned to face Emmy. "I heard you guys talking. Good to see you again, Rory."

Rory shook hands and introduced his wife.

"Where are the kids?" Rochelle asked. "Did they come to the concert? They weren't at the house."

"They're here somewhere," Emmy said. "They wanted to get in line early. I'm sure we'll find them sometime."

"We saw them in June, but they grow so fast," Rochelle said.

"Tell me about it," Emmy said rolling her eyes. "Do they know you are here?"

Kenny shook his head. "I didn't tell them."

"There you are," Father James said walking up to Emmy holding a slice of cake. "I was looking all over for you."

"Is that for me?" Emmy tried to grab the plate.

Father James turned and swatted her hand away. "You can get your own." He paused and stared at Rory. "Well as I live and breath. I finally get to meet you." He offered a hand and Rory shook it. "Emmy didn't tell me you would be here. I'm Father James, by the way."

"Yes, I know and she didn't know we were coming." Rory introduced Rochelle to Father James and turned to Emmy. "I've seen the photos you posted, but it's even more amazing in person. He really does look like your father."

Emmy tilted her head and looked at Rory then at Father James. "Come on. Don't tease me. You guys have met before, right?"

"I don't recall a time," Father James said.

"Nor I," Rory added.

"How is that possible?" Emmy asked.

"Well, you didn't meet your brother until January of 2011, and I moved to Tampa in November of 2012," Rory said.

"How can you remember all that, and I can't believe you didn't meet at some point," Emmy said. "That's almost two whole years. You're yanking my chain."

Kenny scratched his ear. "I'm with Em on this one. I can't believe you weren't at the house at the same time. What about at Diane's wedding?"

Rory chuckled and said, "I wasn't invited for obvious reasons."

"I was at the ceremony, but not the reception," Father James said. "Where is Diane? I saw Carson and Caden earlier."

"They were ahead of us," Kenny looked around. "They are sitting over there with my parents, but I don't see any empty seats at that table."

"What about the barbecue we had for the Fourth of July in 2011?"

Rory pointed a finger at Father James. "That's right! I think we did meet then, but I couldn't stay too long because I got called in and had to work."

"Phew! I'm glad we got that settled," Emmy said.

Father James shook Rory's hand and said, "Glad to meet you again again."

"You guys are dorks," Emmy said.

"Should I save some seats?" Father James asked.

"You can try. Have you seen the kids?"

"There are two tables of kids over there." Father James pointed. "Some of yours might be there."

Eventually, everyone got something to eat, and they found a table with enough seats.

"What kind of cake did you get, Em?" Kenny asked.

"Chocolate and this one is lemon," she answered after tasting it. "Rochelle, did you enjoy the concert?"

"I did. I liked how they coordinated the slide show with songs from the different eras. I thought that little skit with the four men singing was humorous. Did they really wear those loud, plaid sports coats?"

'They must have," Kenny said. There was that short video of them singing."

"That quartet was part of the church long before I came here, but Aunt Doris has told me stories about them," Emmy said.

"Like what, Emmy?" Rory asked.

"Well, her husband was part of the group back in the seventies. I can't remember what she said their name was, but they sang every Sunday, and sometimes they traveled to other churches. She said they had a piano player, a bass player and sometimes a drummer."

"So, the men who sang tonight were not in the original group, correct?" Rochelle asked.

324

"No, I think two of those guys are dead or something."

"So, they couldn't be here, right?" Tony asked with a straight face.

"Duh! Ya think," Emmy answered with a frown.

"It was entertaining," Rochelle said.

"Yeah, that one guy had the deepest voice I've ever heard," Rory replied.

Kenny took a sip of his coffee and said, "That was Mr. Griffith. Someone told me his parents were part of SoHam First Nazarene. That's the church that started this one. It's ironic we are so much bigger than them."

"That's right," Tony said. "At one of the board meetings he passed around some photos of the groundbreaking ceremony. He was a teenager then and was in several of the photos."

"I liked the photos of the inside of the church before they remodeled it," Sloane said.

"It was ahead of its time," Kenny said. "I doubt many churches were designed the way the original building was back in the sixties."

"What do you mean?" Rory asked.

"I'll show you. Can I steal your napkin, Em?"

She handed it to him.

"Do you have a pen?" he asked.

She rolled her eyes.

"I have one," Rochelle said. She pulled it out of her purse and handed it across the table to Kenny.

He thought for a moment, quickly drew a square and let everyone see it.

"That doesn't look very modern or unusual," Emmy said.

Kenny explained, "No, but if you turn it like this." He moved the napkin. "It takes on the shape of a diamond. That's the outside of the building." He added another square inside the original one. "Now all this area inside this smaller diamond, or square, is the original sanctuary. Then all around the outer edges are the entryway, classrooms, offices and storage spaces." He drew some lines to separate the outer area. "I've never seen a church built in the sixties like this."

Rory took a close look at the napkin. "Then they added the building where the school is, right?"

"Yes, that would be on this side," Kenny drew a few more lines.

Emmy faked a yawn and said, "That is so fascinating."

"I could show you the blueprints for the new sanctuary," Tony said.

"Don't tell me you carry a copy around with you," Emmy said.

Tony frowned at Emmy. "No, but I know where Pastor Tyler keeps them."

"Ugh! So boring," Emmy said.

"Maybe another time," Father James said. "Does anyone else need a refill?"

"I could use another cup," Emmy said holding up her cup.

"Splendid." Father James handed his cup to her. "Would you fill mine up while you're getting some for yourself, please?"

"You're lucky I like you," she said and was about to stand up when one of the teens appeared with coffee.

"Does anyone need more coffee? This is regular," the teenage girl said.

"Perfect timing," Kenny said.

"Would you like a refill, Mr. Bertucci?"

Tony waved a hand over his cup. "I'm good, but thank you."

After the teenager moved on, Emmy giggled.

"And what is so funny?" Tony asked.

"She called you Mr. Bertucci like you're an old man."

"I wonder if there's any cake left," Rochelle said.

"I can check." Rory stood up. "Anyone else like more?"

Four people raised a hand.

"Any preference as to the flavor?"

"Chocolate," Emmy said.

"Doesn't matter," everyone else answered.

"Do you need help?" Kenny asked.

"No, Emmy and I can handle it," he answered smiling at her.

326

"Fine! I'll be your waitress."

"You have younger legs than us, Em," Kenny said.

Emmy stood up and pointed to Tony. "He's younger than me. He should get the cake."

"I'm only three months younger, and all those years of playing football have ruined my knees. I'll be fortunate if I can even walk when I'm fifty."

"What a big baby." Emmy rolled her eyes and walked to the dessert table with Rory.

"I don't see any chocolate, Em," Rory said.

"Doesn't matter. I'll take whatever's left," she said and then grabbed a piece of fudge. "I know the lady who makes this. It's so yummy. I'm surprised there's any left."

"Maybe that piece fell on the floor," Rory teased.

Emmy took a bite of it. "I don't care. It's worth it."

"How have things been between you guys?" Rory asked softly.

Emmy grinned but didn't answer.

Rory laughed and asked, "How many years have you been married?"

"Fourteen years this month, and the sex is still great."

"I'm happy for you, Olivia," he said.

"Thank you, Clarence." She used the middle name he hated. "You guys doing okay?"

"We've been married less than a year. We're still practicing," he said. "A lot," he added with a smile.

She smacked his arm almost causing him to drop the two plates of cake. "You are still so bad."

"I thought that's why you liked me."

"Hush, here comes Tyler and Liz. I don't want them to hear us talking about sex," she whispered.

"Emmy, you did a great job tonight," Liz said.

Tyler shook Rory's hand. "Good to see you again. Congratulations on your marriage. I know it's late, but we haven't seen you.

"Thanks, Pastor Tyler," Rory said.

"What were you guys talking about?" Liz asked.

Emmy bit her lip and her cheeks turned red. "Nothing," she said unconvincingly.

Tyler chuckled.

"I asked Emmy how long she and Kenny have been married," Rory answered.

"How long has it been, Emmy?" Liz asked.

"Fourteen years, but it seems a lot longer."

Liz looked puzzled.

"I mean much shorter," Emmy said and then shrugged. "I don't know what I mean. We've been together most of our lives."

"Since grade school, right?" Liz asked. "We need to say good night to the kids. My parents are here and they agreed to take them home. Tyler has to stay and talk to Dr. Schofield and the other pastors who came. See you in the morning."

"Night, Liz," Emmy said. She bumped against Rory as they walked back to the table. "Thanks for bailing me out."

"No problem, Olivia."

"About time you got back," Tony said taking one of the slices of cake from Emmy. "I thought I would starve."

"Why didn't Kristen and John come tonight?" Sloane asked.

Emmy held up a finger and quickly swallowed a bite of cake. "They were getting together with her parents. She didn't say why, but they will be here in the morning."

Just before nine Kenny's parents walked up to the table.

"Are you still going to take the kids home?" Kenny asked.

"Yes, and we're ready to go," Mrs. Colwell said.

Mr. Colwell saw Rory and smiled.

Rory stood up and extended a hand. "It's good to see you, Mr. Colwell."

"You, too, Rory, and I assume this must be Rochelle."

"It is," Rory said.

Emmy spotted her kids running around the gym with Tony and Sloane's younger ones. "Where's Diane and Brady?" she asked.

"They left about fifteen minutes ago. They said they enjoyed the concert," Mrs. Colwell answered.

328

"I'll round them up for you," Emmy said.

"Grab ours, too," Tony said.

While Emmy corralled the children, Rory and Rochelle talked to Kenny and his parents.

"Mom, do we have to leave already?" Ben Bertucci asked.

"Yes, you have to get up early for church, and your little brothers look tired. You need to take baths tonight," Sloane answered. "Go find your jackets."

"Can't I take a shower in the morning?" Ben asked. "I'm not real sweaty."

"All right, but Taylor and Coby need baths tonight."

Tony and Sloane left with their kids. Five minutes after that Grandma and Grandpa Colwell departed with their grandchildren.

"Kenny, do you know that older man talking to Tyler?" Emmy asked.

He looked and scratched his ear. "I wouldn't swear to it, but it kinda looks like Pastor Jantz."

"Who?"

"Rev. Jantz. He was the first pastor here. You've seen the photos in the hall outside the main office, right?"

"Yeah, I guess, but I haven't paid them much attention lately," she answered with a shrug.

"If I had to guess, I think he looks like an older version of his photo."

"Such a dork. He wouldn't look like a younger version. He was the pastor here fifty years ago."

Pastor Ausland and his wife approached Emmy and Kenny.

She saw them and smiled. "It's so good to see you guys. How are you, Carolyn? Is Pastor Herb taking it easy now that he's retired again?"

"I haven't been doing anything more strenuous than spoiling the grandkids," Herb Ausland said as he hugged Emmy.

They chatted for a moment.

Pastor Ausland checked his watch. "We really need to head home, but we will be back in the morning."

"See you then," Emmy said. *I hope you are all right. You look thinner.*

329

"Em, I think Chase wants to talk to you," Kenny said as he nudged her.

Emmy turned just as Chase arrived. "I didn't do it. I'm innocent."

Chase grinned.

"What did I do," Emmy said.

"Nothing I know of, but I'm sure you must have done something. Dr. Schofield has requested a slight change to the service tomorrow. He would like you to sing 'These Things Take Time.'"

"You've got to be kidding!" she shouted. "I haven't sung that song in several years."

Chase shrugged. "For some reason known only to him and God, he would like you to sing it. He said it means a lot to his family."

"If I agree, can we practice it tomorrow? I could use a track, but I'd rather sing with the band."

"I'm pretty sure we can run through it, but I'm sure everyone knows it. It was the title track to your CD."

"Yeah, but that came out ten years ago."

"You wouldn't want to disappoint Dr. Schofield, would you?" Chase asked.

"You're a stinker," Emmy said. "I'm the one who puts a Catholic guilt trip on people, and here you are using it against me."

"Is that a yes?"

Emmy sighed and tried to look angry without success. "Fine! But you owe me."

"I will tell Pastor Tyler to go ahead and make the change in the program."

# Chapter Forty

"We have to drive separately because I have to be there early to rehearse," Emmy said. "You shouldn't stay in bed too much longer. There will be a huge crowd today. You need to get there in time to find seats. Don't forget the service starts at ten today."

"I'm ready to get up," Kenny said tugging on the towel wrapped around her.

"Stop it. I've fifteen minutes to get out the door," Emmy said. She ran to her closet, picked out some clothes and finished getting ready. "I'll see you at church. Don't let Kevin wear the same clothes he wore last night."

"How will I know? I don't remember what he wore."

"Ask Isa. She will know," Emmy said and dashed out of the bedroom. "Kids! It's time to get up!" she yelled. She flew down the stairs, ran down the hall and skidded around the corner into the kitchen.

"Whoa! Slow down, Em," Rory said from an island barstool. "What's the big rush?"

"I need to get to church to rehearse. Why are you up already?"

"I'm still on Florida time, I guess. I made some coffee. I hope you don't mind." He pointed to the coffeemaker.

"Thanks, but I'll take it to go." She grabbed a travel mug from the cabinet and filled it. "You guys are coming, right?"

"Yes, we will be there. Is that a new dress?" he asked taking a sip of his coffee.

"Fairly new. Does it look all right?" She turned around to let him see.

"It's a good color for you."

"How would you know?" she asked racing around the island to the desk.

"Rochelle has taught me a few things," he answered.

"Where did I put my purse?" Emmy muttered rummaging through the mess on the desk.

Rory pointed. "There's one by the landline. Is that it?"

Emmy turned and looked. "Yes, thank you, Rory." She grabbed the purse and her keys which were hanging up in their regular place by the mudroom door. "I'm sorry to rush off. We'll have time to visit this afternoon. See you."

"Knock 'em dead, Olivia!" he said as she disappeared.

Kevin wandered into the kitchen ten minutes later. "Hi, Uncle Rory. Where's Mommy? I'm hungry."

"Sorry, buddy, but she left already. What are you hungry for?"

"Do you know how to cook real food?"

Rory chuckled and replied, "I'm not a gourmet cook like your mother, but I can make eggs and bacon and grits and stuff."

Kevin opened the fridge and pulled out the carton of eggs and a package of Jimmy Dean's sausage. "I'll share if you cook."

Over the next half hour everyone else made it downstairs. Kenny was the last to appear.

"Daddy, Uncle Rory is making breakfast. He knows how to cook!" Kevin shouted while waving a slice of bacon. He quickly ate the bacon and wiped his hands on his pants.

"I can cook," Kenny said. He headed for the coffeemaker and poured a cup. "Good morning, Rochelle. I hope the kids didn't disturb you."

Rochelle waved a hand dismissively. "I woke up before them."

"Ah! You must have heard Emmy's yell as she left," Kenny said as he walked to the stove and took a whiff. "I love the smell of cholesterol in the morning."

"That's bacon, eggs and sausage," Kevin said. "I ate the last of the hash browns, and we're almost out of ketchup."

"Good to know," Kenny said. He looked at Rory.

"Go ahead. Everyone else has eaten," Rory said.


"Emmy, are you pleased with how we played the bridge?" Chase asked. He had taken over the role of band director for this special service.

"Yes, and it makes sense to repeat it four times."

"That's how it is on the recording," Chase replied.

"I suppose I should remember, but I never listen to my own CDs."

"Any other questions before we move on?" Chase asked the group.

The group spent several minutes going over the material.

"There is one small change in the service order," Chase said. "During the offering there will be a video playing. We, the musicians, will not have to play. Other than that." Chase looked through the program again. "This is the plan." He held it up. "If everyone is clear, I will pray and we can get ready."

Emmy raised a hand.

"Yes, Emily?" Chase asked.

"Are we supposed to stay on the platform after..." she checked the program. "Oh, never mind. I guess we can go back to the music suite and watch the service from there. We will come back for the last song."

"Any other questions?" Chase asked.

There were none.

"Dad!" Heather screamed from the bedroom.

Kenny dashed up the stairs around the corner and into the twins' room. "What is it? Who's hurt?"

Heather held up a dress. "No one is hurt, but I can't wear this."

"Why not? Your mother picked it out."

"There is a stain on the sleeve. I can't wear it." She threw the dress on the floor.

Kenny put a hand to his forehead, took a deep breath, sighed and said, "Okay, you can find a different dress. Please hurry. We need to be leaving in fifteen minutes."

"Did Uncle Rory already leave?" Isabella asked.

"Yes, they left ten minutes ago. I have to check on your brother, so meet me downstairs as soon as you can." Kenny darted out of the room, across the hall and peeked into Kevin's room. "You're dressed!"

Kevin stared at his father. "Yeah, I can dress myself, Dad. Been doing it for a couple years. What's the big deal?"

333

"We need to leave in ten minutes," Kenny said scratching his jaw and looking around the room. *I can't remember ever seeing your room this clean.*

"I just need to brush my teeth and I'll be ready," Kevin said. "Could you tie my shoes for me, please?"

"Sure," Kenny said.

Kevin rolled his eyes. "Mom is right. You are a dork. That was a joke."

Kenny stopped and looked at his son.

"Dad, I was kidding. You're not a dork. You're the coolest dad I know. Mom just says that because she likes to tease you. I don't think she really believes it."

"Thanks, buddy. That makes me feel better," Kenny said.

"Anytime, Dad."

The worship team took their positions on the platform as Pastor Tyler prayed. Emmy nudged Liz as Tyler was greeting the congregation and whispered, "I saw that older man talking to Tyler last night. Kenny thought he might be the first pastor who served here. Is he?"

"Yes, his name is Rev. Jantz, and we were surprised he was able to be here."

"He looks pretty old. Do you know anything about him?" Emmy asked.

"Not much, but Pastor Ausland said he's in his late eighties."

Tyler left the platform and took his seat. Riordan glanced at Chase and the band began to play. Emmy scanned the crowd from her position on the right side of the platform. She spotted Tony and Sloane but couldn't see Kenny or the kids.

"Emmy, you're supposed to move to the center," Liz whispered after the worship team sang their fourth song.

"I know," Emmy answered. She moved to the center and smiled as the band played the intro to her song.

"I love hearing you sing that song," Liz whispered when Emmy returned. "Always have."

"When have you ever heard me sing it?" Emmy asked.

334

Liz shrugged and wrapped her long hair around a finger. "I'm not sure, but I've heard you sing it before."

The worship team did one last song and left the platform. They watched the rest of the service on a big screen TV in the music suite. After the message they returned for a final song.

"Can you hear my stomach rumbling?" Emmy asked Liz after Tyler ended the service with a prayer and directions for the potluck.

"Didn't you eat any breakfast? There were donuts in the music suite," Liz said.

"I was too nervous to eat," Emmy answered putting a hand on her stomach.

"You should grab a donut because it might be an hour before we eat," Liz said.

"Why is that?" Emmy asked looking out at the crowd.

Liz grinned and answered, "Because Dr. Schofield and the other preachers are supposed to be the first in line and they're going to be talking forever."

"Maybe I should see if there are any left," Emmy said. She looked out at the crowd. "Can you see Kenny anywhere?"

Liz pointed to the right side near the rear of the auditorium. "He's talking to Rory and Tony."

"Oh, I see him now. Make sure you tell Tyler it was a good service," Emmy said as she headed toward the steps.

"Kenny, would you mind taking the kids home? Emmy asked. "It's almost two o'clock, and they are getting restless. Most everyone has left already. There's just the people cleaning up."

"I assumed they would be going with me. You don't have car seats in your car," Kenny answered.

"I'm going to stop at the store and pick up some stuff to make taco salad. Rory requested I make it while they're here," Emmy explained. "You don't mind, do you?"

He shrugged. "I don't mind. I like taco salad, but you better make two batches."

"I planned to. I know how much you can eat. I'll be quick. I need to talk to Gideon and Bobby about the Fourth of July."

"I will check the pantry and see what we have," Kenny said.

"I made a list. We need just about everything," she said.

He surprised her with a kiss.

"Oooh! I like that. We might have to practice again later tonight."

"Don't take too long. The kids will bug Rory and Rochelle to death," Kenny said.

"I will hurry." She saw Bobby and Gideon out of the corner of her eye. "They're over there."

Kenny gathered the kids and left. Emmy hurried to where she saw the guys.

"Hey, Em, did I tell you how fantastic you sounded this morning?" Bobby asked.

"No," she answered and then rolled her eyes. "I know what you're going to say, Bobby."

"What?" he said as he shrugged.

"Something along the lines of... Never mind. I need to talk about the show. Do you have a second?"

"I always have time for you, Emmy," Bobby answered. "Have you talked to anyone yet?"

"I talked to Jeremy, and he agreed though he had strong reservations about my choice of a drummer."

"He's worried I will steal the show."

"Fat chance," she said. Emmy turned to Gideon and said, "Should I find another drummer?" She stared at Gideon and touched his arm. "Are you all right? You look kinda pale. Not pale, but different."

Gideon put a hand to his heart. "I'm having some chest pains."

Emmy looked at him for a moment. "That's it. I'm calling 9-1-1." She grabbed her cell phone from her purse and punched in the numbers.

"What is your emergency?" a voice answered.

"My friend is having chest pains, and he doesn't look good."

"What is your location?"

Emmy explained where she was and gave the dispatcher some details about Gideon.

"The ambulance should be there in three minutes."

"I'll have someone waiting outside," Emmy said more calmly than she thought possible. She looked at Bobby.

"I'll wait outside and show them where to come," Bobby said.

Tyler heard the last part of the conversation and raced over. "What's..."

"Gideon is having a heart attack!" Emmy interrupted.

Tyler turned and raced into the kitchen shouting, "Genna! Could you come with me, please?"

"What is it, Pastor?" she asked wiping her hands on a towel.

"Emmy just called 9-1-1 because Gideon is having a heart attack!"

"Oh, dear Lord," Genna said. "Not another one."

Genna followed Tyler and saw Emmy kneeling on the floor at Gideon's head. He was lying on his back. "Emmy, could you lift his head a little for me, please?"

"Like this?"

"Yes," Genna said as she took Gideon's wrist to check his pulse. "Gideon, can you hear me? Do you have any nitro with you? Or a baby aspirin?"

He shook his head one time.

Tyler stood by Gideon's feet, shifting his weight back and forth and said, "We have a defibrillator in the office. Should I get it?"

Genna shook her head. "No, because I can feel a pulse."

Emmy rubbed Gideon's forehead and moved his long dark hair off of his face.

"Should I look for some baby aspirin?" Tyler asked. "I know we have some at home."

True to the dispatcher's word, the ambulance pulled into the parking lot in under three minutes with lights flashing.

Bobby waved his hands over his head and shouted, "Over here! Over here!"

337

The driver pulled into position and the two EMTs jumped out.

"Can you show us where to go?"

"Yeah! He's in the gym," Bobby said while pointing. "Follow me!"

The paramedics followed as Bobby raced down the hallway, made a left turn and skidded to a stop. "He's over there!"

The paramedics rushed into position. One of them recognized Genna from St. Bart's and asked, "What do we have?"

Genna quickly told the EMTs everything she knew about Gideon's current condition.

"Thanks, Genna," Nicco Foran said. "Tymir, Genna and I will handle this if you can get the gurney."

Tymir Jones nodded and headed back to the ambulance.

"I'll go with you," Bobby said.

"I appreciate the help," Tymir said.

"You're Tariq's brother, right?" Bobby asked. "I've seen you around."

"And you're the drummer," Tymir said.

They returned to the gym and the paramedics began working on Gideon.

By this time the remaining people had gathered in a circle and were praying for Gideon.

Emmy sat motionless with her head in her hands as she prayed. She looked up as Tyler and Liz sat beside her.

"I'm sure they are doing everything they can, Emmy," Liz said while rubbing Emmy's back.

"This seems worse than the last time," Emmy whispered. She glanced at the paramedics. "Why is it taking so long?"

"It's not like on TV where the guys rush to the hospital right away," Tyler said. "They need to stabilize him first."

Ten minutes later Nicco and Tymir loaded Gideon into the ambulance and roared away.

"Do you want me to drive you home, Emmy?" Liz asked. "Have you called Kenny?"

Emmy shook her head. "Not yet, and I'm going to St. Bart's. I'll call Kenny on the way."

338

"I will head to the hospital as soon as I get Liz and the kids home," Tyler said. "Don't drive like a maniac."

Emmy looked up at him and rolled her eyes. "I am a safe driver."

"Yeah, but even the best NASCAR drivers get into wrecks," Tyler said with a chuckle.

Should I go with you?" Liz asked.

Emmy shook her head. "You need to take care of the kids. I'll be fine."

"Don't forget to call Kenny," Liz said as Emmy walked away.

Emmy grabbed her purse and headed outside. She slipped and almost fell on the wet parking lot as she ran to her car. She started the car, backed out of her parking spot and thought about Kenny. *I'll call him when I get to St. Bart's. There's no need to make him worry about Gideon until I know more.* She made the left turn onto Canton Lane and headed to the hospital. She decided to take Marlboro because it was the most direct route. She made it through several green lights, but then caught a red one at Townsend Avenue.

Emmy pounded the steering wheel and muttered, "Come on change. How long can you stay red."

The light changed. Emmy let out the clutch and hit the accelerator. The front tires struggled to gain traction on the damp pavement.

"Come on!" Emmy yelled.

A split-second later the car was filled with flying glass and the screeching sound of metal against metal as Emmy's car was pushed sideways across the intersection.

# Chapter Forty-One

The driver behind Emmy slammed on his brakes, slid sideways, came to a stop and swore.

"Holy Jesus!" his wife shouted as she was thrown forward. "You better call 9-1-1."

He threw the Ford Escape in park, grabbed his phone, opened his door and tried to get out.

"Your seat belt!" his wife screamed.

He used one hand to undo the belt and stabbed at the numbers with his other one. He lost his balance and fell against the SUV.

"What is your emergency?" the voice answered.

"There's been a hell of a crash! You better send an ambulance and everything you got!"

"What is your location, sir?"

He looked around. "The corner of Marlboro and Townsend Ave. A Suburban or some kind of giant SUV just ran a red light and clobbered a Civic."

Eric Sanders replied to the dispatch. "En route. Less than a minute out." He hit the lights and siren.

"Fire and rescue are on their way," the dispatcher said. "It doesn't look good according to a witness."

"Call for backup," Eric said as he turned onto Marlboro and mashed the accelerator to the floor.

"Will do," the dispatcher answered.

Eric arrived on the scene and positioned his squad car behind the Civic. He jumped out and looked at the Chevy Suburban which had come to a stop fifty feet away as he approached the Honda. He peered into the car and saw the victim. Just then a man opened the driver's door of the large SUV and stumbled into the street.

"Stay right where you are!" Eric shouted. He heard squad cars and could see a firetruck and ambulance approaching. He looked into the Civic again and, even though he knew the victim could not hear him, whispered, "Hang on. Help will be here soon."

340

The firetruck and ambulance arrived and the paramedics rushed over to the Civic. As the first on the scene Officer Sanders issued directions to the other patrolmen. Very quickly the traffic was blocked and the driver of the Suburban, who didn't appear to have suffered any injuries, was placed in the back of one of the squad cars.

"He's a DUI," one of the officers told Eric. "He's oblivious to what happened."

Ten minutes later the paramedics loaded the victim from the Civic onto a gurney and into the ambulance. They immediately left for St. Bart's.

Officer Sanders took a deep breath and looked at the plates on the totaled car. "FAF1996. That plate looks familiar." He called it in and waited for a response. "Thanks, dispatch. I'll take it from here." He put a hand to his face and then rubbed his jaw. He walked back toward his car and retrieved his cell phone. *I can't do this over the network.* He took a deep breath and dialed a number.

"Hello, son. I thought you were working today," Police Chief Warren Sanders said. "Ray, could you check those steaks?" he shouted at his friend Ray Randich, the SoHam fire chief.

"I am on duty, and I'm at the scene of an accident," Eric replied.

Knowing his son would not call under most circumstances, Chief Sanders said, "Give me the details."

Officer Sanders did and then said, "You know them from the old neighborhood, right?"

"Yes, and I should handle the notification myself."

"That's why I called from my phone. I didn't want the media to catch it on the network."

"Smart thinking." Chief Sanders waved to his friend.

Ray Randich walked over carrying a set of tongs and saw the look on his friend's face. "This can't be good."

Sanders ended the call with his son and looked at Ray. "There's been an accident involving someone we both know, and I need to inform the family."

"I'll drive you since my car is blocking yours," Randich said.

341

"Thanks. Wayne, would you take care of the steaks, please?" Warren asked his brother. "We have to leave."

"Will do," Wayne replied without asking why.

"Let's go," Randich said. He led the way around the house to his official vehicle. They got in and he backed out of the driveway. "Where are we going?" he asked flipping on the lights.

"Bristol Ridge," Sanders answered. "The Colwell estate."

Ray looked at his friend and swore under his breath.

"Not him." Sanders shook his head. "It's Emmy. His wife." He used his cell phone to call dispatch and arranged for a squad car to meet them at Bristol Ridge.

Thirteen minutes later they arrived at the exclusive development. The security guard saw them approaching and raised the gate. Chief Randich roared past.

"It's the first driveway on the left. I hope the gate is open."

Fortunately, the gate was open and Randich killed the lights as he drove up the winding, hilly asphalt drive. He parked near the front of the house, and the two men got out. They walked to the front porch, paused for a second and then slowly climbed the five steps.

"I doubt they ever use the front door," Sanders said. He took a deep breath and pressed the doorbell two times.

"What was that?" Kenny asked from the kitchen.

"Daddy! That was the front doorbell," Isabella said as she grabbed an apple from the island and raced away.

"Who would be ringing the front doorbell?" Kenny asked.

Rory, who had just entered the kitchen, turned and waved as he he walked down the hall. "I'll get it. It's probably Emmy trying to be funny." He laughed as he walked up to the double-door and opened it. The site of two men startled him for a split-second. "You're not..." He stared at the man on the right. "Oh, crap!" Rory muttered recognizing Warren Sanders.

Chief Sanders stared back for a moment, and then said, "Porter, right? Rory Porter from Raynor Park?"

"Yes, yes," Rory stammered. "Come in." Rory backed up and held the door open.

The men entered and waited just inside the door.

342

"We need to talk to Kenny," Sanders said without elaborating, but his serious expression spoke volumes.

"He's in the kitchen," Rory said. "I'll let him know you're here."

Rory turned and hurried back to the hallway dividing the house. Just as he turned the corner, he bumped into Kenny.

"Who is it, Rory?" Kenny asked.

"It's Warren Sanders and another man," Rory said quickly and then gulped.

Kenny walked around the corner and up to the entryway where Warren Sanders was staring at the floor while Ray Randich gazed at the high ceiling.

Kenny froze for a second before asking, "Chief Sanders, how can I help you?"

Sanders put an arm around Kenny's shoulders, squeezed and whispered, "I'm afraid I have bad news about Emmy."

Kenny clenched his jaw and nodded.

Rory and Rochelle stood in the hallway watching the scene unfold.

"Maybe you should watch the kids," Rory said. "I might need to take Kenny somewhere."

"She is on her way to St. Bart's, and we're here to take you there," Sanders said.

Rory looked at Rochelle. "I'm going with him."

Rochelle nodded and said, "I will take care of the kids. Call me when you know anything."

"Do I need a coat or my wallet?" Kenny asked.

"No need," Chief Sanders said as Chief Randich walked outside. "We have his SUV and there is a squad car waiting."

The men hurried to the SUV. Sanders opened the rear door for Kenny. Rory jumped in on the other side. Randich turned the vehicle around and raced down the driveway. A squad car was waiting and escorted them out of the development.

Warren turned to look at Kenny, who had his eyes closed. "My son, Eric, was the first on the scene. He said she was alive."

Kenny opened his eyes and nodded.

Check out these other titles by the author. Visit the website:
kennethleemcgee.com

## The Emmy's Story Series

1. We We're 'posed to Get Married
2. One Of The Guys
3. A New Friend
4. Did You Like the Ravioli Tonight?
5. Completely and Forever: A Wedding
6. It's Time To Go!
7. How Difficult Can It Be?
8. Forever... Isabella... Forever
9. The Forgettable Year
10. Turning Thirty
11. Hello, I'm James
12. Remember The Struggle
13. But God! I Write Songs
14. A Lifelong Dream

## The Annie Mercer O'Dell Series

1. Roosevelt High
2. North Park College
3. Smoky Mountain Summer

## Stand Alone Books

1. Growing Up In Kinmundy Junction
2. Grandpa, Lions and Kitty Cats: A Collection Of Short Stories For Children Of All Ages